Saga OF THE Wild Hunt

Annie Mars

DEDICATION

To all the furballs,
both feline and canine,
who insisted on sitting on my lap,
in my arms and on the keyboard as I wrote.
Your paws left marks all over my heart.

CONTENTS

ACKNOWLEDGMENTS

There's this story from my childhood where we were in a store and I apparently went into a full toddler meltdown, kicking and screaming on the floor because I wanted a doll. I was apparently obsessed with Jemima from Playschool (I personally have no memory of this, but the story persists). So there I am, in the store, by a stand of Jemima dolls, kicking and screaming, "I want Jemima!" It's safe to say that I never got that Jemima doll, or any other for that matter.

So, I want to thank my Mum, Francina and my Dad, Mulia. Thank you for putting up with me at my worst all the support over the years and for humoring me that one day I would be a real author. (And especially to dad, for reading through some really, really, terrible crap!).

So yes, mum, I really did name a character Jemima so that I could finally, after almost thirty years, have my very own Jemima.

I guess, I should also think Playschool for inspiring a such a meltdown that that it has lingered in the hearts and minds of this family for decades.

I SEE NOTHING BUT DEATH

The bones dropped from the old woman's fingers, clattering against the soft brownish animal hide spread across the table. One fell outside the confines of the charcoal circle that was supposed to contain the bones for the reading. Brigitta leaned in as far as her swollen belly would allow her to and watched intently.

The old woman's wrinkled face creased into a frown as she watched how the bones fell and shifted before settling into their final positions. Her wizened old face looked up at the woman across from her. Her eyes settled on the young woman's swollen belly, and she shook her head.

"What?" Brigitta asked. The woman just stared at the bones. When she started to shake her head, Brigitta wasn't sure if it was her nerves or the baby. "What is it?" she asked, the panic coming through in her shaky voice.

The old woman's trembling finger pointed at a clustering of the bones. Two small bones were crossed in the centre of the cluster. "I see nothing but death."

Brigitta felt herself go cold. It wasn't the first time she had heard those words. No, it had first started when the nightmares had come, long before discovering her pregnancy. She thought about it more. It wasn't just before they had discovered that she was with child; it had been before she was with child, as though something or someone had known before they did that a child would even be conceived. Dark dreams where she would run through the town or the woods or the tree city, the white blanket she had embroidered with the golden scenes of the gods in battle wrapped around a small, wailing form in her arms. She would look behind her, over her shoulder and there he would be, flanked by creatures she could not identify. He would chase after her until they caught her and took her baby, only to kill the squalling infant before her very eyes. She would wake, drenched from sweat and shivering from the cold, only to be pulled into strong, comforting arms. Closing her eyes, she remembered that feeling.

Then came the lunar new year celebrations, and with it, the contingent of staff and students from Ni Sekai-Ryu or the Two Worlds School in Takama-no-Hara. Kitamura Sensei, a woman much like the dark-skinned woman who sat before her now, had been old and wizened beyond years, likely an offspring of the gods themselves, had offered to read her tea leaves during their welcome feast.

"Buraijita, my child," the old woman had said with her odd pronunciation of Brigitta's name, her previously jovial tone replaced by a solemn and almost reluctant tone.

"What do you see, Sensei?" Brigitta asked, trying her hardest not to peer over her teacup as the old woman inspected it.

Kitamura Sensei shook her head sadly, looking up from the cup to meet Brigitta's, "I see nothing but death..."

In confusion, Brigitta canted her head to the side, a wry smile still on her face to not alert the others in the room that something was wrong, especially her overprotective husband. Ever since head learned of the pregnancy, his protective streak had become nearly unbearable, extending even to her best friend, the school's Weapons Mistress. "I don't understand," she said cautiously.

The old teacher shook her head. "Neither do I, Buraijita." The old woman looked at the cup and the leaves arranged at the bottom. "Your child, though, will not see many days."

Brigitta pushed herself back from the table, "No!" she said forcefully. "There has to be another answer. She can't be destined for death!"

"Child," the old woman said, sitting calmly at her table. "Greatness is feared. Change is feared. Not getting your own way is feared."

"What does that mean?" Brigitta exclaimed.

"The child that becomes within you will either die before her first year is through, or she will go on to be Death's ally."

A soft look overtook her face as she smiled at the old woman. "She... She's a girl..."

The old woman nodded. "Yes, a girl, but all I see around her is..."

"Is death..." Brigitta finished for her. "Could they really be so cruel as to hunt down my child?"

The old woman looked at her. "I cannot say how death will be achieved, but the child will be surrounded by the dead."

"The planes of the dead?" Brigitta asked, resting her hand on her belly as the child that grew within her kicked. "She's a fighter."

The old woman nodded. "Possible. How many fortunes have you had told now?"

Brigitta looked up at her, and a deep sadness filled her eyes. "This is my sixth."

"And they all say the same?"

Brigitta nodded. "Not just that, you all use the exact same words."

"Oh?" the old woman asked, hand hands beginning the task of clearing the bones from the table.

"I see nothing but death. You all say it, starting with Kitamura Sensei and the tea leaves, then Ethelinda with the cards, Menowin with my palm, Vadoma with the stars, and Patrin with the flames... All of you, you say, 'I see nothing but death,' and it scares me."

"As it should, child," the old woman said.

"Is there any future where my child... my daughter lives?" Brigitta asked, reaching out a hand to stop the woman from cleaning up.

The woman shook her hand free and rolled the animal hide up, protecting the bones. "Not in the realms of the gods or the fae. Perhaps in the realms of the dead."

Brigitta stepped out of the old woman's tent. Inside it had seemed strangely silent, the noise of the boisterous camp beyond the fragile fabric almost entirely gone. She stood there and looked around, undecided as to where to go.

She should head back to Nýr Ásgardr. She had a job to return to and a husband who worried far too much. Her recent travelling to find fortune-tellers had left him frantic with concern, but the children at the school needed him. He had tried to even have Astrid talk her out of it, but she had been insistent that this was something that she needed to do... Even if she hadn't told him why.

She started walking slowly towards the base of the tree city. Home. She should go home. Grab the first airship back to Nýr Ásgardr. It was the logical thing to do.

She took the stairs first, walking easily up to the first level, but the child growing within her had other ideas, and she stopped at a flyover that wended its way between the rainbow discs that transported people from the depths of the world's tree's roots to the top.

"Not in the realms of the gods or the fae, perhaps in the realms of the dead."

What did that leave?

The realms of the dead, of course, some managed to eke out a living there, but none of them was any place for a living child. The realms of the gods were out of the question, as were the realms of the Fae, but what about the dark lands of Svartalheim?

Was it possible to maybe go to Vanaheim or maybe Muspelheim? Word was that the two realms were uninhabitable after the great war's destruction of the Nine Realms. No, that wouldn't work. She stepped onto a passing rainbow disc and let it carry her upwards, her thoughts a jumbled mess of confusion and upheaval. She would return to The Bore Tooth Inn, collect her belongings, and return to Nýr Ásgardr. Together, she and her husband would find the right future for their child. She had already missed the festivities of Krampasnacht, and she could not also miss the Yuletide and Hogmanay celebrations. She still had time to make it back to Nýr Ásgardr and even help with the preparations.

Mind made up, she got off the rainbow disc at the entrance to the dining branch. The inner walkways were busy here, with people everywhere. Short, stumpy leprechauns, graceful angels and elegant elves moved between rambunctious Weres and brooding Vampires. A few dark elves scuttled behind their beautiful golden-haired masters, and Brigitta could not help but look away. She hated the elves for keeping slaves, but what could she do?

She stumbled. A cramp shot through her belly, and she cried out. She leaned against the interior of the tree trunk and cradled her belly in her hands. It was too soon. She wasn't home. She hadn't found an answer. She couldn't do this now. Not without Matron Damir or her beloved husband. He had to be there for this.

She tried to take a step forward, but the pain was agonising. Maybe this was what all her fortune tellings had been telling her? Death before breath. No, she couldn't think like that. She had to get to her room at The Bore Tooth. Another step and she was out in the sunlight of the day. The leaves of the tree city blew in the breeze, and she couldn't enjoy any of it. Not the smells of the food wafting from the restaurants, not the blooming flowers that seemed to change from day to day on the tree.

A shoulder slid under her arm, and Brigitta looked up into the eyes of a young angel girl with long dark hair tied in a braid that fell over her shoulder and wide brown eyes filled with concern. She wore the robes of a Healing Initiate, and Brigitta relaxed, the calming presence of the girl easing away her tension. "Are you all right, Lady?" the girl asked softly. Her wing wrapped around Brigitta, embracing her in a warm, healing light.

"My..." Brigitta gasped and swallowed hard. "My baby..."

The girl nodded and rested her free hand on Brigitta's stomach. A warm glow emanated from her hand, and she nodded to herself. "This little one is ready to meet the world."

Brigitta shook her head. "No. No, it's not time."

"It most definitely is, according to this young lady," the angel said. "Come, I'm Yancey, and you are?"

"Brigitta," she gasped out.

"Nice to meet you, Brigitta. Let's get you to the healing house and—"

Brigitta cried out in pain. "No time..." She groaned out.

"Ok, ok, ok," the young angel panicked. "Come on. Are you staying at one of these places?"

Brigitta nodded, hanging on to the young woman. "Bore, ahhhh!" she cried.

"The Bore Tooth?" Yancey asked, and Brigitta nodded. "Ok, The Bore Tooth. Come on." Brigitta allowed Yancey to lead her across the Dining Branch, past the other brightly coloured canvas rooves of the establishments to the one with a roof of green and purple fabric and an awning of shocking orange. The sign of the messenger squirrel swung in the wind, the hinges squeaking. Inside, the dimly lit room was full of noon-day customers enjoying a drink and the fine food offered at reasonable prices. The joviality of a bar ceased at the appearance of the two women.

"Help," Yancey ordered. "Help me get her to her room, and then I need boiling water, lots of blankets and someone to run to the hospital for the herbs I need."

An older man, large and heavily muscled, stood up from a group of similarly statured people. Aside from a woman of the same approximate age as the man, the rest of the group were all young children. Of the six children, the oldest child was maybe fourteen, just about old enough to attend one of the great schools in the new year. They were likely a Werebear Junior Sleuth, the older couple in charge of the small group of children, preparing them for their formal education. The old man stood up. "We'll get her to her room," he said, motioning to the oldest boy, who scurried to stand up as well.

"Water's on in the kitchen," the bartender said after shouting an order through to the kitchen.

A young, lanky boy stood up from the group of Werebears. "I'll run for the healing house," he said, with a look of approval from the old woman, who only nodded in ascent when he glanced at her.

Yancey passed Brigitta off to the two Werebears, "Thank you," she said and pulled out her notebook. She scribbled a list and ripped out the page, handing it to the boy. "Run. As fast as you can. Give this to the matron at the hospital and come straight back when she gives you everything on the list."

"Aye," the boy said, taking the list. He darted out of the bar and disappeared. Yancey followed Brigitta And the two bears up the stairs of the pub and into the room. The two Werebears laid her down on her bed and turned to the Angel. "Is there anything else we can do?" the old man said, his hand on the boy's shoulder.

"Not right now," the angel said. "Send the other boy to me as soon as he returns." They nodded and left the room. "Ok, my sweet. I know that you are in a lot of pain right now," Yancey said, coming over to Brigitta's bedside.

Brigitta grabbed Yancey's arm, her hands like claws, as she gripped the angel. "You have to," she groaned as another contraction hit. Her fingers digging in, bruising Yancey's delicate angel skin. Her wings drew in at the pain, but she said nothing, trying to keep the wince off her face as she willed the woman to speak. "You have to" Brigitta tried again.

"Have to what?" Yancey asked.

A crash sounded downstairs, followed by a scream. Metal clashed against metal as swords met. A bear roared in fury, and the small building shook.

Yancey looked around, her eyes wide with concern and fright but not as concerned and fearful as Brigitta was. Looking back at the woman, Yancey could only see panic.

"My baby."

Yancey looked around. What could she do? What was going on downstairs? She had no idea, but a blood-curdling scream came flying up the stairs, making all her hair stand on end. "We have to get out of here," Yancey declared, and Brigitta nodded, pushing herself into a seated position.

Something ceramic crashed below them. "Come on," Yancey said, glancing over her shoulder at the door. It was closed but not locked. Footsteps on the stairs. Heavy boots and what sounded like more following the leader, calling out. "Open the window," Yancey instructed, then grabbed a chair from the corner of the room and shoved it tight under the door handle.

Brigitta struggled with the window latch and then pushed the heavy frame open. She looked down. The canvas roof of the pub would not hold their combined weight.

"What are you doing?" Brigitta asked as the girl came across the room.

"Getting out of here," she said simply, stepping up onto the bed. She stretched her wings out in anticipation, and Brigitta shook her head.

"We'll never make it," she cried.

"We will," Yancey said. Brigitta backed away. "What are you doing?"

"My bag. I cannot leave without my bag," she said, reaching for the leather bag that held the blanket she had carefully embroidered for her child. She would not leave it behind. The pristine white material made from unicorn hair and the gold thread, a gift from a thankful leprechaun that would ensure the blanket would never stain or be torn. No, she could not leave that behind.

"Leave the bag," Yancey ordered. A hammer collided with the door, smashing the fragile wood.

A head appeared in the gap in the door, an angry, snarling man. "Give me the woman."

Yancey grabbed Brigitta, whose hand just barely clasped the strap of the bag. Yancey pulled her close and then jumped from the bar window, but not towards the branch below. Instead, she leapt over the side. Brigitta screamed as Yancey's wings spread out wide. Their descent continued, the young angel struggling to keep the combined weight of the two of them afloat.

~ * ~

Brigitta finally stopped screaming when they landed, skidding across the smooth, glowing surface of a wide rainbow disc. Yancey kicked out her legs, trying to get a hold of something, anything. She fell backwards, the pregnant woman's weight on top of her and her wings splayed awkwardly beneath her.

"Are you all right?" the angel asked.

Brigitta nodded. "I think so..."

"Who were those men?" she asked, cradling the woman against her as another contraction hit, and Brigitta wailed in pain. The baby was coming fast, and she had nothing to help her channel her magic to ease the labour.

"Nightmares," Brigitta gasped out.

"Is he the father?" Yancey asked, cradling Brigitta against her.

"No. Just. A. nightmare," she managed.

"I'm going to lie you down, ok? I need to go see what's happening with this little warrior of yours, ok?" Brigitta nodded as best as she could, and Yancey shifted herself so that she skirted the edge of the large rainbow platform and crept out from beneath the woman. This was far from an ideal environment to deliver a child, but she hardly had a choice.

"Tell me about the nightmare," Yancey said, looking inside her own bag for anything to channel her magic through. She had needed those herbs from the hospital. She wasn't yet skilled enough to work the healing magics without them.

"He chases me," Brigitta said through clenched teeth. "My baby and I."

"For what reason?" Yancey asked, trying to hide her own panic at the situation. This platform could be going anywhere from Helheim to Midgard or even Muspelheim. Who knew? She sure didn't, not without going through the travel office, and as they were most definitely heading away from the great tree city, she knew they weren't heading back there. It could be hours, days or weeks until this platform returned to the tree city. What could she do?

"I don't know," Brigitta said. "They want her, and her fortunes are all filled with death..." She let out a resounding cry that seemed to carry on the wind.

The world around them changed. The sky changed colour from the bright, luminescent blue of the beautiful day they'd been having in the tree city to a dark, greyish, purplish haze. Svartelheim. Yancey shivered. While not hell itself, Svartelheim was one of the lower realms, if not the lowest, before the realms of the dead. She had never been there herself but knew that in the city of Mörka Fält, they would be able to find help. The city was the largest in the realm and boasted one of the great schools of the Nine Realms. They would have a healing house, healers, and all the right herbs to help Brigitta. It wasn't ideal, but it was far better than this... This... She couldn't even find the words to describe the situation she found herself in.

A bolt of lightning came shooting just over Yancey's head, and she screamed. Brigitta screamed with her. Another bolt sent the platform wobbling.

"No, no, no, no, no, no," Yancey wailed. The magic that animated the rainbow platforms that traversed the realms was fragile. No one really understood how it worked, but Yancey knew that they were carefully tracked and timed. Something like this could set it off course and out of alignment. Anything could happen then. They could wind up anywhere, or worse, the circuit of the rainbow platform might never return to the tree city at the centre of the Nine Realms.

The grey, purplish skies of Svartelheim turned to the hazy, unsure colours of a hot summer's night. So much for making it to Mörka Fält. The town they found themselves in was almost silent as the platform wobbled, tilted and finally collided with a hard, black surface with coloured lines. They fell from the platform, and Brigitta cried out in shock and pain. Around them, light emanated from the buildings, and bright multi-coloured tree shapes seemed to radiate in front of the windows. Music seemed to waft in the air, muted from the confines of the buildings.

"Where are we?" Brigitta asked, pushing herself up from the warm surface of what must have been some kind of road.

"I don't recognise it," Yancey said. She scrambled to her feet and pulled her wings tight around her body despite the night's suffocating heat. She helped Brigitta to her feet, and the woman hung on, the pain and the stress of the night making it hard for her to stand on her own.

She looked up and down the deserted street. Behind them, a large building was bright with light and colour, but the street itself was deserted. The other side of the street seemed very far away, and in the hazy evening light, they could see that a river seemed to run beside the road, and small bridges traversed it, allowing access to houses on the far side.

"Let's go in there," Yancey said, pointing to the building behind them. Despite the strange architecture, something about it reminded her of The Bore Tooth Inn. She was certain that it was some kind of pub or bar.

"Wings," Brigitta gasped out.

"What?"

"Your wings," Brigitta reminded her, and Yancey groaned. She knew that some angels could hide their wings. It was a skill taught primarily to guardians who might spend time in Midgard with the humans. She was not one of those angels.

"We need to get you off the street," Yancey insisted.

"That building there," Brigitta said, pointing to the far side of the river. Directly across from them was a light-wrapped bandstand with a beautiful tree set at its centre.

"It's Yuletide," she realised. "It's Yultide on Midgard."

"Then your wings cannot be seen," Brigitta insisted.

Beside the bandstand was a run-down, dark structure that appeared to have what looked like a tree growing from it. "We can lie low there."

~ * ~

The sun rose to the sound of a squalling infant. Brigitta wrapped her daughter in the white and gold blanket and cradled her against her chest. Yancey slept uncomfortably in the corner, exhaustion having finally gotten the better of her.

A noise startled her, and Brigitta woke Yancey, passing her the baby.

"Stay here," she instructed as she stood on wobbly legs and picked up a thick piece of wood that had fallen from the house.

"What are you going to do?" Yancey asked, holding the baby close to her.

"I'm going to find out who he is and what he wants with my daughter," Brigitta said. "If I don't come back, protect her. Her father is in Nýr Ásgardr, but she will not be safe there if these people are after her. There is a letter there. Make sure she has her blanket, and don't let those men take my baby."

Yancey nodded in awe of the woman before her. Then Brigitta walked out of the dark, dilapidated house, and Yancey never saw her again.

SAGA

Saga was hot. The kind of hot where even shorts and a tank top were too many clothes. Her long blond hair was tied up in a messy bun that perched atop her head crookedly. Loose strands plastered to her face with sweat. Light blue eyes quickly flicked back and forth over the pages of a book as she sat curled up in a chair on the far side of a large living room. A scrawny Christmas tree stood nearby, decorated in clumsy, homemade decorations.

Despite the heat, the pool was closed, and no one was allowed to go swimming. Kids were everywhere around Saga, but no one could be bothered running around, although Saga would have preferred to have taken a run. She found the feeling of the air in her hair, her feet pounding rhythmically against the pavement and the sense that there was no one in existence but her to be calming.

"Ain't no one coming for you," one boy sneered as he walked past the large girl with long blond hair and blue eyes. The girl, Saga, did not need to be reminded of this. No one ever came for her at Christmas. She shrugged and returned to the book she had been reading before being interrupted. "I've got my mum and my dad coming today," the boy announced as though that was a great feat.

"That's great for you, Nick," Saga said, not looking up from her book.

"They'll bring me presents," Nick continued, bouncing around in front of Saga's chair. "My parents are the best." This seemed doubtful to Saga as Nick lived at the group home full time.

"Then go live with them."

"I am!" He announced. "I am going to live with them because my parents love me."

"That's great, Nick," Saga said with a sigh. "Then maybe I can read in peace when you're finally gone."

He reached out to grab the book from Saga's hands. She looked up as her grip tightened around the book. Nick was a few years younger than Saga, having just finished Primary School. Next year, when she entered the ninth grade, he would enter the seventh. He had been at her since she arrived, the day after school had finished for the year. The day her last foster family had had enough of her and her strangeness. It was four days later, and they were developing a burning hatred for each other. She wasn't sure how much longer she could resist punching him.

Stories about everyone's situations flew around the home like wildfire. Saga had been abandoned shortly after birth, but her oddities prevented her from ever being adopted, whereas Nick's parents had gotten into a custody battle so rife with violence that he had been removed from their care. The fact that he said both of them were coming today did not make Saga happy. They would likely argue, and she just wanted some peace before someone started nagging her about going to the next home.

Nick pulled on the book, and Saga pulled back. She was tall for her age and muscled far more than fifteen-year-old girls usually were, but she was lean and athletic in stature. The boy was eager to disrupt her.

The book ripped.

"You idiot!" Saga cried. "I was reading that!" She dropped the broken pages of the book, and the ripped pages fluttered down from her hands. "Why can't you just leave me alone?"

She got up and shoved Nick out of her way roughly, walking past him. She couldn't bear to share the same space any longer. She heard him stumble back and fall. He fell back with a crash, taking down the little Christmas tree with all the handmade ornaments as he went. He landed on top of the tree, crushing branches and decorations alike.

Nearby, Matthew, one of the smaller boys, burst into howling wails of despair at the destroyed tree. One of the adults came running into the room as everyone now stared at Saga, Nick, and Matthew.

"What is going on in here?"

"Saga pushed me over!" Nick shouted, pointing at her.

"He ripped my book!" Saga cried.

"The tree!" Matthew wailed. "The Christmas tree!"

Caroline, their everyday worker who also headed up kitchen duties, stormed over to Saga and grabbed her by the arm. "To your room, now!" She stated forcefully.

Saga tried to wrench her arm from the woman's, but the grip was firm. She was used to indignant and violent children who did not want to do as they were told. "But Caroline!" She cried, careful not to resist too hard for fear that Caroline would be hurt, and she would find herself in further trouble. It had happened before. "He started it!"

"Said every child ever," Caroline declared, starting to direct Saga out of the room while a boy around their age helped Nick to his feet. Matthew was sobbing into the blouse of their other regular worker, Sarah.

"It's not fair!" Saga shouted. "I just wanted to read my book!" Caroline hauled Saga out of the room as everyone watched, no one saying a word in her defence. Everyone knew how odd Saga Joy Carolle was, and no one wanted to be the one caught being nice to her.

Caroline thrust Saga into the small bedroom on the first floor that she shared with three other girls living in the home. Lois was thirteen, put into care when her drug-addict mother had overdosed and died when she was eight. She, like Saga, was awaiting her next foster placement. Heather, fifteen, was there temporarily while her aunt and uncle were assessed to see if they were suitable kinship carers. Lyla, an Aboriginal girl from the outer suburbs, had been taken into care when her parents had been deemed inappropriate carers, unable to maintain her welfare.

Of the girls, Saga liked Lyla the best and loved the stories Lyla told of her family and extended family. They did not sound like horrible, uncaring parents to her. Lyla always spoke of them with love and admiration. She spoke of family gatherings that Saga could not even imagine, having all those aunts and uncles who would love you no matter what. Having a mum and a dad. It sounded magical to Saga.

As the door locked behind her, Saga did not even bother to hammer against it or protest her innocence. Nick had spoken first. Nick was going home. No one was going to rain on his Christmas parade. She bit her lip to ward off the tears threatening to spill from her eyes. She crossed the room to her bed and threw herself upon it, wishing that, despite the heat, she had gone for a run. Her runners, sitting by the door of the room, seemed to mock her.

She hated Christmas.

Not only was it a day everyone always looked forward to, but it was also her birthday. It might not even be her real birthday, but Ms Roskin, her social worker, had told her that they had decided to use December twenty-fifth as her recorded date of birth because that was the day she had been found. Doctors had estimated her to be under a week old, though closer to only a day or two old, as no one had been able to say exactly, they had made Christmas day her birthday.

At least she did not have two days a year to dread like the other kids, though. She knew many who dreaded their birthdays and Christmas because no one ever remembered. No one ever cared enough to remember.

Saga reached her hand out for the top drawer in the little bedside table and pulled it open. She pushed aside colourful ribbons and medals and withdrew a small diary. She laid it on the bed beside her. Saga had tried her best to record everything she had ever been told about herself and her parents. Well, no one knew anything about her parents, but she had been given a letter for her twelfth birthday. According to Ms Roskin, the letter had been found pinned to the blanket she had been wrapped in. Saga had the blanket too. She kept that in her bag. She never wanted to risk losing it or leaving it behind when she was moved to another home, so she rarely took it out for anyone to see.

It was Christmas, though, so Saga reached her hand under the bed to grab the bag that carried all of her worldly possessions and unzipped it. She rifled through the contents until her hand fell on the incredibly soft material of the blanket. No one, not even the foster parents who knitted, sewed and crocheted, had been able to tell her what the material was, but everyone that she had allowed to see it had marvelled at the intricate designs woven into the soft white material in gold, shimmering thread.

Scenes of winged women carrying swords as they flew over what appeared to be battlefields. Crows, wolves, horses, bears, and all kinds of animals intermingled with sword and hammer-wielding men engaging in battle. It had been commented on, what a strange blanket it was to wrap a child in, but Saga held it dear as the only thing her mother had left her.

She pulled the blanket over herself and then unfolded the letter. Her mother's words in her mother's handwriting. Or so everyone assumed.

'To whoever finds my beloved little warrior,
Her name is Saga. It is perhaps the one thing her father and I agreed on. So certain he was that our beautiful little girl would be a son... I knew, though, that he would love a little girl just as much, if not more.
Know that despite my choices here today, she is the hope and the joy of my life, of both of our lives, but there is more at stake than the happiness of one family So much more than can be explained in a simple letter to the strangers who will protect my Saga. I wish I could explain everything, but if I want my girl safe, I need to keep you and her in ignorance.
Keep her safe in a way I never can, for only time will tell what role she has to play in humanity's future.

Brigitta

It was an odd letter. All that talk of great sagas of mythos and gifts from the gods, but it was a letter from her mother. Brigitta. Saga's forefinger traced the letters of her mother's name. No matter how odd the letter was, those were her mother's words about her. *'She is the hope and the joy of my life.'*

"If only she had kept me," Saga murmured into the empty room. Although she never let her thoughts stray further than that because what worried Saga most about her mother was what if she, too, would have given her away once she got to know the girl and her oddities began to show. Not like it mattered. Brigitta had given her away. Just left her for someone else to find, and no one had wanted her in the end.

Self-pity was an easy well to spiral down into, and Saga frequently found herself descending into it around this time of year. Quickly, she folded the letter carefully and placed it back in the small diary before shoving it back into her bedside table drawer.

Despite the heat of the day, she pulled the blanket tight around herself and curled up on her bed, ready to let the day pass her by without anyone remembering that Christmas was meant to be her day.

The call for lunch came and went. Saga had no interest in slinking downstairs to pretend to be sorry for pushing Nick into the Christmas tree. She stayed where she was, the curtains pulled closed and the light barely filtering into the room. She could hear the sounds of everyone gathering for the midday meal. Even if she had wanted to, Caroline had locked the door. What could she do about that?

The sound of the door opening caught her attention as she sat up, bleary-eyed and cautious of what would happen next. "Saga?" Lyla asked hesitantly. "I brought you some lunch," she said as she walked in a put a plate of food on the bedside table.

"How'd you get the key?" Saga asked, staring at the girl in surprise.

Lyla shrugged, sitting down beside Saga. Her fingers tentatively ran over the blanket. "This is pretty."

"My mum gave it to me," Saga said, fingering the blanket as well. "Well... left me wrapped in it when she abandoned me. Sounds better when I say it the other way."

"Oh Saga," Lyla murmured.

Saga shrugged before Lyla could get any ideas to hug her. "Did your parents come?"

She nodded. "Yeah, they stayed for lunch too," she sighed sadly. "I want to go home. I mean... you should have heard Nick's parents. Yelling and screaming at each other. Threats to hurt one another. They were scary."

When Lyla left, Saga pulled the loaded plate onto the bed and started picking at the selection of food the other girl had put together for her. It was all leftovers, but Saga did not mind. Someone had tried for her.

"HELP ME!"

Saga looked up from her food at the sound of the voice. "You're not allowed-," she started to say before seeing him. Nick stood in her room. But not the same Nick she had pushed into the Christmas tree that morning.

He appeared to be wispy, as though he was fraying at the edges and where he was frayed, she could see right through him to the other side of the room. The colour also appeared to be fading; he looked like an old photograph that had been left out in the sun too long.

"Help me!" He cried again. "Help me!"

"Nick!" she cried. She had seen this before. She had seen this when living at the Abrams' house, and their neighbour Mr Grant had died from a heart attack. It had taken people a week to finally listen to her, and all the time, old Mr Grant had followed her around, begging for her help. 'Help me' were the only words that seemed to leave his mouth. Finally, Saga had taken the key she knew he had kept in the fake rock in his garden and went inside. When she had finally called for help, the Abrams had accused her of breaking into Mr Grant's house and making up the story of his ghost following her.

Then there had been the time little Daisy Ridley had fallen into the pool when she had been living with Mr and Mrs Russell. Little Daisy had appeared, dripping, and bedraggled before Saga at the time of her death, scaring her. She, too, had asked Saga to help her. They had complained to Ms Roskin that Saga was too damaged by the death of the little girl for them to be able to effectively care for her along with their other foster children.

There had been a building site down the road from the group home she had been placed in after that. They had been building a huge new shopping centre, with office towers and apartments. A man whose name she had never learned had fallen from somewhere up high. As the emergency alerts had gone up at the site, the man had appeared to her, two words upon his fading lips, "Help me!"

Next, Ms Roskin had found her a place with a family that supposedly specialised in children with traumatic pasts and special needs. They had sent her to counselling, and they had done all kinds of things with her, like meditation and mindfulness. None of it had made the ghosts go away. Near their house, she had seen four ghosts. They had all been extremely faded and frayed, as though they had been dead for an extremely long time. Each of them had asked for her help, their echoed 'Help me,' keeping her aware of one or all of them at all times. She had done her best to ignore them until a new woman appeared. The still-coloured and not-so-frayed spirit of the woman had been the same one Saga had seen on the news. Police had been looking for her because she had been reported missing by her husband. Saga followed that ghost, and she found the burial ground of a serial killer. All five bodies had been retrieved by the police, and Saga was hailed some kind of hero for stumbling upon it.

Eventually, though, that placement ended when the outed killer decided to take her next and broke into the house, hurting Mr and Mrs Henderson in his attempts to get at her.

And now she was here, in another group home with another frayed, fading soul before her.

"Nick!" She echoed her surprise. She got up from her bed, the plate of food forgotten on her covers. She crossed the room, reaching for him, but her hand went right through his ghostly form. "No!" She cried, horrified.

Saga screamed, then pulled open the door. Lyla must have forgotten to relock it when she had left. Saga bounded through the house to where everyone was gathered.

"Nick!" She cried. "Where's Nick?"

"Calm down, girl," Caroline said, walking over with her hands on her hips. "Go back to your room. How did you even get out?"

"No!" Saga screamed in a fury. "Where's Nick?"

"Gone home," Lois said, staring at Saga as though her near hysteria was perplexing.

"His parents had lunch with us, and then they took him," Heather added.

Lyla rolled her eyes. "Yeah, 'cause that's so going to last, the way those two were fighting the entire time."

Saga turned and ran for the door, but it was locked. In three strides, Caroline grabbed her in an attempt to stop her. "You've done it this time, girl!"

"I have to find Nick. Let go of me!"

Behind Caroline, she could see the frayed form of the boy in question standing there. "Help me!" He said again.

"I'm trying!" Saga bellowed. "I'm trying to help you!"

Two more forms appeared behind Nick. Just as frayed and faded as he was, Saga guessed that these were his parents.

"Help me," the three of them said in unison.

"There's been an accident!" Saga cried as Sarah came up to help Caroline restrain Saga. She pulled and struggled against the two women, but despite her hysteria, she knew that if either of them fell, if either of them got hurt, a girl like her would only wind up going one place. "We have to find them!"

"You are being a foolish girl," Caroline said as she wrenched Saga's arms behind her back. Together they lead her down the hall. This time it was not to her bedroom but towards the room in the back with the lockable door and the barred windows. The bed was simple, and there was nothing except a tiny ensuite bathroom. It was the punishment space.

"NOOO!" Saga screamed as the two women hauled her down there. Behind her, she could hear the other kids whispering about what they were witnessing. "You have to find Nick! He's in trouble!" And over the din of their whispering and her screams, Saga could still hear their cries for help.

~ * ~

It was late on boxing day and other than food deliveries by Caroline or Sarah, Saga had had no contact with anyone except for the fading forms of Nick and his parents. Their repeated cries for help could not be blocked out by shoving her head under her pillow and holding it tight against her head. The three of them stood there, unmoving, except when she looked back to find them standing in different locations around the room.

There were not all that many to choose from.

The rest of Christmas day had passed, with her hearing everything going on in the main house. The others had spent a lot of time talking about her outburst, and then, all memory of Saga seemed to fade from their memories as they returned to their festivities. They played games, relaxed and ate good food. Saga had received more leftovers on a plate brought to her by Caroline.

Every time she entered the room, Saga would ask her if anyone had heard from Nick or his parents. Caroline had told her to mind her own business and that they were unlikely to ever hear anything from the boy as he had gone home to his family.

When morning had finally lit up the room — she had forgotten to close the curtains — they were still there. A little more faded than before. All around her, she could hear the sounds of the house waking up for the day. Heavy footsteps in the hall, the opening and closing of cupboards in the kitchen. The toilets being flushed, the showers running and kids talking to each other. Everything from what had happened yesterday to what they would do today.

"Help me," each of them said in unison.

"I can't," Saga cried. "I can't even help myself."

Breakfast was delivered again, toast with marmalade. Saga could not stand marmalade. Still, her only choice was to eat it or starve until the next meal, and if Caroline returned to find her breakfast uneaten, she was just as likely to leave it and not come back.

With great disgust at the marmalade's citrus taste, Saga forced herself to eat the toast in large, awful bites, hoping that the sooner it was down, the sooner she could get the taste out of her mouth. Unfortunately, that left her with massive gobs of bread and marmalade in her mouth at any one time.

Outside the room, one of the little ones had started to cry loud, wailing sobs. They had probably fallen over, or maybe one of the other kids had done something mean. With the little ones, it was hard to tell what set them off wailing. Sarah started to soothe the child while Caroline told off another of the kids. It was pretty much a standard morning at the house, except that Saga was locked up in the isolation room.

She pushed the empty plate back along the small table for meals or homework and slumped in the chair. It was going to be another long, boring day.

She got up, needing to move. She had not been able to go for her morning run, and with the lack of movement the day before, her muscles were feeling tight and tense. She began her usual stretching routine and considered running on the spot, anything for something to clear her mind of their constant cries for help.

Lunch had come and gone when the doorbell rang. Caroline was still ignoring Saga's every attempt to talk to her about Nick, and Saga was now nursing a sore foot from kicking the wall in frustration. The running on the spot had not helped.

She did recall the comments about her having anger issues and a lack of impulse control, usually resulting in some form of violence. Well, maybe if someone ever listened to her, she would not have to resort to such means. Still, she had been trying really hard not to fight back because when she did it, it was a problem. When one of the boys did it, it was normal.

Thumping steps indicated that one of the kids was heading for the door until Caroline called out. "Do not open that door," This was followed by the sharp clip-clop of her shoes as she headed to the door herself.

Noise erupted as everyone wanted to find out who was at the door. Maybe someone was getting placed? Maybe someone's family had come back for a visit. Maybe, maybe, maybe. They all lived a life of maybes. There was never any certainty.

"Yes?" Caroline's stern voice said, presumably as she opened the door. The effect was instantaneous. Silence descended, and Saga wished she were out with the other kids witnessing what was happening. Instead, she was stuck in this small, locked room with no one for company except Nick and his parents, still echoing their first request.

"Help me!" each of them continued to say.

"May we come in?" a voice Saga had never heard before asked. When Caroline acquiesced and allowed the speaker in, everyone scattered, not wanting to be caught eavesdropping.

The silence, caused by everyone wanting to listen, was deafening in itself. Saga's ears rang with an annoying piercing sound that she swore was why she could not hear what was being said between Caroline, Sarah, and the stranger. No, two strangers. A male and a female. Both profoundly serious from the tones of their voices.

Sarah let out a little cry in shock, and somewhere someone started to cry. Saga looked over at Nick and his parents. They no longer opened their mouths to ask for her help. It was no longer hers to give. They had been found, and now they were free to go.

What colours remained in their ghostly forms seemed to fade to white as she watched them, and their edges began to fray even more than they already had. In moments they would disappear from her sight altogether, and she would be free of them too.

To her surprise, the lock on her door jangled, and Sarah appeared. "Saga, come on."

Without argument, question or complaint, Saga got off her bed and followed Sarah out the door of the room. Everyone was gathered in the living room, sitting on couches or on the floor. Holding on to one another. Saga hovered awkwardly in the doorway to the room and waited.

"As I'm sure most of you heard," Caroline said, trying to sound as disapproving as she could, but the hiccup in her words betrayed her true emotions of extreme sadness that she had not yet allowed herself to feel. "Yesterday, as they drove home for their first night together, Nicholas and his family were involved in a car accident. A drunk driver hit the car in which they had been travelling, and as a result, their car spun and flipped. The car proceeded to fall from the bridge. They were killed instantly."

Gasps rang out, and Saga stumbled backwards, her fears entirely realised as Caroline spoke the words. Lois and Heather clung to each other and cried. Two boys who had shared Nick's room stared. They just stared. Neither said anything, but neither did they move. The shock seemed to have paralysed them.

"Saga was right," Lyla mumbled as she allowed Mathew and another of the little ones to cling to her as they wept. Nick had not necessarily been liked, but his death on the day he went home to his parents stung them all.

Caroline's head snapped to Lyla. "Saga's hysterics yesterday have nothing to do with this," she stated firmly.

Saga cocked her head at the woman. "Their car went off the road at twenty-three minutes past two," Saga retorted. "Nick was killed instantly. His parents a short while later. Most likely from their injuries."

Caroline stared back at her in horror. "You... You heard that from the police officers that were here."

Saga shook her head. "What time did I run out here saying we needed to find Nick?" Saga asked her.

Instead of answering Saga, Caroline stormed over, grabbed her by the arm and started to haul her back down the hall to the isolation room. "I will not have you make light of this situation. I will not!" She hissed.

"Ms Caroline!" Lyla called.

"What?" Caroline snapped.

"Let Saga stay with us," Lyla pleaded.

"Absolutely not. If she is going to make a mockery of that boy's death, she can do so without an audience!"

With her grip tightening around Saga's arm, she continued down the hall as fast as she could manage, and Saga didn't even put up a fight as she was thrust back into the room and the door locked behind her again.

At least now, it would be silent in there.

WALHALLA

Silence. There were no longer the cries of 'help me' from Nick or his family. They were no longer standing in various positions around the room, always there wherever she looked. It was a reprieve that was short-lived. Nick was dead. Another person near her, around her, dead. Sure, some she had never met in life, but she was a bad omen.

The day passed slowly. Ever so slowly. She had nothing to do, not even a book to read or lines to write. She would have appreciated having to write lines as it would have given her something to do with the pent-up energy coursing through her with no outlet. If she made too much noise inside the room, Caroline would only punish her further. She stretched, she paced, she ran on the spot, but there was nothing like the feeling of her feet pounding on the ground, eating up the distance, the finish line coming closer and closer with every step. Running on the spot just aggravated her further.

After a day of boredom in the isolation room, it was no surprise that when night finally fell, Saga could not sleep. She had eaten what dinner she could stomach and then shoved it aside, the smell alone making her stomach twist and turn in disgust. She lay on the little bed, curled up so that her feet did not hang off the end and stared at the wall across the room. The house quietened down for the night as everyone went to sleep. Or pretended to until Caroline and Sarah turned in for the night.

The ticking of the clock above the door was the most annoying thing. It had been bugging her since Christmas day, but in the late hours of the night, when sleep alluded her, the sound of the hands moving with their little tick, tick, tick was almost deafening.

By the time they finally struck one in the morning, Saga had already tried walking around the room in lines, then in circles. She had attempted some sit-ups. Then she crawled back into bed and once again tried to sleep. She had counted metaphorical sheep, and after reaching two hundred and thirty-seven fluffy white sheep who had successfully jumped over the farm's fence to greener pastures, she gave that up too.

It was no use. She was awake. She was full of energy from having been stuck in that room for days, and sleep was a prospect that would just never come.

And then, the dogs started to bark. She wanted to scream. The desire was so strong that she gave in. She grabbed her pillow, shoved her face into her mattress and pulled the pillow over her head as tight as she could and screamed into the mattress, hoping no one would hear.

The loud dog was fierce tonight, but she could hear another one. Maybe it was further away or a smaller, less fierce animal, but neither would shut up.

~ * ~

The drive seemed to go on forever, and Ms Roskin said little about where they were going. She just reassured Saga that a great surprise awaited her at the end.

Saga had no idea what this meant but had learned long ago that adults rarely answered her questions. She kept silent and instead watched out the windows of the car as they drove down the freeway. They passed the three turnoffs to Dandenong, then the turnoff to Narre Warren and the big shopping centre there sometime later. After Berwick, it was as though all possible routes off the long straight road led towards neighbourhoods and suburbs that Saga recognised in name only. Even further out, those freeway exits became the exits to small towns with names like Koo Wee Rup, Nar Goon and Labertouche. They drove on past Warragul, and after that, the road just seemed to run through the towns as the main street where all the shops were gathered.

Ms Roskin finally stopped the car in Yarragon to use the facilities. They had been on the road just over an hour, and it had seemed endlessly straight. They had not taken a single turn since turning onto the freeway.

When they emerged out of the public bathrooms and started back to the car, she pointed towards a building, the last row of shops where they had turned into the little parking area.

"Do you want anything to eat?" Ms Roskin asked, pointing towards a bakery near where she had parked the car.

Saga started to shake her head but then thought better of it. Ms Roskin had woken her early, or at least sometime after she had finally fallen asleep and said they had somewhere to be. Saga had thought that she meant another home. Another foster family. Another... Everything. With that thought on her mind, the cereal and toast offered for breakfast at the home had lost all appeal to her, and she had reluctantly followed Ms Roskin out to her car, her bag of meagre possessions slung over her shoulder, certain that she was not coming back to the children's home.

Now that she thought about it, Caroline had been less than thrilled with Ms Roskin, and Saga had heard Caroline talking tersely to the social worker. Probably about Saga's behaviour over Christmas.

"Yes, please," she finally answered.

"Ok, let us go look at what they have," Ms Roskin said, putting some cheer into her voice.

Saga walked a few steps behind Ms Roskin as they crossed the road. Saga bit her lip as they walked. She had been dying to ask her what they were doing ever since she had picked her up. Where they were going? All of that, but she still dared not to and biting her lip was a way to prevent herself from opening her mouth and blurting out all the questions she had bubbling up inside her.

Ms Roskin paused at the door to the bakery and opened the door. Then she stood there, waiting for Saga to catch up. With a quickened step to not keep her waiting, Saga stepped into the bakery and smiled. She really, truly smiled when she saw the colourful baked goods behind the counter.

"What shall it be?" a man behind the counter asked, looking at them as they inspected the baked goods. Saga eyed the strudels, croissants, colourful cupcakes, and raspberry tarts. Next to that were chocolate éclairs, apple turnovers, lamingtons, and meringues. The choice was endless!

"What do you think, Saga?" Ms Roskin prompted.

Saga looked at her. "I can pick anything?" she asked, and Ms Roskin nodded. Saga looked back at the display and grinned to herself. She pointed at a large domed cake with white frosting. "That one."

"Apple cake," the man behind the counter said. "Good choice." He retrieved a white paper bag and some tongs, then opened the display case and retrieved the delicious treat. Saga could not wait to enjoy it. She rarely had treats like this, coach discouraged it, but just this one wouldn't hurt.

Ms Roskin ordered a chocolate éclair for herself, and after paying for them, the two walked out of the shop. Saga opened her white bag as soon as they were outside and stared in delight at her cake.

"Go on, eat it," Ms Roskin said as they walked back to the car.

"In the car?" Saga asked, surprised. Everywhere she had stayed, the foster parents had always banned food in their cars... or the bedrooms... or the couch. Anywhere that was not the kitchen table.

Ms Roskin shrugged. "Unless you would rather sit at that picnic table and eat. It is really nice out today. Not too hot, not too cold." She did have a point. Saga agreed to eat at the table. They ate for a few minutes in silence before she spoke again. "I keep waiting for you to ask..."

Saga looked up at her, taking in the woman's face. She had known her for maybe five years, and despite not all the foster families being kind to her, Ms Roskin had always listened, always been kind, and appeared to be on her side. "I..." Saga paused and put her cake down on the table. "Am I being sent away?"

Ms Roskin shook her head. "No. This is only a day trip for you to see somewhere very important."

"So... Caroline doesn't want me gone?" She hated how small and unsure her voice made her sound, but there it was, the effects of years of shifting around and the last few awful days.

Ms Roskin sighed. "Caroline is... She's concerned about you." Saga harrumphed. She did not believe for a single second that Caroline worried about her. "She says that your behaviour is worrying."

"Oh," Saga muttered. "What? She's worried I'll hurt someone?"

"Yes," Ms Roskin said. "Yourself. Then there was this thing with young Nick and his parents."

That made Saga finally look up from her cake. "What did she tell you? I bet she never told you the truth!"

"Saga," Ms Roskin said calmly. "There's no need to get riled up with me. I've heard every tale there is about you. I don't know how or why, but I do know that you have never been wrong about these things."

"You believe me?"

"I always have," Ms Roskin finished her éclair and got up from the table. "Come on. Finish that in the car. I think that it's really important that you see where we're going."

Saga wrapped up her apple cake and got up from the table, hurrying to catch up to her caseworker as she headed back to the car. "Where are we going?" she finally asked.

"That," Ms Roskin said dramatically, "is a surprise."

The drive continued much as it had on the way to Yarragon. Straight and without any turns. Through Trafalgar, which Saga thought was funny because the small town held no resemblance to the only Trafalgar she had heard of before this, in London.

In Moe, pronounce Moh-ee, not mow, they finally turned off the Princes Freeway. They passed a McDonald's next door seemed to be some sort of museum. They drove on, not stopping, still full from the pastries they had bought in Yarragon.

A few turns later and Ms Roskin was driving out of town. Then, there was nothing but the wide-open countryside and then dense forest. They followed the long, winding road and travelled higher and higher into the mountains. The forest gave way to open farmland, and Saga enjoyed looking out at the views of endless, rolling pastures.

They passed through another small town named Erica but again did not stop. The next town seemed so small that the shopping district appeared to have only one shop, while the others were all boarded up, waiting for the day someone once again brought life to the diminutive town.

They seemed to pass that town in the blink of an eye because, after the tiny primary school, they saw a few more houses and open land before descending into dense forests and winding roads. They went up and down on the ever-winding road. Saga watched Ms Roskin handle the car with ease, as though she travelled roads like these frequently.

They passed a train station in the middle of nowhere that Saga had to ask about. "Well, they run a tourist rail line here, using the old path of the goldfields railway that operated back when these were mining towns," Ms Roskin explained. "The line used to run all the way to Moe but was abandoned until the historical society started to rebuild it. They use the tourist funds and donations to continue extending it. It only runs to Thomson now, which used to be an actual stop on the rail but is no longer a town, just a stop in the middle of nowhere."

When they finally pulled into another town, it was perhaps the smallest and oddest one Saga had seen that day. To her inexperienced eye, the town seemed to exist on only one road, the high mountains on either side making it difficult to build, and the roads that did go up were extremely steep. She saw signs that pointed up a precipitous walking track to a cemetery. Small wooden buildings made up shops and houses alike, some of them showing their age, maintained for historical accuracy. A couple of new places had been built, maybe to deal with tourists, and Ms Roskin pulled her car to a stop on the side of the road across from those newer places.

"Come on," She said eagerly, "We're here."

She waited by the side of the car, locking the door as soon as Saga had closed her door, then led the way, not to the shops, but across a small wooden bridge that crossed the gurgling river that passed through town next to the road.

"Welcome to Walhalla," Ms Roskin said. Saga had seen that name on the signs and many buildings they had already passed. "Established in eighteen sixty-two and during the height of the gold rush, around four thousand people populated the town. Today, there are only about twenty permanent residents."

Saga gaped at her. "You mean to tell me that there are fewer people in this town than there are in some of the homes I've lived in?"

Ms Roskin paused her recitation of town facts and blinked, startled by Saga's comment. "Well..." She thought for a moment. "Yes, I guess you're right." Ms Roskin led her up a rickety flight of stairs into an old bandstand that stood there for all to see on raised stilts. "Do you know what this place is, Saga?"

Saga shook her head as she slowly walked around the small space of the bandstand. She could see a walking trail leading up behind the stand, heading higher up the mountainside, across the road to the new and old shops and even an old shack nearby. "What is it?"

"It was right here, in this town, where you were found."

Saga's slow traverse around the bandstand halted instantly. Slowly she turned to look at Ms Roskin. "Here?" she asked.

Ms Roskin nodded. "Yes," she pointed at the little shack not far from the bandstand. "The couple that found you used to own that property. They didn't live there, but there had been rumours that lights had been seen there. That someone was using that property. After finding you, they thought that maybe it had been your mother hiding out there, especially after finding evidence of someone having been there."

Saga walked over to the banister and stared out at the little shack. Were they right? Had that been the place she was born? Where her mother had hidden with her until deciding that she didn't want the child she had given birth to?

"There are police in Rawson, but that station does not operate twenty-four hours. They called around until eventually being told to drive to Moe..."

"They didn't come?" Saga asked. "I mean... an abandoned child, and they didn't come?"

Ms Roskin shrugged. "I don't know. I believe the opinion was that in Moe, they would also be able to take you to the hospital, and it would save time if the couple brought you there themselves." They stood in silence for a few moments, Ms Roskin waiting to see if Saga would say anything, ask a question, anything. Eventually, she continued. "Your blanket, the one with the gold embroidery... Everyone always thought how odd it seemed to portray the Norse god Odin and other Norse battle scenes."

"Why?" Saga asked, still gazing at the shack.

"The name of this town, Walhalla — it being so similar to the Norse plane of the dead, Valhalla."

"Plane of the dead," Saga said under her breath.

"The plane of the dead where the Valkyries brought the chosen slain to Odin so that they could train for the great battle to come, Ragnarök."

"But that's all fairy tales," Saga said, resuming her slow walk around the bandstand. It had a high domed roof that, like the pillars and walls, was painted in a yellowy creamy colour. The walls and pillars were accented in burgundy and the wood floor. It was all so cold to leave an unprotected infant. Saga turned on her heel and stared at Ms Roskin.

"Why are you showing me this place?" Saga asked, her fingers digging into the wood of the banister. "What are you trying to prove to me? That no one, not even my own mother, has ever wanted me? I know all this already. Everybody makes sure that I know!"

"No!" Ms Roskin tried to reassure her. "Just look at that blanket. That's the sign of someone who genuinely loved their child."

"No one has ever loved me or wanted me, and you throw in all this crap about Norse gods and Valkyries. To do what? Make it all seem like some stupid story." Saga pushed off the railing and stepped toward Ms Roskin. She was shaking, she didn't know if it was an attempt to ward off the tears that were threatening to fall or in a fury at the woman's words, but she could not stop as she pointed her finger at the woman. "It's not some stupid story, not for you or to be passed around over coffee as you and all your friends think, 'oh, poor Saga, but what a story!' It's not a story. It's my life!"

Unable to keep the thoughts in her head from fuelling her anger or denial, or confusion, Saga retreated to her safe place. She ran, fled past Ms Roskin and ran down the rickety old steps of the bandstand. She went back over the little bridge, Ms Roskin calling her name over and over again as she raced after Saga. Ms Roskin's steps were far more unsteady as she tried to keep the same speed as the girl, but the heels she had worn that day, even if they were short and sensible, had not been designed for rickety old stairs in small mountain towns. Especially when her quarry was junior state champion runner. She could do nothing but hobble along as the girl ran across the road and past a small collection of shops before she was out of sight.

~*~

Saga ran. She was so mad and confused that she could not stand to be near Ms Roskin a moment longer. Over the years, she had been told bits and pieces bout the day she had been found or how the letter left by Brigitta had been used to form her name.

So close to Nick's death, after being held in the isolation room and the lack of sleep the night before. She was angry. It did not matter how or why, but she had not been prepared for this trip or this place.

The path she had chosen seemed to run behind a café, and besides an old hotel, she had no idea where it would lead, but she would run until she calmed down. That always worked. Running would calm, then... then she would go back to Ms Roskin. Apologise for yelling at her and listen to what the woman had to say.

A dog, big and black, started to run beside her. Saga had no idea where it had come from, but the animal loped along easily beside her, almost guiding her even. His large head, looking up at her expectantly, those wide doggy eyes seemed to be trying to say something to her when she looked down at him. In those moments, his solid body seemed to nudge her away from a flat road and up a ridge that ran behind the old hotel.

She stopped to catch her breath and get a look at her surroundings. She was quite a bit higher than she had been before. She could look down upon the town over the roof of the old hotel. She could see the bandstand clearly and Ms Roskin hobbling along. Maybe she had broken a heel?

She wanted to feel guilty about running off, but something inside her prevented her from running back down to the woman. Or maybe it was the dog, the massive, wolf-like animal that was rubbing itself against her legs.

Saga crouched down, and the dog licked her face. She ran her hands through his long shaggy fur until her arms were wrapped around his body. He was so warm and soft against her. He sat up, his paws resting on her shoulders as they looked at each other.

"Hey, who's a good boy?" Saga asked, ruffling the dog's fur energetically. "Where's your collar, boy?"

The dog licked at her face, it's tail wagging so fast it was almost a blur. Then he jumped back from her, looking around eagerly. He ran off a few metres and then looked back at Saga. Seeing that she was still crouched where she had been hugging him, he bounded back to her, looked into her eyes briefly and then ran back up the path.

Saga stood and smiled affectionately at the dog. When he returned a second time, she realised he wanted her to follow him.

"Where are we going?" she asked. He bounded along the path, stopping only briefly to check if she was following before allowing the trees on either side of the path to swallow him up.

Stepping under the canopy of the trees, Saga could barely see the dog. Every few metres, he strayed in front of her. He would run back, rub himself against her legs, and then continue. They continued like this until they reached an intersection in the path.

Saga leaned forward, her hands on her knees, and took several gulping breaths. The dog kept up a fast pace that he had not allowed her to slow, and the path seemed to rise up the mountain steeply. The next bit appeared to be even steeper.

The dog barked once and moved further up the mountain path before starting his up-and-down circles between her and the path in front of them.

"Where are you taking me?" she asked him. "I should be getting back..." she added hesitantly, but the dog responded by barking excitedly and breaking into a full-out run as he burst from the trees into a great expanse of sunlight.

Not having a better plan, Saga followed the dog into the open air and was surprised to find that a cricket ground was at the top of the mountain. Even from the edge of the oval, she could see the pitch located in the centre of the field for the wickets and... Well, she did not know all that much about cricket. But she did know that this was a cricket pitch on top of the mountain.

Two Blackbirds flew high above the oval, cawing down at them as they circled. One dived down before pulling itself up from what would have been a lethal crash landing and landed calmly on the head of the dog.

The dog looked back at Saga. He ran up to her, circled her, and then, without warning, took off running across the empty field. The bird screeched in displeasure before spreading its wings and launching itself back into the air as the dog ran.

"Hey!" Saga called out. "Wait for me!"

She ran across the field, following the dog and out of the corner of her eye, she saw both of the blackbirds flying in the same direction.

Still half a field away, Saga saw the dog run up and be embraced by a woman. She was crouched down, allowing the dog to have his paws up on her shoulders as she ruffled his fur and allowed him to nuzzle her face.

As Saga approached the woman and the dog, the woman stood up, the dog sitting beside her, thumping his tail against the grass and panting from his excitement. Saga saw that, like her, the woman was bigger, taller, and probably stronger than most women. The breeze was blowing her wild, blond ringlets all over the place, and she had to brush the hair away from her face several times. Blond ringlets should have looked delicate and regal, but on her, with the wind blowing, it looked strong and fierce. Saga did not think she had ever seen a person like this woman. Her flawless skin seemed to almost glow, or maybe it was reflecting the sunlight, it was hard to tell.

She stepped forward, a warm smile on her face. "Hello, Saga."

ASTRID

Saga's forward momentum halted instantly. She stared at the woman. "How do you know my name?"

The woman smiled and held out her hand. "I know many things, Saga, the most important of which was that you would be here today."

"I—" Saga started. "I didn't even know I would be here today," Saga said softly. She took the woman's hand and shook it as she had been taught. As Saga had guessed, the woman was strong.

Once again, she smiled that oddly gentle smile. "While that is true, there are things that will happen that have been known for long before either of us existed."

Saga frowned. If this woman talked in riddles, she was going to leave. She had had enough of people talking in fairy tales to her. "Your dog should really have a collar on," Saga said instead. "Something to I.D. him as yours."

"Oh, Shadow here isn't my dog," the woman said, reaching down to ruffle his head. Shadow looked adoringly at her as his tail thumped harder against the ground. "He just likes to follow me around."

Saga looked around awkwardly. She had no idea what was going on here. She looked back at the woman, who was watching her intently. "Who are you?" Saga finally asked after several tense moments.

"My name is Astrid Grunborg. I am the Weapons Mistress at Toserra Sorose Academy." She said this as though it was the most obvious thing in the world and as though Saga would know what Toserra Sorose Academy was.

"Umm," Saga murmured. "Ok." They stared at each other, Shadow panting happily as Astrid stroked his head. "What's that?" She asked.

Astrid blinked several times, a look of complete non-comprehension coming over her face to match Saga's expression. "What?" She blinked several more times. "You don't know what Toserra Sorose is? Did Brigitta not tell you anything?"

Saga was startled at hearing her mother's name, and she felt a tightness in her chest that she had not felt since the day she had first been given the letter. "You... you know my mother?" she gasped, clutching at her chest as though it would help her breathe.

Shadow seemed to realise that something was wrong and leapt up from where he had been sitting, enjoying Astrid's attention and came over to her, sniffing. He rubbed his body against her legs, and without thinking about it, Saga crouched down and wrapped her arms around his furry neck, burying her face in his fur before tears could spill from her eyes.

"Saga, where is Brigitta?" Astrid asked, crouching down beside the girl and the dog. Concern was evident in her voice, and Saga wondered why.

"How should I know?" Saga wailed, looking up from the dog, her face streaked with tears she had not meant to let the woman see. "She left me in this town fifteen years ago and never looked back."

Astrid's face darkened at her words. "She did what?" Confusion fought with anger as she started to pace. She would go about three or four steps before turning, repeating the action as she spoke. "Bri and I worked this out. I would be here, today. She would be here with you..."

"She didn't name me or anything, just wrapped me in a blanket and left me down in that bandstand for strangers to find."

Incredulity and anger flashed across Astrid's face, replacing the initial confusion she had shown. She stopped her pacing and crouched there silently before Saga, stunned. "I can't believe her... she said that..." Words seemed to escape her as she tried to come to terms with whatever she had thought was supposed to happen. "So... who brought you here today?"

Sage sniffled and wiped at her eyes, trying to erase the evidence of her tears. "Ms Roskin... my social worker..."

That perplexed look seemed to consume Astrid's face again. "A... a social worker? What's that?"

Saga sighed. "She basically decides everything important for me, like where I live and what I do... or where I go to school."

"But... I... you..." Astrid sighed and seemed to take several deep breaths. "So... you don't know... well... anything?"

"Anything what?" Saga asked.

"Come on," Astrid said. "Let's sit down," and with that, she sat down cross-legged on the grass. Saga followed suit and sat across from her. Shadow settled between them, his head resting in Saga's lap. She sighed and looked at Saga as though she was assessing the girl. Trying to figure out where she should start. "Brigitta was supposed to raise you to know all this stuff. What happened to her?"

Saga shrugged. "I was abandoned at birth. So, they tell me. All what stuff?"

"Everything I now apparently have to tell you. I cannot believe that this is happening," she sighed dramatically. "Not only about yourself but about Toserra Sorose."

"About me? What about me?"

"Saga... it's... I mean you... you're not like other kids — other people."

"I could have told you that," Saga interrupted.

Astrid's eyes widened. "So, you do know!"

"Know what?" Saga repeated. This woman was weird.

"About the dead. How you are meant to guide them to Valhalla."

"Say what?" Saga sputtered. The dead — Saga's greatest fear. The source of her constant ridicule. What did this woman want from her?

"You can see the recently dead, right?"

"Well, yeah, I can see dead people," Saga replied, too surprised to even bother trying to come up with a lie or a snarky remark. "And not just the recently dead."

"What do you mean?" Astrid asked. Saga explained about the incident with the serial killer and how several of the dead who had come to her had been dead for months, if not years. Astrid nodded along. "The unsettled dead who needed a voice so that they could seek their own closure."

"You're saying that I'm not a freak?" Saga asked.

"A freak?" Astrid asked. "Absolutely not. You're a Valkyrie."

"A what?"

Astrid sighed. "Do they teach you nothing in these Midgard schools? I mean, seriously, have you never heard of Odin's Hall of the dead, Valhalla?"

"Well... like in the movies and stuff, sure." Saga said softly. "But... what is... I mean... what do you mean that I am a Valkyrie?"

Astrid looked up at the sky warily. "This was never meant to be my conversation. Brigitta was supposed to prepare you for all of this. For the dead, school, for... for what is to come."

"You're not making any sense," Saga told her.

"No, I suppose I'm not," Astrid agreed. "You, Saga, a good old Norse name, by the way."

Sage raised an eyebrow. "Why do people always bring up old Norse stuff with me? It's like everyone expects me to know what they're talking about."

Astrid laughed softly. "Girl, life is like that. People will always expect you to know what they know. "Anyway, as I was trying to tell you, you are a Valkyrie. You are the first Valkyrie to appear in Midgard or anywhere since Ragnarök, two hundred years ago."

~*~

The big black birds that had dived at the dog earlier circled above them as they spoke. One squawked loudly, pulling Astrid's attention to it. "People are looking for you in the village. We should get you back there."

"What? How do you know?"

"Hojar told me," Astrid said, pointing at one of the birds. Saga could not tell the difference between the two birds, but Astrid pointed confidently at one of them. "A woman is quite panicked about your whereabouts."

Saga frowned. "That would be Ms Roskin."

"Saga, if you are not trained in our ways... the dead... they will begin to consume you. I want you to come to Toserra Sorose. I want you to learn to be the Valkyrie we need."

Saga shrugged her backpack off her back and hauled it into her lap. Shadow woke up with a start, barely managing to prevent his nose from being squashed by the bag. He dropped his head into Astrid's lap with a disgruntled huff. Saga pulled out several articles of clothes, and as she did so, several award ribbons fluttered out, A book, her phone and finally, from the bottom of the bag, the white baby blanket with delicate gold thread depicting winged warrior women. "These, are these Valkyries?"

Astrid leaned over, her hand scratching the dog's head idly. "Oh. Oh my." She gasped in awe. "That... that is Brigitta's work. Yes, yes, those are the Valkyries. That would be," Astrid tentatively ran her finger over the gold thread work of the Valkyries' forms. "Róta and Ölrún. Two fierce warriors. May I?" She asked, indicating that she wanted to take the blanket from Saga. Saga hesitated. She rarely showed the blanket to anyone, but to let someone else touch it or take it from her hands made her heart constrict. It was all she had from the mother who abandoned her, and she feared losing it. Finally, she nodded, agreeing to let Astrid take it from her hands.

Astrid was gentle, almost reverent, in her movements as she handled the blanket. "This is Odin, the All-Father of the Æsir. That is his wife, Frigga," Astrid explained, pointing to a female figure beside the figure of Odin. The birds above them squawked again. "Ok, ok," Astrid called out, waving them off as they dived at her, eager for her attention. "Myjor, I get it. The Rainbow Bridge comes."

Saga watched the bird as it swooped down to Astrid, then back up again to the sky where its friend still circled above them. "The what?" She asked.

Astrid handed the delicate gold-threaded blanket back to Saga. "The Rainbow Bridge. It is——" She paused as she watched Saga return the blanket gently to her bag before repacking every item within it. "It is a remnant of what used to be called the Bifrost bridge. A shimmering bridge of light that connected Midgard to Asgard. But those are lessons for another day. Today, I have left you much to think about."

Astrid started to get to her feet, and the two birds circled lower until she stood straight. Then they settled, one on each of Astrid's shoulders. "It was nice to meet you, Saga Joy Carolle."

"But!" Saga objected. "You said——" She cried, jumping up to stand beside Astrid.

"Yes, I said I want you to come to Toserra Sorose, but these things must all happen in time. A time that includes the adults in your life."

Saga scoffed. "There isn't anyone here that cares about me. Not a one." She felt a little guilty about Lyla, but the girls had only known each other a short while, and both would have been separated at some point to be moved on to another home, another house, or drummed out into adult life before long.

"Saga," Astrid said, turning to face her, even as her eyes kept glancing to the sky, looking for something that Saga could not identify. "There are rules that must be followed."

A colourful platform of light came swooping at them from nowhere suddenly. It shimmered and glowed, the colours rippling like fire against not only every other colour on the platform but against the landscape of wide-open blue sky and the green of the cricket pitch atop the mountain.

"It is here, and I must go," Astrid said, carefully stepping onto the platform as it slowed near her.

"Wait!" Saga cried out as the platform started to move again.

"Shadow!" Astrid called to the big dog standing several paces away from where they had been talking. He bounded up towards Astrid and Saga, his tongue lolling out of his mouth as he ran. His infinite energy had him circle the moving rainbow platform several times as it crossed the cricket field. Saga turned around, trying to keep him in sight as she followed Astrid and the broken piece of rainbow.

His little jaunts around the shard became smaller as he narrowed in on Saga until he managed to trip her over. Saga flailed her arms as she attempted to catch herself on anything she could before falling to the ground in a great heap. Saga's hands grasped onto the first thing she could and suddenly felt herself being dragged along. Her feet could not get any purchase against the grassy field as she held on to the rainbow platform, which suddenly rapidly began to move upwards instead of continuing across the field. The dog kept running and jumped up beside her.

"Shadow!" Astrid barked, her voice the only thing Saga could take notice of as her feet lost all contact with the ground. "No!"

Saga screamed in fear, and she could hear her scream echo off the nearby mountains, ricocheting its way down the valley. "Help!" She cried out as she reached for another handhold, anything that would help pull her onto the platform so that she would no longer be hanging from its edge. "Help me!"

Startled, Astrid crouched down, "Take my hand!" She cried. Saga's hands refused to cooperate. Her feet kicked wildly at the wide, open air beneath her.

And then she did the thing she absolutely should not have done. She looked down. The ground was retreating away from them at an alarming rate. The cricket pitch and, even further below that, the tiny town of Walhalla were mere specs on the ground. She felt her heart stop as her sweaty palms slipped.

"Give me your hand!" Astrid ordered. But Saga could barely hear her over the whipping wind around them and the fear that paralysed her where she hung. "Saga!" Astrid cried.

Saga's pounding heart made it even harder to hear anything going on around her as her eyes stared dumbfoundedly down at the ground as it continued to retreat away from her.

"Shadow!" Astrid commanded, and without further warning, the dog was atop her, his long snout and jaw grabbing into the back of her shirt and backpack as he began to shimmy backwards, trying to haul Saga onto the flying rainbow shard.

Astrid grabbed hold of the girl, aiding the dog in his efforts until Saga was sprawled across the colourful platform. Astrid knelt beside her, awkwardly patting Saga on the shoulder as she heaved deeply to take in air.

"I take it you don't like heights," Astrid said serenely.

Saga gasped three more times as she wrapped her shaking arms around Shadow's thick, fluffy neck. "Heights?" Sage asked incredulously. "This is not 'heights'. This is flying through the godforsaken air on a freaking rainbow!" Shadow barked in agreement, his tail wagging excitedly. "What the hell?"

"Well?" Astrid said, eyeing Shadow suspiciously, "I guess we will go to Yggdrasil together."

"Ig what?"

"These Midgard schools really do teach you, children, nothing."

~ * ~

Saga was sure that she would never get a feel for flying. Not in a million years. Nope, absolutely not. It would not happen. The shimmering platform of light brought them up high, well above the cloud cover, startling birds and even once passing an aeroplane.

"Can't they see us?" Saga asked.

"Of course not," Astrid replied. "Their mortal eyes do not expect to see a rainbow disk with two women and a dog upon it. Therefore, they do not."

"It cannot be that easy," Sage argued.

"It's not, but that is how the magic works. It makes us invisible to them because what we are is inconceivable. There!" She pointed at the horizon where they could see a ginormous tree extending high above the clouds, even higher into the atmosphere, its many branches extending seemingly into forever. "Yggdrasil, the World Tree. It connects every plane of existence."

The sight of it took Saga's breath away. The mere size of the tree, the breadth of its trunk and its far-reaching branches were beyond anything she had ever even imagined. Glittering lights sparkled between the leaves as the wind moved the tree gently. As the rainbow platform beneath them sped them closer towards the tree, Saga thought that she could see flowers of every colour and shape blossoming from between the leaves until she realised that they had moved. Reds and greens and blues, dashing to and from between the branches and leaves of the tree.

"Wow," she breathed out. As they came even closer, she could hear them and realised that the colours she saw were not flowers but people. People were walking around on the tree's giant branches, and, if she was not mistaken, there were buildings, tents, hovels, and stalls. People lived in the tree. "Are those... people?"

"Yes," Astrid replied, "The city within the tree came to be as Asgard fell, and those who had lived within those hallowed halls fled but were unable to reach the other planes due to the destruction of the Bifrost bridge, they made a home..." As she spoke, the platform they were riding started to run over an extended branch. Astrid expertly dodged leaves and small twigs that extended over the runway, and Saga covered her face to prevent herself from being scratched.

"Jump on off," A voice called, and Astrid stepped off the shimmering rainbow platform and onto the rough brown bark of the branch beneath her feet.

"Come on," Astrid ordered, and Shadow jumped down beside her. Saga started as the platform continued to move. "They don't stop. You've just got to hop on down."

She walked beside the platform as Saga stared at her once more in incredulity. "What?"

"They're just broken pieces of what was once a bridge that crossed the realms of existence. Jump down, Saga, or who knows where you'll wind up," she offered her hand and tentatively, Saga took it and jumped down from the floating platform as it continued to glide across the top of the branch, turning before it hit the massive trunk of the tree and heading off into the great unknown.

Stepping off the moving platform, Saga stumbled and only managed to stay upright because of Astrid's help. "Wow," Saga murmured.

"All Rainbow Express passengers are asked to vacate the landing area."

"Come on," Astrid said as soon as the announcement passed. Without checking to see if Saga or Shadow followed, she started towards the tree trunk.

As they left the landing area, they entered a gap within the tree trunk resembling a door. The two birds resting on Astrid's shoulders left her, flapping their wings, departing for parts unknown. Saga was surprised to find that the interior of the tree's trunk was hollow and that stairs were spiralling around the walls and crisscrossed with walkways at various intervals that led out via other gaps or archways to other locations of the tree. Small discs of rainbow light moved up and down between the walkways, various people getting on or off for an easy trek up or down the levels of the tree. Astrid led Saga and Shadow up, taking the stairs that seemed to run up and down the tree as far as the eye could see.

"Where are we going?" Saga asked.

Astrid looked down at her three steps above from where she was. "Right now? To the Bore Tooth Inn for some food. We can talk there... and hopefully, Headmaster Gotts will be there."

Saga followed her, scrambling up the stairs, eager to keep up with Astrid's punishing pace. She turned confidently out of an archway, two flights up from the landing area.

Shadow raced out ahead of them, running past the archway that led onto the street upon the branch. Strings of light glistened from the low-lying smaller branches, lighting up what appeared to be a collection of dining establishments.

Saga guessed that this branch held maybe four separate establishments, their buildings made of wood and cloth, making the place look as though it was temporary. The multi-coloured fabrics of the tents made it hard to discern just how many establishments were operating on this branch, but Astrid strode confidently towards one with a roof of green and purple fabric and an awning of shocking orange. A wooden structure seemed to erupt above the fabric roof, looking for all the world as though it had just been propped atop the tent.

She brushed a flap of thick red fabric aside and stepped inside. The interior was crowded. People sat around large, rickety wooden tables. A musician strummed at a lute on a little stage made out of what had probably once been a crate.

"Hadar," Astrid said, striding through the crowded tables to a small one in the back corner of the half shack, half tent building.

"Astrid, did you—" he started, but then he spotted Saga, and his words stopped mid-sentence. He just stared, and Saga felt as though he was attempting to stare right through her, into her very soul. Saga's head felt as though cotton wool was engulfing it, and she stumbled.

"Hadar!" Astrid cried softly, trying to catch the man's attention.

The man suddenly looked away from Saga, and her head instantly cleared up. The cotton wool feeling disappeared in the same instance that their eyes ceased to look into one another. "She... she really is."

Saga looked from the man Astrid had identified as Hadar to the woman herself. "Really what?"

Astrid grabbed a chair at the table and motioned for Saga to take the other one. As she moved through the narrow space left between occupied chairs, she noticed that people stopped to watch where she went. The conversations around the bar seemed to have stalled around them, and Saga could feel their eyes on her back as she took the seat Astrid indicated.

"A Valkyrie," Hadar breathed. "I didn't think they existed anymore."

"Well, I told you that they did," Astrid said, sitting down. "Saga, this is Hadar Gotts, the Headmaster of Toserra Sorose Academy in Nýr Ásgardr. Headmaster Gotts, this is Saga Joy Carolle."

Saga took the time now to look at the man across from her at the table. She could now take in his features, unlike when she had first entered, and their eyes had locked. His eyes were a dark brown that seemed striped with different shades of browns and golds. Now that she could look at him without that cotton wool feeling engulfing her head, she could see just how unusual they were, almost like a gemstone she had once seen on display called a Tiger's eye. He wore a deep, ruby-red jacket with black accents that seemed to darken the five o'clock shadow adorning his chin. The whole effect made the straight black hair that he had shaved on one side and pulled back on the other side. It all made him seem younger. But Saga was not fooled. For some reason, she could tell that this man, with his deep-set, brown eyes was older and far more menacing than she could ever imagine.

"A Valkyrie... I don't think that I ever saw one before... not even when they were standard fare on the battlefield," Gotts murmured, staring back at Saga as she appraised him.

Behind her, she could hear the word 'Valkyrie' whispered again and again by the other people as they talked to one another, occasionally glancing surreptitiously towards their table. A few people close to them even tried to move further away from her, although their attempts at discretion were always disrupted by the scraping of chair legs against the roughhewn floor of the bar.

"What's the big deal?" Saga asked, looking around.

"Every Valkyrie of the day, every last one that survived the great battle of Ragnarök, vanished in the days after Odin's death," Astrid said, leaning in so that they could speak without others listening in. "No one knows what it means that a new Valkyrie has appeared in the world. I want to bring Saga to Toserra Sorose in the new school year."

Gotts shook his head. "Too many people will not like it."

"We cannot allow the girl to wander off alone in the world."

"A Valkyrie? A Handmaiden of battle, at Toserra Sorose?" Gotts shook his head again. "Astrid, you have lost your mind. As one of the Æsir, you should be frightened of this prospect. More frightened than any of us."

"She is Brigitta's child. I will not abandon her back to that Midgard society," Astrid stated.

"Drinks?"

Everyone at the corner table jumped. Gotts looked around as if trying to decide if anyone other than the server could have heard. Astrid straightened, her face falling back into a stern expression. "A Storm Pale Ale," Astrid stated as though she had not been almost startled out of her skin by the server's appearance.

The young woman looked from Astrid to Gotts. "And you, Sir?"

"An Elven Ruby Red," the girl noted the order down, and while she looked at Saga, she refused to make eye contact. She also did not speak.

"Umm," Saga said, looking around awkwardly. "You got a Coke Zero?" Astrid, Gotts, and the serving girl all stared at her in confusion. "Umm," Saga mumbled. "Whatever... like a diet soda or something..."

The poor serving girl looked helplessly at Astrid and Gotts. Who, much to Saga's dismay were also looking hopelessly at each other.

"How about a Jelly Melon Cider?" Astrid suggested.

The serving girl looked positively relieved as she made a note of the order. "Anything else?"

"Actually, I'm famished," Astrid declared. "I'll get some of the day's stew as well. Hadar, Saga?"

Hadar Gotts shook his head. "No, thank you, Astrid. I have an appointment later today for my meal."

Astrid nodded as though this statement made perfect sense and looked at Saga, who had thought that the headmaster's choice of wording was quite peculiar.

Saga thought about food. She had not had much breakfast, and she did not know how long it had been since she had eaten the apple cake with Ms Roskin. "Yeah... Umm, what Astrid's having."

"Right," the serving girl said. "A Storm Pale Ale, an Elven Ruby Red, a Jelly Melon Cider and two stews of the day."

When it was indicated that there would be nothing else for them, the serving girl hurried away through the tables of patrons to the far side of the ramshackle building.

Hadar Gotts looked at the Saga intently, his strange, striped, brown eyes roaming over her face before he turned his attention back to Astrid. "Hmm, yes. Where were we?"

"I was telling you that Saga would be joining us at Toserra Sorose," Astrid stated flatly.

"We offer no program for Valkyries," Gotts objected.

"No one does, but she sees the dead. We cannot allow her to roam alone in a world that has forgotten what we all are."

"You speak of which you have no understanding, Astrid. You were but a babe in your mother's arms in the aftermath of the war. I see no way for this to work."

"You know," Saga said, speaking up. "It's great and all that you two are trying to decide my future as though I'm not here, but there's still an awful lot that I don't understand. Starting with where we are and moving on to what the hell everyone means by the fact that I'm a Valkyrie to everything in between. You think one of you wants to start explaining that?" Neither Astrid nor Gotts spoke. "You can start anywhere... I mean, really... anywhere."

Gotts ignored her and looked at Astrid. "She's seeing the dead?" Astrid nodded. "Fine. But she is your responsibility. You and only you."

"I'll be her guardian," Astrid stated, ignoring Saga's request.

"You know!" Saga interrupted loudly. "I am here!" Around them, the conversation stalled as people turned to look at them. "I'm here, and would one of you please acknowledge me!"

~ * ~

By the time Astrid led her up to a small bedroom above the inn, she had no more answers than when she had entered the bar.

"We don't have all that much time to get you everything you need for school," Astrid said idly as she sat on the small bed, running a brush through her golden ringlets. "There's your uniform, work gloves, riding uniform, hmm. First, years do not need their own weapons until they select their own... Textbooks for languages, herbalism, history, and planarography. Hmm, with Gotts insisting that you be enrolled as an Angel, you'll be doing World Religions... You'll also need an astrology book, astronomy book and telescope, and a planar star chart. Oh, with being with the Host, you'll be expected to do an instrument at some point, but that should be able to wait until the second semester."

Saga stared at Astrid. It had seemed as though everyone had spent the evening staring at her, so it was quite fulfilling to be able to be the one doing the staring. Astrid just kept rambling about the school things she would need to attend Toserra Sorose, and the classes she was talking about seemed slightly out of this world. That seemed to be everything she had encountered since the large black dog had led her up the mountainside.

Standing by the window of the tiny second-floor room of The Bore Tooth Inn, Saga looked out into foliage scattered with tiny little lights. She could still hear the noise from downstairs and the other restaurants. She could not believe it. She was staying in an Inn in a tree! A tree!

Behind her, Astrid was still going on about the things she would need before starting school at the end of January. "And with everything Shadow did, you will have nothing to your name... I'll need to set up some sort of allowance. Something that allows you to survive in Nýr Ásgardr city."

"It's a boarding school, isn't it?" Saga asked, turning back to Astrid.

"Well... yes," Astrid stated, "But... the students live in residential houses around the town. Only two of them have a dorm-like structure, but even so, without family support, you will need access to money. The house you're assigned to provides breakfast and dinner, but not lunch."

"So, you mean I won't be with you?"

"No, Saga. I live in town, but no, all students are expected to live in school housing."

"So, what are the houses like?"

Astrid shrugged. "Depends on the house. Each has its own characteristics. Specific things that are looked for in the students that are assigned there. I'm not entirely sure how it is decided, but everyone always gets assigned where they ultimately belong."

"You work there, and you don't know?"

Astrid chuckled as she put her brush down on the bedside table. "There are some things they keep a mystery from the Weapons Mistress."

"And those classes you were talking about before? What about Maths and science, French and P.E. Where's that stuff?"

"There are other classes you can take as you progress through the year levels, but these are pretty standard in this world for any proposed career path," Astrid stated. "Horse riding is only mandatory in the first year."

"Ok." Saga was still confused. "And what's planarography? And Weapons craft, Astrology? These are actual classes?"

"What would you want to study?" Astrid asked.

"Want might be a strong word, but I would be expected to take like English and Geography and-."

Astrid cut her off. "There! Geography. That's Planarography!"

"Why not call it Geography?"

With a laugh, Astrid shook her head in amusement. "There are nine planes that extend off the World Tree. Now, as for your other class, while I am completely capable of answering most, if not all, of your questions, sometimes it's better to experience things firsthand. Like a good surprise, don't you think?"

No, Saga did not think that. In fact, she hated surprises.

THE TREE CITY

In the days since she had come to Yggdrasil city, Saga had noticed that Shadow would come and go at his own will. Astrid had insisted that he was not her dog and that he was free to do as he pleased. She had also explained that Shadow was not a dog but a wolf. When he was around, though, Astrid allowed Saga to go off alone with the animal and spend their days traversing the branches, running up and down the tree's central trunk, exploring every aspect of the vertical city as they could. It was as though Astrid trusted the dog or wolf or whatever he was to keep Saga out of trouble.

Shadow sat beside Saga as she ate breakfast, his head resting in her lap. People in the bar, the servers, and the regulars had stopped muttering about her, and she no longer felt as though her every move was being watched as she ate her meals or went to the tiny room she was sharing with Astrid. Outside in the town, it was a different story, though.

Shadow looked at her, his head shifting slightly, allowing his sad little doggy eyes to catch her attention as she attempted to put her bacon into her mouth.

"What?" Saga asked. "Didn't you eat before you came?"

His head turned a little, almost as though he was attempting to shrug and say, "Who me? Why would I do that when your food is for the taking?"

Saga sighed, bit a large piece of her bacon piece, and handed the leftover piece down to the dog. It was gone in two seconds as he practically inhaled it, finishing by licking his lips expectantly.

"More?" Saga asked. "Really?"

He cocked his head to the other side as though showing off his cutest side. "Fine," Saga relented. "But no more," she said as she handed him her last piece of crispy fried bacon. The dog's eyes continued to stare up at her. "What?" Saga cried, exasperated. "You've already eaten half of my food."

"Oh good," Astrid said, striding over, a piece of parchment in her hand. "Oh, even better. Shadow is here too." She put the parchment on the table. "I have made a list of what you will need for school. I know that I was supposed to come with you, but I'm afraid that something has come up that I must deal with. Think you can handle arranging this in the marketplace?"

Saga looked over the list. There were standard things. Blank workbooks, one for each subject, textbooks, quills apparently, and ink jars, the kind of stuff you needed no matter what school you went to. Ok, some of them were a little odd, but it was your standard school list.

"I should be able to handle this," Saga said, putting more confidence into her voice than she felt when she spotted items like a herbalism kit, telescope, and riding accoutrements. "Umm, what are riding accoutrements?"

"You know, helmet, boots, uniform," Astrid said easily. "But that place is not in the marketplace. You'll have to go down to the base of the tree. They also sell horses and well... You know... Horses and heights..."

Saga did not know, but it seemed to make sense. She looked over the rest of the purchase list and sighed. It would be a long day. "But... How am I going to afford all of this? I don't... I don't have any money..." While in the days that they had been together, Astrid had bought Saga little things here and there so that she had toiletries and a few changes of clothes, she could not expect Astrid to just pay for everything on her booklist. It looked as though it would be really expensive.

"I have a Toserra Sorose discount as an instructor. Take this," Astrid handed over a small card that detailed Astrid's position at the school. "And this," Astrid handed over a rather large bag of coins. "You're familiar with money, and you just need to remember that we primarily deal in drachmae and obols. Six Obols make one drachmae. A triobol is a half drachma or three obol, a diobol is two obol. Honestly, no one should be dealing in anything less than an obol, but we do have hemiobols which are half an obol and a few others, but as I said, you shouldn't have to deal with Tetartemorion or Hemitetartemorion. I mean, no one really deals in less than an obol these days... Now, I have not given you anything larger than a drachma. You really shouldn't have any need for anything costing a Didrachm or higher at any one place, but... no... You should not need any. Now, you must get everything on that list, no matter how strange they appear to you."

Saga looked back over the list, her head reeling with the monetary knowledge Astrid had just presented her with. She was never going to remember any of that... And apparently, there was more! What could Astrid mean by that? "Combat leathers?" Saga asked because asking about the money was likely to make her head explode in confusion.

"Armour for class. It's necessary that it is correctly fitted for the student, and no class sets are available, even in the first year."

"Astrid..." Saga said softly, holding the list and the bag of coins. "I'll pay you back. I swear. I will."

Astrid smiled distractedly at her. "Never you mind that," she insisted. "Just make sure that you buy everything on that list, and if you have anything left over, keep it for during the school term. Living in the town will have its expenses."

"This list is huge," Saga said in awe as she read through the various required books and class accessories, then the uniform items, many of which were needed multiple. Then there was the equestrian uniform, the combat leathers, and all the usual school stuff.

"Make sure you get all your uniform items fitted," Astrid added. "Nothing worse than ill-fitting jodhpurs."

~ * ~

With the equestrian stables at the base of the tree, Saga set off there first. Astrid's insistence that uniform items should be fitted made her eager to get those items out of the way before the shops could become overly busy with other back-to-school shoppers. So, as soon as she had finished the last of her breakfast, with Shadow's assistance, she had bid Astrid goodbye, wondering where the older woman was going, as this seemed like a day that Saga could have used her assistance.

"Come on, Shadow," Saga said as she stepped off the last of the steps inside the tree to step for the first time in almost two weeks on the actual ground. At that time, she had wondered what had happened to poor Ms Roskin, left in that quaint little mountain town all on her own. What would have happened after Saga had not come down the mountain? Did anyone other than Ms Roskin even miss her? She had wanted to ask Astrid about Ms Roskin but could never find the right time to do so. The green grass spread out before her, making a soft, almost inviting field that begged for her to sit down or wrestle in the grass with the big dog at her side.

There were a few buildings scattered in the shade of the tree, one of which was surrounded on one side by a large paddock and, on the other, by several large barns where she guessed that travellers' horses were stabled during their stay at the big tree city. A few people seemed to have made camp on the other side of a small road leading to the tree's entrance.

She stopped short when she saw a young woman, maybe a few years older than herself, or at least Saga guessed that the woman was only a few years older. Saga had never seen anyone like her before. Her skin was not what people called black on Earth... or Midgard, as Astrid always called it. The girl's skin was blacker than the night sky. The deepest pitch of black that Saga had ever seen in her life. Long white hair trailed down her back as she pottered around a small campsite preparing breakfast.

A boy emerged from the tent, also older than Saga. He spoke to the girl, maybe his sister? Saga did not know, but he, too, had skin so black it seemed unreal. His pure white hair, as white as snow, just like the girl's was cut short and stuck out from his head at all angles.

"What you looking at?" He barked suddenly, and Saga realised that she had been staring at them intently as they had gone about their morning routine.

"Edun," the girl hissed. "Quiet. We will not cause trouble."

Edun, for Saga guessed that this was the boy's name, scowled at his sister. "Weakling," he hissed back at her before turning a scowl on Saga and storming off. He made sure that as he passed Saga, their shoulders collided. Shadow barked loudly and was about to chase after the angry young man.

"No, Shadow," Saga ordered. "Stay," She looked sheepishly at the girl, who was now standing with two younger girls, all with the same night sky skin and snow-white hair. "I'm sorry," she called out, "I didn't mean to stare!"

The oldest of the girls shook her head. "No one ever does," and she turned back to her food preparations.

Feeling as though she had done something horribly wrong, Saga hurried past the little campsite and into the big wooden building next to the paddock. Shadow looked at the door of the building, gave a little bark of alarm and bounded off. She was used to this from him, so as she always did, Saga let him go off and do his own thing. He would most likely return when she left the building anyway.

The big man behind a counter called to her without even looking up. "Which school?"

"Umm..." Saga murmured as she looked around. Several other kids her age were inside the shop, each with someone attending to them. She noticed that the riding clothes they were showing the parents and kids were of different colours and had different logos on the breast pocket of the riding jackets. She noticed at least four different school riding uniforms being fitted.

"Well, girl?" the big man bellowed across the room, causing everyone to stop and look at her.

"Toserra Sorose," she finally managed to say.

The big man harrumphed something about flighty girls and pointed her towards one of the women currently measuring up another girl. "Over there, wait for Sarita to measure you up."

As Saga waited, she watched the people go about picking their required school riding uniforms, watched as their heads were measured for the correct helmet, and they inspected what Saga guessed to be items from the horse care kit she was supposed to pick up.

The door to the large workroom opened, and a distinguished lady walked in. Her thick mane of black hair was tied intricately atop her head, and she looked frustrated. The well-dressed man beside her looked just as frustrated.

"I swear that boy is never where he's supposed to be," the woman hissed loudly to the man.

"Come now, Gisette, he's a young man exploring the city for the first time on his own. He will be here," apparently, the man's frustration was with the woman and not the missing boy she was complaining about.

Behind the counter, the large man once again did not look up. "Which school?"

A displeased consternation crossed Gisette's face as she looked across the room at the large man. "Excuse me? Is that any way to address your customers?"

At the sound of her crisp, stern voice, the man looked up and, in an instant, also straightened up. "Oh... My apologies Lady Harding. That will be Toserra Sorose for your youngest, yes?"

"Exactly," she added, her voice a little less crisp. "If that wretched boy ever gets here," she added.

The man, whom Saga guessed to be Mr Harding, was looking anxiously at what Saga considered an old-fashioned pocket watch and sighed. As he slipped the ornate device back into his pocket, the door crashed open, and a young man appeared. He was tall and slender, with shaggy black hair as thick and as dark as Lady Gisette Harding's. Dark blue eyes scanned the room. "Mother, Father," he said, taking long strides towards them.

Saga watched his every move. Something about this boy was so remarkably familiar, but she could not place it. He glanced at Saga, caught her looking at him, and they both quickly looked away, embarrassed to be caught looking at the other.

"We will have Sarita fit Emory out," Lady Gisette announced, striding over to where Saga was waiting.

"Move, girl."

Saga blinked in surprise but was saved from having to say anything by the large man. "I'm afraid Sarita has a queue this morning Lady Harding."

As if this was a new phenomenon, Lady Harding looked from the woman currently measuring up another girl to Saga and then to the large man. "Yes, starting with my Emory."

"Ma," the boy, Emory, hissed. "Come on, just wait until Sarita is done with those girls... Or we can go to one of the others."

"Sarita is the best. You will be seen by no one else, and you will not wait in a mere queue behind this nobody girl as though——" Saga turned to look at the woman, and maybe it was the fact that, for the first time, they were looking directly at each other, or maybe it was the fact that Lady Harding was now confronted with Saga's large form, long blond hair and piercing blue eyes, but she stopped short. "I... well... oh... of course, you go right on ahead of us."

Emory looked between Saga and his mother. Saga blinked awkwardly in surprise. "Umm... thank you," she said softly as Lady Harding wrapped an arm around her son and steered him away from where she had been waiting to be seen by Sarita.

The wealthy family were finally seen by one of the other outfitters, much to the elegant woman's disdain. Saga left with a large bag full of her riding uniform, helmet and horse care kit slung over one shoulder. She looked outside the establishment for Shadow, but he was nowhere to be found. She lingered for a while, hoping that the dog would appear. The campsite across from the farrier's looked abandoned now. The tents were closed up tight, the fire put out, and all small odds and ends were out of sight from possible prying hands. Saga wondered where the small family had gone.

She walked slowly past the paddock, where a horse was munching on the lush green grass near the enclosure's fence. Saga had only ever once before seen a horse this close. They had taken a group of kids on an excursion to a horse farm where they had been given very short but extremely fun riding lessons. Saga had loved it there, and her horse had nuzzled at her and eaten from her hand so enthusiastically. She had laughed every time his large tongue licked her hand as he sought out the treats she had been feeding him. It had been over all too soon, but she looked forward to the opportunity to learn to ride for real.

The horse looked up from its grazing and wandered over along the fence line to where she was standing, admiring him. The horse popped his head over the fence and knocked his head gently against her shoulder, just like the horse from that excursion.

"Hi there," she said softly, raising her hand to pat his face. "Well, aren't you just gorgeous, huh? Don't suppose you've seen a large black dog running around out here, have you?" She asked the horse.

She patted him a little longer and realising how much time had passed, she sighed, patted the horse one last time on his large nose and backed away. "I gotta go, but if you see that dog, you send him after me at the marketplace, ok?"

She looked back at the list Astrid had given her that morning and noticed a notation next to 'Herbalism' stating that the best shop to buy her tools from was also located on the ground in the shade of the tree city. Saga departed from the horse and found her way back to the path that circled the tree, branching off to unknown parts that lead off into the blinding sunlit fields beyond the tree's branches.

She eventually stepped into another small wooden building roofed by a colourful green canvas. It was dark inside, but a beautiful blonde girl with translucent, glittering wings protruding from her back stood inside, inspecting gardening tools. Beside her, a boy with the same startling bright and beautiful features stood.

"No," the girl said. "Tasso, you can't just take any junk like those non-people before," she stated haughtily. Across from her, the old woman who had been showing a kit of tools to the boy looked angry, but as she noticed Saga looking at her, she smoothed her face out.

"Ah, good morning there," she called over as if she were glad for a reason to get away from the beautiful people. "Oh, I suppose it's just about midday now, isn't it? What can I do you for this fine day?"

As she managed to extract herself from the two winged beings, she hurried over to where Saga stood, Astrid's list in her hands. "Oh... umm, I'm looking for..." Saga looked back at her list. "An eleven-piece gardening kit that must have a—"

"You going to Toserra Sorose, Aquino Beccara. No, you're not fae or angel, Ehras Magna or Rinsunid Cantera, dear?"

"Toserra Sorose," Saga answered.

"Right, right, you'll be looking for the kit with the shovel, trowel, shears, ah yes, small rake," she bustled around the shop looking at different kits, trying to decide which one she thought would be best for Saga. All the while, the beautiful blond, winged girl looked as though she had never been more affronted in her life.

"You were serving us," she stated.

The woman looked over at her. "Well, you were not yet decided, were you? Continue your deliberations, and I'll be right with you."

The boy, an identical image of the girl in every way, except that he was male, and his silky blond hair fell only to his shoulders instead of to his waist as the girl's hair did, spoke up. "I'll have this one, Madam Laiona."

Madam Laiona nodded, "Of course, dear boy," She placed a set of tools down on the counter, "Inspect these and see if they're to your liking, dear girl, while I go see to this young man's purchase."

Saga looked over each tool, not knowing what she was looking for but biding her time until the woman returned from the other two.

It took another ten minutes for the girl to finally settle on a set of tools with sparkling pink handles and for her to allow her brother to purchase the set he had been willing to accept at the beginning as well.

Madam Laiona sighed in relief as they left, "Faeries," she muttered harshly under her breath. Then straightened herself and returned to Saga. "So sorry that took so long, my dear. How are these, or would you like to see another set?"

Saga shook her head. "These are fine. I really don't know all that much about gardening," she waved her hand over the selection of tools. "I don't even know what all of these are, let alone what they do," she said miserably. The longer she had stood there staring at the tools, the worse she had felt about 'Herbalism' class.

Madam Laiona laughed. "Never mind that. The plants will either like you or they won't. Never fear; they do appreciate a good set of tools, though." Saga paid for the set, and as she went to put the kit of tools in her bag with her equestrian gear, Madam Laiona added. "The secret is to talk to them. Talk about anything, a bad dream, a good memory, your friends. Plants, they're great listeners, and they grow better for the conversation too."

Saga smiled. "I'll remember that. Thanks, Madam Laiona."

Outside, Saga was disappointed to discover that Shadow had still not returned, so she slowly made her way back to the large tree trunk stairwell. She looked at the stairs, then at the little floating discs of coloured light that went up and down through the tree. Without giving it a second thought, she hopped on one that appeared to be heading up.

And instantly regretted it.

The straight upwards motion was similar to that of an elevator going up at speed, but the lack of walls, handholds, or anything to support herself. Her legs wobbled, and the disc, which was even smaller than the one she had ridden with Astrid, left her no choice but to look at everything beneath her if her gaze drifted anywhere near her feet.

Where was she supposed to get off again? The marketplace was just on branch twenty. But she had already lost track of where she was going.

And how did you stop the thing long enough to feel comfortable stepping onto one of the catwalks?

She held her arms tight to her body. Her shopping bag clutched against her body in the fear that she might drop it.

A streak of black up one of the staircases. People screaming about a mangy dog, but Saga could not find a focus on what they were talking about.

A bark suddenly resonated from beside her. She thought that she saw Shadow, his sleek, dark form, running up the staircase that spiralled around the tree's interior. He looked as though he was trying to get higher than her.

"Shadow!" she cried, and the dog barked back at her, never pausing in his long, galloping stride. He circled her, the stairs taking him up and up, above her now.

A catwalk appeared above her, and she caught sight of the large dog's head hanging over the edge of the walkway. He was waiting for her. Her faithful companion since coming to this place.

The rainbow disc she rode upon did not slow as it started to near the walkway where Shadow waited for her. Saga kept her eyes fixed on the dog. Her only friend in the world. As the disc came level with the platform, Shadow reached out to grab hold of her shopping bag and tugged. She felt her momentum forward, and when she went to step off the disc, she stumbled. The disc had already risen above the level of the catwalk as it continued its journey upwards towards the uppermost heights of the huge tree city.

People were watching as Shadow attempted to pull her down towards the catwalk, but as soon as the shopping bag fell from her fingers, Saga tumbled forward, unbalanced by the movement and the loss. She fell to the platform, laying sprawled against it as horse riding tools, gardening tools and her uniform fell from the tattered bag, most of it into a heap on the catwalk by Shadow, who redirected his attentions to her from the remains of the bag between his teeth. His mouth snapped towards her hands, trying to grab hold of her. As Shadow hauled Saga down from the platform, the horse-riding helmet, rounded and smooth, slid down the length of the catwalk, spinning around and around like a tortoiseshell in a Mario video game. And just like a spinning tortoiseshell, an unsuspecting little man dressed like a leprechaun for St. Patricks Day was knocked over as it barrelled through his stubby legs. Another young man managed to elegantly jump over the torpedoing riding helmet.

Saga fell, landing heavily on the catwalk beside Shadow. She clambered to her feet and awkwardly picked up each item that had fallen to the floor before taking off after the helmet, accidentally knocking the leprechaun back down just as he got to his feet.

"Just you watch out, girly! I'll get you!" he yelled angrily behind her as she chased her helmet down the catwalk, her arms full of her previous purchases.

"I'm sorry!" she cried back at him. "I'm really, really sorry!"

Behind her, Shadow weaved in and out around the other people on the catwalk until they both stopped in front of a man holding the errant riding helmet.

"Is this yours?" he asked, his voice low and almost regal.

"Yes, sir," Saga panted. "I'm so sorry. I... I... I didn't mean to cause any trouble."

Despite his calm, regal appearance and voice, the man scowled at her and Shadow. "You will need to be more careful." He stated, then handed her the riding helmet.

The man stalked off, and as Saga's breath returned to normal and she attempted to juggle all her purchases without the large bag she had just broken, she noticed how quiet it was around them. The angry leprechaun was no longer spewing curse words in her direction or threatening all kinds of financial ruin. He stared at her, just as most other people were now doing. It was not the amused stare of people who had just watched the debacle of her dismount from the rainbow disc but a silent stare that seemed to radiate fear.

An old woman who was now beside the leprechaun refused to catch Saga's eye as she looked around the centre of the tree.

She could not figure out where she was now for the life of her. Looking around the silent, still watchers, she asked, "Which way to the marketplace?"

~ * ~

Both the horse care and gardening tools had come in carrying bags, so Saga had been able to use their handles to carry them. She had unceremoniously stuffed the work gloves and riding uniform pieces into the bowl of the riding helmet. This had worked for everything but the riding boots she had bought to go with her uniform. They were long, knee-length boots that had left her with no choice but to change from her comfortable runners and put on the brand-new boots. She had tied the laces of her runners together and let them hang around her neck as she had seen ice skaters do with their skates in movies.

Shadow still walked beside her, sometimes running ahead, before stopping and running back to her side as though trying to hurry her up as he had on the mountainside. They emerged out on a large sweeping branch in the middle of the tree. Here most of the structures looked old and about as permeant as one could when one was made out of wood and canvas. The canvas all along the sweeping branch was bright and eye-catching. Yellows and blues and reds and greens and purples, many had sewn on patches of different colours, all attempting to pull the shopper's eye to their little shops and stalls.

"What do you think, Shadow?" Saga asked the large dog. "Weapons shop or Book shop?"

The dog barked and bounded off through the crowd of people. He jumped excitedly when Saga caught up to him and then ran off again to wait for Saga to find him among the crowd of people undergoing their shopping. Lots of families were out and about, getting their children everything they needed to start the new school year at their respective schools.

"Watch out, girl!" someone barked at her as she scooted around a table of trinkets.

"Sorry!" she called back to him, but not before she caught sight of someone else trying to make their way to the shopkeeper without being seen.

Again and again, as she passed people, she would hear them mention the word 'Valkyrie' as she went by. Their voices were hushed, and the only indication of whom they were talking about was in the direction their eyes were looking.

She found it disconcerting just how often people would do that and did her best to ignore it. The dog stopped excitedly before a shop with a fantastic suit of armour outside, tables, barrels, and shelves full of weapons and armour. The area was full of families, but instead of looking at the shop and going through their book and equipment lists, everyone seemed to be staring at a ruckus being made just in front of the weapons shop.

Saga stepped away from the suit of armour and walked towards the gathering crowd, sliding herself through as people unconsciously made space for her and Shadow. At the centre of the crowd looked to be what would soon be a fight.

A very one-sided fight.

FAERIES AND ELVES

A group of girls around Saga's age were standing around a white-haired girl significantly shorter than they were. The group of girls were tall, their long and elegantly styled hair shimmered in the sunlight, and gossamer wings protruded from the backs of their elegant and colourful clothing.

As Saga approached, people made way for Shadow's exuberant form. Getting closer, she recognised one of the elegant faerie girls. She was the girl who had irritated the old lady at the gardening store. Looking around, Saga realised that the faerie who had their back to her was the boy who had been with the faerie girl.

"No one wants you here, Dark Elf," one of the faeries Saga did not recognise was saying to the small white-haired girl.

"T... t..." The girl looked around at the four beautiful faeries wildly, and Saga could tell she was terrified of these people. "T..." So much so that she was having issues speaking.

"Tee. Tee. Tee," the faerie taunted. "Can't even speak like a real person!"

The girl's eyes were wide and stood out even more because of the darkness of her skin. "This o... o... one needs to g... g... need to buy school stuff," she managed.

"School stuff?" the first faerie said. "What would you need with school stuff?"

Saga walked closer. She recognised the small, dark-skinned, white-haired girl from that morning as well. She had been one of the kids in the camp she had been observing on her way to buy her horse-riding equipment. Saga thought that maybe she was one of the girls who had stuck her head out of the tent tentatively to see what was happening.

"They don't let freaks like you in at the schools," one of them said, but Saga was concentrating on the girl. Her fear was so palpable that she was sure that everyone around them could feel it, but no one stepped up to do anything.

At the girl's feet was a set of leather armour, delicately inlaid with beautifully embroidered flowers. It was the kind of thing a young girl would want to own and, at the very least, to admire. Saga crouched beside the girl and picked the leather shirt up in her hands before standing up to her full height.

"I think you dropped this," Saga said to the girl.

"N... N... N..." she shook her head, looked back up at Saga and said, "Navi, thanks you," then took the shirt into her own hands.

"Nuh. Nuh. Nuh," one of the faeries mocked.

"My gods, whom the hell called in the Jotun," the pretty faerie Saga had seen before sneered.

Saga frowned. "I have no idea what that means," she stepped up to the faerie and smirked when the faerie seemed to gulp as she looked up to see eye-to-eye with Saga. "But I do know that you need to leave this girl to do her school shopping."

"It's not like a slave can afford that kind of armour anyway," the faerie to her left commented cruelly.

"Slave?" Saga cried. "You have slaves?"

The girl shrugged. "What else would you do with the black and white freaks?"

Saga turned to face her. "I've been told that it's my job in life to choose the slain upon the battlefields..."

"Valkyrie," the boy who had not spoken muttered. "She's a Valkyrie, not a half-Jotun..."

"Don't be stupid, Tasso," his sister shot at him angrily. "There's no such thing as Valkyries. This one's just another freak like the bicoloured one there."

"Tonya," the boy hissed back. "I'm telling you."

"Shut up," she shot back at him. "Amita, Gheree, what do we do with freaks?"

The girls on either side of the one identified as Tonya looked at her, shock in their eyes. "Umm..." one of them said. "We..."

"Amita!" Tonya hissed.

Amita shook her head, grabbed a stick from the nearby weapons barrel, and tossed one to Tonya before grabbing one for herself and one for the third girl. The boy seemed to back away, not wanting to get involved. Smart but cowardly. Saga was used to kids like him. Kids who hung out or trailed along with the bullies but neither participated nor objected.

Saga grabbed two sticks as well and handed one to the small black-and-white girl. "I guess that this is on, then."

"W... w... what?" The girl asked, her voice high-pitched, almost as though she was squealing.

"They're only faeries," Saga objected.

"Only faeries?" Tonya challenged as she slid into a fighting pose.

Saga smirked. "I've seen all the Jackie Chan movies. You're so totally going down!"

"No, no, no, no, no, no," the small girl, whom Saga still did not know the name of, was repeating the same word over and over again.

"Who in the Nine Realms is Jackie Chan?" Gheree asked.

"Only the greatest martial artist to ever be in film!" Saga retorted.

"Not good, not good, not good," the girl behind her repeated.

Around them, people were talking to one another, and Saga was sure she saw coins change hands. This was getting ridiculous. The five girls all stood, ready with the weapons held. The three faeries looked confident and elegant in their postures, the small dark elf girl was trembling where she stood, and Saga did her best to imitate her movie hero in posture, trying to look as though she knew what she was getting herself into. The crowd around them had surreptitiously moved, making a larger space, almost circle-like, for the fight to happen.

The shopkeeper came running out of his shop, finally noticing the commotion. He stared at the five girls and cried out. "Not my weapons!" at which the crowd surrounding them jeered at him. Someone nudged him and whispered something in his ear. The man frowned, then sighed. "Winner gets the weapons they're holding."

The faeries did not look impressed by this feat, but Saga smirked down at the small dark elf. "Then I suppose we had better win, huh?"

The girl looked up at her. "A... a... a... are y... you crazy? W... w... we don't stand a... a... a chance!"

"But I do believe in Jackie Chan!" Saga said, but the girl looked far from reassured at this fact.

"This one's sister I... I... is going to kill Navi." The girl moaned but took a stronger grip on the long stick and faced the faerie Saga thought was called Amita.

Tonya struck out first, trying for a sneaky shot to Saga's knee, but Saga jumped out of the way and used her staff. Yes, she liked the term staff better to stick. It sounded more weapon-like than 'stick.' Beside her, Saga caught sight of the smaller elf girl. She moved with an effortless motion that distracted Saga for a moment. The girl's trembling fear only moments before had not prepared her to see the girl move as though she was an action movie star.

"Be the Jackie," Navi muttered again as she moved. "Be the Jackie!"

Tonya and Gheree took that moment to attack together, but a cry from the audience alerted Saga to the danger and tucking her weapon in close to her body, she launched herself into a roll and just before she made to stand up, several feet away from the faeries, she heard the clash of their weapons meeting. Staying low, Saga spun, keeping the staff parallel to the ground, and swept at their feet. Gheree cried with pain, but Tonya, seeing what happened to her friend, jumped back into the circle of Amita and the elf girl's fight.

The elf girl struck at Tonya's head before turning on the spot and aiming for Gheree. Tonya clutched her head with one hand, loosely holding her staff in the other. The end of Saga's staff went up, between Gheree's hands and trapped her there, unable to do anything but drop the weapon or travel with the movement. She allowed the staff to direct her, and Saga flung her away, where she was unprepared to move with her weapon and stumbled to the ground, the staff clattering away from her. Saga turned to Tonya and saw Amita drop her weapon out of the corner of her eye as the elf girl rapped her staff down on the faerie's hands.

"You lose faerie girl," Saga announced, and the crowd cheered. The crowd that had wanted nothing to do with assisting the little elf girl cheered. Coins again began being swapped amongst the onlookers as they started to filter away, the spectacle now over.

"Do you," Tonya hissed. "Do you have any idea who I am?" she cried, still waving the staff one-handed at Saga. It bobbed and weaved, and Saga just stared at her, not afraid of the weapon she barely held.

"Don't particularly care," Saga stated as she saw the store owner walk up to the faerie girl and take the staff from her hand.

"Don't, just don't," he muttered in disgust as he retrieved the weapons that had been wielded by Amita and Gheree as well.

He pointed at the little dark-skinned elf and saga, "You two, though, that was quite the show."

The little elf girl beamed. "This one's sister is a prefect this year at Toserra Sorose," she beamed, and Saga noticed that the girl's stutter did not afflict her now that the stress of the event was over, and she was beaming in pride.

"Navi!" a voice called out.

"Navi!" a male voice this time.

"Where are you, Navi?" the third voice, older and firmer than the other two, called out, and suddenly three more black-skinned and white-haired elves burst from the remaining crowd. "Navi?" the oldest girl asked.

Navi, the little elf, beamed at her sister, so full of pride. "Look!" she said, holding out the staff. "Navi won this in a fight!"

The oldest girl blinked in surprise. "You what?"

The shopkeeper smiled. "True to my word, girls, winners get to keep the staves they were holding at the time," he sighed and looked at Saga. "You didn't have to take my prettiest ones, though?"

Saga looked down at the staff she was holding and noticed that, like the little elf girl's staff, it was engraved with delicate flowers, much like the leather armour Navi had been admiring when the faeries had descended upon her. She smiled. "They are very nice, Sir. Did you make them?"

He nodded. "I did. The young schoolgirls were always bemoaning the masculinity of my work and buying the girly and far inferior stuff from down the way. Those will last the two of you far longer than your school days.

Wield them well," he stated. He looked at Navi, "I expect to see you on your school team."

"Really?" Navi asked, and her siblings echoed the cry.

"Sir, we cannot accept such generosity," the oldest girl stated firmly.

"Nonsense," the storekeeper said. "The little one here won that fair and square in front of many witnesses. There can be no retribution for the young dark elf possessing such a fine piece of equipment."

"Ziva!" Navi moaned. "Please!"

Ziva sighed and looked at the other two, who stood a little behind her. They looked excited. Then she looked at Saga. "You again," she said.

"Umm... Yes."

"She was amazing, Ziva," Navi beamed. "She stood up to those girls, and then we fought, and it was amazing!"

"Navi," The other girl exclaimed. "You're not stuttering!"

"Navi knows, Annis!" Navi beamed. She looked up at Saga. "By the way... What's your name?"

Saga smiled at her. "Saga. Saga Joy Carolle."

Navi held out her hand. "Navi Jensyn," they shook, and Saga allowed the girl to pull her in for a full hug. "And these are Navi's sisters, Ziva the prefect and Annis, and that is Navi's brother Edun."

Edun looked far from impressed. He scowled at Saga and his sister. "Great. Now we're never going to shut her up," he groaned.

Ziva chuckled. "This one does not think she has ever heard you say this much." She looked at Saga. "Thank you, Saga Joy Carolle. For protecting Ziva's sister from those faeries. That Bonnedras girl," She heaved a deep sigh but did not say anything else on the matter.

Ziva looked at the storekeeper. "This one's sister did actually come here for leathers," she stated.

He looked the dark elf siblings up and down, taking in their shabby clothes and the scant few bags they carried compared to other families. "I suppose you won't be wanting the matching set for that staff?"

Ziva shook her head. "No."

"Your usual then?" The girl nodded, and the man back-tracked into his shop to come back out with a small, almost child-like set of leathers that looked like they had seen better days. "And for you?" the man asked, looking at Saga, then hopefully at the embroidered leathers.

Saga glanced at Navi, who still looked wistfully at the beautiful set and shook her head. "No... But I would like to know your recommendation for a first-year."

The man nodded as he accepted the money from Ziva for the set she had purchased for Navi. "Let me think, a big girl like you." Saga frowned but tried to ease the expression from her face. She knew that the man was only trying to help, but people had been commenting on her abnormal size all her life, and she hated it. Still, the shopkeeper was trying to help, and she would let it go.

Behind her, she heard the siblings talking. Edun wanted to move on, but Navi wanted to wait for Saga and see where she was going next.

"You really want someone else to watch us bargain hunt for second-hand scraps?" Edun whispered to his oldest sister.

Saga turned to him. "I've lived of second-hand scraps all my life and usually had to fight to keep it too. I have very little to call my own, and what I'm buying for school... I will one day have to pay all of this back to Astrid."

The three older dark-elves eyes widened. "Astrid?" Ziva asked. "Astrid Grunborg?"

Saga nodded. "Yes," she replied hesitantly.

"The Weapons Mistress at Toserra Sorose?"

"Yes..." Saga repeated.

Annis and Navi were watching the exchange with interest. Edun looked as though he did not care. "Well... I..." Ziva shrugged. "Ziva doesn't know. That was unexpected."

"You're telling me," Saga said. "I had no idea that any of this even existed... I had no idea people like you, those faeries, or anyone here existed."

"You're from Midgard?" Annis asked in surprise.

"That's what Astrid keeps saying," Saga replied unsurely.

"So, where to next?" Navi asked. "Have you got your books?"

Saga shook her head. "I still need to get my books, uniform and telescope." She looked around. "Has anyone seen a dog? He's big and black and—"

"No," Navi said, looking around.

"You had a large dog with you this morning," Ziva said. "That one?"

Saga nodded. "Yes. That one. His name is Shadow."

The dark elves all looked around but eventually shook their heads. "No, sorry," Navi said.

Saga sighed. "Ah well, he'll be back."

Ziva showed Saga to the shop where she could buy her telescope for astronomy. Then, after explaining that they hoped that the class schedule and living arrangements would allow them all to share her telescope, they continued after Saga made her purchase. She was glad to have new bags again and rearranged everything so that the combat leathers and riding uniform all fit in one and the gardening tools, horse tools and telescope fit in another.

Saga's old sneakers still hung around her neck as they moved along together towards the uniform shop, Navi and Saga walking proudly with their staves. Edun often looked at his younger sister, a look of spite and jealousy in his eyes, but Saga put that down to sibling rivalry.

At the uniform store, Ziva took Navi to a back room while Saga spoke with one of the seamstresses about her uniform.

"There are so many pieces... and," Saga sighed, looking at Astrid's handwritten list.

"Let's start with the easy pieces, dear," the kindly lady said. "Stockings, gloves, scarves, hats. How do you like to do your hair? What hair accessories would you like?"

"Umm," Saga said, running her hand through her long, blond hair. "I usually just plait it."

The lady nodded and retrieved a pack of hair ties in the Toserra Sorose colours. "Bows?"

"Absolutely not!" Saga retorted.

The lady laughed. "I thought so. You didn't look like a frilly bow kind of girl, but I will recommend a headband. You may find it useful in combat weapons classes." Saga nodded as the woman talked on about useful accessories a girl should have when going to boarding school. "Ok, now let me get my measuring tape, and we will find you your jackets, blouses and skirts."

Saga already had a fluffy woollen winter hat, a school scarf, a set of gloves, a belt for her skirts, a large and, in her opinion embarrassing straw hat for summer. She remembered mocking the kids from the local private school who wore them whenever they appeared in public. There was even a ribbon in dark blue wrapped around the hat that tied into a bow at the back, the tails of the bow falling over the brim of the hat. She was going to look ridiculous in that. The lady had also shown her how to tie a ribbon around her neck under the collar of a shirt, as was required for girls at Toserra Sorose.

Next came a thick winter jacket because it snowed in the city where the school was. The seamstress bustled around her, measuring her arms, hips, and length, before bustling back into the storeroom and retrieving a jacket. "Try this on, dear," Saga tried it on and found the jacket fit. It was not too tight or too tight in some places while loose in others, and it was warm. So very, very warm. Not like anything she had ever owned before. If it were not for the day's heat, Saga would have never wanted to take the jacket off.

"How is it?"

"Perfect," Saga breathed out.

"Ok, why don't you pop behind that curtain and try this skirt and blouse?"

Saga did as she was told and changed her clothes, trying on the new school uniform items. The skirt was red, checked with black, and the blouse was white with a black line around the collar and ribbing down the front that she found herself playing with.

"How is it, dear?" the seamstress asked. Saga could not recall having ever owned a brand-new school uniform, let alone as many pieces as Astrid's list dictated, and it took her a moment to compose herself before she stepped out from behind the screen to face the seamstress. "Oh," she beamed when Saga stepped out. "Perfect. Now add this," Saga was handed a sleeveless button-down vest.

The bell above the door to the shop opened, and a family walked in. With a voice Saga recognised, the woman was berating a young dark-haired man. "And what exactly were you doing that was so important?"

"Ma," the boy said. "I had stuff to do."

"What stuff?" the woman practically wailed.

Saga watched them and recognised them from the horse-riding shop earlier that morning. The boy glanced to where she was standing, barefoot and unstockinged, in her school skirt and blouse, buttoning up the vest.

"Now, try on the blazer, dear," and Saga followed suit, allowing the woman to slip the stiff, dark blue jacket with red trim over her arms to settle it on her shoulders. "And your tie. Perfect."

Saga looked away from the boy and down at her toes, wiggled them, and then looked back up. The boy was no longer watching her but had a thick winter coat, similar to the one she had just purchased, thrust upon him.

"Good, good," the seamstress said. "Now let me see your list again. How many items did you need? You go change, and I'll get all of this together for you, dear."

Saga disappeared behind the screen again as she heard Ziva and Navi re-emerge from the shop's back room.

"And you can share with Ziva and Annis," Ziva said.

"Don't forget, you need to rethread your blazer with the gold trimming of a prefect," Navi reminded her sister. "Navi's awesome Prefect sister."

Suddenly, silence seemed to descend upon the shop, and Saga found herself hurrying to redress into her clothes.

There was a huff from the far side of the shop. "Who let them in?" and Saga once again found herself disliking Lady Gisette Harding.

Saga bounded out from behind the screen, hopping on one leg as she attempted to pull her boots back on. Ziva looked between the woman and Saga, and her back straightened. "Saga, we will meet you outside when you are done with your purchases. Come along, Navi."

Navi looked up at her sister, then at the older noblewoman and then at Saga, who smiled reassuringly at her. "Sure, no problem. I'll just be a minute." Ziva hustled Navi out of the shop, and Saga glared at the woman.

Gisette Harding harrumphed again. "Beasts meet beasts, I suppose. Come along, Emory."

"But I don't have—" he started to say, but his mother interrupted him.

"We will complete your shopping elsewhere," and she directed her son out of the shop. The boy looked back at Saga as his mother steered towards the door, their eyes meeting briefly before he was shepherded out. There was something familiar about those deep blue orbs of his that Saga could not place.

The seamstress re-emerged from her back room, laden with clothes she deposited on the counter. "Was that Lady Harding?"

The young tailor who had been fitting Emory Harding for his uniform nodded. "She departed after witnessing the Jensyn girls in here."

The seamstress shook her head but said nothing on the matter. "Now, dear, this should be everything you need for every situation at school."

Saga looked around. "Navi said that Ziva needed gold lining for her blazer. Did she buy any?"

"No, she left before she could," the tailor replied.

"Then I'll get some of that, too, please."

~*~

They managed to purchase their books without any further incident. Saga had never done so much shopping in her life. Not for herself, anyway. School supplies had always been handled for her, and the cheapest materials were passed on to her from whoever had bulk-bought them for the children in care. Her uniform was new, rather than second hand, and she now owned a school skirt rather than just being told to wear a boy's uniform because of her size.

Ziva looked around after they had finished at the bookshop. "We should go," she said to her siblings.

"But!" Navi cried.

Ziva shook her head. "No... Saga has to get back, and so must we."

"Good, it's about time," Edun muttered. "This one does not understand why we had to drag her along all day just because she won Navi a stick!"

Saga turned on the boy. "Navi won that all on her own. She didn't need me for that."

"Y... y... yes, Navi did," the girl stated, her stutter returning for the first time since the fight outside the weapons shop.

"I saw you," Saga insisted. "You were amazing, and you heard what the man at the store said. You need to try out for the school team!"

"No point!" Edun interrupted. "They would never let the likes of us on their precious school team."

"Come on," Saga said. "My turn to insist on something. Ziva, you helped me find so many great bargains today that I want to take you all to dinner with my savings."

"What?" Ziva cried. "No, Ziva can't allow that."

Saga would not take no for an answer, though, especially when Shadow came bounding up to them. He leapt up, his big paws landing on her shoulders as she crouched to meet him. "Where've you been getting off to all day, boy? Huh?"

"Is that your big dog?" Navi asked.

"Well... He's Astrid's, I think," Saga said as she stood back up. "But then again, she said he was not hers either, so I have no idea. Shall we go?"

Edun trailed along behind them as the girls decided to follow Saga back to The Bore Tooth Inn. As usual, conversation stopped as she entered, and all remained silent as the four dark elves entered with her, but when Shadow snarled at them, everyone returned to their drinks, food, and conversations. Saga found her usual table empty, and the group deposited their numerous bags of purchases around the side of the table as they then climbed over the bags into seats.

Shadow settled down, stretching himself along with the mess of strewn bags and school equipment, content with laying his head on the bag of school uniform items.

Saga ordered them all a stew of the day and a Jelly Melon Cider each. "This one has never had Jelly Melon cider," Navi announced excitedly. "Is it good?"

"The best," Saga replied ecstatically as she turned in her seat. "Astrid got me one on my first day here, and I had no idea what it was. I had just wanted a Diet Soda."

"A what?" Annis asked. The silent girl had followed them all day.

"Apparently, it's only a drink in my world," Saga told her, "Anyway, Jelly Melon Cider is the best thing ever!"

"Why does everyone have to stare at us?" Edun muttered as he wrapped his arms around his middle.

"What makes you think they're looking at you? They've been staring at me since the day I walked in here," Saga told him. "Staring at me, talking about me, avoiding my gaze..."

"You're an oddity, like us," Ziva said. "No one has seen a Valkyrie in centuries."

"So, everyone keeps telling me," Saga muttered.

Their food arrived, and despite all of his complaints, Edun tucked in with gusto, just as his sisters did.

Suddenly, Ziva stopped eating and pushed her chair back, standing up. "Mistress Grunborg."

Edun and Annis followed suit quickly, and Ziva waved awkwardly at Navi to follow their lead. "Good evening, Ziva, Annis, Edun," Astrid said as she stood a little away from them, her path blocked by the sleeping dog and all of their shopping. Her gaze turned towards Navi. "You must be Navi. Are you looking forward to starting school?"

Navi nodded. "Y... y... yes. N... Navi is," she managed to say but said nothing else as she put her hand in front of her mouth and looked crestfallen, obviously ashamed by the re-emergence of her stutter.

Astrid looked down at everything. "Did you get everything, Saga?" then she paused. "Wait, where's the trunk or travelling case?"

"What trunk or travelling case?"

"The one you're going to need to get everything to school," Astrid stated as though it was the most obvious thing in the world. "Where's your list?" Saga leaned over and dug the list out of one of her shopping bags.

"Oh no!" Ziva cried.

"What is it?" Annis asked.

"Lady Harding startled me so much at the uniform shop that I forgot to get the gold trimming for my blazer..."

"Oh, oh, oh, oh," Saga cried, still hanging off the side of her chair, as she renewed her search inside the bags. "Hang on!" she sat back up, her shopping list in one hand and a roll of gold material in the other. "The seamstress said you didn't buy it, so I got you a roll." She handed the spool of gold ribbon to the flustered girl and then handed her shopping list to the flustered weapons mistress.

"Oh... I never put one on the list. We'll take care of it tomorrow, then."

Ziva stared at the roll of gold trimming in her hands, and Saga could have sworn that she saw tears in the girl's eyes. "Thank you," she murmured.

Astrid looked affectionately at Saga, then at the four Dark elf siblings. "You kids have a good night. Saga, make sure Shadow goes with them when they head back to their lodgings, all right?"

Saga nodded. "Of course."

Astrid turned to leave but spotted the two staves leaning up against the booth on Saga and Navi's side. "Why do you have staves?"

"We won them," Navi announced, her stutter miraculously gone again as she spoke of the afternoon.

"You won them?"

"Some faeries were hassling Navi," Ziva stated. "A duel broke out between them and those two."

"A duel?" Astrid exclaimed, looking at Saga. "How could you be so reckless?"

"What?" Saga cried. "If there's one thing I can't stand, it's a bully, and those girls were bullies... I just... they grabbed staves first, and the shopkeeper promised that the winner won the staves they were holding."

"And they should try out for the school stick fighting team," Annis added.

"Well, then I suppose I'll see you two at tryouts then, won't I?" Astrid asked them pointedly, and the girls nodded eagerly. Astrid shook her head and walked off. "Duels with faeries... what have I gotten myself into?"

LE SPECTRE ÉCLAIRÉ

The sound of staff meeting staff echoed throughout the courtyard. A few people from the surrounding establishments watched as Saga and Navi sparred with their staves.

Navi jumped gracefully as Saga swept the long staff across the ground, and as she landed back on her feet, she brought her staff down to try and catch Saga on the side of the head. Saga ducked out of the way, using the staff to anchor herself as she spun around.

A slow, deliberate clapping started from the doorway of The Bore Tooth Inn. The girls stopped, sweat dripping from their brows as they breathed deeply from their exertions.

"Ok, ok, I'll admit you two aren't half bad," Astrid said from where she leaned against the door frame. "Don't think that little demonstration will guarantee either of you a spot on my team, though. First years aren't supposed to compete."

Saga grinned. "Yeah, well, we'll show everyone!"

"Especially those faeries," Navi added. With the staff in her hand, the sweat of combat dripping down her, her stutter vanished as though it had never been there. Her confidence seemed unstoppable at moments like these.

"Go," Astrid said, pointing inside. "Wash up and put your uniforms on. Navi, you did bring yours, right?" The girl nodded, her wild white hair blowing all over the place in the morning breeze. "Good, we have to be at the dock in a little over an hour, and you two must be in your school uniforms when we arrive. How are your siblings getting there, Navi?"

"Ziva has a Prefects meeting, and Annis and Edun are meeting with friends."

In the days after their meeting in the marketplace, Saga and Navi had found a comfortable friendship. Astrid had taken her presence in stride, and Saga often got the idea that she greatly approved of the burgeoning friendship. She talked fondly of Navi's sisters and only a little about her brother, as though her words may not be as kind about the boy.

They made their way inside and up to the room Saga shared with Astrid.

"Where's Shadow?" Navi asked as she shed her clothes.

Saga shrugged as she kicked off her shoes. "I don't know. I haven't seen him in two days now."

"Is that odd?"

"I don't know... I've only been here for three weeks... I wouldn't say he's been my constant companion, but yeah... I guess I've seen him less and less since the day we met."

Navi paused in her actions as she looked up at Saga from across the room where her old, tattered travelling trunk was thrown open. "Maybe... Maybe he doesn't like Navi...?" The sad, defeatist question hung in the air, but Saga was quick to disagree that the presence of the young elf could be the reason.

"Astrid told me early on that he does his own thing. Comes and goes as he pleases," Saga buttoned up the vest over her blouse and stared at herself in the mirror. "I've never had a school uniform this nice..."

"This one has never been to school," Navi said, coming up beside her. She was busy trying to tie the little ribbon under her collar.

"What?" Saga asked, startled by the comment.

"We couldn't afford it, and not many people want us around and all... Our mother did her best to teach us at home. Well, Ziva did impress the Master's wife, which is why we are allowed to come here..." She trailed off softly before looking back up, her bright smile on her face. "Here I am, going to a real school for the first time!"

"Saga! Navi!" Astrid called from outside the room. "You girls dressed?"

"Yes," they chorused together.

Astrid entered and stopped short when she saw the two girls standing before the mirror, doing up their ribbons. There was a stark contrast between the two girls. Saga's pale skin, Navi's midnight black skin, Saga's glimmering blond hair, tied back in a plait down her back, Navi's white hair, straight down her back, a red headband in her hair.

"You two," she said affectionately.

Saga reached over to her bed to grab her blazer and pulled it on over her blouse and vest. "How do we look?"

Another contrast between the girls that Astrid did not want to pull attention to. Saga's uniform, brand new and correctly sized, looked like it had been made for her. Navi's, the offcasts of her older siblings or the purchases from the back room at the shop looked more faded, worn, and not as well fitted. With time Astrid was sure that something could be done for the small girl.

"You look like Toserra Sorose better be ready for the two of you," Astrid said. "And that's one of the things I wanted to talk to you about." Saga looked at her, confused, as she repacked her hairbrush and other toiletries into the large travelling trunk Astrid had bought for her. "The familiarity we have enjoyed... It can't... Well..."

Saga straightened, and she could feel Navi watching them. "No one ever wants to admit that they know a teacher outside of school," Saga said easily. "Really, it's like the fastest way to confirm your social downfall. There was this kid at one school I went to, and his next-door neighbour was our classroom teacher, and she would bring him to and from school... It was... Well... Not good for him, the tormenting he got."

"There are so many rules..." Navi whispered behind her. "Navi doesn't know any of these things... Navi does not want to be a social outcast..."

Astrid shook her head. "Those Midgard schools... I swear... Navi, you will be fine. Saga, I was referring to our familiarity level, particularly during school hours or class. Toserra Sorose uses the formal terms of Master and Mistress for the teachers. I am Mistress Grunborg during class, all right?"

Saga raised an eyebrow. "Master and Mistress? Really? That's so... so..."

"So what?" Astrid asked, crossing her arms over her chest and staring at the girl.

Saga shook her head. "Nothing Astrid," and when Astrid made no move but to raise an eyebrow at her, she quickly followed with, "Nothing, Mistress Grunborg."

Astrid relaxed and smiled. "Good. Now, if you remember that, you won't get into trouble with your other teachers."

~*~

Astrid insisted on taking the floating rainbow discs to the airship dock, and they were standing on the catwalk, their trunks beside them, as they waited for one large enough to appear.

"I can carry it," Saga insisted, trying to ignore how uncomfortable the idea of riding one of those discs further up the tree made her. The stairs that spiralled around the tree's interior seemed like a much safer prospect. "I swear I can."

"Good for you," Astrid stated. "But we're going to the very top of the tree city, and you cannot carry it, let alone walk that far up."

And so, with Astrid and Navi hustling her on board a large rainbow disc headed towards the top of the tree, Saga pulled her trunk on, deliberately trying not to look down and trying not to let the memory of her last excursion on the discs overwhelm her. "Saga, you have to look where you're going!" Navi said, stopping short before she tripped over Saga's trunk. She struggled to realign hers with the space Saga had left.

The disc took them up, past floors that seemed to become more and more elegantly decorated, the people who walked past dressed in unimaginable finery. They passed a family waiting for the rainbow discs that Saga could have sworn were the Hardings, that pompous family with the son who looked as though he might be in their year at school.

She also thought she saw the faeries, Tonya and her two friends, Amita and Gheree. She did not see Tasso, the pretty faerie boy who looked just like his sister, anywhere. A disc shot past them, and a glimpse of shocking white hair pointed out Edun, but she did not recognise the boys he was with.

Finally, they arrived, and Saga hauled her trunk off the floating death trap and onto the secure branch of the tree. She felt her heart hammering in her chest as though it was trying to beat its way out into the open as she waited for Astrid and Navi to disembark the disc.

"Wow," Navi breathed as she looked out past Saga's heaving form. "Wow!"

Astrid beamed. "It's a sight, isn't it?" She asked.

"Yes," The small dark elf breathed. "Navi means... Wow."

"What?" Saga asked, looking over her shoulder at what they were both staring at. First, there was the fact that from where they stood at the very highest point of the Yggdrasil tree, they could see everything. The plains, the mountains, the seas, the deserts and the polar ice caps, as far as the eye could see, depending on the direction you looked. She had caught glimpses of this view from between the leaves and branches of the tree as she wandered the city but had never imagined it would look like this. She had never imagined that anything could take her breath away so completely. "Oh... Wow..."

And then there was the sight that Navi and Astrid were looking at. The endless number of sails that rose high above the floating harbour of ships. One stood out amongst the others, sporting the crest of Toserra Sorose Academy, but the first thought that came to Saga's mind when she saw it was "The Black Pearl..." she murmured.

"What?" Astrid asked. "The ship so evil. No, no, that is Le Spectre Éclairé. All interplanar travel by airship is banned for the day as the airships are requisitioned to bring the staff and students to the great schools of the realms."

Around them, they could see students in four distinct uniforms milling around and heading towards one of the four ships currently docked at the top of the great tree. A few other uniforms were intermingled, heading to towards smaller vessels, their groups less organised and more ragtag than the organised chaos of the great schools.

"They're built around the floating discs," Navi added. "They allow large-scale travel between planes. We go to the Idavoll Plains in Asgard. The first of the great planes to have life after Ragnarök."

"Very good," Astrid said. "That is correct. "Toserra Sorose is the oldest of the schools and is located in the Nine Realms. But you will learn about all of this during History and Planarography."

"First Years for Toserra Sorose," A voice called loudly as someone else called for first-years to Ehras Magna Were Skoli.

"You two get along. I'll see you in Nýr Ásgardr," Astrid said and then strode off in a direction that had no students nearby.

"Where's she going?" Saga asked.

"The teachers take a speed craft to the schools to ensure that everything is ready for the arrival of the students," A boy said from behind them.

"W... w... w... what do you want?" Navi asked, stepping back so quickly that she almost tripped over her trunk.

The blond-haired boy with delicate, gossamer wings looked down at his feet as they shuffled on the spot. Finally, he looked back up at Navi. "I... I wanted... I wanted to apologise for my sister," he finally said. "She can be needlessly cruel, and... going to a bigger school has given her so many more targets that are not me. Also, our parents can no longer watch her every move."

"Tasso, right?" Saga asked.

Surprise etched upon his flawlessly beautiful face. His head swivelled to look at her. "How... How did you know that?"

"I heard your sister call you that."

"Tasso Bonnedras," the boy said with a nod at her, then quickly at Navi.

"Saga Joy Carolle and this is my friend, Navi Jensyn."

"Really, I am very sorry for the trouble my sister and her friends caused you the other day," he reiterated.

Navi shook her head. "I... It is not your job to apologise for her. This one would never stop apologising for Edun if that were true," she murmured. "And we won these great staves."

Tasso's eyes lit up. "You were amazing," he said to Navi. "And you haven't even been to Mistress Grunborg's classes yet!"

Well, they were not going to tell him that Astrid had been tutoring them in private in the days since their adventure at the marketplace. They had practised at every moment they could and pestered Astrid until she had finally given in and given them some pointers on correct stance and movement.

The three of them pulled their trunks along the uneven tree bark to the person calling for Toserra Sorose first years and waited in line behind a group of boys jostling each other.

"There's Ziva," Navi exclaimed excitedly, waving and trying to catch her sister's attention. Ziva didn't seem to notice her though, as she talked with a handsome, fair-skinned boy with delicately pointed ears, and long blond hair tied back away from his face. His blazer, like Ziva's, was outlined in gold, marking him as another of the prefects.

"I think she's busy," Saga said, eyeing the two elves.

"Perfect stuff, maybe," Navi said idly, but Saga caught Ziva laughing at something the boy said and wondered if that was true.

Tonya, Amita and Gheree wandered past, just walking through to the front of the line, and Saga was surprised that people just let them. "What the?" she asked.

"That's just like her," Tasso said softly. "Him too," he said under his breath as Emory Harding followed in their wake.

"Names," a tall girl, maybe eighteen years of age, with gold trim around her blazer, asked.

"Tasso Bonnedras," the faerie boy answered.

"Go on," she said, ticking his name off a list.

"Navi Jensyn."

The prefect looked Navi up and down, ticked her name off the list and motioned for her to board the big ship. "You?" she asked Saga.

"Saga Joy Carolle."

The girl stopped and looked at Saga, longer than she had spent looking at Navi, and it unsettled her. "The Valkyrie?"

Saga squirmed where she stood. "Yes."

"Right," she said, ticking Saga's name off her list. "Go on. Your possessions are your own to handle for the voyage. Keep them with you until told otherwise in Nýr Ásgardr. Listen for any announcements. They will contain further instructions."

The three of them nodded and, glancing at one another, continued further onto the ship. Saga and Navi looked up at the towering sails in awe, but Tasso seemed to take them for granted. "You two look like you've never seen an airship before."

They instantly looked down, taking a moment to glance at each other in embarrassment before looking at Tasso. "We haven't," Saga admitted.

"Oh boy," Tasso said, turning and walking towards the front of the ship. With a shrug at each other, Saga and Navi followed him.

"Hmm," Tasso grumped when he spotted a group of people in the spot he had been heading for. He stopped short, Saga running into his back. Two boys were surrounding a girl who had sat herself down on a seat at the very point of the ship. She had a book in her hands and was trying to read. She was not looking up at them, trying to ignore them.

"We said that this is our spot. Now scram," a tall boy, who wore a hooded cloak over his uniform, said.

"Vampire," Navi hissed under her breath.

"Say what?" Saga gasped. "They're real?"

The boy in question looked over while his friend began to laugh. "Look at her shiver!"

The vampire stared at Saga. His pale skin and red eyes scanned her from head to foot from beneath the hood of his thick navy-blue cloak. "You never seen a Vampire before?"

Saga pointed up. "Sun's shining."

The boy pointed at his cloak. "Block out material."

"Huh."

"Do not touch me," the voice was soft but harsh.

"Hey, Konishi," the tall, gangly boy with wild hair said, trying to draw the Vampire's attention away from Saga. "Watch this!" And with that, he reached over and took the sitting girl's arm. She screamed as though he had struck her. The book tumbled from her hands as she wrapped her arms tightly around her legs and, if possible, attempted to curl into an even smaller ball.

Saga's hand tightened on the flower-engraved staff in her hand as she released her hold on her trunk. Navi noticed her and discreetly released the handle of her own trunk, shifting her weight into the standard combat position Astrid had taught them.

"Do not touch me. I told you not to touch me.," the girl muttered again. She started to rock, and the unidentified boy laughed hysterically at her reaction.

"Vihaan," Konishi growled. Vihaan kept on laughing, though, as he proceeded to poke at the girl, who rocked and keened, unable to get away from him. Saga stepped forward, making her presence known. The staff presented before her. Before she had a chance to speak, though, Konishi crooned, "Ooh, what are you going to do?"

"Saga!" Navi called hesitantly. "Navi does not think this is a... a... a good idea." And there it was again. Saga glanced over at her, but she saw that her grip was as firm as her own, and Tasso looked between the boys and the two girls. He, too, dropped his hold on his trunk.

Konishi scoffed. "A dark elf, a faerie and a—" he paused and looked Saga up and down again. "What exactly are you?"

"She is a Valkyrie, dead thing," Tasso spat.

Konishi went still, as behind him, Vihaan kept hassling the girl. "Vihaan!" he snapped.

"Yeah?"

"Stop it."

"But!"

"But nothing," Konishi interrupted. He turned to Saga, Navi, and Tasso. "I will remember this. I will remember this always."

"Beat it, Vampire, before I remember what I did with my garlic," Saga taunted.

The Vampire stepped closer to her as Vihaan attempted to poke at the terrified girl again. To his surprise, he found Navi's staff in his face as he wheeled backwards, stumbling as he attempted to regain his balance.

"Y... you too, Hyena," she said, her confidence wavering. "Leave her alone."

Konishi the Vampire bared his teeth at Saga. She started in surprise, having not expected him to have two extra-long, sharp teeth protruding from his mouth like fangs. He took another step towards her, and she lowered her staff, letting it protrude into his stomach as he tried to come closer.

"You can't intimidate us," Saga said easily, ignoring the startled look from Navi and the curious look she got from Tasso.

Konishi frowned and looked back at Vihaan. "Let's go," he stated with as much confidence as he could muster. "We'll leave these losers to their own for today. But this isn't over." Then he walked away, his cloak flapping around his ankles with a false sense of confidence and elegance, only enhanced by the way Vihaan scrambled after him, his long limbs seemingly not within his control.

Navi stared after them before turning her wide eyes on Saga. "W... w... what did we just do?"

"The same thing you did to my sister," Tasso said with a grin, but it did not seem to reach his eyes as he glanced sidelong at the retreating forms of Konishi and Vihaan.

Saga crouched in front of the girl that the two boys had been hassling, careful not to reach out and touch her gently as instinct kept telling her to do. "Hi. My name is Saga." When she got no response other than the girl rocking back and forth as she held her knees tightly, Saga sat back on her heels.

"Now what?" Tasso asked.

Saga looked up at him. "We wait."

"For what?"

"For her to be ready to talk to us."

"How long will that be?" Navi asked as more people passed them by, looking for the perfect place to sit with friends as they made the voyage from Yggdrasil City to Nýr Ásgardr.

"Depends on how scared she is," Saga said as she sat down next to the girl, careful not to touch her. She motioned for Navi and Tasso to sit as well, making a small circle to include the unknown girl.

~ * ~

"Jemima."

Saga, Navi, and Tasso all looked around. Tasso had just finished telling them about his sister's reaction to the loss of the fight in the marketplace and the rampage she had gone on because not only had she and her friends lost, but Saga and Navi had won the weapons maker's best staves. She had wanted staves to match the beautiful leather armour Navi had admired when it had all started.

Navi looked at the silent member of the group, the girl whom none knew. "Jemima, is that your name?" she asked.

The girl looked up and slowly, delicately stretched her legs and arms out while rolling her head around, loosening up her joints. "Yes. I am Jemima."

"Navi."

Jemima nodded. "You are Dökkálfar, and you have a stutter."

"Umm... Ye-es," she said tentatively, drawing her words out as though she was unsure of what she was saying.

"The faerie is Tasso Bonnedras. He is a twin. The rest of you do not like her." The girl's head turned slightly to look at Saga. She said nothing for a long moment until finally, she spoke again, just as the others started to get restless. "You are called Saga, but I do not know what you are." She had listened to them, even if she had not been speaking.

"They tell me that I am a Valkyrie," Saga replied.

"You do not know?"

Saga shrugged. "I apparently don't know much of anything, having grown up in the real world."

"This is the real world. Everything in all the planes of the Bifrost bridge are the real worlds."

"Astrid said that the bridge was destroyed, and all that remains are those floating rainbow discs everyone uses to get around," Saga said. Beside her, Navi coughed.

"Are you thirsty?" Jemima asked.

Navi shook her head. "No," but she looked meaningfully at Saga, who did not notice.

"You are strange," Jemima decided. "Very strange indeed."

"So?" Saga asked, looking around awkwardly, "I don't know if this is rude or not, but umm... What are you?"

At this point, Navi's pointed coughing turned to choking, and she just about rolled off her trunk, which she was using as her seat. Beside her, Tasso put his head in his hands in complete dismay. "Saga..." Navi gasped. "You... you cannot ask that."

"Why not?" Jemima asked. "If everyone just asked what they wanted to know, would everything not be simpler?"

Tasso shook his head. "Questions like that put people off, especially the Vampires and the Weres."

Jemima cocked her head to the side and gazed at Saga, contemplating something. "I am an Angel."

At this, Navi really did need a drink because her pointed fake coughing choke had become real, and Tasso hurriedly jumped off his trunk and dug around inside. "Here," he said, shoving a bottle at her. She took it and gulped it down.

Once done, she stared at the half-empty bottle. "Jelly Melon Cider?" she asked. The boy nodded, and she grinned at him. "Thanks."

"How can a melon be jelly or a cider be jelly. That name makes no sense," Jemima said, looking at the two of them.

"The melon is called Jelly Melon. And no, I don't know why," Tasso said, situating himself back upon his trunk and getting comfortable once more. "I just like the drink."

Saga nodded. "Me too... It's one of the best things I've tasted since being here."

"You've eaten since boarding Le Spectre Éclairé?"

"No..." Saga frowned as she looked at Jemima. "I uh... since I arrived in this world. We don't have anything like it on Earth... I mean on Midgard."

"You grew up on Midgard? Is that why you do not know what you are?" Jemima asked. "And all the Valkyries disappeared after Ragnarök. You cannot be a Valkyrie."

Saga shrugged. "Tell that to everyone else who keeps whispering about me," she muttered and to prove her point, a group of older girls passed by them, one pointing Saga out to her friends.

Navi looked at her. "She could have been pointing at me. People are always pointing at us."

"Us?" Jemima asked, looking at her. "You are only one person."

"This one's sisters and brother," Navi stated. "Navi has two sisters and a brother."

"There's a dark elf girl among the prefects. Is she your sister?"

"Because she's a dark elf, we have to be related?" Navi snapped.

Jemima looked unphased by Navi's retort. "There are not many Dökkálfar who attend Toserra Sorose. Only four, in fact. Three girls and one boy. It is only logical to assume that all of the Dökkálfar who currently attend the school are your siblings."

Navi pursed her lips and looked away, her arms crossed over her chest. "Well... yeah."

"Tasso!" The faerie groaned as he attempted to ignore the shrill call of his name.

"Your sister is calling for you," Jemima said helpfully, and the faerie looked up at her in consternation.

"Yeah. Thanks," he said sarcastically.

"You are welcome," Jemima said, a small smile gracing her features.

"I wasn't—" he started but gave up as Tonya Bonnedras stormed up to their little group. He sighed and turned on his trunk to face her. He sighed even harder when he saw that she was flanked, as usual, by Amita and Gheree. "What do you want?"

"The freak show just keeps on growing, doesn't it?" Tonya said, staring at the little group. She spotted Jemima. "What's wrong with you?"

"Nothing is wrong with me," she replied.

"You're making me look bad," Tonya said in a huff, even going so far as to stand there with her hands on her hips. She accentuated her point by stomping her foot angrily upon the deck of the ship.

Saga giggled. She really could not help herself. Navi was looking from person to person, waiting to see what would happen next.

"What are you laughing at?" Tonya snapped, her voice going shrill and her foot stomping the deck again. Saga's giggle burst out into full-blown laughter. Navi was hiding her face in her hands, but her body was shaking as she attempted not to make a noise and draw the faerie girl's wrath.

"You," Saga managed to say. "You! You're so... so..."

"So what?" Saga was laughing so hard that she had problems answering, which only enraged the girl further.

"You little...!" Tonya hissed, stomping her foot angrily as she couldn't think of what to say.

"She's actually quite large, especially compared to Navi," Jemima interrupted.

Tonya stared at Jemima as though she had grown a second head. "Who are you?"

"I am Jemima Dove."

"Freak," Amita sneered.

Saga stood up, her hand grabbing her staff as she did. Navi followed her. "Want to repeat that, Faerie?" Saga asked.

A boy with gold trim on his blazer walked by. "Is there a problem here?"

They looked at each other, recognised him as a prefect, and shook their heads. "We were just leaving," Tonya sneered.

"All students, we are arriving in the town of Nýr Ásgardr. First years arriving in Nýr Ásgardr are to report to Clock Tower in the centre of town to hear of their Residential assignments. All other students are to head straight to their accommodations and prepare for the evening Assembly. Prefects are to join the first-year students at the Clock Tower. That will be all."

A sudden burst of confidence seemed to overcome the faerie girl as she ran her hand through her shimmering blonde locks. "Well..." she looked at Navi. "I suppose you'll be in Dorbe Manor..."

"So, what if Navi is?" Navi asked. "This one doesn't want to be around you any more than Navi has to be."

With a huff, Tonya turned, her two followers pausing only to sneer at the group before they all stormed off. Saga watched them go and smirked at Navi. "So... What's wrong with Dorbe Manor?"

"Dorbe Manor tends to be where the poorer students live. However, there is no evidence that this is how they are selected," Jemima stated. "Are you poor?"

Navi's mouth twitched as she thought about what to say. "We are... Not rich," she settled on.

"So... Some houses are better than others?" Saga pressed.

"Well... Of course," Tasso said. "As a faerie, I want to be in Limomoux Heights. As an Angel, Jemima probably wants to be in Nollet Hall."

"Why would I want to be in Nollet Hall just because I am an Angel?" Jemima asked. "I have no preference for my location as long as it is quiet and small."

"So not Queenette Dormitory then?" Navi asked.

Jemima seemed to shiver at the name of the Dormitory. "No... not Queenette Dormitory. Too many people."

Saga nodded in understanding. "Large group homes have no privacy," she agreed. "I shared my last room with three other girls. Your own belongings are always going missing."

"She's right, though. This one probably will be assigned to Dorbe Manor... Ziva is Prefect there, and Annis and Edun were assigned there in their first year."

A GHOSTLY QUARREL

Prefects with gold-trimmed blazers started to direct first-year students to the exit points of the ship. Jemima stared at the stampeding hoard of students who seemed to come out of every nook and cranny of the ship, all carrying or pulling their trunks and travelling cases as they went. She looked terrified of joining the halting and jostling line.

Saga saw a large group of cloaked students making their way towards the exit. "How many vampires are there?"

"Oh, lots," Tasso said.

"Lots has actual value," Jemima said. "What is lots? Saga asked, 'How many' and 'lots' does not give her a clear answer to her question. Not even 'more than the Weres or there are more vampires than faeries' which would then lead to the next question of how many Weres, or faeries are there."

Tasso sighed. "I don't know how many Vampires there are," he stated, cutting her off.

"Um... it's ok," Saga intervened. "Really... I got the point..."

"I don't know how. That answer held no useable knowledge."

"Navi! Saga!"

"Hey, Ziva," Navi called out. Saga waved to the older girl.

Ziva grinned happily and turned around for them all to see. "What do you think?" The gold trim on her blazer sparkled in the sunlight, and Saga beamed.

"It looks great!"

Navi nodded. "And to think you almost came to school without it."

Ziva shushed her. "Hush! Don't go telling everyone that," she grinned at Saga. "Thank you. You're a lifesaver."

"Don't mention it," Saga said as she heaved her trunk over the lip in the walkway that connected the ramp to the dock.

"No, really," Ziva insisted. "Arye Tait, the Prefect of Rottport House, showed up to the meeting with his trim dyed black, and Mistress Grimaldi practically ripped him a new one... This one didn't think Angels ever yelled..."

"That is a gross misconception," Jemima stated. "Angels are capable of anger. My Aunt Seraphina constantly yells at me and states that this is a sign of her displeasure."

Ziva glanced at Jemima and then at Tasso. "New friends?"

Navi nodded. "Jemima Dove and Tasso Bonnedras."

"Bonnedras? Ziva thought you two duelled a Bonnedras?" Ziva exclaimed.

"That was my sister, Tonya," Tasso said easily. "She had it coming."

Ziva shook her head. "Ok. You lot know where you're going?"

Saga shook her head. "No."

"Come on. This one'll show you to the clock tower, then."

"Can't y... y... you just tell me which house Navi is in?" Navi asked, nerves descending upon her again as they made their way through the town.

Saga looked around the town. "Where's the school?"

Jemima pointed towards a large building in the distance. "That is the main building, Sorosian Hall or College Castle. My Aunt Dina has used both names to refer to the building... Most classes are taken there, but many more are taken around town, and the student residences are around town. Nýr Ásgardr and Toserra Sorose are intertwined with one another."

"Wow," Saga murmured. "It's like going to university."

"Going where?" Tasso asked.

Saga shook her head. "Never mind." She noticed that many people were lining the town's streets as the students made their way from the air ship dock to the Clock Tower. Older students, their trunks already away in their residences or walking, their trunks rolling along behind as they kept glancing at the first-year students.

"How many people... No... Wait, what's about to happen?" Saga asked, looking at Ziva.

The older dark elf girl winked at her mischievously. "Why would Ziva tell you that?"

Navi nodded solemnly. "She has not e... e... even told Navi."

Ziva glanced at her sister and sighed. "This one has a sacred responsibility as a prefect to ensure that all of you have the full Toserra Sorose welcome experience."

Tasso shook his head. "Isn't it all based upon race, finances, and gender?" he asked. "How much of a surprise could it possibly be when this is over?"

"Oh, look who knows everything," Ziva crooned. "Is that what you really think?"

"The houses choose you," Jemima said.

"How does a house choose you?" Saga retorted.

"I do not know," Jemima admitted. "But it is the houses that choose the residents. That is what we are going to do. We are going to be chosen by the houses. That is what my Aunt Evangeline says."

Ziva pointed towards a large square where people were gathering to watch. Near the centre, at the base of a large Clock Tower that rose above every building in its immediate surroundings. Masses of students stood there with their trunks, waiting. A dais stood beneath the clock tower, and several people were wearing formal academic robes, the kind Saga had seen when watching television shows about university graduations. They looked regal and fancy, but looking at the dais, she could see nothing that would indicate how the students would be allocated into the houses. Listening to the other students around her, no one else knew either. Students and watchers were still striding into the square, and the build-up of anticipation was electrifying the air around them.

"The Deputy Headmistress will be speaking soon. This one needs to go join the other prefects for the choosing."

"Ziva!" Navi wailed as her sister began to stride away. Ziva just laughed and waved as she weaved her way through the crowd.

"She was useful," Tasso said cheerfully.

"No, she was not," Jemima interjected. "She provided us with no additional information."

Tasso sighed. "I know that. I was being sarcastic."

"I wish people would just say what they mean."

A loud bell rang through the square, and the chatter of students and observers died away. People quietened and stilled as all eyes turned to the dais.

A rather unremarkable woman crossed to the centre of the dais to stand beneath the clock tower and looked out upon all of the waiting students. Her height was average, her hair tied back into a simple twist, and her clothes, aside from being slightly more ornate than the academic robes of the other waiting staff, were simple and dark blue, with a red stole that hung around her neck.

"A very warm welcome to each and every one of you. I am Kelda Athanasios, the Deputy Headmistress of Toserra Sorose Academy. People of Nýr Ásgardr, my dear and respected fellow staff and teachers, to our returning students and, most importantly, to our brand-new class of first years, a very big and warm welcome to Toserra Sorose Academy." The woman spoke out, her voice effortlessly projecting across the entire city square, though there was no microphone in sight.

"How does she do that?" Saga whispered.

"She's a Siren," Navi answered. "Their voices are... well... like that."

"You should hear a siren sing," Tasso added.

"No, you should not," Navi and Jemima chorused together at him.

He blushed and held his hands up to ward them both off. "Ok, ok..."

Around them, several other students shot them dirty looks as the Deputy Headmistress continued speaking. "At last, this beautiful day has arrived, and it is a beautiful day to arrive at your new home for the coming year. I am sure that you all have been eagerly waiting for this day to come, some more than others. The fact that not everyone has a love of coming to school is not surprising, and it is known to your teachers. We endeavour to provide you all with an education that is well-rounded, practical and engaging while recognising that catching up with your friends, meeting new friends, meeting your favourite teacher or just making sure that you can get a Pegasus tart at the Rolly Polly Kitty Eatery are just a couple of reasons, why we cannot avoid coming back to school." With that, everyone laughed.

"They're the best damned Pegasus tarts in the Nine Realms!" someone called out to more laughter.

"Anyway, before going any further, I am delighted to think the presence of the personality that hardly needs any introduction. It is none other than Mistress Grunhilda Grimaldi, your Residential Administrator and your port of call for any house-related issues you may have throughout the year. Mistress Grimaldi will shortly lead the choosing where all our dear, first-year students will be placed into their new residential houses for the coming year and, possibly, their entire Toserra Sorose experience." There was polite applause for the short, round woman standing beside the Deputy Headmistress. Thick, curly grey hair sprouted from her head beneath her plumed bonnet and her eyes were hidden by huge, round glasses with black frames that made Saga think of a certain boy wizard with similar glasses. The most interesting thing about her was the great grey wings that sprouted from her back.

Mistress Grimaldi spoke up. "It is a great pleasure seeing you all gathered here for this year's choosing after what feels like an eternity of vacation. Without taking much of your time, as I am sure that you are all eager to find your lodgings, get to know your new housemates and prepare for your first day of classes tomorrow, I want to mention a lesson that personally inspires me to do and achieve more despite failing a hundred times."

Around her, people were shifting awkwardly and anxiously as they surreptitiously looked at one another. As the people began to talk softly again, the fact that Ziva had said nothing useful about what would happen to them next settled on Saga's shoulders like a weight she could hardly bear. She could recall terrifying Family Days where potential adoptive parents would come, spend time with her and other kids and then, like magic, some of the kids would find themselves new homes. Saga looked around, trying desperately to figure something out, to determine what would happen next but all that happened was that Mistress Grimaldi kept on speaking.

"And so, allow yourselves to start this new year at your new school with hopes and dreams that no matter how limited you might be or seem to yourselves, you will do your best to achieve those dreams. Also, there is something magical about success and I don't just mean our Arcana classes. If I asked you to name the first man to win the Interplanar Pentathlon, I am pretty hopeful that I will get a bunch of answers. However, if I asked you who the second person was, I doubt I would get any answers."

Saga's thoughts kept dragging her away from the speech being made by Mistress Grimaldi. All this talk was just like the speeches of togetherness and family and all those things she had always wanted as a child but had never been chosen for until the day had come when they had decided she was too old to still attend the family day events... or had that coincided with her beginning to see the dead? What if none of the houses wanted her?

"Because we traditionally do not value the second or third positions as much as we should. After all, in battle, it is only the victor who matters. No one ever recalls the conquered. Now, I am sure that each of you is eager for what comes next. Do not allow me to hold you back, and further, but before I call the first student forth, allow me to welcome you, each of you, new students and returning students, to Toserra Sorose Academy."

Applause. This time, eager and impatient erupted from the crowd. Saga clapped, but her chest felt like a vice was squeezing tighter and tighter around her, forcing all of the breath out.

Mistress Athanasios handed Mistress Grimaldi a long scroll, and Grimaldi nodded thoughtfully. "All right," She looked around, noticed that the Prefects had appeared behind her and nodded again. She turned to her other side, where Saga was startled to notice twenty-six transparent people standing. She gasped, her hand covering her mouth as she tried not to cry out.

"What is it?" Jemima asked. "Are you not well?"

Navi and Tasso were looking at her curiously now too. Saga shook her head in panic. "No... no... no," she murmured to herself.

"Saga?" Navi asked concern etched across her face. "Saga, what's wrong?"

Saga shook her head. "Nothing."

"Something is very wrong," Jemima stated. "Something has scared you. What?"

Again, Saga shook her head. "Nothing is wrong," she sat down on her trunk and took several deep breaths.

"Umm, Saga?" Tasso asked cautiously. "Are you sure?"

She nodded. "Just... just give me a moment." She could not tell them what it was she was seeing. Every time she had told people of her nature, every time people had suspected, every single time she had been cast out. Just now, with these people, for the first time in a long time, she felt she could build real relationships and have friends. She would not risk that because of a few stupid ghosts.

Several minutes passed, and Saga had no idea how many students had been up by the time she finally stood back up, her back straight, her breathing back under control. Like everyone else, she stared at the stage as Grimaldi called up the next student. Saga watched in horror as the twenty-six ghostly figures surrounded the boy. A pale-skinned, black-haired boy Grimaldi had called Avery Amani. Several ghosts turned away instantly, obviously not interested in the boy. The remaining ghosts stood talking around the boy, who could not see or hear from the way he stood there, waiting for something to happen. Three more ghosts left the conversation as two male ghosts seemed to stare each other down for the boy.

With a huff, the tall, stately ghost turned and joined the waiting ghosts, leaving the smaller male ghost in his white robes to look at Mistress Grimaldi and nod.

"Nollet Heights," she announced, and a cheer went up from the spectators.

"He must be an angel," Navi whispered. "Only angels get into Nollet house."

They watched as Konishi Beroun, the Vampire who had hassled Jemima on Le Spectre Éclairé, was picked by a dark-haired ghost with a wooden left leg, and a hook for a right hand was chosen for Rottport Hall.

Tasso was called up after a girl called Bindi Billingsley, who was sorted into Bridelow Cottage.

"Werewolf," Jemima stated, and Saga's eyes went wide.

"Really?"

"Yeah, really," Tasso said, looking at the three girls one last time before making his way nervously up to the front of the crowd. Navi and Saga smiled reassuringly as he walked up the few steps to the dais and waited.

The ghosts began their debate again, and a short man in green turned away, not interested. A regal woman in a crown and heavy velvet robes also turned away, as did the dark-haired man with the wooden leg and hooked hand. Slowly, other ghosts started to turn away until a delicate small woman with fluttering, almost non-existent wings stood on one side of Tasso, and the tall, stately man with a sword at his hip stood on the other. They appeared to be talking animatedly over the top of Tasso's head. The man pointed out into the crowd, his finger pointing at where Saga saw Tonya waiting. With a sigh, the delicate little faerie ghost slumped across the dais to the other waiting ghosts.

"What are you watching so intently?" Jemima asked.

Saga glanced at her as Mistress Grimaldi stepped forward and said, "Knightrich Dormitory." A humongous roar went up from the male students, and Tasso was led away by a tall, good-looking boy with a gold-trimmed blazer.

Tonya was called up next, and the little faerie ghost was once again left arguing with another ghost over the top of Tonya's head. The woman with the crown and the heavy velvet robes waved her hand dismissively, looking at Tonya and walked away. The faerie ghost did not look ready to give up, but as a woman, bedecked in more jewels and gold than the regal crowned woman, laid her hand on Tonya's shoulder, and the little faerie ghost stomped her foot in fury as Mistress Grimaldi announced. "The Estievillers."

"Ooohhh..." The sound resonated through the crowd as a tall, elegant girl stepped forward to lead Tonya away.

The scene repeated itself, again and again, as the ghosts would squabble over the students. A boy called Darragh Byrne was selected by an odd little ghost in a green top hat for Ainsli House.

"Leprechaun," Tasso announced, coming up behind them. A new pin decorated the lapel of his blazer. A shield with a mounted knight looking as though he was about to charge.

"Leprechaun?" Saga asked in amazement. "This place," she murmured to herself as Tonya's friend Amita Cannavale wound up going with the Faerie ghost to Limomoux Heights.

"Saga Carolle," Grimaldi announced, and Saga stood frozen to the spot.

"Go on," Tasso said, having returned to them. "It's not that bad."

She glanced at him out of the corner of her eye. "That's easy for you to say."

With her head held high, imitating a feeling of confidence that she did not feel because she was still finding it hard to breathe as she stepped up the stairs and onto the dais. Over with the teachers, she spotted Astrid, who smiled reassuringly at her before Mistress Grimaldi made Saga face the crowd.

The ghosts wandered over to have a look, all except the one who had selected Tonya. She stayed where she had been. Was Saga not good enough for her?

The faerie girl looked at her. Then shook her head. "Not interested. She's not a faerie."

Saga looked at her but said nothing as several others shook their heads. "Not a Were," and a group of five ghosts disappeared on her.

"She's a curious one," the man in white robes said as he looked her over.

"Yes indeed," said the tall, stately man with the sword.

"What are you doing, Knightrich?" the regal woman asked. "Does she look male to you?"

"Mind your own business Queenette. You're not telling Nollet off, and she is most definitely not an Angel."

"Isn't she?" the robed man asked. "I feel as though she has the touch of the Gods upon her."

Another man sidled up and looked at Saga. "Can you see us, girl?" he asked.

Having them hovering around her, discussing her, dismissing her as if she were irrelevant was grinding on her. She looked straight at the odd man but said nothing.

"Hmmm..." he mused thoughtfully as the regal crowned woman looked her up and down. "Yes... Nollet, I do feel the touch of the Gods upon this child... But she is not one of mine," and he turned away without another word, making his way to wait with the other ghosts that dismissed Saga with barely a comment.

The white-robed man nodded. "Uchechi is correct. She is not mine. Touched by the Gods, yes, but not an Angel."

Saga clenched her fists within the folds of her skirt as they talked. Everyone was watching her, Navi, Tasso, and Jemima, as well as the people of Nýr Ásgardr, the new students and those who had wandered in to watch. They could not see the ghosts. They could not hear the ghosts. These were things she was certain of, but she also knew that while they talked, the minutes ticked on, and people were getting restless.

"Valkyrie," she said under her breath, and the ghost the other had called Nollet stopped short in his retreat back to the other ghosts. Saga's fingernails were biting deep into the flesh of her palms as she waited for them.

A ghost who had not spent any time inspecting students until now stepped forward as the crowned and velvet-robed ghost retreated away from her and several others. Nollet just kept staring back at her over his shoulder.

"So, you can see us," the new ghost said. He was young. Young in appearance, at least. He circled Saga, then stopped before her, looking into her eyes, his face coming as close as he could without touching. "A Valkyrie. Of course, you can see us. That is one of the things that separates you from the angels. That and your prowess on the battlefield."

"A Valkyrie. They've not been seen in two hundred years..." The ghosts were all talking. They were talking about her and speculating as to what her existence meant.

The strange young ghost in front of her smiled. "You can come with me," he said softly before turning to look at Mistress Grimaldi, who was starting to look extremely uncomfortable by the ghosts and their reactions to her.

She beamed when the answer came. "Jimpsee House." Tentative applause went up. Maybe they were all tired of waiting.

The ghost, who must have been called Jimpsee, smiled at her again before motioning to a prefect. "Tymberlee, would you please take care of Miss Carolle while I see to our next residents."

A tall, dark-skinned girl with closely cropped, dark hair approached Saga with a grin. "Welcome to Jimpsee House. I am Tymberlee Kaia, the house Prefect." Ziva waved discreetly as Tymberlee led her by the other prefects and teachers. Astrid beamed and nodded in encouragement. Saga waved to both of them, a small, discreet wave as Tymberlee led her from the dais.

Out of immediate view from everyone, Tymberlee dug into her blazer pocket and pulled out a small bronze pin. She carefully attached it to Saga's lapel. "This is the sign of our house. Each student is supposed to wear their house pin. It is now an official part of your uniform."

Saga looked down at the pin attached to her blazer and smiled as she lifted her hand to trace the embellishments of the pin. It was shaped like a shield, with a sword running down one side. Upon a shield was a fire-breathing animal that Saga did not recognise. She saw the same pin upon Tymberlee's lapel and smiled broadly. She had never belonged before, and right off the bat, she already belonged to this group. This Jimpsee House.

"Thank you," she murmured. "What is the animal?"

"It is a Chimera, and you are very welcome. I must get back in case he chooses another student. I will explain the importance of the Chimera to Jimpsee House tonight when we go back to the house to celebrate. Go, join your friends. I will find you and any others again after the ceremony."

The Choosings continued as Saga returned to the others. The ghost of Bridelow house selected Brea Cavandish. So, another werewolf. Jemima was wringing her hands together as Mistress Grimaldi read out another name, and the student stepped up to be chosen by the house ghosts.

"Jemima Dove," Mistress Grimaldi called out, and the girl stood completely still as she stared at the stage. She looked at all the people she would have to pass to get up in front of.

"I don't want to go up there," she whispered. "Everyone will stare."

"It's not that bad," Tasso said. "You just stand there, and Mistress Grimaldi says the name of your house after a while."

"Yeah, but how does she do that?" Navi asked. "Navi means... she looks at something and then nods like—" She stopped and looked at Saga. "You know... or you saw or something, didn't you?"

"Jemima Dove?" Grimaldi asked again, looking around the crowded square.

"Come on," Saga said. "I'll walk with you," Jemima nodded nervously and together, they walked side by side to the dais. At the stairs up, Saga nodded encouragingly to the girl and watched as she took the steps very tentatively.

The ghosts converged around Jemima as she stood there, trembling. She glanced at one of the teachers, who gave her a reassuring smile and motioned for her to look back out at the crowd. The ghost of Nollet Heights seemed to shake his head in apprehension while several others had turned away. Their houses were that of Weres, leprechauns and boys. But Jemima was an Angel. The ghost of Nollet Heights could have at least glanced at her. Sure, Jemima was nothing like any angel Saga had ever imagined, but she thought them just plain cruel at that moment. She looked up as the regal, elegant ghost of

Queenette Dormitory shook her head and left the search. Saga looked, trying to find the young male ghost of Jimpsee House. The one that had chosen her. She spotted him, hanging back from the crowd of ghosts, watching Jemima intently. Suddenly he turned his gaze, and they were looking at each other. His eyes seemed to bore into her as though asking what she was after, and she nodded her head towards Jemima.

As two more ghosts left the circle around Jemima, he approached, circled her as he had with Saga and looked back at her. "You sure?"

Mistress Grimaldi stared at the ghost and then at Saga in surprise. Perhaps she had never seen anyone other than herself or the prefects interact with the ghosts. Saga ignored the portly teacher, nodded at the ghost, and mouthed 'Please' to him. The Jimpsee ghost nodded and looked at Mistress Grimaldi.

"Umm," she said, still looking oddly between the ghost, Jemima, and Saga. "Jimpsee House."

Tymberlee went to lead Jemima away, and Saga nodded her thanks to the ghost. He nodded his acknowledgement back to her. She, too, looked oddly at the ghost but said nothing as she led Jemima away from the stage, and Grimaldi went on to call up the next student.

As Saga waited, Bridelow Cottage claimed another werewolf named Elayen Eastwood, and Ouwste House claimed a big, bear-like girl named Harriet Frazee. They just kept coming. There was a murmur of intrigue when Javaid Glairnet was assigned to Glairnet Hall.

Jemima was trembling when Tymberlee guided her back through the crowd long after her choosing had been completed. Tymberlee led Jemima, careful to stay close but extra careful not to touch the girl, as though she had already encountered that experience. "Saga?" the prefect asked. "Can you take care of Jemima?"

Tasso and Navi came up behind her, dragging their trunks as well as Saga's and Jemima's. "Of course," Saga said, nodding gratefully to the faerie and the dark elf. "Come on, have a seat on your trunk. We need to see which house Navi's going to be assigned to."

Jemima nodded but looked up at them with plaintive eyes. "How much longer?"

Tymberlee looked around awkwardly. It did not appear as though she wanted to leave the newest member of Jimpsee House, but her responsibilities as Prefect meant that she had to return to the ceremony proceedings. "Still a while."

"Emory Harding," Grimaldi called, and Saga could not help but watch as the tall, black-haired boy wended his way through the crowd and up to the dais with long, confident strides. Standing on the assigned spot, he stood tall and proud, confident of his looks and abilities. His eyes met with hers, and they held.

The ghosts wandered around him. The Ghost of Timbergard and the Ghost of Bridelow seemed interested and then turned away. Finally, she witnessed the Jimpsee ghost wander up after most of the ghosts had retreated from the boy. He circled him just as he had done with her and Jemima and then nodded to Mistress Grimaldi.

"Jimpsee House," she announced.

JIMPSEE HOUSE

Tymberlee looked around in surprise. "What?" She asked, looking up to the boy. "A Harding?" She looked around some more, maybe trying to see the ghost. "What is he thinking?"

"What do you mean?" Saga asked.

But that was answered for her when Emory Harding gave an outraged cry. "What?" He cried. He turned to Mistress Grimaldi as Tymberlee hurried back up the steps of the dais to meet with him. He looked at her before turning to face the other Prefects. The Prefect of Timbergard and the Prefect of Bridelow seemed to look anywhere but at Emory Harding.

"What's going on?" Saga whispered to the others.

"The Hardings are werewolves," Jemima provided. "Influential, important werewolves... It was expected that he would be in Bridelow like his father or Timbergard like his mother... Although generations of Hardings have been in Bridelow..."

"Even Knightrich would have been something... or the Xayvion. Something no Harding has achieved," Tasso added.

"There's status around the houses?" Saga asked. "How?" How could there be status to something no one had any control over? What would you do, bribe a ghost you did not know existed?

"There just are family legacies, standing in the school community. That kind of stuff," Navi added. "This One's siblings are all Dorbe Manor, but we have no history beyond Ziva, who was the first Dark Elf to attend Toserra Sorose. The Hardings," She glanced at Tasso, "The Bonnedrasses, these are old, powerful families that have long legacies at Toserra Sorose."

Tasso nodded. "Tonya getting into the Estievillers will be a boon for my parents... My not even getting into Limomoux... that will... well..." He shrugged but said nothing else. Saga wanted to tell him that the Limomoux ghost had fought hard against the Knightrich ghost but did not know how to get into that conversation. She wanted to tell him that the decision was bigger than any of them had known, but she did not want to ruin what friendship she hoped was building between the four of them.

On the dais, Emory Harding was being led away by not only Tymberlee but by the Deputy Headmistress as well. The boy was fuming. With a look of apprehension, Mistress Grimaldi carried on, calling out students' names. The ghost of Ainsli house chose Ronan Healy, and Shiquita Ivanek was chosen by the tall, scary ghost of Rottport Hall.

"Navi Jensyn," Mistress Grimaldi called out, and Navi walked up the stairs onto the dais, not looking at anything or anyone. Her eyes were closed against the sight of everyone watching her. Unlike Saga, the ghosts were quick to step aside for one. An old woman, someone who had died in their later years, a stark contrast from the young man who seemed to determine the residents of Jimpsee House, looked at Navi first. She nodded to herself and then turned to Mistress Grimaldi. It was a quick and simple decision for the old ghost, and Ziva was beside her sister even before Mistress Grimaldi said, "Dorbe Manor."

~*~

"If all new students would please meet with their House Prefect, you will be escorted to your residences for your welcome feast and orientation," Mistress Grimaldi said as the last student was led away by their prefect. "Once again, Welcome to Toserra Sorose, and we will see you all in class tomorrow. Oh, and keep an eye out on the notice boards in your house foyers, assembly times and other important messages will be placed upon there, and attendance is mandatory."

Saga did not know how she did it, but Ziva seemed to be beside them, her arm around Navi's shoulder, even before Mistress Grimaldi had finished speaking. Annis seemed to materialise out of nowhere and took Navi's other side. Astrid also came over another teacher beside her.

"Aunt Dina!" Jemima exclaimed, showing more excitement about this woman's appearance than they had seen her give on anything all day.

"Mistress Bess," the kindly woman chastised the girl. "How are you feeling?"

"I…" Jemima looked around at Saga, Tasso, and Navi. "I am good."

"How many aunts do you have?" Saga whispered to Jemima.

"Nine," she stated. "Aunt Dina is the Religious Studies teacher here."

Astrid nodded approvingly at the group. "You'll all do great this year."

"Well, come on, Sis," Ziva said, turning her sister away from the group. "We have the Dorbe welcome feast for you and the others."

Tasso looked around. "I had better find the Knightrich group. See you tomorrow in class?"

The girls nodded, and Tasso took up the handle on his trunk before heading off to find his new housemates.

"What about our class schedules?" Jemima asked Dina Bess.

"Your Prefect will have them," she eyed Ziva. "Have you gotten yours for your students?"

Ziva looked chagrined. "I'll uh… well… come on, Navi, Annis." If the girl had been able to go red in the face from embarrassment, Saga was sure she would have. The three sisters went off, Navi dragging her trunk behind her.

Astrid shook her head. "It's always exciting when your sibling gets assigned to your house," she glanced at Dina Bess. "We have that staff meeting now, don't we?" With a sigh, Jemima's aunt agreed. "Then, I will see you in class, Saga."

"There you two are!" Tymberlee exclaimed, pushing through a crowd of Queenette girls, Emory Harding trailing along behind her, a scowl on his face.

"I'm telling you," he kept saying. "There's been a mistake."

Tymberlee turned to him, her patience with him wearing thin. "I do not make the decisions, and you have spoken to Mistress Grimaldi and Deputy

Headmistress Athanasios. "Both have told you that the decision is final and not up for debate until the new school year. Maybe next year, you'll manage to get away from us freaks. That was what you called the residents of Jimpsee House, wasn't it?"

Saga and Jemima watched the boy recoil from the faerie girl's rant. "I... I didn't mean it like that!"

"Didn't you?" She asked. "Because you sure as hell sounded like you meant it." She turned to Saga and Jemima, plastering a smile on her face. "Girls," her voice held a different quality from when she spoke to Emory, but that did not hide how frazzled she looked. "Shall I show you all to Jimpsee House? I am sure that all three of you must be starving, and everyone else will want to meet with you."

The walk was awkward and silent. Saga glanced over at Jemima, but she too seemed to think better of saying anything as Emory trailed along behind them, his head hung in shock. From the square, it was only a short walk to Jimpsee House. Saga figured that this was good. It would be harder for her to get lost when going to and from classes. Tymberlee opened the door and held it open as the three new residents of Jimpsee House hauled their trunks in.

"Welcome!" A huge cry went up from the front room when the last of them, Emory, had settled their trunk into the hallway of the house. Eight other students, their uniforms in various levels of dishevelment, stood there. A big banner that said 'Welcome First Years' hung over the mantel place and lots of streamers and food around the room.

"Welcome to Jimpsee house," A tall girl with feathered wings of gossamer said as she approached and shook hands, first with Saga, then with Emory, and when she tried to shake Jemima's hand, Tymberlee seemed to shake her head, and the girl just said, "Welcome!" Again. "I am Onorati Forridel, the other Jimpsee fourth year."

"We're Percival and Perdita," a boy said, indicating himself and the girl beside him. They looked so alike that Saga guessed that they were siblings. They were short, with the same mousy brown hair as each other.

Beside her, Saga heard Emory sniff. "Rabbit?" He asked curiously.

Percival looked the boy up and down. "Wolf?" He looked at Tymberlee. "Really, a werewolf? We already have a Vampire and a Werehyena. It's like a den of predators in here!"

"Hey!" A boy who had been hiding in a corner cried. "When have I ever made to eat you!" He still wore the heavy cloak of the Vampire students but had the hood down so they could see his pale face and red eyes. "Gedde Rafi. Resident vegetarian Vampire."

"So you claim," Perdita said, one eye on him and the other on Emory.

A tall, awkward boy with long limbs boy waved from where he stood at the back of the room near Gedde. "Mannish Hijriyyah. Resident predator with a taste for rabbit stew." Perdita seemed to jump out of her skin with a squeak, but the boy just laughed. Percival glared at the boy but said nothing. Nor did he move. Saga thought maybe he was trembling.

A short, squat girl waved her hands. "Oh, shush it, the lot of you. I am Siobhan Bradigan, the only female Leprechaun and that silent one over there, tall, good-looking, brooding? That's Vespers Ina, the only male Siren... ever."

"See what I mean," Emory whispered under his breath. "Freaks. Every single one of them."

"And you," Siobhan continued, going up to Saga. "Are the Valkyrie, right?"

Saga looked at the short girl uncomfortably.

"Valkyrie, huh?" Gedde asked.

Saga looked sideways at Emory. "So, what does that make you?"

After a festive dinner, Tymberlee led Saga, Jemima, and Emory upstairs. "We're two to a room here. Saga, Jemima, you will be sharing this room."

Jemima looked startled. "I... I have never shared my space with another person before."

"I'm an old hand at it. Usually, there's more than just one other person," she grinned at Jemima. "I'm usually pretty tidy." The girl nodded, but the uncertainty was clear on her face.

"I'll leave you girls to settle in," Tymberlee said and then handed them each a scroll. "Your timetables. I'll have a house schedule up tomorrow with everyone's class schedule that you can refer to, but these are for you to keep." Then turned to Emory. "You'll be sharing with Mannish," and she led him down the hall to another room.

Saga and Jemima looked around their room. Two wrought iron beds stood, their heads to the far wall, a window over a long cupboard of draws. The other side of each bed had a desk for each girl, with shelves running up the wall for any books or knick-knacks they wished to place. Across from the beds were two tall cupboards, one for each of them. There was not much space in the room, but it was their own, and the space was neatly organised so that they could arrange not to get in each other's way.

Jemima set about unpacking right away. She opened her trunk and started unloading her uniforms and her street clothes and arranging them in the cupboard across from one of the beds. Saga positioned her trunk next to the other cupboard and opened it. She stared at the neatly folded clothes in there, along with the new schoolbooks and equipment she had bought. She set her staff up against the side of the cupboard and stared at the things inside her trunk. She had never owned so many things.

"Are you not going to unpack?" Jemima asked as she settled her nightwear into a drawer closest to her bed.

Saga unbuttoned her blazer and dropped it over the desk chair on her side of the room. "I..." She looked from the trunk to all the cupboard space and shrugged. "Maybe later." What if all of this were a mistake, and she would have to leave Jimpsee house? If she forgot something in the effort to repack, she would never get it back.

She picked up the scroll Tymberlee had handed her and unscrolled it. "First class tomorrow is World History... Followed by Ancient Languages... Great..."

"You are being sarcastic, right?" Jemima asked, looking up from her scroll. "Which Class Group are you in?"

"One."

"Me too."

Saga looked over her should at the girl and smiled. "Good."

Jemima started to arrange her books and possessions, and the effort she put into ensuring everything was in its proper place made Saga uncomfortable.

"I'm going to have a look around the house. Find the bathroom, that kind of stuff."

"Ok," Jemima said.

Saga opened the door and stepped out into the hallway. She was glad that Jemima could be so comfortable unpacking everything, but it would be some time until she felt as comfortable doing the same thing. There were four bedrooms on this floor and two bathrooms. The bedrooms all had names on the doors elaborately written and decorated, except for their own. It looked as though the residents of Jimpsee House had decorated their doors. The room she now shared with Jemima had a blank door with a small piece of parchment tacked to it with a pin. It bore only their names. A door hidden behind the stairs up to the third floor seemed to lead outside, and Saga opened the door and welcomed the fresh air she felt. She stepped outside and walked across the expanse. Small lights, what she would have called faerie lights back in her world, were strung across the open sky, lighting up tables, chairs and couches that seemed to be scattered in the outside area that she guessed was above the kitchen of the house.

She walked over to the railing and leaned against it. It was cool and quiet outside, but she could hear the revelry from the town as other student houses celebrated the arrival of their first-year students.

"Most first years are busy unpacking and perfecting their space at this time."

Saga whirled around. She had not heard the door open. Standing behind her, tall, elegantly dressed and completely ethereal, was the Jimpsee ghost.

"Oh..." Saga said in surprise.

"That was some choosing today," he said with a grin as he floated around her to stand at the railing next to where she stood.

"Was it different from usual?" She asked.

"Well, there was you. No student has ever seen us before. Even the Prefects must be given the ability to see us, and so does Mistress Grimaldi." "He looked at her. "You, though... you are an enigma to all of us. There has been much talk of you among us ghosts since the choosing."

"Oh..." Saga said, looking back out over the city. "More talk about me..."

"You do not sound pleased to be the centre of conversation everywhere," he said jovially, his ghostly arms sweeping the view of the city.

"Would you be?" She asked.

The Ghost was silent for a moment. "In life, I often was the centre of everyone's attention. Perhaps that is why I lived little further beyond my eighteenth birthday, but like you, I was the only one of my kind at this school."

Saga's eyes widened. "You went to school here?" She asked in amazement.

"Yes... Over a few centuries ago, the school opened its doors to the first class ever. A mere twenty-six students were in that class..."

He trailed off, and Saga thought. "Twenty-six students... twenty-six houses..."

He beamed with pride. "Exactly." He held out his ghostly hand to her. "Tremblay Jimpsee at your service. Do not hesitate to ask me if you ever need anything. Young Tymberlee can only see me when she wears her Prefect's badge and if I want her to, but you... You and I could be friends."

"Friends, huh?" Saga asked.

"Hello? Is there anybody out here?" Saga once again found herself looking around. As she did so, she spotted Tremblay Jimpsee, his finger to his mouth.

The window to a room that looked out over the outdoor area swung open, and Emory Harding stuck his head out. "Oh," he said. "It's you." He looked around. "Who were you talking to?"

Saga looked away from him and realised that Tremblay Jimpsee was gone as she did. Must be nice to be a few centuries-old ghosts who can vanish and appear at will. Emory stepped out of the window and walked over to the railing where he stood exactly where the ghost had been standing... floating?

"No one," she said.

"Could have sworn I heard..."

"I was talking to myself..." then added, as a dig to him, "Freak, remember?"

Emory leaned against the railing. His hands clasped as he looked at her, trying to catch her eye. He still wore his uniform blazer, but the tie all the boys had to wear was dangling from around his neck, untied. "I didn't mean..."

"Yes, you did," she stated. "The pretty, rich boy didn't get what he wanted, so he lashed out, but you did mean it."

"My family," he started. "They put a lot of stock into... well, everything." When she did not say anything, he went on. "You heard them down there... The Vegetarian Vampire? The male Siren... a female leprechaun... Wererabbits! For crying out loud, Wererabbits... The Gods only know what's wrong with that Hyena or those faeries."

"And me," Saga added for him before he could say it.

"You're a Valkyrie," He said, "Everyone knows that."

She glanced sideways at him. "In your own words, that makes me a freak. At least I'm used to it, though. I've been a freak all my life. I never expected that to change just because I'm in another world now."

The look on his face softened as she spoke. "You were raised in Midgard, right?"

Saga straightened, standing tall and looking out over the city. "Yes." A cold wind blew over them, rustling her skirt and making her shiver. The day had been warm, but the night was significantly colder than she had bargained for when she had left her jacket behind in her room.

She heard Emory moving but did not bother looking at him, so she was surprised when suddenly, she felt the heavy weight of his school blazer over her shoulders and the warmth it suddenly encompassed her in. Tentatively, she reached for the sides of the jacket and pulled it tight around her. "Thank you," she said softly.

They stood there in silence, listening to the city. Saga wrapped in the warmth of Emory's jacket. There were several other student residences near them, and Saga was sure that they were hearing several of the welcome parties from where they currently stood.

"I see you everywhere," Emory finally said. Saga looked at him, remembering all the times they had encountered each other in Yggdrasil City on the day she had gone shopping for her school supplies. But it had not only been then. Afterwards, she would spot him as she wandered through town with Navi. Never with Shadow, but the big dog had come and gone at his own will. He had been in The Bore Tooth Inn with friends one night while she had been there with Navi and her siblings. There had been other times throughout Yggdrasil City when they had seen each other. This was perhaps the longest conversation they had ever had with one another.

"One might have thought that you were following me," Saga said with a grin.

"Me?" He asked. "You... you were everywhere."

"So, you admit that I was always there before you!"

"That wasn't what I—" He shook his head and smirked. "Who are you?" He asked in a strange, questioning voice. He was looking at her so intently that she was taken aback for a moment.

"Saga..." She replied hesitantly.

Emory was quick to shake his head. "I know that it's more..." He sighed and stood up straight. "You know what? It's just me being weird. We should probably turn in."

She nodded, and as she slid his jacket off her shoulders and immediately missed the warmth. "You're probably right," she said, handing him his jacket. "Good night." She started to walk away after handing him back his jacket and only just heard his whispered good night as she opened the door to the main house.

"Holy hell," Emory cried suddenly, and Saga turned in surprise, her hand on the door, about to go inside. She walked back over to stand beside him and stared at where he was standing. Together they stared at a building, far out in the distance, past the walls of Nýr Ásgardr City as it burned. "It... it just suddenly... I don't know... exploded."

But Saga was not listening. She was watching. She could see something that the boy could not because what she saw as she looked out at the burning buildings in the distance were hundreds upon hundreds of mounted warriors riding over the countryside. The noise they were making was astounding, and she cried out in fear as she watched them rampage and burn everything they came into contact with.

"Saga?"

"Oh my god..." She whispered, her hands covering her mouth as she watched the riders fade away just as quickly as they had appeared.

A bell started ringing somewhere in town, and people came streaming out of their houses, but Saga was not taking any notice of that as she watched the riders move across the night sky.

"You see them, don't you?" Tremblay Jimpsee asked, suddenly appearing on her other side, and she nodded. "I thought so."

"Saga?" Emory asked again. "What is it?"

She shook her head. "I... I don't know."

The door to the balcony burst open and the twins, Percival and Perdita, came running out to look. Then, Vespers and Siobhan, Mannish, Gedde and lastly, Jemima.

"What happened?" Siobhan exclaimed as she seemed to walk through Tremblay to stand at the railing beside Saga.

"It just suddenly exploded," Emory said, glancing away from Saga for a moment, but as the others started to talk excitedly, he leaned in close to Saga. "What did you see?" he asked. She looked at him, not wanting to say anything, but he added quietly. "I heard... a long time ago that Valkyries see the dead... like... maybe the supposed ghosts of the houses." When she did not answer, he went on. "And maybe whatever caused that," he nodded towards the raging fire that people were now streaming out to fight. "It's the fourth sudden fire in as many months on this plane."

"I don't know what I saw," she said, resolute on not telling anyone about her ability to see the dead, if that was what she had seen, riding through the night sky.

CLASSES BEGIN

Saga awoke to find Jemima busily arranging her school bag for the day. On the desk beside her bed, Saga found a stack of books and several pens and notebooks. She had not left them there the night before.

"Did you unpack my things?" Saga asked cautiously as she sat up in bed, trying to get a look around the room through half-lidded eyes.

"No. Only the things you needed for today. We have the same schedule for this semester," Jemima said. "You should hurry and get dressed."

Saga rubbed her hands over her face, digging her fingers into her eyes to try and wake herself up. The lid of her trunk stood open, but everything within it was just as neat as she had left it, except for the things Jemima had set on her desk. She knew that she should say thank you, but she hated anyone going through her things and figured that not yelling at the other girl for touching her things was as polite as she could be on the matter.

It was tempting to give up on that resolution when she saw a fresh school uniform draped over the desk chair, though. Jemima was already dressed and closing the clasps on her school satchel when Saga swung her legs out of bed. "Yeah... I'll be down in a minute."

She stared at the books, neatly arranged on the desk, the bag waiting next to it so that she had the opportunity to pack it herself. With a sigh, she undressed and put on her school uniform. She knew that she should thank Jemima for her thoughtfulness, but it would not happen. Not today, anyway.

Five minutes later, she was downstairs, with her bag packed and her hair plaited down her back. She still had to grab her shoes from the self by the front door, but she could do that before they left for the day. Tymberlee had insisted that this was a shoes-free house, and Saga wondered just how hard and fast that rule was.

"Come on," Siobhan called out as Saga entered the dining area. Almost everyone was sitting there eating, the long table laden with food. Saga stared. She had never seen so much food for breakfast.

"You three ready for your first classes?" Perdita asked.

Jemima nodded. "Yes. I have everything ready and have done the prescribed reading too." There had been prescribed reading? Saga thought. She glanced at Emory and saw that he, too, looked stricken by the idea. That idea relaxed Saga a little. At least she was not alone.

"Where are Tymberlee and Onorati?" Emory asked, biting into a thick piece of bread with a strange green and orange spread.

"The fourth years were all called to help out last night. If they're back, they'll still be asleep," Siobhan answered. "You'll have to ensure you don't lose your class schedules. Tymberlee has not had a chance to complete the house schedule as she had promised."

They nodded, the images of the burning buildings still fresh in their minds. Saga sat down next to Jemima and looked at all the food. Mannish was digging in as though there had not been a feast the night before while Jemima ensured that her food was neatly placed upon her plate.

"Will you three be all right to find your way to class?" Perdita asked. "What is your first class?"

"World History," Emory answered after swallowing.

"Us too," Jemima said, indicating herself and Saga.

"Oh good, at least you three can go together," Siobhan said, packing her bag. "I'm sure you've all noticed that your academic classes are in the morning and practical classes are in the afternoon. That will alternate every semester." They nodded. "Make sure you do pop by here to pick up your other uniforms and equipment. There's not always lunch, but we have leftovers from last night, so you should be able to eat here for free today."

Theirs was the only student residence on the street, so they did not encounter another Toserra Sorose student until they hit the square, the huge clock tower looming over them all as shopkeepers opened their stores for the day. Students streamed past the clock tower to the large, ancient building set apart from every other building in town.

"We are on the third floor for World History," Jemima said. "Room fourteen."

"We should hurry," Emory said, looking up at the clock tower. "Or we'll be late."

They hurried towards the building, pausing only briefly when they ran into Tasso and Navi, arriving together. Emory looked around awkwardly as the four friends greeted each other and compared schedules.

"Hey, this is great!" Tasso exclaimed. "We're all in Class Group One."

Navi nodded excitedly. "Shall we?"

Jemima nodded, and together they started to walk towards a large sweeping staircase that led up to the second floor. Saga stopped when she noticed that Emory was not following. "You coming?" She asked.

Looking at her, then at the others, he nodded. "Yeah..."

She nudged him playfully with her shoulder when he fell into pace beside her. "Don't tell me you're nervous about my friends."

He glanced out of the corner of his eye at her. "No," he said a little too forcefully, but he did look awkwardly at Navi as she bounded up the stairs, Jemima and Tasso at her side. "I was just looking for some of my own friends."

"Oh," Saga said. "Right. You haven't mentioned any..."

"Because we know each other well enough to know everything about one another?"

"Touché," she answered.

"Too what?"

Saga shook her head. "Nothing."

They passed another group of first years who were staring at their schedules and a map of the school in complete confusion, and another group of third-years hurried past them without stopping. Jemima led the way up the second flight of stairs, not as sweeping and grand as the first and then confidently led the way down the third-floor corridor.

"Yasen!" Emory called in delight and broke away from them.

"What's with the rich boy?" Navi asked as he brushed past her to a boy waiting outside the same classroom door as them.

"Emory!" The other boy greeted. "Those the girls from Jimpsee house? They're cute." Emory looked at Saga but said nothing to confirm or deny the other boy's opinion.

"Nothing," Saga answered Navi. "Just... housemates. Now, what about you and Tasso?"

To her surprise, Tasso went bright red and tried to answer in Navi's stead. "We... We just met at the town gates. "Dorbe Manor isn't far from Knightrich and... well... we ran into each other... and you know... Why walk alone?"

"All right everyone, inside, find yourself seats quickly and quietly," The door behind them opened, and a tall, grizzled man stood there. He looked old enough to have witnessed history firsthand, in Saga's opinion. She sat next to Jemima in the second row of the classroom and grinned when she saw Navi and Tasso at the desk across the aisle from them.

The scraping of chairs ceased, and everyone looked at the front of the room. The grizzled old man took chalk to the blackboard and began to write. "I am Fermin Berfelan. Master Berfelan to all of you," he stated. "This is World History. We will cover everything from the great Gods to the fall of Asgard and the rebuilding in the aftermath of Ragnarök."

Master Berfelan unscrolled a long scroll. "There are twenty of you in this class. I expect to see you all here at every class," he cast a distrustful eye over all of them. "Your reading done; your homework ready to be submitted at the beginning of every lesson. Do I make myself clear?" Everyone looked at each other, but no one said a word. "Do I make myself clear?" he bellowed.

"Yes, Master Berfelan," they chorused awkwardly.

"Good," he murmured. "Konishi Beroun," Saga and Navi both turned in their seats to see the Vampire boy, his cloak over the back of his seat as he leaned back on two chair legs. Beside him, Vihaan was smirking.

"Here, Master Berfelan," Konishi said, rocking forward on his chair with a loud thud.

"Chairs are to be on the floor with all four legs," Berfelan said without looking up from his scroll. "Bindi Billingsley." The girl, a werewolf from Bridelow cottage, announced her presence from beside a squat, red-headed boy Saga recognised from the Choosing. She thought his name was Darragh and that he was a leprechaun. He was followed by Tasso and Tonya, answering Master Berfelen's call.

"Amita Cannavale."

The faerie girl beamed from her seat next to Tonya, and Saga noted that Gheree seemed to be scowling at the girl. There was friction there already. "Here, Master Berfelan."

He nodded, barely looking up to identify the girl, his eyes gazing at his list. "Saga Carolle."

Saga straightened in her seat. "Here, Master Berfelan," she said.

At the sound of her voice, he did look up, a scowl on his face. "The Valkyrie, right?"

Saga really hated that question. Everyone seemed to ask it, and like Berfelan, they always seemed unhappy or even angry about it. Hadn't the Headmaster insisted that she be enrolled as an Angel or something else? How did everyone know that she was a Valkyrie? "Yes, Master Berfelan."

Berfelan seemed to growl low in his throat as he stared at her. "I knew Valkyries... Bloody scavengers, every one of them."

Saga blinked in surprise. Hadn't Astrid told her that no Valkyries had been seen for two hundred years? Did that mean... Just how old was Master Berfelan? Around her, the others in the class seemed to be whispering and questioning his words.

"Silence!" Berfelan roared, and all sound ceased instantly. They stared up at the man from their seats, waiting for what would happen next. He looked straight at Saga. "I'll be watching you, girl," And then he went on marking the attendance. "Seona Cerdan."

Saga glanced first at Jemima beside her, but when she shrugged, she glanced across the aisle to Navi and Tasso.

"Dayan Chagmion." Master Berfelan was still going over his attendance list. "Jemima Dove."

"Here, Master Berfelan," Jemima popped up from beside Saga.

He grunted in response and went on. They also had the Werebear from Ouwste house, Harriet Frazee, in their class and the boy who bore the same name as his residential house, Javaid Glairnet. Berfelan paused to look at the boy, and as a result, everyone turned to look at him. He was a tall, muscled boy, nothing like Harriet. Harriet's strength was evident in her size, but Javaid also looked fast and agile. Saga could not help but wonder what he was.

"Emory Harding."

Behind her, Emory spoke up, responding to Berfelan, but the teacher seemed to ignore him as he went on. "Essa Izadi," an extremely pretty girl seated next to Javaid Glairnet answered, her voice loud and musical. "Pados Jenika."

A boy in the front of Saga answered. "Here." Berfelan glanced up at him but did not reprimand the boy for not addressing him as he had ordered all the students to do so.

With a grunt, Master Berfelan called out Navi's name. The girl looked around awkwardly as if suddenly, realising that she would have to answer him in front of the entire class. "H... h... h... here... M... Master Berfelan," she called out tentatively, and Saga felt for her. Over the time she had known her, the stutter had become almost non-existent until she got stressed out at events like this.

"Another Jensyn?" He shook his head. "They just keep letting you dark elves in. Untrustworthy creatures, I keep telling them, but no... Their children have a right to an education." He glared at Navi, and she seemed to shrink in her seat. "You are another one I will be watching." He shook his head in disgust and looked back at his list. "Dökkálfar and Valkyries... What is this school coming to? Oisin Murphy."

"Here, Master Berfelan," the squat red-haired boy seated a few rows away called. In quick succession, Vihaan Naveli and Gheree Nollar answered to their names, followed at last by Yasen Torrey, the boy seated next to Emory.

"Let's see what you lot all know about your world, shall we?" Berfelan asked, walking down the aisle between the desks. "What was Fenrir, and who did he kill?" Jemima's hand rose, as did several others around the room. Contemplating his choices, Berfelan walked back down the room and stood in front of Saga. "You." He ordered.

Saga looked up at him wide-eyed. She had no idea who Fenrir was nor who he had killed. She knew nothing of this world. She looked at Jemima, but with Berfelan standing right on top of them, there was no way for anyone to pass her an answer. "Umm..." She said, trying to make time. "He uhh... he slew, ummm..." She heard sniggers behind her and was sure it was either Tonya or Konishi.

"A Valkyrie, who doesn't even know that Fenrir was the wolf who killed and was killed by Odin himself? Useless," Berfelan sneered. He turned and continued his questioning. "On what plane was Thor killed?"

Again, several hands went up, but again Berfelan pointed at Saga. "You."

"I..." Her chest was tight, and she wished he would pick one of the people who actually wanted to answer the question.

"Just giving up, girl?" he bellowed. "Do you know anything? Have you never been to school before?"

The question stung because she knew that for Navi, this was her first time at school, and Saga had been to many schools. Just never a school in this world. Hell, she barely even knew what world she was on.

"I went to school in Midgard," Saga said softly.

"What was that?"

"I went to school on Midgard," She repeated a little louder.

"Midgard. The plane where Thor was killed. How about that?" Berfelan asked, standing beside her desk, towering above her and Jemima. More snickers burst out from around the classroom. He looked at Saga intently. "Who was the war even against, Girl?"

Saga blinked rapidly. She knew this. She knew this. She had read it somewhere in a book. The war... The war... She membered reading about an Irish druid who could work with iron and regularly blamed things on the dark elves, not that she had ever mentioned this to Navi, but he had known about... Not the events of Ragnarök, but the coming of it. She looked up at him defiantly. "The Ice Giants."

Berfelan stared at her in surprise. "Well... yes." He turned and marched back to his desk. "And what are the Ice Giants called?"

"I don't know," and damn it, she was fairly sure that same book had told her that too, but she could not remember. Berfelan seemed to ignore Navi's presence despite her attempts to answer the questions, and he never called on her to answer, usually deciding to pick Saga over anyone. "I don't know the history here. That's why I'm in class. To learn it." As soon as the words had left her mouth, she regretted it. The anger that flared in Fermin Berfelan's eyes was not to be ignored, and the way he seemed to lean in over her in response said even more about his mood. She was in trouble.

"Detention. With me. After tonight's school assembly," he declared, and Saga's eyes widened. Detention? Already? Astrid was going to kill her.

~*~

The end of class could not have come any sooner for Saga.

"Detention?" Navi exclaimed as soon as they passed through the door of the classroom. "Detention?"

"What was that guy's deal?" Tasso mused.

"Aside from being a little rude after considerable harassment, I see no reason," Jemima stated. "But he is the teacher."

"But detention on the first day of school?" Navi whisper-shouted at Jemima across Tasso and Saga.

"And why aren't you fuming about how he treated you?" Saga asked, her hands wrapped around the strap of her satchel to prevent her from moving them.

Navi shrugged. "Ziva, Annis and Edun warned This One about him. Honestly, it's fine. He disregarded them so much in class that he could barely remember their names, so when marking assignments, they were graded fairly because he didn't know which person on his list was the dark elf. "What's next, Jemima?"

"Planarography," the angel answered. "First floor, room three."

Group one all headed that way together. Tonya and her two sidekicks walked past, sniggering as they did. Emory and Yasen hurried on by them as if Emory did not want to be seen near the girls from Jimpsee House.

Saga glanced back at the doorway to their World History classroom, and standing there in the doorway was Fermin Berfelan, watching them with his hawk-like eyes as they left his classroom. His eyes never left Saga, and his stare made a shiver run down her spine.

"So, Planarography," she said as she hurried along with the others. "Umm... What is it?"

Tasso stopped walking so abruptly that Saga walked right into him. Navi and Jemima were staring at her.

"Didn't you do any of the reading?" Navi asked.

"How can you not know what Planarography is?" Jemima asked.

"Ohh... boy." Tasso groaned as he checked to make sure he still had everything.

"Why does everyone keep mentioning the reading?" Saga asked. "What reading? And when will anyone remember that I have only been in this world one whole month!" She exclaimed. They had resumed walking, and several people in the hall stopped to glance at her outburst.

"This is not going to be good," Navi said, looking at Jemima. The angel nodded as they went ahead, talking. Saga was sure she heard Jemima mention how she had had to prepare Saga's school things for the day.

"This day sucks," Saga whined. Tasso just laughed as he went on ahead to catch up with Jemima and Navi.

Their class settled into new seats in the circular room that Planarography was held in. The room was on the first floor of the grand old school building and was the base of a tower. The interior was completely circular, and the teacher's desk was situated in the middle of the room, and two semi-circular tables surrounded it. Ten on one side of the room, ten on the other. Jemima, Saga, Navi, and Tasso sat down next to each other on one side of the room, the rest of the class finding seats for themselves. Tonya sat between Amita and Gheree on the far side of the room from them, while Emory and his friend Yasen sat down opposite Saga and Jemima.

"Good morning, everyone," a jovial man in a long red, embroidered coat walked into the room. "Welcome one and all to Planarography. Now, I know for some of you, this is your first foray into formalised education, but basically, Planarography is the study of the Nine Realms and The Extended Planes. Who has been to Yggdrasil City?" About three-quarters of the room raised their hands. "Good, good. And how many of you rode upon the rainbow discs to get there?"

Looking around the room, the raised hands were fewer. Saga's remained up as she recalled with a sickening gut-wrenching feeling the flight from Walhalla to Yggdrasil, half of which she had spent hanging off the disc.

"Interesting," the man went on. "Anyone use them to skip the stairs?" More hands went up. "So, who can tell me what those flying discs are?"

"Magic set up by the gods?" Essa Izadi, one who had never ridden upon the discs, guessed.

"Not quite," their teacher said. "Anyone else?"

Saga thought. What had Astrid told her what seemed like a lifetime ago on a mountaintop cricket field in Walhalla? She raised her hand tentatively.

"Yes? You there," their teacher said, pointing at Saga.

"They're the remnants of the Bifrost Bridge?" Saga asked, questioning her answer as she said it, but she was sure that that was what she remembered Astrid saying.

A slow grin blossomed across his face as he pointed excitedly at her. "Yes. Yes. Yes." He accentuated each word with another jab in her direction. "Remnants of the Bifrost Bridge. Exactly right! Well done. Someone has been doing their homework!"

Saga went red at that. She had done no such thing, but after the debacle of World History, she was not about to open her mouth and disillusion this nameless teacher with the notion that she was a well-versed student.

Tasso leaned over Navi to look at her. "Really?" he mouthed, and she nodded, unable to hide the grin of pride on her face.

"And who can tell me what the Bifrost Bridge was?" he went on. On either side of her, Jemima's hand and Navi's hand went up. So did a few others around the circular room.

"You," he directed a hand to Jemima.

"The Bifrost bridge once connected Asgard to Midgard," Jemima explained. "The broken remnants now circle between the Nine Realms at a set pace, with some only moving up and down the World Tree."

Again, their nameless teacher bobbed his head excitedly. "Yes. Exactly. I might have to dub this the clever corner," he said, motioning to where they sat. Nearby, Saga heard Konishi mutter something to Vihaan while Tonya glared angrily towards her brother, where he sat leaning over Navi's book. Across from her, Saga could feel Emory's eyes on her, and she tried to focus on an interesting knot in the wood of her desk than on looking up at him. "Yes, very good indeed. The World Tree itself was what connected the planes of existence, but the fall of Asgard during Ragnarök shook The World Tree to its core and the flames that consumed Asgard also consumed the Bifrost bridge. Ultimately a good thing because the bridge's destruction prevented Midgard from being destroyed. As a result, the bridge cracked, leaving behind the rainbow discs that have been extensively mapped and timed to allow travel. Now, which plane do we live upon?"

"Asgard, sir," Emory said.

"Yes, yes," excitement danced in his eyes. "What a clever group you all are." This caused the class to snicker in derision. Their teacher, who as of yet was still unnamed, seemed a little over-excited about basic knowledge. He then picked a stack of scrolls up from the circular table in the middle of the room and started to walk around, passing them out to each of them. "There, you have a map of Yggdrasil and the Nine Planes of existence," as he returned to the centre of the room, he took a crystal from a drawer in the desk and placed it in an ornate holder at the centre of the circular desk. Suddenly, an image emerged before them, as tall as the room of Yggdrasil. "Mark on your maps what is here. Placement is everything." Tonya raised her hand. "Yes?"

"Excuse me, sir, but who are you?" she asked, and around the room, several people nodded in agreement and even as much as she did not want to agree with Tonya Bonnedras, Saga did want to know who this teacher was.

The man stopped and turned in a circle, looking at everyone around the room. "Did I forget to introduce myself again?" When they nodded, he removed the crystal from its holder so that everyone could see him once again. "My most sincerest apologies, everyone. I am Master Byrge Iacono. I will be your Planarography teacher for the year. Any more questions?"

A unanimous shaking of heads resulted in Iacono replacing the crystal in the holder on his desk and the image of the tree reappearing in the room. It circled slightly, allowing everyone the chance to get down the names of the planes and their placement concerning the tree and the former Bifrost bridge.

"This guy is a lot cooler than Berfelan," Saga whispered.

"Well... I mean, I know he is wearing that long coat and all, but what makes you think he is cold?" Jemima asked.

Saga looked at her in disbelief, but upon seeing the blank looks on Navi's and Tasso's faces, Saga sighed. "I... I didn't mean cold... umm... cool means like... umm... great... better... umm... awesome..."

"Why is being cold awesome?" Navi asked. "It's not... Navi means really... It isn't."

"That's not... it's just... never mind... it has a lot of uses... but umm... forget it." Saga looked back at her image of the old World Tree and started ensuring that she had labelled it correctly.

PINGU

The kitchen was crowded when Saga and Jemima returned to Jimpsee House after Planarography. They had split off from Tasso and Navi, who were headed back to their own residences for lunch and to get their gear for their afternoon classes. Music was playing in the background, just barely audible over the din of multiple conversations.

"Mistress Grunborg was just brutal today," Siobhan told everyone as she showed off a spectacular black eye that shone like a black hole against her flame-red hair.

"Oh my god," Jemima exclaimed, looking at the girl. "What happened to you?"

"Just a bit of a scrabble in Combat class. Who do you guys have for combat?" she asked.

"I thought Leprechauns were supposed to be lucky," Emory said, filling his plate. Saga had no idea where he had come from because she had not seen him after Planarography and had not seen him come into the kitchen.

"Well... You should see Fergal Kavanagh," she added with a laugh. "Serves him right for all his loud mouthing about me."

Perdita laughed, almost bouncing in her seat like the rabbit she was. "It was great! That stupid Leprechaun had been going on and on with a couple of the werewolves about how I'd make a fine rabbit stew, and then, like magic, he was paired up with Siobhan and yeah, he got that good whack in at her, but look at her... And he's off to the hospital to get his nose reset."

Tymberlee and Onorati were seated at the far end of the table, eating silently as the others talked. They looked weary and tired, but they were dressed in their uniforms, likely ready to start their afternoon classes despite the evening's disaster.

"Do you know what happened last night?" Saga asked them. The chatter around them seemed to fade away, curiosity causing everyone to stop their conversations.

Tymberlee shook her head. "No... just that the Arsinee Farm was destroyed..."

"Completely... it wasn't just the house either," Onorati added. "It was..."

"Everything," Tymberlee continued when Onorati could not find the right words. "The farm animals, the outbuildings, the house... the... the trees... it's all just flattened and burned. It's so weird."

Saga thought of the riders she had seen and the noise of their onslaught. Hundreds upon hundreds of mounted men and perhaps women, beasts of myth that she had never imagined existing, converging upon that one place and then leaving again as though nothing had happened.

"Oooh, oooh!" Perdita bounced up and turned up the gramophone, releasing the tension in the room. "Saga, you must hear this song!" she cried excitedly. Percival was shaking his head, a grin on his lips as he did so. A woman's voice rang out from the gramophone... Or at least that is what Saga thought the device looked like.

"Here we go, to war again, all the heaven-sent soldiers,
When they ride, they shall have all the weapons they're proud to wield,
Arrows and bows, maces, and swords, all the weapons for them to wield."

Saga thought that the voice and the tune were eerie, and as it went on, her opinion was solidified, but she also understood why Perdita had thought she should hear the song.

"Down on the battlefield, the Valkyrie,
doth choose the slain, to serve the Gods
The brave and the true are called to serve
In the hall of Valhalla."

"I love her music," Vespers said, reclining in his seat. He had been singing along, his soft voice accenting that of the ghostly female singer.

"Here we go, to war again, all the heaven-sent soldiers,
When they ride, they shall have all the weapons they're proud to wield,
Arrows and bows, maces, and swords, all the weapons for them to wield."

The words of the song stuck in Saga's mind as she settled into a seat, the empty plate on the table before her, waiting still to be filled with food.

"Saga?" Emory asked. Once again, he had been watching her. His deep blue eyes followed her every move.

Saga looked up. "What event is she singing about?"

"Ragnarök, of course," Onorati answered. "Where the slain warriors were called to serve in the great war once more."

"No," Tymberlee disagreed. "I thought the song was about the Wild Hunt."

"What's the Wild Hunt?" Saga asked.

"An old fae tale," Onorati answered, "About the fae riding upon Midgard, causing havoc, but unable to step down from their mounts for fear of crumbling to dust... something to do with time." She shrugged and stood up, putting her empty plate on the counter. "I've got to get ready for class."

"Me too," Tymberlee said, getting up. She pulled the pin from the gramophone, and the music stopped. She eyed Saga, Jemima, and Emory. "Do you three know where you're going?"

"We have Animal Husbandry," Jemima said.

"You lot better get moving," Percival said, looking up at the clock. "You need to be right across town."

"Where?" Emory asked, looking at his schedule.

"Go back to the town square," Tymberlee instructed, "Ignore the main school building and follow the road directly across from this one, past the clock tower. Get out of town. To your left is Herbalism on the farms. To your right are Horse riding and Animal Husbandry at the stables. What have you got after animal husbandry?"

"Combat training," Emory said, shoving his schedule back into his satchel.

"Geez... they got you lot running all over town, don't they?" Siobhan asked. "Combat training's down on this side. Not the gate closest to us, that's religious studies for you heavenly types, but the next one over. Anyway, from Animal Husbandry, don't come back into town."

"Yeah," Perdita agreed. "You're better off running around the outside of the town walls. That time of day, the streets will be packed full of people, and you'll wind up being late."

The three of them looked at each other and nodded, feeling less confident than they were projecting.

"Go on, go get your stuff," Tymberlee instructed.

The town was bustling as they ran. Students streaming towards classes in various directions, and townspeople going about their day. Saga had yet to have an opportunity to explore the town, and it did not look like today would be the day. Not with the school assembly and her detention with Master Berfelan.

"Who thought it would be a good idea to spread a school across an entire town?" Emory wailed as they passed the clock tower, found the street Tymberlee had been referring to and passed by two more student residences near the town gates. Students in outdoor wear seemed more common out this way than students in uniform, so they figured they were in the right place.

"That way," Jemima said, pointing at a large building surrounded by an open equestrian field. They entered and found Navi and Tasso already there with most of the rest of their class. Gathering at the far side of the hall they were in was another class, all in their riding uniforms.

"Class One?" A stern female voice asked from a doorway that seemed to lead into the darkened expanse of a large row of stalls behind her. When they nodded, she continued. "I am your teacher, Gretchen Anhora."

"Oh dang," Navi whispered under her breath.

"What is it?" Saga whispered back.

"An elf."

Saga looked from Gretchen Anhora to Navi. Their teacher was tall. So many people around here were tall, Saga thought. Maybe not the Leprechauns, but so many others. She was not unusual here like she had been at her old school. Aside from her height, Saga noted the same pointed ears as Navi, but Gretchen Anhora's skin was pale, and her features delicate and fine. Navi's dark skin made those same features seem sharp and angular. "You're both elves, though... Right?"

Navi shook her head. "I... I... it's not that." That damned stutter was back.

"The Ljósálfar kept the Dökkálfar as slaves," Jemima added in a hushed tone. "Master Berfelan, no matter how rude... Was not wrong. It is unusual to see Dökkálfar in schools, and Navi's family are the only ones that attend Toserra Sorose... or any school as far as I'm aware."

"Come on through all of you," Mistress Anhora said, waving at them to follow her further into the building. With curious glances at one another, Class One did as requested.

The space beyond the doors was a large barn or stable. Corrals lined both sides of the central aisle for as far as they could see. "Toserra Sorose cares for a large number of magical and non-magical beasts, as you will come to realise in the coming years. To aid us in this, each student is assigned an animal that is their responsibility for the duration of the school year," she turned from facing them in the dim light of the barn. "Your care of these creatures and your presentation on their ecology and development form the basis for your grade as well as your developed knowledge of every creature in your class group."

They were surveying the space around them, eager to get a look at the animals they would be caring for, but could see no further than their immediate group, the lighting being so dim.

"Go, investigate. Each stall is individualised to the animal type. Today," she passed around heavy tablets and chunks of chalk. "Get to know the animals and use your textbooks to identify each animal." Mistress Anhora stopped short before handing Navi her tablet and chalk. They stared at each other, neither saying a word as the rest of the class watched them. With a deep, heaving breath, Anhora allowed Navi to take the tablet and chalk before continuing to Essa Izadi, who had been beside her. "The animals will choose you. Not the other way around. Make sure you note on your tablet what animal is yours for the course duration. You are also free to name your partner. Spread out. I do not want to see an entire class in one stall."

Bags were dropped on the floor as everyone retrieved their textbook, *Myth to them, Real to Us* by Perdita Abtahi. Emory and Yasen went in one direction, Tonya, Amita and Gheree in another. Konishi and Vihaan selected a stall and went in.

"Shall w... w... we?" Navi asked, glancing suspiciously at Mistress Anhora.

Tasso nodded and pointed towards a stall. "Here?" They all nodded and followed him in.

In an instant, it was as though they had been transported to another place. The dimness of the barn was gone, and they were bathed in a brilliant light. A gentle breeze blew, and the trees, there were actual trees in there, which rustled in the slight gusts of wind. A bit off in the distance, they saw a flock of what looked like birds. Slowly, they approached, certain that whatever they were walking towards was not a simple predator bird.

"H... h... holy damnation!" Navi gasped. "Those things are ugly!"

"What are they?" Saga asked, opening the textbook but not knowing where to start. "It's like a weird kind of chicken lizard thingy."

"Chicken lizard thingy?" Jemima repeated, each word coming off her tongue slowly. "Oh. Oh!" she suddenly gasped, grabbing her book and flipping excitedly through the pages. They watched her as she jabbed her index finger at a page. "Here!" They all peered over her shoulders, crowding in around her, until she ducked away from them, backing away, a look of panic on her face. "Not so close!" she begged.

"Sorry!" Saga gasped. "We're sorry, Jemima." Navi and Tasso were nodding wordlessly along beside her.

Jemima took several deep breaths, holding the book close to her chest as she did so. They stood there awkwardly, waiting for her to speak again. "Cockatrice," she finally said. "They are cockatrices."

Tasso nodded eagerly, grabbing his book and flipping to the right page. He ran his finger quickly over the lines of text and looked from the sketch in the book to the creature. "Yeah. Yeah, they are!"

"Score!" Saga exclaimed. "One down. No one's being targeted by the creature, right?"

They stared at the chicken lizard-type creature, but the cockatrice had no interest in any of them, so they marked the number of the stall they had entered and listed it as a cockatrice, then headed out to find the next one.

Back in the huge barn, Yasen Torrey was being followed by a strange creature shuffling along on what looked like three legs. A long stalk seemed to bear two eyes that tracked Yasen's location, despite his attempts to escape from the creature.

"Help! Get that thing away from me!" He cried, but Emory, standing by the door to the stall they had entered, doubled over with laughter. A rotten odour permeated the barn.

"Oh... That's just..." Saga groaned.

"The worst!" Navi agreed.

Gretchen Anhora walked up to Yasen and put her hands on his shoulders, stopping him in his tracks. His eyes opened wide as she looked meaningfully at him before turning him to face the creature.

"It would appear that you have been selected," she said simply. Emory's laughter ratcheted up another level, and it sounded as though he was laughing so hard that he was having problems breathing.

"Shut up!" Yasen shouted at his friend, but that seemed to egg Emory on even further.

"Have you identified it?" Mistress Anhora asked.

"Yes," Yasen groaned. "Otyugh, right?"

She nodded. "That's right," she held her hand to her nose. "Mr Torrey, would you mind returning your animal to its stall?"

Yasen whirled on her. "How?" he wailed.

Saga quickly wrote down the animal's stable number and name, noticing Tasso and Navi doing the same thing before they slipped into the next stall, unnoticed by Mistress Anhora.

"That thing was disgusting," Jemima exclaimed.

"And it stunk so bad!" Navi cried, taking in deep, heaving breaths from their new environment.

Two short, stocky boys were moving back towards them. "Where'd it go?" the first one asked.

The second one shook his head. "No idea!"

"Let's get out of here!" They decreed to one another and turned to run, only to run straight into Saga, Navi, Jemima, and Tasso.

"Move!" Darragh Byrne cried. "That thing is a beast!"

"You don't want to go out there!" Navi told him.

Darragh shook his head. "Yes. Yes, I do!"

"We really do!" Oisin Murphy agreed, and they could see that both Leprechauns were covered in what appeared to be cat scratches. From a very big cat.

Saga looked around. "What are you running from?"

"The cat!" Darragh exclaimed, pointing as clouds covered where they were standing, and a large paw came into sight, followed by a head of a ghostly, grey-white colour.

"A bezkira," Navi exclaimed, and the animal looked at her.

"You drew its attention!" Oisin cried. "We're doomed!"

Navi stepped forward, though. "Hello there."

The large cat-like creature stopped approaching Darragh and Oisin and turned all its attention on Navi. It cocked its head to the side, its eyes looked hungry to Saga, but she watched, her heart hammering in her chest as Navi insisted on approaching the creature. She looked nervously at Tasso, but his eyes were locked on the small dark elf and the large cat.

At two meters long, it was no house cat that Saga was used to. Suddenly, the cat stretched, its long front legs low to the ground, it's huge, rounded behind, high in the air with its tail sticking out as far as it could go.

"Yeah, that's right," Navi crooned, and the cat looked up at her as it lowered itself to the ground.

"What the?" Oisin whispered as they all watched.

When Navi reached out to scratch the huge cat between its ears, Saga heard Darragh take a deep breath of shock. She, herself, was not sure if she was even breathing. The animal nudged its head against Navi's small hand, just like any cat Saga had ever seen. It even appeared to be purring. Navi looked back at them. The smile on her face said everything.

"She... She..." Oisin cried. "How did she?"

"The dökkálfar have a special relationship with the bezkira," a voice said behind them. They all turned on the spot to find Mistress Anhora behind them. She was staring at Navi, stroking the ethereal fur of the big cat. She shook her head. "I suppose the girl will have the Bezkira as her project for the year."

Saga was starting to feel irritated. Navi had her bezkira, which she had decided to name Ephyra. Jemima had spoken with a strange dragon lion-type thing she was naming Kaia and was talking away with the large beast as though they were best friends. Tasso was playing fetch. Yes, fetch with a dog that did not run after the ball but appeared to teleport and catch it mid-air.

Emory had an extremely weird creature sitting on his shoulder that, when it smiled, showed off hundreds, if not thousands, of razor-sharp teeth. Yasen was still trying to escape his trash monster, and Tonya Bonnedras showed off her cute miniature dragon with butterfly wings. Harriet Frazee had changed into her bear shape to compete with an odd, exceptionally large bear-type creature with a beak and feathered wings for arms.

Mistress Anhora was trying to get a cockatrice to leave Gheree alone, but the animal had chosen the faerie girl, much to her alarm, especially with Amita having a Unicorn as her project for the year. But Saga had yet to bond with any animal, and she was feeling left out. Not that it was unusual for her, but since meeting Astrid, things had been a lot better for her.

She walked into the last stall, all but ready to give up. What would she do if no animal chose her? This stall seemed to be an extension of the barn, and she walked in, eyeing the additional stalls she saw on either side of her. Most of them had the head of a horse sticking out from them. With a start, she realised that they were not horses. Not with gigantic, elegant wings protruding from their backs. One rustled its feathers, allowing her to see them.

"Pegasus," she breathed out in wonder. Almost every animal in there was a startling bright white. There was one, a dazzling deep black, just like Navi. He looked at her with deep, intelligent eyes and his head moved around, looking to and fro. It seemed to direct her to the only stall not to have an animal looking out at her from it. Tentatively, Saga walked towards the apparently empty stall, her eyes on the big, black pegasus as she did so. His gaze seemed to hold hers, and as she reached the stall door, he looked as though he nodded to her.

Saga looked into the stall she had been directed to and gasped at what she saw. Curled into a ball in the back corner of the stall was a winged horse, small compared to the ones she had seen so far. Maybe it was younger? A baby?

"Hi there," she said softly. The animal looked up at her, and she was amazed to see that it was vastly different from every other one she had seen.

It was not the startling white of the majority of the pegasi nor the solid black of the male who had pointed her towards this stall. A mane of snow-white, a body of midnight black. It clambered to its feet, and she saw that tufts of hair around the feet were also white, as was the tail. "You are beautiful," she whispered to the pegasus. First, it stretched one wing out and then then the other. She saw that while most of the wing feathers were black, a strip of feathers at the base of his wings was white.

The pegasus walked towards her, curious eyes meeting hers as it walked. "I was wondering whom he would choose." Mistress Anhora had once again managed to arrive out of nowhere without warning.

"Has he picked me?" Saga asked as the dual-coloured pegasus popped his head over the top of the stall gate to nudge at her. She raised her hand to stroke his nose.

"I would say so," Mistress Anhora said. "You're the only one that has even noticed that he was in there."

"Does he have a name?"

"No," Mistress Anhora said quietly. "No one quite knows what to do with him. "He... does not fly... his wings are fully grown. They appear to work, but he does not fly."

"Why not?"

"We do not know. As such, we had to bring the family down from their mountain nest to the stables. Onyx took to the move well. He is very protective of his foal... the mother not so much."

Saga looked away from the creature, nuzzling her to look at her teacher. "He... I..." She looked back at the horse and gave in to a burning desire to hug his nose. "It's ok. It's ok beautiful... I know what it is like to not be wanted." She chuckled softly. "You look like a big penguin."

"A... a what?" Mistress Anhora asked.

Saga looked at her. "You've never heard of penguins? They're flightless birds... and they like the cold usually... well... the ones from where I'm from prefer the cold, but they're black and white like him."

"Pen-gwen," Anhora said, trying out the word. "I have not ever heard of these birds. I should like to, though. And what will you be calling him?"

Saga looked at the pegasus and smiled. "How about after the most tenacious penguin there ever was, huh? Pingu?" The pegasus whinnied at her, shaking his great head and allowing his mane to shake all over the place, tickling her nose as he did. She giggled at the feeling and hugged his nose once again.

"Good," Mistress Anhora said, marking something down on her scroll. "Come along. Bring Pingu," she said, glancing back at the Pegasus. She must have thought that it was a most unbecoming name for the animal, but she had said that they could name the creatures themselves.

Out in the main barn, the cacophony of students and animals was still ongoing and Mistress Anhora's piercing whistle cut over all the noise. Students, in various states of dishevelment, turned to look at her. Harriet was still in her bear form, and it looked as though she had been fighting with the large bird-like bear with her. Others were staying far away from her, sporting injuries that looked like they had been swiped at by the creature rather than their projects.

"Quite the selection this class has amassed," Mistress Anhora said, looking around at them. She pointed to Harriet. "Make sure to go to the hospital for those injuries. As I said, these animals will be your responsibility for the semester, potentially to the end of your schooling with us. Your primary assignments will be about your animal and its development. Now, if you will supply me your name and the animal's name, I will mark that down for future reference, and you may be off to your next class."

Saga looked at Pingu and grinned. "I guess it's you and me, boy?"

The pegasus unfurled its wings and whinnied, shaking his mane back and forth. Saga thought he agreed with her, and she grinned. Jemima was still talking with her strange dragon lion creature, but Tasso had the odd dog sitting beside him sedately. Navi's giant, ethereal cat, was standing, its paws on her shoulders, trying to lick her face.

Konishi, first in their class by his surname, approached Mistress Anhora with a huge dog beside him. It was considerably larger than Tasso's and looked like it would melt into the shadows at a moment's notice. He cleared his throat and said quietly to Mistress Anhora. "Maybelle."

Saga stared at the gigantic black dog and stared at Konishi. There seemed to be a complete disconnect between the animal and his chosen name, but who was she to judge? She had named a Pegasus after a cartoon penguin that could turn its beak into a megaphone.

STAVES. ASSEMBLY. DETENTION

They took Siobhan and Perdita's suggested route and did not re-enter Nýr Ásgardr. While the road outside of town was busy with travellers, farmers, and marketgoers, they could keep a steady pace.

"This one would never have thought of this," Navi said as they walked at a fast pace. She and Tasso had been quick to agree to the plan, as had Emory's friend Yasen, though for him, it may have been the lure of escaping his Animal Husbandry project at the fastest rate possible.

"Siobhan and Perdita were pretty adamant," Saga said.

The six of them cut across the furthest paddock from a small farmhouse of property that backed right up against the town wall, hoping the landowner did not catch them. Every so often, Yasen would look behind him, checking to see if he was being followed. This doubled in frequency when, halfway to the combat grounds, Emory's odd flying creature came flying towards them. It grabbed him and held on as though its life depended on it.

"Hermes!" Emory complained. "What are you doing here?" He tried without any luck to pull the creature off his head. Its wings had wrapped around his head so tightly that he could no longer see where they were going. Emory flailed to the ground, the strange batlike creature still around his head.

Yasen was continually looking behind him to see if the creature he had named Blackjack would follow him as Hermes had followed Emory.

"That is a homunculus, yes?" Jemima asked, looking at the creature wrapped around Emory's head as he struggled to his feet.

"Yeah," he snarled. "Stupid thing won't leave me alone..."

"At least yours doesn't stink like a rotten dung heap!" Yasen intervened. "And don't you four try to object on that one... You all got something cool. A Pegasus, a Bezkira, a Dragonne and a damned teleporting dog!"

Tasso laughed. "Cronin is the coolest thing out, isn't he?" Emory was still busy trying to pry Hermes from around his head.

"He took to you quickly," Jemima was now flipping through her textbook. "According to this, homunculi form incredibly strong bonds with their masters. In this case, they dislike being further than five hundred meters from their masters. The stables to the training yards are easily a kilometre."

"You mean I'm stuck with him?" Emory cried. "We live across town from the stables!"

"Guess Hermes is going home with you," Navi laughed.

"As long as Blackjack doesn't come home with me. They'll kick me out of Bridelow if he does..." Yasen moaned.

"We're going to be late if we don't hurry," Tasso said. "Come on, Emory." Emory finally managed to pry the homunculus's wings from around his face and situated the creature on his shoulder, scowling the entire time.

Despite Emory's disaster, they were the first to arrive at the training grounds. Astrid crossed the large field to meet them. "Ah, you're here!" She called. "I was hoping you would be in my group!"

"A-."

"Mistress Grunborg," Navi said loudly, overriding Saga altogether, causing the others to look at her. She rarely spoke loudly in their experience, especially not to teachers.

Saga coughed awkwardly. "Right... Mistress Grunborg."

Emory's scowl deepened as he narrowed his eyes at the two girls. "I saw you all together at The Bore Tooth!" he exclaimed suddenly.

"What?" Navi cried. "No! Of course, you didn't... N... N... Navi means... Saga, and this one ate there... but... not anyone else... except for this one's brother and sisters..."

Tasso laughed. "I saw you too."

They turned on him. "What?" Saga cried.

He held his hands up in surrender. "Relax," he said, an easy grin on his face. "So, what if you know Mistress Grunborg."

"What is the relationship?" Jemima asked.

Saga and Astrid looked at each other. "If you want to tell them, hurry up," Astrid said. "The rest of the class is coming," and then she paused. "What in the Nine Realms happened to you lot?" she asked, getting a better look at the whole class as they came closer.

"Harriet got an Owlbear for her project," Oisin mumbled.

Astrid blinked. "Ok..." Then she looked at Emory again. "You had Animal Husbandry?" They all nodded glumly. Most of them sported some injury, if not from their animal, then from Harriet's erratic and vicious furry and feathered friend. "Well... is this everyone?"

"Harriet had to go to the hospital," Javaid Glairnet explained. "Mistress Anhora's orders. She should be along once they're done with her."

Astrid nodded. "Ok... well... I am Astrid Grunborg. For those that don't know me, I am the Weapons Mistress at Toserra Sorose. Aside from teaching my classes, I also handle all weapon assignments and competitions. Anyone wishing to try out for the Tourney teams must go through me. Might I make a suggestion?" They looked at each other, and several class members nodded hesitantly.

"There's no rule regarding your uniforms for Animal husbandry... perhaps wear your combat leathers to that class too..."

"We can do that?" Bindi Billingsley asked.

"Most students do," Astrid said. "Never on the first day... everyone has this first-day mishap... But yes, you can. Now go on and change. Boys through that way and girls over there. And once you're done, grab a staff from the rack over there..." She trailed off and eyed Saga and Navi. "Unless, of course, you have your own."

When they were changed, Saga and Navi headed out to the training field. Jemima had to go past the weapons rack to collect one for herself. Several people watched them and the staves they both carried.

Tasso leaned over to Emory and Yasen with a smug grin on his face. "They won them back in Yggdrasil City after whooping my sister and her friends into the ground!"

"What do you mean?" Yasen asked, leaning on the weapon he had selected for the class.

"Tonya and her shadows," he motioned over to where the three faeries were scowling at Saga and Navi, "Were hassling Navi. You know, the whole Dark Elf thing... anyway, in comes Saga like some kind of avenging angel and all of a sudden, Tonya's grabbing weapons, and so Saga does too, hands one over to Navi, and away they go. Around me, bets are being made by the crowd as to who'll win, and the shopkeeper offers the winners the staves they're wielding."

"Two against three?" Yasen asked in surprise, but Emory was only half listening. He was watching Saga as she and Navi showed Jemima some moves.

"You should have seen them!" Tasso exclaimed.

"Navi's different with that staff in her hand," Emory said after a while.

Tasso nodded. "Yep. Strong and brave and confident and..."

"And?" Yasen and Emory asked together, one eye on Tasso and the other on Navi.

Tasso gulped. "Nothing." The two werewolves laughed as Tasso went a shade of red, similar to tomatoes.

"Ok, everyone, line up," Astrid ordered. They did so and watched her. "The staff is perhaps the most versatile weapon you can ever wield." As she spoke, she moved fluidly, the staff striking, hitting, defending, parrying and just effortlessly moving around her, sliding through her hands and back again, doing exactly as she demanded. "You can hold it, here, here or here. You can move easily between these positions. You're free to attack and defend in any way you please." She then proceeded to teach them what she called a simple strike and parry. They did it together, repeating first the strike, again and again, and again, before she made them practice the parry. "Ok, pick a partner and practice those moves. No, not you two," she suddenly called out to Saga and Navi. They stood still, weapons loosely in their hands, waiting for her to continue. Hoping that she would change her mind. "Navi, you go with Ms Dove," she said, indicating Jemima. "And Saga... you go with," she looked around the class, cringed when she watched Emory strike at Yasen and shook her head. "Saga, you go with Mr Harding. Mr Torrey, if you wouldn't mind," she motioned to Seona, an angel with whom Jemima had been about to partner with.

Astrid walked up and down between the pairs, correcting stances, posture, and how they were holding their weapons. She would watch as they struck at each other before having a go with each pair member and saying a quiet compliment to them before moving on to the next pair.

"Just how well do you and Navi know Mistress Grunborg?" Emory asked as he deflected a strike to his belly.

Saga shrugged, resetting, and striking again. "Well enough..."

"What does that mean?"

Saga sighed. "Your turn," she said and waited for him to attack her. "She's my guardian."

Emory stumbled, his attack going wild and missing her completely. "What?" he asked, looking over at where Astrid was readjusting Dayan Chagmion's attack on Bindi Billingsley. "How?"

Saga shook her head. "Wouldn't want you to think that I'm any more of a freak than you already do. You going to attack or what?"

"I don't think that you're a freak!" Emory growled, striking harder than he had intended. Saga jumped out of the way, deflecting most of his overzealous attack with her staff, but she got clipped on the side. She grunted in pain before stepping in to attack him over the top of his head.

Emory grunted as he moved enough to catch the blow on his shoulder. He stepped back, sweeping her legs out from under her as he moved. Saga fell to the floor hard but leapt back up. "You were pretty damned quick to run off after one of your own this morning. Escape from us freaks!"

"What?" Emory cried as she jabbed at him hard with the move they had been taught. "You and Jemima ran off with Navi and Tasso first!"

"Well, sorry if the freaks have more friends than the pretty, rich boy!" she snarled as his staff attempted to get a strike at her. It got caught in between her arms, and as he moved to try and dislodge her from the end of his staff, he sent her flying across the training ground floor.

"Saga! Emory!" The cry echoed across the field as Saga stood back up and saw that everyone had been watching their heated argument. She was unsure how much they had heard, they had been whisper-yelling at each other, but they had garnered everyone's attention. "That was not what we were practising. Everyone else, back to work," she ordered before stalking over. "Just what exactly was that little display?"

"Nothing," Saga answered meekly, not looking at Astrid or Emory.

"Nothing?" Astrid asked. "Nothing, Saga? You two were having an all-out duel there, and you say nothing? What do you have to say for yourself, Emory?"

"We were working some stuff out," Emory said, looking sideways at Saga.

"Working some stuff out? Well, not with weapons in your hands, you won't!" Astrid declared. "An angry warrior is a dead warrior. I want the two of you to remember that."

"Yes, Astrid," Saga said as Emory said, "Yes, Mistress Grunborg."

"What was that, Saga?"

"Oh... crap..." Saga muttered to herself, at which Astrid raised an eyebrow. "Yes, Mistress Grunborg."

Astrid chuckled. "Get back to it, the both of you and stick to what you were shown."

Astrid walked away, leaving them to get back to work. "I don't think that you're a freak," Emory said, grabbing Saga's arm before she could walk away from him. "I was angry yesterday. I said some things that I regret... and I already told you this last night."

Saga wrenched her arm free from him. "It doesn't matter. You said it because you meant it or at least thought it. I said that last night too. Let's just work."

They finished the rest of the class silently, not talking to one another. Instead, they would take jabs just that little bit too hard. Unexplainable anger boiling in both of them.

"Ok, good work today," Astrid declared. "Look at your training partner and remember who they are because they will be your training partner for the rest of the semester." For some reason, she stared right at Saga and Emory as she said this. They looked at each other, but upon noticing that the other was looking at them, they instantly looked away again.

Emory followed Saga and Jemima home. They had time to change into their uniforms and have dinner before going to the evening assembly. Everyone had filtered off in the direction of their various residences, the idea of food an alluring thought after two gruelling classes.

"Why were you and Emory trying to kill each other today?" Jemima asked when they were alone in their room, changing for dinner.

"No reason," Saga said, not looking up at her roommate.

"It looked very heated."

"It was nothing."

"It was something."

"Just leave it, all right? Emory Harding is a hypocritical jacka—"

"Ahem," Perdita stood in their doorway, a look of disapproval on her face. "Dinner's ready."

"Coming," Saga replied, grabbing her blazer from her bed and walking out of the room. This day just would not end. There was still the assembly and her detention with Master Berfelan.

She sat down at the far end of the table, as far from Emory as she could get. Once again, there was food with no explainable explanation as to how it had gotten there, but everyone seemed as ravenous as each other.

"First-day hunger," Mannish explained to the first years. "Everything's all so new, and we're all so tired that you'll eat anything and everything in sight."

"No," Vespers said, nudging the werehyena over until he moved seats. "That's just you. You literally never stop eating."

Mannish looked at the siren and shrugged. "But first-day hunger is still different."

"How?" Onorati asked. "I don't notice any difference in how much you eat today compared to every other day."

Saga was glad for the banter between the older residents of Jimpsee house. It meant that she did not have to speak. She could eat, except that she had no appetite and just kept swirling her food around her plate instead of eating it. When she looked up from her plate, she would catch Emory staring at her and wondered what his issue was. He was always looking at her, and if not that, he was confusing her with his snarky comments and sweet behaviour.

And it had only been twenty-four hours.

"Jimpsee House sits over here," Tymberlee said, guiding them into a large auditorium. The whole school was making their way in, going towards seats engraved with the same crests they wore upon their uniforms. At the back of the stage, behind a podium, the Toserra Sorose crest was displayed proudly for all to see, the twenty-six smaller crests of the houses surrounding it. Teachers were making their way in. Saga recognised the Deputy Headmistress Athanasios and their teachers from the day, Berfelan, Iacono, Anhora and, of course, Astrid.

"Why are school assemblies at night?" Saga asked. "At all my other schools, they were like, Monday Mornings..."

"Headmaster Gotts is a Vampire. He prefers the night time so that he doesn't have to wear that huge cloak," Tymberlee explained.

"Really?" She thought about the night she had met Gotts with Astrid, her first day in Yggdrasil City. "What's Elven Ruby Red?"

"Blood from Ljósálfar," Tymberlee answered. "The expensive kind. Why?"

Saga shook her head. "It doesn't matter... just something I heard once."

A gavel hammered against the podium, and everyone stood. The first years looked towards their seniors and followed along uncertainly.

"From the fires of war, a school grew," the students began to sing at Mistress Athanasios's direction. The first years looked at each other in bewilderment.

"We're going to do just the same," Locking eyes with Emory again, Saga turned away, her gaze staying forward at the front of the auditorium.

"Learning and training together."

"What is going on with you two?" Jemima asked again, leaning over to whisper in her ear. "It's been a day, and you already hate each other?"

"Proud to uphold our name," the combined voices of the rest of the school rang out loud, making sure nothing they said could be heard by anyone.

"I don't hate him," Saga whispered back.

"Really?" Jemima asked. "Because you two looked ready to kill each other."

"Toserra Sorose our school."

"Why didn't we know that there was a school song?" Saga asked. "We could have learned this."

"I know it," Jemima said, non-plussed.

"We wave our banners true."

"Of course, you do... Your Aunt."

"No, student guidebook," Jemima answered. "Haven't you read it?"

"Always striving for the best."

"Ummm..." Saga murmured but looking around at all the other confused first-years, she did not feel that bad. "No..."

"In everything we do," everyone finished and reclaimed their seats.

A man Saga recognised as Hadar Gotts stepped up to the podium. "Welcome. Welcome one and all to the new school year. To our new students, I hope that your first day has been everything you hoped for and an indication of the coming year."

Saga kind of hoped he was wrong about that. Her day was long from over, and the fight with Emory fresh in her mind... It irked her that she had let his comment get to her so much. She was so used to being considered a freak by other people that it usually rolled right off her back, but for some reason, she kept feeling the need to dig at him. "To our fourth years, our graduating class. Two hundred years of prestige belong to the name Toserra Sorose. A name you will carry with you always as you embark upon your adventures through the Nine Realms.

"I understand that Mistress Athanasios, my Deputy Headmistress and Mistress Grimaldi have already welcomed the first years to our school, so this is a reminder to the whole student body that the city of Nýr Ásgardr hosts our school and that all students represent our school at all times, even when not wearing our school uniform. Be respectful of the townspeople, the shop's proprietors and the town as a whole." He shuffled his papers, looking for his next topic. "The School Tourneys will occur at the end of every month during the first semester, and the Interschool tourney team will be formed from those winners for the second semester."

There was an excited muttering from the student body about the school Tourney. Saga glanced at Jemima and whispered, "What's this tourney thing?"

"Only the biggest event of the school year," Jemima whispered back. Saga raised an eyebrow at that. Jemima laughed quietly, a little embarrassed. "I forget that you don't know these things... Especially after watching you fight Emory in class today... The Tourney has rounds in swordplay, staves, archery, riding, jousting, werebattles, Pentathlon, stuff like that..."

"Right..."

"You should compete for a staff fighting entry..."

"A reminder again that students must be inside their residences by ten o'clock unless they are coming or going to Astronomy. Students caught outside their residences after this time by the city guard will be disciplined."

As Headmaster Gotts rounded out his welcome speech, Saga's gaze fell on Fermin Berfelan. He sat on the stage in line with all the other teachers and seemed to scowl at every student there. Around him, the other teachers, Astrid, Dina Bess, Byrge Iacono, and Gretchen Anhora, sat there, eyes following Headmaster Gotts or eyeing misbehaving students.

Thoughts of her upcoming detention swam in her mind. She was no stranger to detention, but nothing at this school was like anything she had ever experienced before. She doubted Berfelan's idea of detention was like sitting in an empty classroom for an hour writing lines.

She was right. When Saga had left the auditorium, Master Fermin Berfelan had appeared right behind her. She had been about to leave Jemima and the others from Jimpsee house to locate his office when his voice had barked her name.

"Saga Carolle."

Saga had cringed and turned to look at the grizzled old man. "Yes, Master Berfelan?" she asked, trying to be as polite as possible. She really did not want another detention or to get this one off to a bad start.

"Where do you think you are going?"

"To your office as instructed, sir."

As he stared at her, he let out a sigh that sounded more like one of Shadow's growls. It was as though he was attempting to decide her level of truthfulness. She stood there, knowing that the others were watching. Without a doubt, the story of that morning's history class would be told to the entire house before she returned home for the night. Emory would likely regale everyone with the story. Jemima was just not that chatty.

"Then come this way," he finally said, shooting a disdainful glance at the rest of Jimpsee House.

Saga also looked back at them, her concern about what was to come evident on her face. The older members of the house watched with slight amusement, but she saw the worry in Jemima's eyes and surprisingly enough, Emory appeared as if he was ready to claw Master Berfelan's eyes out. The little homunculus on his shoulder sneered its razor-sharp teeth at the old history teacher.

They walked in silence to Berfelan's office. Saga had no idea where it was, aside from the fact that it was not near the classroom they had used earlier. She followed him, her pace keeping her just two steps behind him the entire time. She did not want him to think that she was trying to escape, but this silence was almost suffocating and scared her. These things, these she was used to. Those she could wrap her head around, but what was punishment like in this strange place? What could a man like Fermin Berfelan do to her? And what laws protected her? Were there any?

They stopped at a door, and Berfelan pulled an old key out from his pocket. Saga watched as he inserted it into the lock, jiggled it, and then turned it. The door swung open on shrieking hinges that echoed down the hall of the school building's administrative wing.

A head popped out from one of the other offices. A young, ragged man that Saga recognised as her excitable Planarography teacher. His tousled hair and crumpled clothes almost made him impossible to recognise. Berfelen scowled at him as the other man shook his head in exasperation. "Oh, it's you, Fermin," he said, looking from him to Saga. "Detention already? It's only the first day…" He seemed to take a double-take when he realised who the student in detention was. "And it's one of my clever corner girls!"

Saga did not dare look over her shoulder to see the look on Master Berfelen's face, but his tone said everything she needed to know when he spoke. "Mind your own business Iacono," and then he ushered Saga into the unlocked room.

The room was a mess. Saga had no idea how, one day into the school year, this man's office could look like someone had released Harriet Frazee's Owlbear in it, but it did. Maybe it always looked like that, and he just did not bother. Bookshelves overflowed with fine leather-bound books and rolled scrolls stuffed into individual shelves. Papers, books, scrolls and other unidentified things scattered the desk and the chairs that faced it. The walls not taken up by overflowing bookshelves were covered in ancient parchments and tapestries. On one such wall, between two large bookshelves, was a tapestry of some kind, the details of it obscured from view by a thick cloth thrown over it. Every available space on the floor and surfaces was covered in even more books and scrolls. A pedestal was next to what must have been Berfelan's chair. It looked like the only clean space in the entire room, with only one thing on top of the pedestal.

Saga just stared. Her feet had stopped moving when she spotted the thing on the pedestal.

"Move along, girl," Berfelan said gruffly, and Saga took a tentative step forward. Her foot seemed to kick an unsteady pile of books, and it tumbled to the floor, scattering more books and papers across the path Berfelan had meant her to take.

"I'm sorry," Saga said quickly, crouching down immediately to try and clean up the mess she had made before Berfelan could yell at her. Concentrating on that meant that she did not have to look at the thing on the pedestal.

"Clumsy oaf," he growled. "Up. Never mind that." Saga stood up again, looking at him. What on earth did he have in store for her? He walked around the room, seeming to know his way around the masses of books that littered his office floor. He sat as soon as he reached the chair behind the desk. The one next to the pedestal. He looked at her, those old, grizzled eyes observing her every move as she carefully moved to stand before his desk. Waiting. Endlessly waiting with this man for something to happen.

Finally, he turned from the pedestal and said. "How should we punish this impertinent little Valkyrie for her rudeness?"

Saga's eyes were fixed on the pedestal. She could no longer help it, and her eyes widened as she was fairly sure she gasped in fear as the human head upon the pedestal began to speak.

13

BAD MOON RISING

It was dark when Saga stepped out of Sorosian Hall. Dusk had almost completely set when the assembly had finished, but now the street lanterns seemed to create these small wells of light along the streets. Shadows danced against the side of buildings in the light as the trees rustled, and a cat ran across the square, screeching as something fell, clattering in the night.

Carefully, she stepped down the stairs that had seemed so impressive and looked out over the empty town square. She had yet to explore the town beyond the route from their house to the school or other associated buildings. As late as it was, she was exhausted, and she still had not started any of her homework. She would at least need to do the reading for World History, as she had another round with Master Berfelan during the second period the next day.

She looked down at her hands. They were still trembling from what had just happened. Her feet, so eager to escape from Berfelan's office, seemed to no longer want to move now that she was outside. Instead of continuing to Jimpsee House, she let herself slide down to sit on a step at the top of the stairs. If she just gave herself a minute, she could move on. To put one foot in front of the other and make it home.

Still, her hands shook. She could see the tremors in the light of the moon, and she breathed deeply, trying to calm herself down as she had been taught.

She looked up suddenly when she heard footsteps, but she did not see anyone not coming toward her from the town or from behind her from the school. The old building almost seemed to glow in the moonlight, and she could not help but admire the old building. She thought she saw someone looking at her from a window on the third floor... Berfelan? The thought had her up in an instant. She turned away from the building and started down the stairs at a run.

As she neared the last step, she halted again. Too soon? Could the man in the window still see her? But there, at the base of the steps, was a shadow. A dark silhouette of a large animal. Eyes seemed to glint in the moonlight, and Saga gasped.

"Shadow?" she asked, and the animal barked. A joyous-sounding bark before running up to her. Giant paws wrapped themselves around her waist, and she hugged the dog, burying her face in his dark, luscious fur. "Where did you come from?" she asked. "I thought you stayed in Yggdrasil city?"

With a glance back at the school, Saga could not see anyone watching from any of the windows, so she shook it off, hoping that she had imagined it. "Come on, boy, let's go home."

Shadow disappeared as she climbed the stairs to Jimpsee House. With a sigh, she watched him go, disappearing into the darkness of the street, but she had been grateful for his escort home. She had not relished the idea of attempting to navigate her way back to the house from the school in the dark.

She used the key she had been given to let herself in and closed the door as quietly as she could behind herself. Sneaking back into the house unnoticed was unfortunately thwarted by the open-plan nature of the common area where almost everyone was gathered doing homework.

"You're back," Jemima exclaimed, and those who had not already noticed looked up from their work to see what was happening.

"Umm. Yeah," Saga said, trying to move along the hall to the stairs.

"Anything we need to talk about?" Tymberlee asked from a table where she sat with Onorati, going over something.

Saga shook her head. "Uhhh. No." She shrugged. "Would have thought Emory would have told you all about it gleefully."

"He might of," Mannish agreed. "If he'd been here."

The door opened, and Emory entered, proving their point. They looked at each other for a moment before Saga turned back to the stairs. "I've got homework..."

She dashed up the stairs to the room she shared with Jemima before anyone could stop her. As she searched for her history book, she could hear footsteps on the stairs and quietened, not wanting to draw attention to herself, even though everyone already knew where she was.

~*~

There was the sound of a sword being sheathed to one side of her, and on the other, someone was sharpening an axe. She strode through a field of men dressed in a gown of the purest white. Men everywhere, preparing for battle. Weapons and armour glimmered by firelight as horses and other animals stomped their hooves and knickered, their breaths coming out in bursts of warm steam in the cool air.

The energy was of anticipation as they mounted up. The leader, a man of snowy white hair with a beard braided down his chest, reared his horse up. The animal swivelled on the spot as they turned to face the massing warriors. Up above them, two great black birds circled the leader, their cawing reaching across the field, even over the noise of preparation. The man of snowy white hair looked upon his force with his one eye, and almost as though that single eye focused upon her, he reared up once more, sword raised high into the air. With a loud battle cry, he turned the horse around and galloped into the distance, the men around echoing the cry as they waved their own weapons at the man. By foot or by mount, they charged after him, their bellows echoing across the countryside and down the mountains, warning all of their coming. Hundreds... no thousands of hooves and feet hammered across the ground as anything that stood in their way was trampled and burned to the ground.

She found herself above them, spear in hand as they rode, not into battle, but into the hunt. A joyous, ruckus moment in time. Everywhere they went burned.

Saga awoke. Being used to sleeping in rooms with other people, she did not make a sound as she attempted to sit up and regain her breath. A weight held her down as she struggled up, and it took her a full minute to figure out that there was a large animal draped over her bed. She blinked, trying to clear her eyes of sleep.

"Shadow?" she gasped quietly.

The big black dog looked up at her with sleepy eyes. He sat up, stretching, and looked as though he was about to run off before Saga wrapped her arms around him, holding him close to her body and burying her face into his fur.

She took several deep breaths, replaying the dream over and over again in her head as she did so. It had felt like she was inside the stampede that had destroyed the Arsinee farm and all the land around it.

Shadow looked at her with questioning eyes. Saga sighed and looked at the clock on the dresser between the two beds. It was early, just barely five in the morning. No one would be up yet, but she still had her world history reading to do before class. "Go on, off you go. Tymberlee will have a fit if she finds you here."

Without a second glance, the dog jumped from her bed and slid out of the open bedroom door. She heard his claws clattering across the hardwood floor and guessed someone must have left the balcony door open. She would close it when she went out. She found her robe, put it over her nightwear and dug into her school bag to find *Realities of Ragnarök* by Saorise Taliesin. The book was big, bound in heavy, dark brown leather, embossed with scenes she thought she recognised.

Quietly, not wanting to wake Jemima, she made her way over to her trunk. She opened the lid and rifled around for her old backpack, which had carried her every worldly possession from home to home back in Midgard. She emptied it of those old-world things that she no longer needed. Her old sneakers, an mp3 player, some leftover candy, and a small amount of Australian dollars. Her most prized possession was at the bottom of the bag, where nothing could get to it. The blanket she had been wrapped in when she had been found as a baby. The soft white material was accented by golden embroidery of winged warrior women and ancient gods.

She extracted it carefully and, looking back to ensure that she had not disturbed Jemima, left the room with her textbook and the blanket.

She turned towards the stairs but remembered the open balcony door and went to close that instead. The air that came in smelled fresh with early morning dew, and she breathed it in. Instead of closing the door, she went outside. There were seats and lights enough outside to read by.

Saga settled on a large bench designed for someone to recline in and put the book on her lap. She stared at it before moving the book to the side and unfolding the old blanket. She looked at them side by side for a while. The picture was different, but the work looked similar enough that the work of the same artist might have inspired the embroidery.

"You're up early," Saga looked up, surprised, and the book slipped off the bench.

"Ohh... uhh... yeah... I have to do that reading for Master Berfelan," Saga said, bending over to retrieve her book.

Emory Harding stood in the window to the room he shared with Mannish. He watched her, and Saga wondered how long he had been standing there. "I hear that it helps to open the book when reading," he said with a smirk.

"Well, you're just full of useful tips, aren't you?" she said, putting the book on her lap.

Emory stepped out of his room and crossed the balcony. "May I?" he asked, indicating a place beside her. She frowned slightly but nodded. Emory looked at her after he sat. "That's a nice blanket... bit small for you, though..."

Her frown turned to a scowl. "It was my baby blanket, if you must know," she said, turning away from him to look like she was going to do that homework reading she needed to do.

"And you kept it?" he asked incredulously.

"It's all I have," she said softly, not looking at him. Silence settled between them as if Emory no longer knew what to say, but it was comfortable, and after a while, Saga felt inclined to speak again. "I was... I just thought that the cover of this book looked a lot like the pictures on here..."

"Can I have a look?" Emory asked. Saga handed him the textbook. "I know *Realities of Ragnarök*," he said smugly. "The blanket."

Saga hesitated, her hands softly stroking the blanket. Astrid had been the first person she had willingly shown the blanket to. Fear of losing it always in the back of her mind every time she had handled it in any home she had lived in, but here... this house, this school, this place... It was supposed to be hers.

As if sensing its importance to her, Emory handled the blanket with great care and gentleness. "It's very fine work," he said. "My mother would even appreciate this," he said wryly, and Saga remembered Emory's overbearing mother well. Then he glanced at the book. "The picture is different, but..." he trailed off, leaning in to look better at both images. "This one, a Valkyrie, I think... I think that they're the same one..."

"What?" Saga asked, and he handed the blanket to her, holding the book up for her to get a better look at. Saga eyed both of them carefully. The face, as much as you could see on embossed leather and embroidered thread, did look the same. The way the hair flew in the wind and the armour the two figures wore. "Coincidence?" she asked.

Emory shrugged. "Probably... But... At the same time, whoever made this blanket must have known the work of Oji Kamal..."

"Who?" Saga asked.

"Oji Kamal is a famous artist. He has done many paintings representing or inspired by the battle of Ragnarök. Odin's Battle with Fenrir, Thor's battle with the serpent. The Jotnar... He even depicts the Wild Hunt of Odin..."

"Huh," Saga said, looking at the book and the blanket. "So... my... my mother... she must have come from here to know this, right?"

Emory shrugged. "No idea. Come on," he said, getting up. "Breakfast awaits."

Saga looked around, noticing how the sun had risen, and she looked back at the book. "Crap!" she cried. "I still haven't done the reading!"

Emory laughed. "Jemima has really good notes. Check with her. I'm sure she'll let you borrow them."

~ * ~

The first lesson of the day was Ancient Languages. Yes, Ancient languages, as in the plural. That meant that they were not just doing one but six ancient languages, which they could then choose one of in their second year to continue with. Mistress Abanda Chikerotis, a sandy-haired, short woman with glittering transparent wings, lead them into a room with five small tables with four chairs around each, like little conversation groups. Mistress Chikerotis's desk was angled in a corner facing the room but out of the way.

She started the class by explaining the differences between Latin, Gaelic, Norse, Sanskrit, Ancient Greek, and Hebrew. Saga was sure that everything Chikerotis had said had gone over her head. Jemima had seemed to suck everything up like a sponge, while Navi had looked as bewildered as Saga felt, and Tasso had been fine with the Gaelic, almost fluent from Saga's opinion but seemed to lose a little of his confidence as they had moved on to Latin and Old Norse, before losing all comprehension as they had tried Sanskrit, Ancient Greek and Hebrew.

When they had finally filed out of class, no one said anything as they headed upstairs to Master Berfelan's World History classroom. Saga was dreading the upcoming class. Despite reading over Jemima's notes at breakfast, Saga was far from ready.

"Ragnarök was not the first war fought by the Æsir," he started as soon they sat down. He eyed them all as he stalked up and down the room between the desks.

"The Æsir and the Vanir," Dayan Chagmion said, but as Berfelan's stony eyes turned on the sturdy weretiger boy, he seemed to shy away, and he quickly added, "Master Berfelan."

Silence fell over the room as everyone turned in their seats to watch. Everyone anticipated a scene similar to every other encounter with the cantankerous teacher. From the look on Dayan's face, he did not just expect it, he feared it and with good reason. Previous classes had shown them that Master Berfelan did not do well with students who spoke out of turn.

Saga, for her part, kept her head down and avoided looking at Master Berfelan as much as she could. She was glad that Dayan had attracted his ire but, at the same time, felt guilty about it. As the class proceeded, Berfelan, who had not yelled or screamed at the boy like many had expected, berated him with every question, just as he had done with Saga. Often belittling him when he did not know the answer.

The ringing bell had them all packing up before Berfelan could order them to read Chapters three, four and five of *Realities of Ragnarök* by Saoirse Taliesin before their next class. That was not until the next week, which had more than one person breathing a sigh of relief. Saga walked out of the classroom, head down, trying to hide her height behind that of Harriet Frazee,

Javaid Glairnet and Dayan Chagmion, who was also trying to hide as they left the room en masse.

Saga and Jemima darted back to Jimpsee House, right across town. Emory followed, but none of them said anything as they ran through town, eager to collect their things for their afternoon Horse Riding and Herbalism classes. Saga was excited about the prospect of riding and wondered when she would ever be able to ride Pingu, but then she remembered that the animal had wings and was meant to fly. She hated heights.

Saga changed into the riding uniform that had been the first thing she had bought for the school and looked at herself in the small mirror inside her cupboard door. She scoffed. "I look like some rich girl going to her fancy riding lessons..." Jemima glanced over at her from where she was busy scouring a book at her desk. "What are you doing?"

"Checking the uniform requirements for Herbalism," Jemima answered.

"Oh..." Saga answered. That was a good idea. Their afternoon classes varied so widely in what they did and what they were required to wear that she dreaded the prospect of carrying multiple uniforms and her schoolbooks.

"Ok. Here... riding uniforms can be used as a base for weapons... Weapons, leathers and riding uniforms can be worn for animal husbandry... Ah, here, Riding uniforms can be worn for herbalism. Seems like they're pretty easy in the afternoon as long as we have the requirements for each class."

"Good to know," Saga said, picking up the small kit bags of gardening tools and horse care tools. She found the textbook for herbalism sitting on her desk, along with a guidebook on horse care. She glanced at Jemima. "Thank you." She said softly, then picked up the book. "Where did this come from? I don't recall it being on the book list."

"It wasn't," Jemima said easily. "I've been riding since I was very small and have lots of books on horses. I thought that maybe you would like to do some additional reading."

Saga grinned. Ok, the idea of additional homework did not excite her, but the idea of horse riding did. She slung her satchel over her shoulder once it was packed with *Flora and Fauna of the Nine Realms* by Iseldir Omar-Ming. "I have got to do some homework tonight."

"That and we have to see our animals," Jemima added. "We should do that before coming home for dinner, I think. Otherwise, we'll be running all over town half the night."

Saga nodded. "Sounds good. Lunch?"

"Let's go!"

They met back up with Tasso and Navi at a place on the clock tower square called The Rolly Polly Kitty Eatery where Mistress Athanasios had mentioned something about pegasus tarts being the reason everyone came back to school. Seeing one, Saga guessed that they were similar to angel cakes, but with pastry, wings protruding from the tart. Shortly after sitting down to order, Emory walked in with Yasen Torey. The four glanced at each other until everyone was staring at Saga.

"What?" she asked in a hushed whisper.

"Do we ask them to join us?" Navi asked.

Saga glanced at Emory, and their eyes met for a moment. She remembered sitting on the balcony that morning, showing him the blanket and just talking. They had the oddest conversations, but most of the time, he irritated her until moments like that where they just sat and talked. "Why are you asking me?" she finally asked.

Tasso raised an eyebrow at her. "You just about killed each other in class," he said wryly.

"We did not," Saga said stiffly before raising her hand to wave the two werewolves over.

They, too, were dressed in their riding kit and carried the two extra bags of tools.

"So... that was something with Master Berfelan, wasn't it?" Yasen asked as soon as he was seated.

"Yeah... How's Dayan? Do you know?" Navi asked.

Yasen shook his head. "Nope. He disappeared back to his residence..." He looked questioningly at Tasso. "Dayan's at Knightrich, isn't he?"

Tasso nodded, his expression turning just as thoughtful. "I don't recall seeing him on the route there... or when I was getting my things..."

"Maybe he wanted to be alone for a bit?" Saga suggested. "Master Berfelan seems to have that effect on people."

"Yeah!" Tasso agreed, looking at Saga. "What happened in your detention? You write lines about not talking back or something?"

Saga blinked in surprise. She shook her head, though. "I wish," she muttered and was saved from having to elaborate further by their food arriving. Tasso had suggested a serving of lucuma pie with pacay for himself, to which Jemima and Navi had excitedly agreed. Saga had shrugged and agreed, having never heard of either item before. She hoped she had not made a mistake. She had requested jelly melon cider as her drink, and in the end, they had wound up with a jug of the drink to share among them. Emory and Yasen had also decided to have the pie, so the server suggested that, as a group, they buy a pie and save some money.

She cut the pie for them at the table, serving each of them a piece while Navi poured drinks. Sage watched her, curiosity flooding her as she passed drinks to Emory and Yasen without looking at them. She very deliberately kept her eyes down and never looked at either boy. When she did the same thing to Tasso, the faerie boy looked ready to hit something, but Jemima, in a rare moment of contact, put her hand on his arm, and to his surprise, his anger seemed to flood away as she shook her head.

"So, who's ridden before?" Jemima asked, removing her hand from Tasso and looking at her pie.

"A little," Emory said. "Horses tend not to like us too much unless they're battle-hardened or too young to know better."

Yasen nodded in agreement. "Yeah... it's not easy when you smell like a wolf."

"Never," Navi said, her eyes on her food.

"Tonya and I had riding lessons since... Oh, I don't know when, just not on horses usually... I'm expected to make the jousting team. What about you Saga? Jemima?"

"Once." Saga shrugged. "We got taken out horse riding a few years ago, but it was more like we sat on a horse, and they led us around."

"Oh, I've been riding for years," Jemima admitted.

"You going to try out for the riding team?" Yasen asked, his pie already half gone.

Saga put some on her fork and inspected the food. She had eaten a lot of strange food since coming to this world and was sure that it would only get weirder, but this one seemed like normal pie. She ate it and nodded to herself, enjoying the flavour. The Pacay was odd, too, a little like candy floss. She liked it.

"Maybe," Jemima said. "I don't know..."

~ * ~

Horses were waiting for them when they strode into the barn that afternoon. Master Carson Toshiji was waiting for them, leaning against the railing of the paddock.

"I'm afraid we have a slight issue," he said when they were assembled. They looked at each other before looking back at the riding instructor. "We only have nineteen horses, and there are twenty of you. Winx had a bit of a fall, and while he'll be ok, he is not able to be ridden today. Someone will need to double up. It's not ideal, but we will make it work for today. We shall start by selecting a mount."

There were instantly questions from other students who had their own horses, but Master Toshiji quickly quelled those with a reminder that first years did not need their own horses unless they were on a school team.

"What about a mount that belongs to the school?" Saga asked suddenly.

Toshiji looked at her. "Sorry?"

"What about a mount already in the school's care?" Saga asked again.

Behind Master Toshiji, Saga saw Jemima's eyes widen as the other girl seemed to realise what Saga was getting at. "And what mount would that be?" He asked.

"A pegasus."

"A pegasus?"

"Yes. A pegasus. My Animal Husbandry animal is a pegasus," and after a pause, she added, "Who doesn't fly..."

Toshiji stared at her for a moment before allowing his gaze to wander over to the stable of magical creatures. "I—" He stopped short, noticing everyone looking at them. "I should not allow it, but for today I will." He stated. "You will have to figure out the differences in saddling a pegasus to a horse on your own, though."

Saga nodded eagerly and, with his permission, left the field to go and retrieve Pingu. She had no idea what had made her ask, but excitement brimmed within her the nearer she got to his stall.

"What are you doing here?"

Saga stopped and addressed Gretchen Anhora. "Mistress Anhora, I have come to get Pingu."

"Oh, have you now?" she asked.

Saga nodded. "We are a horse down for Riding lessons, and Master Toshiji has given me permission to ride Pingu."

"Oh... has he now?" Saga waited awkwardly for Anhora to give her blessing or send her back, but instead, she walked away without a word, and Saga followed her. "You'll be needing this," she said when she finally stopped. She handed Saga a large, oddly shaped saddle. "Pegasi are different from horses. They need the freedom to move their wings even if there is no intention to fly."

Together, they walked to the Pegasi stall and entered the odd realm where the second stable full of glistening white pegasi awaited, along with the charcoal one and, across from him, the black and white misfit of Pingu.

The pegasus eyed her with intelligent eyes that seemed to remember her. He let his head hang over the barrier of the stall as she patted him on the nose. He liked that and nuzzled harder into her hand.

"Like horses, he will enjoy apples and carrots, so he will be fine with anything you feed him during class," Anhora said, opening the stall. "Are you sure about this? He's a skittish young man who has never been trained to ride with a rider."

"I'll be fine," Saga said, hoping she did not sound as unsure about her decision as she suddenly did.

Saddling Pingu had been harder than she had expected. Doing his harness and bridle, though, was not any different from what everyone else was doing, except Pingu was much more fidgety than the other horses. Eager anticipation seemed to dance in his every step. He was just waiting for the opportunity to be ridden.

A LIT SPARK

Wednesday morning, Saga and Jemima went to the library. A free morning with only one class seemed like a good chance to catch up on the never-ending amount of homework that was piling up around them. Saga had also wanted the opportunity to look up the Tourney rules before deciding what she would apply for if anything.

"Have you transcribed your alphabet yet?" Jemima asked as she opened her Ancient Languages homework.

Saga shook her head. "No... I tried to finish it last night but kept messing the characters up." The unfamiliar characters had felt like abstract drawings, and after a while, her attempts to copy them down from her textbook had driven her to complete frustration. Instead, she had spent the night working on her homework for Planarography. She had mapped out the Bifrost bridge's old and new routes easily enough before sleep had dragged her into bed.

They kept careful track of the time, ensuring they had enough time to cross the town once more to the Temple complex on the outskirts of town. Before they had left, though, Jemima had taken pity on Saga and helped her transcribe the complex characters for Hebrew, Sanskrit and Ancient Greek.

"I haven't seen Navi or Tasso today," Saga said as she walked with Jemima. They passed through the square and took the time to walk past the shops rather than hurrying through as they had every day so far.

"And you won't now," Jemima said.

Saga raised an eyebrow. "Why not?"

"World religions is for heavenly host only. Angels and demi-gods usually. You're considered a heavenly host as a Valkyrie; therefore, you were put in this class... or at least that's what I'm guessing."

Sags thought about that. "Ok... so... What, Tasso's going to, some faerie class?"

"Arcana."

"Ar-what?"

"Arcana. It's a form of magic that faeries can cast. They need to study it for proficiency. Unlike us, who can give up World Religions after the first year, they must keep doing Arcana until they graduate. Weres do 'Shifters through the ages', and as long as they join a pack by the second year, can drop the class. 'Vampiric Law' is required by all first-year vampires, and Sirens have to do 'Music and Song.'"

"Huh," Saga said, stopping short and holding Jemima back as a horse-drawn cart barrelled down the street in front of them, not even noticing the passing students. "What class is Navi doing?"

"I... I do not know..." Jemima admitted, looking a little rattled. "Umm... I think the Ljósálfar can do either Arcana with the faeries or Music and Song with the Sirens. It usually depends on whether or not they have developed any magic. Elves are very closely related to faeries, so it does happen that they can perform Arcana... Navi though... I do not know much about the Dökkálfar... Not enough to tell you which class she would be assigned to anyway..."

"I hope she gets to go with Tasso," Saga mused, but when Jemima looked at her curiously, she added. "A friendly face an all."

"Tonya will be in that class with Amita and Gheree..."

"I know... But those two seem to have become fast friends," Saga pushed. "Like... really fast."

Jemima beamed as soon as they entered the classroom within the temple complex. Nýr Ásgardr and by extension, Toserra Sorose recognised all religions, and the temple complex was a harmonious place made up of churches, temples and shrines in every cultural style Saga could think of and many she could not identify. There was a pretty woman that Saga recognised from The Choosings at the front of the classroom. The room looked more like an old church or the kind of schoolrooms she had seen on old television shows where the school was in the village church.

Long wooden pews with connected tables ran down the length of the bright room, with space for maybe forty or fifty students. The woman turned to face them. Mistress Dina Bess raised an inquisitive eyebrow as a mere fifteen students wandered into the room.

"A small class this year," she said, looking over them all in interest. The pews looked like they could hold about five students each in a crowded situation. "Hmm... let's only fill the first two rows. What do you say?"

There were a few disgruntled comments, but Saga followed Jemima into a front seat and was followed into the pew by a girl Saga had seen around but did not know the name of. She was tall, with chocolate brown skin and hair braided into hundreds of colourfully beaded braids that jangled together as she walked or moved her head. Jemima's eyes widened comically as the girl sat herself down in their row, but she said nothing.

"Good, good," Mistress Bess said as the last of them settled into their seats. "Welcome all to World Religions. As you are all aware, this is a compulsory class for all first-year angels, Demi-gods, and other heavenly beings," she seemed to eye Saga with that last comment but not in that scary, foreboding way Master Berfelan did. Before moving on, Dina Bess went so far as to smile at Saga. "We are not in the habit of ignoring one religion over another. We have all been born of the gods. As such, our future lives will be dictated by this. You might be called to serve a member of the Æsir or maybe to serve the Jade Court. Mount Olympus may utilise your skills or any number of other pantheons. We are here to provide you with the knowledge and skills to serve at any heavenly hosts with dignity, grace and skill."

Saga leaned over to Jemima. "I thought angels were created by the god they served?"

Jemima looked at her in incredulity. "Who told you that?"

"And I, like all of your other teachers, do not accept talking in my class," she said, eyeing the two girls. The mysterious girl beside them seemed to edge away, not wanting to get caught up with them. "But I understand why this might confuse some of you. We angels are born. Nothing more than blank canvases ready to be taught to serve. The religions we are exposed to give us a greater breadth of understanding and serve to make us more employable, but until an Angel comes of age, they are just an angel, not an angel of any one god. No, you must impress your future employers with your knowledge and skill. I hope you will all continue with World Religions after the first year... but not many do anymore."

From World Religions, it was easy to get back to Jimpsee House. Saga felt as though something she had believed all of her life had been thrown out the window with that class and was silent on the way home. They quickly gathered their things for Herbalism and Weapons Craft before running back out again to find lunch.

In Herbalism, Master Iseldir lead them through the school farmlands. Gardens that the school maintained for this class and aiding the town. He talked of flowers and their properties in healing. He pointed out a pretty yellow honeysuckle flower that could be used in treating skin rashes or inflammation, then showed them the begonias and talked of their properties to soothe and heal sores and burns.

Jemima was writing intently, taking notes on everything Iseldir said and as he moved them along to Chrysanthemums and how they were effective in soothing tired eyes when applied to the eyes as a paste but in treating fevers and colds when consumed as a tea. Golden Poppies caught Saga's attention when Master Iseldir told them how they could relieve anxiety and stress.

In actuality, the whole class seemed foreign to Saga. Natural medicine had been scorned around her as hogwash for as long as she could remember, and she did not believe that any of it would work. Navi, like Jemima, was busy scribbling notes, but Tasso seemed to have glazed over a little.

Saga leaned over to Jemima. "What are you thinking? Some of this will help us get through all the coming homework?" They were not even a week in, and so far, the schedule had left very little time for homework, and most teachers had given significant reading assignments. It would only be a matter of time before the homework started to pile up on top of everything else they had to do.

Once again, they had to cross town to get from the farmlands to the training grounds, and while the majority of the class split up into small groups to make their way through the town, Saga, Jemima, Navi, Tasso, Emory, and Yasen ran around the outside of town, clutching their bags tight as they jumped fences that got in their way. The path existed, but it went around the massive property, so they quickly ran across the backfield, certain that no one could see them and jumped the fence of the other side to get back on the track.

They arrived at the training grounds before anyone else to find Astrid setting out large wooden barrels of weapons. She eyed them curiously as they ran onto the field. "You're early," she said eyeing a clock set on a pole at one end of the field. Then she straightened from her task and looked in the direction they had come from. "You didn't come through town, did you?" she asked. "No, don't answer that. It's obvious that you took the shortcut around the outside of town, but you better not have been jumping fences. Old Mister Rishi and his wife hate it when students do that," she eyed each of them in turn. "And they are both awfully good with a crossbow."

Navi looked wide-eyed at Astrid before looking at Saga and the others. Saga shook her head, "No," she said. "Of course, we didn't jump any fences."

"Hmmm," Astrid mused. She did not look as though she believed Saga, but she could say nothing else as the rest of the class began to arrive. "Go on, get," she said. "Go and get changed."

Astrid introduced them to the sword in this class, and Saga found herself once again paired with Emory. Something about the sharp weapon kept them from going all out on one another, but Saga found the weight of the weapon comforting in her hand. She liked the feel of it as it cut through the air, slicing at their shared training post.

Yasen left them after class, heading back to Bridelow Cottage, but Navi and Tasso came back with them to Jimpsee House, eager to see the insides of another student residence. They entered to find Percival and Perdita on the couch in the living room, looking over a textbook together. They seemed very cuddly, but maybe that was the rabbit in them.

"Ohhh," Perdita said dreamily, looking up at them.

"Friends," Percival added, his tone as sleepy and dreamy as his sister's.

Mannish appeared from the kitchen, cleaning his hands with a towel. "Friends?" He asked, waggling his large eyebrows and grinning, revealing his big teeth that seemed even longer given his lanky stature and tall height. "For dinner?"

Navi, ever nervous about meeting new people, stared at the twins before Mannish caught her full attention. "F... f... f... friends f... f... for dinner?"

Saga felt bad for her. She really did, but even the presence of everyone around her could not stop her from bursting out in loud, uproarious laughter.

"Saga?" Perdita asked cautiously.

"And you think you're not a freak?" Emory asked. Saga looked up, all humour seeming to drain from her until she saw Mannish waggling his eyebrows and licking his lips as he watched them. Saga looked back at Emory and saw a sparkle in his eyes that she had never seen before as he grinned at her. "You back?" he asked.

Saga nodded, somewhat dazed. "Yes... I just..." She saw Navi looking cautiously at the werehyena from a little behind Tasso and could not help herself.

"Nope, she's lost it," Tasso said, eyeing her cautiously.

Her bag started to slip down her shoulder, and Emory reached out, grabbing it, before putting it down with his own beside the nearest chair. He looked at the others and motioned for them to do the same. "Care to tell us what has you in hysterics as one of your best friends quivers in fear from our hyena?" he asked.

The twins laughed at that. They had long since given up on their reading to watch the unfolding drama and grinned as Tasso and Navi cautiously followed Emory's direction to drop their bags. Jemima was already sitting but staring at Saga as though she had grown two heads.

"Umm... well..." Saga gasped out. "There's this story... Well... Movie or series of movies really... about these baby dinosaurs... And well... they're all herbivores, and they meet this little baby Tyrannosaurus or Sharp Tooth as they called him, and he's so excited because he's made these new friends and has invited them over for dinner. He's really sweet about it, too, looking for all the things they might like to eat because he knows that they don't eat meat like him. But all the while he's preparing dinner for them, they're all thinking that he's 'having' friends for dinner well and they all sing about it, little Chomper about his search and the other baby dinosaurs about the various foods he might turn them into..."

"Dinosaurs do not exist and even if they did, they would not sing," Jemima said simply, looking at Saga without too much consternation. But the stunned and bemused faces that looked at Saga from the others seemed to finally catch her attention.

"Baby Dinosaurs?" Emory asked.

Mannish laughed, chomping his big teeth toward Navi and Tasso. "Singing baby dinosaurs," he laughed hysterically, much as Saga had originally, as he turned and headed back into the kitchen. "Just wait until I tell Vespers about this!" He said, disappearing into the other room, even though they could still hear his laughter.

Tasso leaned over Navi and looked at Saga. "What's a movie?"

~ * ~

The rest of the week passed by without incident. Ancient Languages was probably always going to confuse Saga, and she had no idea what language she would pick come second year. Jemima seemed to absorb everything that came at her in that class, and Saga realised that primary school Indonesian and high school French were not going to help her here. Navi approached each class with enthusiasm. She did that with everything, though, even when she found them hard, like this one.

They had their first every Astrology class, where Mistress Kaushalya Satark explained to them how it was possible to tell a person's future by the placement and movement of the stars and planets. Well, now, Herbalism did not seem so ridiculous.

Their afternoon had been a good one, too, with Animal husbandry and Horse Riding. Saga had been able to spend the entire afternoon with the black and white Pegasus after discovering that no alternative mount had been found for her in the class. He seemed to really like the attention he was getting from Saga and the rest of the class.

The last day of the week had had them present in the circular tower room that Master Iacono used for his classroom first thing in the morning for a lesson on Asgard before they had dashed out, splitting up to head for their different classes. Saga and Jemima headed across town to the temple complex for World Religions with Jemima's Aunt Dina, but after that, they had a free afternoon and Saga planned to relish it. She had not been so busy before.

They met back up at the Rolly Polly Kitty Eatery. It seemed that many first years had considered a free afternoon a good opportunity to enjoy a long, stress-free lunch at the town's favourite eating place. Once again, they shared a jug of jelly melon cider and a lucuma pie with a big bowl of pacay to top their pie with.

"So, where are we going to study?" Jemima asked, scooping up some pacay from her plate.

"Library?" Navi suggested.

"Hmm... the library has private study rooms on the top floor that we can book," Jemima agreed.

"Then we can take food and drink with us!" Tasso suggested.

"No!" Jemima exclaimed. "The library says no food."

"No food in the stacks," Saga corrected. "The signs don't say anything about the study spaces."

"You're going to use our first free time in how long, to study?" Yasen asked in disbelief. "Seriously? Isn't it about time we cut loose?"

"I can't afford any more trouble with Master Berfelan," Saga groused.

"And those Ancient Languages are so hard," Navi whined.

"Too true," Saga agreed.

"And we can go out tomorrow," Tasso said with a nod to himself, assuming he had everything planned in his head.

"But tomorrow is the first school Tourney!" Yasen exclaimed, looking at Emory for support.

The werewolf widened his eyes. "Crap!"

"Oh, man!" Tasso exclaimed. "Has anyone signed up?" he asked.

Yasen nodded. "Yeah. Sword and stick fighting."

Tasso hung his head. "If I don't sign up for the joust, my mother will never forgive me."

"Where do we sign up?" Saga asked.

"Message board in the centre of town. Near the clock tower," Jemima explained. "It will be there monthly for students to put their name down for whatever events they wish to participate in."

"Most points at the end of the semester win the tournament. Most points in a single area win that event," Navi added. With a grin, she looked at Saga. "Stick fighting?"

Saga's eyes brightened. "Hell yeah!"

"My sister is doing that one," Tasso said glumly.

"Another chance to beat her then," Saga said, still grinning. "Jemima, you going to do the riding events?"

The angel girl shrugged. "I... I don't know."

"After we've eaten, let's sign up for the events we want and then go to the library," Tasso said.

The signup sheets had overflowed with names as they had added their own to the lists. Saga felt herself regret putting her name down for the stick fighting, but she enjoyed doing it, at least with Navi. Even Emory gave as good as he got.

Saga looked at Navi. "We should practice tonight."

"Sounds good," and then they headed to the library, where they received permission to use a room on the third floor that looked out over the farmlands owned by the school and even past that to further fields that seemed to run on as far as the eye could see.

There was a great consensus on the difficulty of ancient languages, so after hearing endless complaints from each of them, Jemima offered to tutor them as long as Tasso tutored Gaelic, as it was actually his native tongue.

He begrudgingly agreed, and they started with their basic phrases from the common tongue they all spoke in school, which to Saga seemed just like English, to Gaelic.

"Girl?" he said. "Anyone?" when they all stared at him in non-comprehension. Well, no, Jemima had her hand up as though they were in class. "Yes, Jemima?"

"Cailín," she replied, and they all dutifully wrote it down.

"Woman?"

Again, it was Jemima who knew. "Bean."

"Boy? Yes, Jemima?"

"Buachaill,"

Tasso nodded and looked down at his notes. "Man?"

Tentatively, Navi raised her hand and even though Jemima was waving hers eagerly at Tasso, he chose Navi. "F... f... fear," she said softly.

He nodded. "Uhh... Yes..." He looked at Jemima. "Want to carry on with the others?"

Jemima nodded and had them repeat the same four words in Latin, Greek, Old Norse, Sanskrit and Hebrew. Saga was running her hands through her hair and tugging on it in frustration when she looked up at her friend. The girl was right in her element. She loved to teach them languages from the looks of it.

"They will ride, side by side."

"Huh?" Sage asked, looking around. Around her, the others seemed to pause and look at her.

"Want me to explain it again?" Jemima asked, looking up from her pronunciation notes.

Saga shook her head. "No." She glanced around the room again, trying to see who had spoken. It had been male, but not Emory or Tasso. Yasen had decided that there was no way he would spend his only free day studying and had gone off to find some other first-year Weres to hang out with from Bridelow Cottage or Timbergard Hall.

"Mounted upon endless dread." She looked up again, trying not to draw their attention to her, and she saw him. Standing in the corner of the room, she realised now that she had recognised the voice. She had heard it only once, but it had also sent shivers down her spine then. *"Fear for where they tread."*

Saga's face went white as she spotted a growing plume of smoke outside their window. It was coming from the far-off farmlands, past the land owned by the school. "Fire!" She cried.

The unrelenting voice continued, *"Grows in the hearts of man,"* the face looked at her, their eyes meeting as they had that night.

"Oh my god!" Jemima cried, looking where Saga had been looking. "Raise an alarm!"

Tasso pushed his seat back. "I'll tell the librarian," and with that, he ran downstairs. They could hear someone scolding him for running in the library as he went.

"As sounds the beacon," around her, Jemima, Navi and Emory were pushing back their seats to get a better look out of the window, but Saga was rooted to the spot, staring at the ghostly figure that no one else could see. *"Of the one true rule."*

"Saga?" Emory was looking away from the scene far off in the distance "Saga?"

"Beware the shining jewel," with a final cry, the ghost vanished, and Saga looked up at Emory. He had moved to stand behind her, his hand awkwardly hanging there as if he had been trying to decide whether or not to touch her.

"Who did you see?" he asked softly.

"No one!" she whispered, even though she knew that face. Had seen it back in Master Berfelan's office on her first day of school. That ghost. That ghost was the head that had sat on the pedestal in Berfelan's office and had decided upon her punishment. She looked up at him, her eyes wide and her skin pale. "No one."

A loud bell began to ring. It was coming from the clock tower but rang in a different chime to the tune that usually rang on the hour every day. They had heard it ring late on their first night in town when the Arsinee Farm had been destroyed, killing the farmers, the cattle and every farmhand that had lived on the property. The land was also now completely burned out, and rumours were flooding around the town that it would not be usable for years. Not that anyone would ever live there again after all the people who died there.

Emory made to sit down beside her, but Saga shot out of her chair, the heavy wooden chair almost falling to the ground in her haste. Emory reached his hand out to catch it as Saga pushed her way up to the window to look outside.

"They're riding!" she gasped out.

The first instant someone had spoken, Saga had fled. She was not even sure who it had been but like with Tasso before her. She had heard calls of admonition as she had run down the library's stairs and out into the street.

It was mid-afternoon, and the town was in a flurry of activity as fourth-year Toserra Sorose students and citizens alike organised and, with the unity of a town in distress, headed towards the farm that was being attacked and for the potential incoming injured. Saga wandered after the crowd a little to where they gathered at the gates of the town to watch the first teams head out to the farm. She wondered who owned it and who would be listed amongst the dead this time. It had not even been a week since the last time this had happened.

Far in the distance, she could see the rampaging riders destroying and pillaging everything in sight. She thought that she could also hear the noise of their pillaging and ransacking of the land. Fire bloomed around them, but they were unaffected.

"Another fire this term," A woman nearby said to her friend.

"They were only happening rarely until now," Another woman said.

"I hear that there's a Valkyrie at the school," the first woman attempted to whisper to her friend, but she had to speak so loudly over the crowd that Saga heard her easily.

"Those vultures?" The second woman asked. "No one has seen one of them in centuries."

"School hasn't even been in long, and the attacks picked when they started."

Wide-eyed and afraid, the second woman looked at her friend. "Isolde!" she exclaimed. "You don't think?"

The first woman, Isolde, looked at her friend. "How many will die today at the Valkyrie's will, Varela?"

Isolde and Varela never noticed as Saga backed away from them. "No," she murmured to herself, "No, no, no!" she wanted to cry out that it was not her fault, but she knew better than that. No one had ever believed her in the homes. Who would believe her here? Were people dying because of her? First, she had shown her freakish nature to her friends, and now this. Saga backed out of the crowd watching the burning fire with no real understanding of what was happening. She ran.

Running had always been her thing. The only thing she had ever been good at. She had won almost every distance in almost every school athletics she had ever taken part in. It seemed like only a matter of moments before she passed the clock tower, the bell high at the top of the tower still ringing its ominous alarm before she entered the street where Jimpsee House sat.

She had no idea what made her return there, but she found the house empty except for Tremblay Jimpsee, wringing his transparent hands as he floated up and down the main hall.

"Saga!" he exclaimed upon seeing her.

Saga blinked her eyes. The last thing she really wanted to see right now was another ghost, and she found it hard to focus on him. "Tremblay!" she exclaimed, wiping at her eyes and realising that she had been crying as she ran through the town.

"Is it true?" he asked. "Is it really true? Winokur Sheacku just pulled us to the netherworld. Said another horde rode across the farmlands!"

"Who?"

"Winokur Sheacku," Tremblay cried. "The ghost of Sheacku Cottage!" That was when Saga remembered. Sheacku Cottage and Pouinie Cottage were located right next to the gate everyone was gathered. The rescuers had ridden from the gate closest to those student residences. "Is it true?" Tremblay cried again. "Does the Wild Hunt ride again?"

TOURNEY

No one spoke of anything else but the two fires that occurred in the first weeks of school. The second attack resulted in the death of everyone at the Jisook farm, two Nýr Ásgardr citizens and a fourth-year Toserra Sorose boy from Pouinie cottage. The lanky werehyena had been one of the first on the scene, his speed allowing him easy access. He was said to have been pulling debris from bodies to rescue any survivors when suddenly, he had been struck down as the building had collapsed upon him.

In the aftermath of the tragedy, the school cancelled that month's Tourney event. The most recent assembly had praised the efforts of rescuers from the city and school alike before becoming a memorial for Sindre Mozhan, who had turned out to be the Prefect of Pouinie Cottage. That week then passed by listlessly after the excitement of the first week. Students, particularly fourth years and werehyenas, were frequently seen holding each other and mourning the loss of one of their own.

Vihaan Naveli, the werehyena and constant tag along of Konishi Beroun of the first-year class group one was quiet, rarely speaking unless spoken to, and his connection to his animal husbandry creature, the startling beautiful couatl seemed to be a source of comfort as the animal appeared to take notice of Vihaan's mood in a way that his best friend did not seem capable of.

All the while, rumours flew around town about what had caused the two tragedies. First, the Arsinee farm on the first day, and then a mere few weeks later, Jisook farm. People were scared, and many spoke of previous fires that had destroyed properties and an entire swath of land as though an unseen, unknown force had ridden through it. The 'Valkyrie at the school' seemed to resonate through town, and Saga felt those who knew what she was were staring at her. She avoided eating in town at the Rolly Polly Kitty with the others, often skipping lunch or grabbing extras from breakfast and going off to eat alone before afternoon classes.

In Weapons, they started on Archery, and Saga relished the opportunity not to be paired with Emory as she strung her bow and practised shot after shot at the target.

It was not until the Saturday of the first Tourney event, that they managed to catch up to her, ending her self-isolation. It was breakfast at Jimpsee House, and as successfully as she had avoided everyone by eating in her room or always needing to be somewhere else, Tremblay had stayed with her, and they had talked. The young ghost had led an interesting life... And an even more interesting afterlife.

"Saga!" Emory had yelled through the house. What had surprised Saga, however, was when Jemima's voice echoed his call. They were both looking for her. "Saga!"

She was partially interested in why they were looking for her but, at the same time, wanted to be left alone.

"You should see what it is they want," Tremblay said, his head sticking through the closet door to where she was hiding.

Saga shook her head. "No."

"You, my dear girl, are being childish," Tremblay Jimpsee declared. He eyed the book she had grasped in her hands and shook his head. "The Valkeric Accounts? Really?"

"I need to know what I am!" Saga hissed at him.

"Saga!" Jemima cried out. The door to their room burst open, and Saga could hear the angel sighing in frustration just before the cupboard door creaked open as Tremblay backed out of it. A moment later, Jemima wrenched the door open and stared at her in disbelief. "You have got to be kidding me!" she exclaimed, looking over her shoulder to call out. "Found her!"

Emory came in before she could fully crawl out of the closet and stared at her, half in and half out. The book clutched awkwardly against her until it fell to the floor.

"What are you doing?" he asked incredulously.

"Nothing," Saga said as she picked up the book and pushed past them.

"We need to talk," Jemima insisted.

"I don't want to talk about what happened at the library," Saga stated angrily, slamming the book down on the desk. The heavy leather cover cracked satisfyingly against the wooden top, and Saga felt slightly better. She could see Tremblay in the corner of the room, arms crossed and shaking his head as though he was disappointed with her.

Emory shoved a scroll in front of her. "It's not about what happened at the library."

"How many events did you sign up for in the Tourney?" Jemima interrupted.

That caused her to stop short and actually look at them. "What?" It had not been what she had been expecting.

"How many events did you sign up for in the Tourney?" Jemima repeated, enunciating each word slowly.

"Two. Stadion and Stick fighting," Saga replied, looking at them both. Why were they so panicked?

"Then why are you listed for all of them?" Emory cried, waving the unfurled scroll in front of her face.

Saga ripped the offending paper from his hand and stared at it. It listed every member of Jimpsee house and their Tourney events. The older house members had their events listed as well as placements and awards from previous years listed. Jemima was in for riding as she had wanted, and Emory was listed for swordplay, hand-to-hand combat and stick fighting as he had wanted, but under Saga's name was listed every event. Stadion, dressage, archery, hand-to-hand combat, swordplay, stick fighting... And jousting.

"What?" She cried. "But I didn't."

"The first events start in thirty minutes," Jemima said, reaching into Saga's cupboard to grab her riding uniform and leathers, only to find it mostly empty. She looked around wildly before throwing open the lid to Saga's trunk. "You actually did sign up for the stadion, so get a move on and get dressed," she shoved the clothes in Saga's arms and then ushered Emory from the room. "Out, out, out. Out, out, out!"

The hurried dressing and run from Jimpsee House to the arena had served as a good warmup, and Saga was lined up at the starting line with twenty other first years. Apparently, the school made their sprint runs as a free-for-all, putting all the competitors up against one another.

Saga was not sure how she felt about that. Having run from one end of town to the other with Emory Harding and Yasen Torrey regularly, she knew that werewolves were fast runners. It made her wonder about the hyenas and other Weres. How did a weretiger run?

Bashiir Abassi, a tall, lanky werehyena from Pouinie Cottage, stood next to her on one side and on her other was Disha Killoran. The girl looked as though she was all muscle. Her Glairnet Hall pin identified her as a weretiger, and Saga realised that she would get an answer to her question sooner than she had anticipated.

She looked back to where Jemima and Emory were waiting. Navi and Tasso had joined them, and Navi held up her thumb, copying the gesture that Saga had taught her to show her support. She looked back at the other end of the track. It was only one hundred and eighty metres. A mere sprint to some of these creatures, and it came to her at that moment that she was the only non-were running in this event. They were eyeing her in curiosity as though they knew that she did not belong there.

"What are you wearing?" Gretta Pillsbury, a werewolf from Queenette Dormitory, asked as she stared down at Saga's feet.

Before running out of her room, or before Jemima had been able to drag Saga out, Saga had taken the moment Jemima left her to reach into her trunk, where she stored all her 'real world' belongings and grabbed the sneakers she had been wearing the day she had met Astrid. They were good running shoes, and she had won many races in them. They just looked particularly odd underneath her riding breeches and the undershirt she wore instead of the blouse.

"Running shoes," Saga said, looking down at them with a grin. She shuffled her feet against the dusty ground and noticed several people looking down at them. Maybe they would all get so distracted by her feet that she could win.

Still, Saga had sprinted at the state championships and had form and technique behind her. They just had raw, animal power. She chuckled at her own wit but looked towards the end of the starting line.

Saga tried to get the teacher's attention, but he didn't seem to notice her as he called out, "Everyone to your places!" Master Tillson Everard handled everything related to the Tourney. Arranging teams, sending notices to the various houses, and organising competing students on the day. If anyone could get her out of this mess with the events, it had to be him, right?

Again, Saga got strange looks when she crouched, arranging her feet as though she had starting blocks to run from.

"We're not running in animal form," Rafi Shoniker, another tiger from Glairnet, said snidely from further down the line. Saga just looked up at him and grinned wickedly. Running was her thing. She had been trained and coached on the best ways to sprint, and she would go into this against all of those Werecreatures with every ounce of training she had been given at school.

A horn sounded, and Saga pushed off, her feet launching her forward, almost to the surprise of Bashiir and Disha on either side of her. Javaid Glairnet and Dayan Chagmion were ahead of her, and she caught sight of Vihaan Naveli on her left.

She was running, and she could feel the smile form across her face as her back straightened and she looked ahead, her eyes never wavering from the finish line. Her arms pumped at her sides, from her hips up to her mouth, then down again. Her strides became longer as she fell into the familiar rhythm of running and every other person seemed to fall away from around her.

And then it was over. She had reached the other end, and Dayan was two steps behind her, grinning. "Damn, Saga! I never saw that coming."

Javaid was not panting, but he had his hands on his knees as he looked up at her. "Where did you learn to run like that?"

Saga just shrugged. "I used to run for my old school."

"I have never seen a non-Were win the stadion," Master Everard said as he came up and picked up the large horn he had been using to be heard by the surrounding crowd. It was early yet, and the stands were nowhere near full yet, but everyone from Jimpsee House, as well as Tasso, Navi, and her sisters, were there, cheering as though Australia had just won the soccer world cup.

Vihaan glared as he came up in the bottom five of the group. "You cheated," he hissed and looked towards Everard. "She cheated!" he cried, pointing at her shoes. "Those things helped her win!"

Tillson Everard looked from Vihaan to Saga, then to the rest of the group. "Does anybody else wish to complain?" he asked.

Dayan and Javaid shook their heads. "No, sir," they said together.

"Master Everard?" Saga said, trying to get his attention, but she was interrupted by a group arguing and pointing angrily at her. Saga looked away and tried to catch the Tourney coordinator's eye.

Gretta Pillsbury looked like she wanted to complain, but Disha Killoran elbowed her to quiet. Rafi Shoniker spoke up. "I want to know what she was doing!"

"But there are no other complaints about the outcome of this race?" Everard questioned again. Getting no further complaints, he turned to Vihaan. "The placements stand."

Saga had come in first. Dayan Chagmion in second, and Matvey Wallette, a weretiger Saga had never even noticed, had come in third. Javaid Glairnet had made it into fourth, while Vihaan had come in the bottom five of the group.

Tillson Everard informed the bottom five that no further applications to stadion would be accepted for them and sent them off from the field, then announced the top three to the waiting crowd. If possible, the little group from Jimpsee House seemed to get louder, and the group was hustled from the area before Saga could attempt to say anything else.

"That was amazing!" Ziva exclaimed when Saga returned to the group.

Saga laughed. "No... it's just... well... that's how I was taught to run."

"You were great!" Tymberlee said, nudging Ziva out of the way in a, 'I'm her prefect, not you' kind of move. Ziva backed off with a grin, wrapping one arm around Annis and the other around Navi.

"You beat every Were out there," Emory said in disbelief.

Yasen Torrey was hovering nearby, grinning. "They're going to be whinging about this for years!"

"I just can't believe that we made it in time," Saga said, looking back at the field where the second years were undergoing the same challenge. Mannish was running in this group.

"Don't get too comfortable," Navi said, thrusting Saga's staff at her. "We're up after the fourth year stadion."

It did not take long for the second, third and fourth years to run their one-hundred and eighty meters before they called for the first-year entrants into the stick fighting challenge.

Half of first-year seemed to flood into the arena, including Saga, Navi, Emory and Yasen.

"Go, Navi!" Ziva and Annis called out.

"Saga!" Jemima cried out.

Tillson Everard raised an eyebrow at seeing Saga again but did not say anything to her even as she tried to get to him once again. He paired them off into groups, and Saga found herself face-to-face with Tonya Bonnedras.

"You will score points for each hit. You can also score style points for your defence and attacks. Mistress Grunborg will judge along with me," Master Everard explained. "Just because you lose your match will not automatically disqualify you from further competition if you win on style. You must win your match to win today, though."

Saga grinned at Tonya. "Ready to go again?" she asked, brandishing the flower-engraved staff she had won in their last fight.

Tonya glared, her fingers flexing on the staff she had picked up from the school supply. "Just you wait," she hissed.

"Aaaaaaand, fight!"

Tonya's first move was to sweep at Saga's feet fast. Saga turned to try and escape the attack but realised she could not move fast enough without going through it. Instead, she launched herself over Tonya's staff, tucking her own in tight to her body and managing to roll and come back up on the other side.

Tonya looked dumbfounded as Saga jabbed at her before raising her staff above her head to block an incoming blow from the faerie girl.

"Why can't you just stay down?" Tonya hissed. "You've corrupted my brother, and he's hanging out with that doxie girl all the time!"

"Way I hear it, you were never nice to Tasso... always treated him like garbage," Saga accentuated her statement by sliding her staff under her arm and taking Tonya by surprise.

"You don't know anything!" Tonya accused, leaping out of the way.

"Maybe I do, maybe I don't," Saga replied indifferently, "but unlike you, I listen."

Nearby, Navi was holding her own against a large weretiger girl, and Emory had already defeated a Ljósálfar boy who could not meet his strength and speed. Yasen was somewhere, but Saga had not laid eyes on him since Tonya had started her attack. Their staves clashed against one another before they both pulled back. Saga defended as Tonya went for another headshot, but as they collided, Saga stepped out from under her staff and allowed it to fall, supported only by one hand and swung. It came around in a full swing before catching Tonya unaware as it came back and her on the side of the head.

They walked back to where Jemima was keeping seats for them with Tasso and passed by a group of panicked boys from Knightrich. "I signed up on a dare!" a young leprechaun, Saga thought his name might have been Eion, was exclaiming to a couple of older boys. "I don't want to do it anymore! It was a mistake!"

"A mistake?" a tall, well-muscled boy said, leaning against a light pillar. "They don't handle those well."

"What do you mean?" The leprechaun asked. "It's hand-to-hand combat. Look at me!"

"You can't pull out!" the older boy said. "They'll never let you make any interschool team if you do!"

"What if I don't want to?"

"What if you change your mind?"

The leprechaun looked around, his pale face even paler under his shock of red hair. His freckles seemed to be the only source of colour on him. "I don't want to, I don't want to," he murmured again and again.

Saga cursed silently to herself. Was that true? If she pulled out, would she never compete at larger events? She hurried away from the boys and found Jemima, not waiting for the others to catch up.

She sat down beside the angel, with Navi sprawled out on her other side. Emory and Yasen seemed to slump in their seats when they sat. Jemima eyed the four of them. "You seem tired," She stated. Tasso was too busy laughing at them to say anything.

"What?" Navi asked, craning her neck back to look at him.

"You all won, and you all look like you just fought to the death," Tasso grinned.

"Didn't we?" Emory asked. "Did you see Devina Aribo? She's twice the size of Navi!"

Navi grinned at him with more confidence than Saga had ever seen. "Yeah, and she fell twice as hard!"

When Tasso asked about Tonya, Saga sat up somewhat uncomfortable. "Apparently, it's all my fault that you spend your time with us undesirables."

"Speak for yourself!" Emory huffed, motioning to himself and Yasen.

"You two went on the longest," Tasso pressed.

Saga shrugged. "She's good... but don't tell her I said that."

"Hadn't you all better get your horses?" Emory asked. "The joust will be up after Archery and the riding not long after that."

"Oh, man..." Saga groaned. She turned to Tasso. "I have no idea how to Joust!" she cried hysterically. "What am I going to do?"

Tasso stared at her dumbfounded. "Then why did you sign up for it?"

"I didn't!" Saga wailed.

"Someone went and put Saga's name on all the events," Jemima explained.

"I need to get out of these!" Saga exclaimed. "I've been trying to talk to Master Everard, but I haven't been able to."

"No!" Tasso and Emory cried together.

"What?" Saga asked, confused. "I didn't sign up for the events. Why should I do them?"

"One of the boys at Knightrich signed up on a dare, and there's all this talk about how it's taboo to pull out. You're better off trying and failing miserably!"

"he's still trying to get out of it," Saga muttered into her hands. She looked for the timekeeper. "I don't have time to go and get Pingu from the stables if I have to do the archery too!"

"And as your assignment animal, he's unlikely to go with anyone else," Jemima reminded her.

"I'm going to lose and won't even be there!"

"You should get up earlier," Jemima said stoically.

"Not helping!" Saga exclaimed.

"Go!" Ziva stated from behind them.

"What?" Saga asked, turning to look at her. Ziva was standing there on her own, but a few steps away a boy Saga was sure was the prefect of the Ljósálfar house, Yeatwens, stood waiting and watching. He was trying to look as though he was uninterested in what was happening, but his eyes followed Ziva.

"Go!" Ziva repeated. She looked around as though trying to find someone, her lips curving up slightly when she spotted the boy but eventually turned back to Saga. "This one'll talk to Annis. We'll draw out our staff fighting matches, try and make it drag on!"

~*~

Tasso had already moved his mount to the arena stables, so it was up to Saga and Jemima to collect theirs. They were not the only ones in the stables collecting mounts for later events, but they were the only ones that ran in, Jemima barely able to catch her breath as Saga practically dragged her along.

"You... you," she panted as Saga let go of her hand, and she could lean over, heaving for breath as she held onto her knees for support. "You..."

"We'll ride back," Saga promised, looking at her.

A third-year girl walked by them, leading her horse, and eyed them. "Where did you come from? And what did you do to her?"

Jemima attempted to stand up straight but coughed and went back to leaning over and heaving for breath. "Ran..."

"We just ran up from the arena," Saga clarified.

"Then why don't you look like you've broken a sweat?" the third year asked, a hand aimlessly petting her horse.

"Because," Jemima tried again. "She won the stadion."

That seemed to catch the third year by surprise, and her hand stilled on the horse's nose. In protest, the animal nudged its head against her hand to get her to restart her ministrations. "You what?"

Saga shrugged. "I don't get the big deal. I've run competitively back home."

"But the Weres?" The third-year pointed out.

"Lost," Jemima said, pride filling her voice now that she could breathe again. "Every single one of them."

The girl's eyes widened in surprise then. "Oh my god! Oh my god!"

"What?" Saga asked.

"Pentathlon!"

"Huh?"

"Pentathlon," the girl repeated excitedly. "We haven't had a good pentathlon team in years! Mainly because the Weres keep beating out everyone in the stadion, and no, none of the non-Weres even give it a go."

"I can run," Saga said, stepping back. "But I can't do much else."

"Won her stick fighting match," Jemima corrected.

"Points?" the girl asked, eyeing Jemima.

"Top five per cent of the pack."

The girl's slow grin grew as she held out her hand. "Donetta Coccio. Vice-Captain of TS's Pentathlon team."

Saga shook her hand. "I... Saga... Saga Joy Carolle."

"Nice to meet you, Saga Joy Carolle... What other events are you in?"

"All of them," Saga mumbled, "But I only signed up for two. I didn't want to do them all. I don't know anything about archery or swordplay or... The archery!" She wailed, turning back to Jemima. "We've got to get back!"

It did not take long to saddle up Jemima's horse and Pingu. Donetta Coccio even helped. They were out of there sooner than expected.

"I can't believe you have a pegasus for the riding competition," She exclaimed as they mounted up. "This is going to be great! Aerial Archery is going to be a steal for us!"

Saga paused one foot in Pingu's stirrup. "Aerial? Aerial?" She could feel the panic rise within her. "No. No. No. No. No!"

"What is it?" Jemima asked.

"I don't do heights. Absolutely not," Saga exclaimed as she swung her leg over Pingu's back and settled herself into his saddle.

"You ride a pegasus, and you don't do heights?" Donetta asked.

Saga looked at the older girl smugly. "He doesn't do heights either!" Then she kicked her heels into Pingu's sides, and they were off, riding out of the stables and into the open fields surrounding the riding school and the exotic animals' stables.

"We can't go this way!" Jemima called as they neared the Rishi farm on the outskirts of town."

"We don't have time to go any other way!" Saga called back, just before Pingu leapt the Rishi farm fence.

"She can ride too!" Donetta cried excitedly as she and Jemima soared over the fence after Saga. "Just wait until I tell Deluca about this!"

Despite Astrid's warning, they had run over this field frequently between classes. Still, riding Pingu outside of the riding school was a freeing experience that Saga had never expected. As they built speed, Jemima and Donetta behind her, the fun she was having hazed out everything else. The wind was blowing in her face, the grass smelt freshly cut, and the only sounds were that of horses' hooves hammering into the ground and the whistle of a missile flying by her face.

That pulled Saga out of her reverie as she turned her head to see a man running towards them, a crossbow in his hands that he was lowering for another shot.

"Mister Rishi!" Jemima screamed in terror. Behind him, they could see a little old woman half-running, half-hobbling as she held up the skirts of her long dress, to catch up to her husband, a crossbow in her other hand. Mister Rishi lowered the crossbow again and fired. The bolt was closely followed by another from Missus Rishi.

"Ride!" Donetta ordered, and they kicked up the speed of their mounts, crossing the field in a matter of moments. Behind them, Mister Rishi was screaming and cursing at them, but they barely heard him as they soared over the fence that led back to the main road, and they were back on their way.

Saga slowed when they were a good distance from the Rishi farm. "Everyone ok?" she asked.

"Yeah," Jemima said, petting her horse. "But I can't wait until I can bring Sir Hoofington to school."

Saga looked back at Jemima. "Your horse's name is... Sir... Sir Hoofington?"

"Yeah? What's the problem with that?"

"Nothing," Donetta threw in with a laugh. "Nothing at all."

Tasso was pacing up and down the centre aisle of the stable when they rode in. "There you are!" he cried. "Annis and Ziva held up their bouts as long as they could, but you've got to get out there!" he exclaimed to Saga.

"But I have to put Pingu-," She tried to say.

"Go!" Tasso ordered, pointing out to the arena where the archery boards were being set up and the bows were being placed, along with arrows, by each placement. "You don't want the wonky bow!"

"Who cares about a wonky bow!" Saga exclaimed. "I have no idea what I'm doing!"

"You did fine in class," Tasso reassured her, helping her dismount from Pingu. "You won't win, but you shouldn't be in the bottom ten per cent either."

"What about Pingu?" Saga pressed.

"Pegasi love faeries," he said. "Go." He petted Pingu's nose and although the animal stared after Saga forlornly, the young Pegasus snorted aloofly and stomped his hoof, but allowed Tasso to lead him off to a stall to be rubbed down and readied for the jousting match that would take place after the archery. All the while, shooting a forlorn look in the direction Saga had disappeared.

Tasso had been right. Saga had not won, but she also had not placed so low down that she would be disqualified from re-entering the archery tournament in the future. Donetta watched from the sidelines and held her hand up for a high five as Saga walked past. "How many classes?" She asked.

"Not many."

The girl's grin grew. "You and I need to have a talk with Deluca later."

"No," Saga said, walking past. "You said aerial. I don't do heights."

ALL THINGS GOOD AND BAD

Trembling, Saga stood on the sidelines of the jousting field. She had one hand wrapped in Pingu's reins, and the other kept rubbing against her leg. Her sweaty palms were driving her crazy. A hand suddenly grasped hers, and she looked up. Tasso squeezed her hand and smiled softly.

Two jousters clashed in the centre of the field, the lance of one missing the mark and the lance of the second colliding with the chest of the first rather than the shield strapped to his non-dominant hand. The rider went flying from the back of his horse and fell to the floor with an impact that made Saga jump in surprise. The horse ran on, only to be caught by two stable hands at the end of the field.

"Saga?" Tasso asked. "Saga?"

She glanced at him out of the corner of her eye, and he could see the obvious fear there. "What is this?" she whispered to him.

"The joust," he said uncertainly, but his face indicated that his answer was the most obvious thing he could have said.

Saga shook her head and waved a hand aimlessly at the field where two new riders were setting up for their bout. "This... What's the point? Hitting each other with extra-long sticks?"

"It's a noble representation of knightly courage and skill."

Saga watched as the next two competitors charged at one another, their long lances lowered and pointed at one another as they sped by each other on either side of the barrier. They both missed and sped to opposite ends of the field before reining in their horses and turning to charge each other again.

"What skill?" Saga whisper-cried in his ear. "All they do is charge at one another."

Saga felt his hand tighten around hers, which helped her anxiety a little until the crash happened and the lance that struck seemed to splinter, sending wooden shards all over the field. The struck rider fell from the saddle, but a foot got caught in the stirrups and dragged behind his horse until the stable hands could stop the galloping horse and untangle the poor first-year student.

"I'm so going to die!" Saga cried.

Tasso released her hand but pushed her shoulder so that they were staring at each other. "Listen to me," he said firmly. "You just need to ride. Ride and aim. You can shoot, so you can aim-,"

"That thing is heavy!" Saga hissed. "How am I supposed to aim that with one hand?"

"Tasso Bonnedras!" The announcer called, and Tasso looked up in surprise, "I have to go," he said. "You'll be fine."

Full-blown panic encompassed Saga as Tasso led his horse away. Saga stared after him, her chest constricting in fear, so much so that she never heard who Tasso's opponent was. She clutched Pingu's reins tightly and rubbed her free hand up and down her riding pants. If she did not calm down, she was never even going to make it onto Pingu's back, let alone be able to charge whomever she would be up against.

To make matters worse, she was the only female student among the eager first years. All of whom were Faerie, Angel or Ljósálfar. Not one of the Weres were participating. She felt Pingu nuzzle at her, offering what little comfort he could.

The match went by, with Tasso riding with a confidence Saga rarely saw in him. It was easy to watch him. He looked as though he was filled to the brim with courage as he charged. She watched. She took in his posture, how he wielded his lance, and how he moved his horse. This was the first time she had ever seen any jousting matches. It was not something that they had covered in riding class, nor had they covered the basics of using a lance in weapons.

Tasso's unknown opponent went down, and he rode past her victoriously, holding his lance high above his head. There was more to him than the rich little faerie boy he portrayed to everyone.

"Omar Barzilay," Tillson Everard called, and a tall, long-haired boy stepped forward, leading his horse. He was already wearing his helmet, but his hair flowed out around his shoulders. Saga did not remember his name from prior classes, so she had no idea what race he was. "Saga Carolle." Saga's stomach fell from her body. Her feet would not move as people in the audience seemed to snicker at hearing her name again. She stood there, willing her feet to move, but they would not. "Saga Carolle," Everard called again, looking around for his missing competitor.

Pingu nudged her softly on the shoulder, and she stumbled forward. She led the Pegasus up to the stand where she was directed. She stood across the arena from Omar Barzilay. He was being suited up in armour and being issued a lance. The two stable hands on her side did the same for her, and Astrid appeared at her side.

"What in the Nine Realms are you doing?" she cried.

"Don't," Saga wailed. "Please don't. I didn't do this," A thick leather armour with additional padding was set over her leathers, and they startled to buckle it tighter around her body.

"Jousting?"

"I didn't sign up for it!" Saga cried. "I didn't sign up for any of them..." She was pulled slightly off balance by one particularly hard tug at her padded armour, and when she straightened, she sighed. "Well... Stadion and Stick fighting, sure, but not this! Not any of the others! Can't I get out of this?"

Astrid shook her head, "No. Well, yes, but the consequences would be far-reaching. The dishonour alone."

"Why? It was a mistake! I didn't do it. Surely someone could see that the handwriting is different or something?"

Astrid just shook her head. A thought suddenly occurred to her, "Do you even know how to hold a lance?" Astrid exclaimed, and the look on Saga's face must have told her everything she needed to know because she sighed visibly and picked up one of the long weapons from a nearby stand. She then proceeded to show Saga how to hold it, and as soon as she was let go by the armourers, she handed the long, oddly shaped weapon to Saga. To her surprise, it was balanced and did not feel as unwieldy as she had originally thought.

"Hold it steady," Astrid said, taking the weapon back from her as she mounted Pingu. With her free hand, she handed Saga a helmet and watched as the girl settled it onto her head and strapped on the shield before handing the lance back to her. "Hold it steady, and don't lose your nerve."

Saga nodded, but her confidence was still swimming somewhere near her feet. At least she was not entirely certain that she was about to die. "Thank you."

Lining up to charge at Omar Barzilay was more nerve-wracking than hanging from the rainbow platform after Shadow had knocked her on. The horn blew and Saga lowered the lance as Astrid had described, as she had watched to previous competitors do. Then she kicked Pingu's flanks, and they ran.

He was a fast runner, and they charged along fast enough that there was no time for Saga to think before she and Omar met in the middle of the field. Her lance grazed off his shoulder, but he was a good enough rider to keep his balance. The blow had knocked his lance off course, and it had just barely missed her. They rode on to their respective ends of the field and wheeled their mounts around, ready to do it all over again.

Again, Pingu charged down the straight line of the field. She had not been ready for the moment of contact. Omar's lance slid across her shield and connected with her chest. It unseated Saga from Pingu's back. She felt herself go flying through the air, and her lance fell from her hand, clattering to the field mere moments before she crashed to the ground.

The pain was like nothing she had ever felt before, and despite hearing a commotion from the far end of the field, where the stable hands were trying to get a hold of Pingu until Mistress Anhora's voice silenced them all and she took control of the panicked pegasus, she couldn't move. She could barely breathe. The blow to her chest, the fall from the horse. She lay there, people moving around near her as Tillson Everard announced Omar the winner of the bout, and Astrid crouched down beside her. "Hold tight," she said softly, taking Saga's hand. She tried to move, but Astrid put a firm hand on her shoulder. "Don't move," Astrid stated firmly. "Not until Matron Damir says we can move you."

A small woman approached, and Saga could tell that she was an angel, unless she was dying, she was pretty sure that the woman was an angel. "Let's have a look at you, dear," it was a familiar course as this same woman had looked over each fallen competitor before they had been allowed to stand back up. "Can you breathe?" Saga tried to speak, but nothing came out, so she shook her head. "Gently, dear, gently." The woman said softly. "I would say bruised and winded, but let us get her off the field and into my tent."

Astrid and Healer Damir both helped Saga stand, and she found that her feet would not support her at that moment. One on either side, the two women held her up as they walked slowly across the field.

"Aunt Raffi! Aunt Raffi," a voice called, and despite attempts to turn and look, Saga was certain that it was Jemima. So, the little healer was another of her aunts. As she was led into the tent, she noticed that Navi, Tasso, and Emory had followed Jemima. Tymberlee and Onorati entered a few moments later.

"My, what a full house we have here," Raffi Damir said. "I will need a few moments with Miss Carolle before any of you can be told anything," Jemima looked as though she wanted to contradict the healer's statement, but she got there first. "That includes you, Jemima. Out, everyone but Mistress Grunborg."

~*~

Everything hurt. Saga sat in the healer's tent; poultices meant to ease pain and bruising covered various parts of her body. In the cots on either side of her were all the other jousting competitors who had fallen harshly to the unforgiving ground.

"Drink this," Raffi Damir said, holding a glass of a foul-smelling concoction to her lips.

"Must I?" Saga asked with a groan.

"Yes. And before you ask why, because I said so," her comment brooked no response, and Saga drank down the concoction, trying not to gag as she did.

"When is the next match?" Saga asked.

"What next match?" Raphaella Damir asked. "You, my girl, are down and out for this round. There is no going back out there for you."

"But—" Saga argued. "What about—"

"Withdrawal due to injury does not prevent you from re-entering the rounds you will be missing this afternoon. However, you will no longer be able to enter the Joust. Just as well, my waiting area is full of your friends, and I am starting to feel that if I do not let them in, I will soon have a stampede."

Against the wishes of Raphaella Damir, but at the pleading of Saga and Jemima, Saga was released from the healing tent and allowed to return to the arena stands to watch the rest of the competition.

It also became evident how hungry she was, so Navi offered to find them all some lunch. Tasso predictably went with her to help as he was not part of the upcoming swordplay tournament. The fourth-year jousts were just finishing as Navi and Tasso disappeared to search out the various vendors. Saga had not had an opportunity to have a look at them herself, and moving was just too hard at the moment. Emory disappeared with Yasen to prepare for the contest, and various members of Jimpsee House made sure to regularly pass by them. Ziva and Annis had also passed by, checking on her and commenting about other competitors.

When Navi and Tasso returned with food, they enjoyed a picnic of fried lotus chips, something Saga had not seen before, and strange, skewered meatballs coated in a sweet but salty glaze that stuck to her fingers. She almost feared to ask what the meat was. The final item was a set of large pie-looking items that Saga guessed to be like fried pasta filled with meat and vegetables. She had not yet found a food she did not like, and they cheered Emory and even Yasen in their matches. Emory placed in the top ten per cent of participants and won his personal bout, while Yasen had made enough points to not be ranked near the bottom, had lost his.

Navi perked up when she noticed Edun out on the field with the other second-year competitors. "This one's brother is up," she announced, and they cheered him on for her. Edun was a ruthless swordsman. He kept up a constant barrage of offensive moves against his opponent, who had no choice but to stay completely on the defensive. Any attempt to attack might have resulted in serious injury. It was no surprise when he won, beating his opponent into submission until the other boy was carried off the field by Raphaella Damir's assistants.

Navi stared at her brother in shock. "What was that?" she asked hoarsely.

"He just won. Isn't that a good thing?" Tasso asked.

Navi shook her head. "Well... yeah... but... he's so angry, s... s... so not like himself."

Edun had avoided spending time with them back in Yggdrasil city when Ziva, Annis and Navi took Saga around. Even around school, Saga rarely saw him and Navi's reaction to his brutal defeat of the other boy said a lot about her concerns for her brother and Saga wondered what Ziva and Annis had thought of the spectacle. Emory wandered back at that time, and Navi plastered an insincere smile on her face to congratulate him on his win.

Emory sat down next to Saga and plucked a lotus chip from the packet in her hands. "How are you doing?" Saga shrugged and instantly regretted it. The move caused her to cringe, resulting in even further pain, and she was silent for several moments.

"Saga?" Jemima asked. "I'll go and get my aunt!"

"No!" Saga managed. "Don't..."

"You're as white as I am black," Navi said stoically from where she stood, presumably torn by her concern over her brother and her concern for her friend.

"I'm ok... Really..." Saga insisted, passing the packet of lotus chips to Emory so she did not have to worry about holding it. "I shouldn't have moved, though."

"I should get my aunt," Jemima said uncertainly.

"No," Saga insisted. "I am just going to sit here and not move."

"You're not sitting out here to watch our bouts, are you?" Emory asked, enjoying having the chips in his hands, but he spotted the meatball skewers on the seat between Saga and Tasso and waggled his eyebrows at the faerie boy. "Pass me one?" Tasso shook his head but held out the half-empty packet of meatball skewers. Emory picked one up, instantly ripped one of the meatballs from the skewers, and ate it like the wolf he was. "Mmm, good! I gotta get back out there for the hand-to-hand," and with that, he stood and, after handing the packet of lotus chips to Navi. He grabbed two chips, sticking them in his mouth as he ran off again.

Jemima stood and brushed her hands down her riding pants. "I'm going to go and ready my horse," she eyed Navi and Tasso. "Make sure you get my aunt if she gets any worse."

Tasso mock saluted Jemima as she walked away to the stables. "Yes, ma'am!"

Emory did not place as high in the hand-to-hand bout as he had in other matches, but he was not placed in the bottom so he would be able to compete again. Edun appeared again when the second years had their bouts. Again, his bout was fast and vicious, barely allowing the other student a chance to respond before Raphaella Damir was back with her assistants to carry Edun's victim from the field.

Navi was biting her lip as Edun left the field, her hands worrying her fingers as she sat there, tears in her eyes threatening to slide down her cheeks.

"Navi?" Saga asked, tenderly reaching out a hand to grasp Navi's hands and stop her from picking at the loose skin around her fingernails. "What is it?"

"Edun," she said softly, her eyes tracking his progress across the field. She freed one of her hands and swiped at her eyes before the tears that were forming there had a chance to fall. "H... H... He," she shook her head. "I... It's nothing."

"Navi, you're scared of something," Tasso said, taking her other hand in his. "What is it?"

She shook her head adamantly. "I... I... It's nothing... N... N... Navi just doesn't know... He's so... ever since he started school, it's as though he's so angry and Navi does not know why," she sighed, took her hands back from Saga and Tasso and rubbed at her eyes again. "We'll figure it out," she said, perhaps trying to convince herself more than her friends. They joked about the rest of the second years, admired the third years, and cheered on Onorati during the fourth years.

By the time the arena had been set up for riding events, Navi was looking happier, and Emory was back. He slumped in his seat with a huge sigh, drawing everyone's attention to him.

"What?" Tasso asked.

"What, what?" Emory asked back.

Navi picked through the remains of their lunch and found another lotus chip, the last in the bag they discovered when Emory took it after her, looking for more food. "So... Not going to take on so many events next month?" She asked innocently as she bit deliberately into her chip.

Emory watched her in dismay as the chip vanished into her mouth but sighed. "Don't know. I'm not out of any." He glanced at Saga, taking in how she sprawled across the stands trying to alleviate the pain. "Any idea who signed you up for everything?" he asked.

"Next month?" Saga exclaimed, not even realised that he had asked a question. "We have to do this again next month?"

"Well, no, you don't 'have' to do anything," Navi stared. "But this one is totally going for a first in stick fighting!"

"Oh really?" Emory and Saga exclaimed together.

Navi laughed at their incredulity. "Of course!"

Saga laughed and winked at her. "Not if I get a first!" she declared.

Navi beamed at her. "You're on! At the end of the semester, we shall see who is better. Saga or Navi!"

They were still laughing at Navi's sudden burst of confidence when Emory asked again, "So, any idea who signed you up for all the events?"

Saga resisted the urge to shrug and instead shook her head. "I've been wracking my brain but not coming up with anything. Maybe Tonya?" She asked with a glance at Tasso, who just shrugged.

Out on the field, Tillson Everard announced the first rider to take the dressage course. Somehow, looking at the course, Saga was glad she had been given an out. The riding event suddenly seemed harder than she had expected, and as the first rider began, she became sure of it.

"I ran into Deluca Goett," Emory said. "You would have seen him in the fourth years," They all nodded, and Saga recognised the name. "Apparently, Donetta Coccio approached you about the Pentathlon team?"

Saga did not look at him and had been bout to shrug when she remembered the earlier attempt and decided against it. "Jemima and I met her in the stables when we went to get our horses."

Emory nodded thoughtfully, and Saga could see Tasso and Navi staring at her wide-eyed. "Apparently, you said no."

"That's correct."

"Are you insane?" Navi exploded. "An invitation to Pentathlon?"

Navi's sudden eruption startled Saga so much that she jumped half off her bench and stared at the girl before the pain of her ever-growing bruises gripped her. "Oh," she gasped. It had not been what she had wanted to say in response, but it had been all she could get. "Ow..." She breathed heavily for several moments, noting the concerned looks of those around her.

"Jemima's Aunt?" Tasso asked uncertainly.

"Navi is so sorry!" Navi exclaimed. "Saga, this one is so, so, so sorry!"

"I'm ok!" Saga tried to ease their concerns. "Please don't bother Matron Damir. She is busy enough."

"You're seriously going to turn down a position on the Pentathlon team?" Tasso asked. "I'm with Navi. You're insane."

"I can't ride very well. I really don't know how to use a sword, a bow, or fight and apparently, there's an aerial component." Saga shook her head. "Nope. I am not doing it."

"There are two pentathlon versions," Emory said. He leaned forward, resting his elbows on his knees. "They're always looking for the full package. A team member who can do it all, run, shoot, ride, but it was discovered that this could be a huge strain on a single person, so they made a kind of relay version," Saga eyed him as he spoke, also listening out for Jemima's name to be called. "The relay version is why we have a pentathlon team. Basically, they look for the best competitor in each field, and it is a race to see who can complete the course first," he shrugged. "Some members of the team have only one skill, but Toserra Sorose has lost the last so many years because our runners or stadion competitor lacks. Even amongst the Weres. There are also good reasons why the Weres never join the pentathlon team, even as single event relay members," he shrugged. "The only ones likely to run a traditional Pentathlon are Deluca and Zibby, the fourth years on the team."

"So, I wouldn't need to fly?" she asked tentatively.

"Maybe if you're still on the team in our Fourth year, but they want you because you can run and you stick fight well, you would also be a suitable second for that event."

"It's a relay?" Saga asked again.

"Yes."

"Huh."

"Jemima Dove," With the announcement of Jemima's name, they turned their attention back to the arena where Jemima was seated upon her school mount. She was eyeing the field as she waited to be allowed to start.

"Then why do they call it a pentathlon?" Saga asked.

"It's supposed to be run as a pentathlon, one person doing all five events," Emory said, leaning in and whispering, "But schools were having a hard time managing studies and Pentathlon competitors, so they run it in a relay for the first few years."

"Huh."

Jemima and her horse wound their way through the course, doing the assigned tasks. On the far side of the field, another rider was doing identical moves, their horses moving in the same ways.

Saga shook her head, "I could never have done that."

"You haven't seen anything yet," Tasso commented. "This is the show of training component, and Jemima's doing well, but she doesn't know that horse, and it doesn't know her. She would be doing much better with her own horse. But my point is that they leave the riders until last because the event is longer. They have two tasks to complete. This shows how calmly and competently they and their horse can complete those assigned tasks in the right locations and times, but after dinner, they'll have the show jumping."

"Really?"

"Yeah," Tasso said. "Jemima's good, apparently, but the horse worries me."

"You said after dinner, right?" Emory said, leaning back against the bench behind them and stretching his legs out in front of him. "I could eat."

"You haven't stopped," Navi commented. "And you didn't pay for any of it either!"

"Uhh," He sat up suddenly and looked at each of them in turn. "Well...
I..." They stared at him, "All right, all right! I'll go and find more food.
Tasso?"

"Coming."

Jemima did not return between the dressage show and the jumping
segment of her event, but Emory and Tasso returned with more food, which
the group enjoyed together until the second half of the equestrian event began.
The course had once again been set up, with various obstacles of differing
sizes that the horse would be required to jump. Two identical courses lay side
by side in the arena.

"They're running a match race," Tasso said, pointing out the two identical
courses. "Two riders, timed, so not only do they have to run their best course
and not knock over any of the barriers, they gotta do it with the best time
too."

"And how much of this is in the Pentathlon?" Saga asked.

"Just jumping. They call it dressage but do not care about the skills-based
show you just saw. They want the jumps. They choose their teams from the
best performers in the individual events, but they're all different."

"Huh." Saga said again, her thoughts far away as she thought about it.

"Pentathlon is the prestige event. We compete competitively in all the
other events as well," Navi added. "This one can't wait until people start
bugging you about running stadion against the other schools. They're always
complaining that we have too many Weres for stadion to be fair, but you ran
them into the dust."

Saga laughed. "The way they were running, it wasn't hard."

"What do you mean?" Emory asked.

"Didn't you see them, all hunched over? It's like they were trying to run in
their animal forms but had to run as humans and had no idea how to."

"Well, I mean, they do a stadion event, but there's not an actual class in it
or anything," Emory said defensively. "It's not like you can teach someone
how to run. They either can or they can't." He caught the look on Saga's face
and trailed off, "Right?"

Saga just shook her head. "If that's the thought around here, no wonder I
won."

Jemima's return to the group was met with applause and congratulations. She bowed as modestly as a winner could and lapped up her victory.

"Did they ask you to join the team?" Navi asked.

"Not everyone gets asked straight off to join a team. Some of us actually have to compete and collect scores to make the team!" she said with a pointed look at Saga, "but I really need to get Sir Hoofington here. I should write to Aunt Azrael."

Saga blinked. "You have another Aunt?"

"Yeah, how many do you have?" Tasso asked.

"Nine," Jemima said. "Nine Aunts. Aunt Dina and Aunt Raphaella. Aunt Azrael, Aunt Cassiel, Aunt Angelica, Aunt Muriel and Aunt Seraphina, Aunt Evangeline. Ohh, and Aunt Gabrielle, I'll need to get a message to her so she can take it to Aunt Azrael as soon as possible, so Sir Hoofington can come.

As everyone got up, Saga watched them. It had been a long day, and she wanted desperately to join them, but she suddenly feared getting up would be hard. She had been careful to keep movement to a minimum, little more than reaching out for things, and the sudden thought of walking back to Jimpsee House seemed to seize her entire body into immobility.

NOW COMES THE NIGHT

The weeks passed in a flurry of classes and sporting events that Saga had never imagined. She loved school. For the first time in her life, she loved being around people. She loved the lessons they were learning. Master Berfelan still hated her, and Ancient Languages was still so hard that she wanted to hit her head against a table every time they had a study session, but she loved school. By the time the mid-semester break came around, and students from the school took the opportunity to go home for a week and visit friends and family, she had only received one other detention from Berfelan that had dragged her back into his office, and that mysterious head, whose ghost was once again following her around the school.

"Tremblay!" Saga begged as she rolled over in bed. Jemima had gone home with her aunts for the break and had the room to herself. "Make him go away!"

The ghost of Tremblay Jimpsee hovered over Jemima's empty bed, looking as though he was sitting there, watching her. Saga rolled over in bed, pulling her pillow out and shoving her head underneath to keep out the moaning, cryptic voice.

"I can't," Tremblay said sympathetically. "He has a power I cannot explain."

Saga sighed. "I just want to sleep, and he won't shut up!"

"Perhaps you should listen then," Tremblay suggested.

"Uggh! You are no help!" Saga complained, crying into her pillow.

"He does say some pretty interesting things," Tremblay added. "I mean, it's just a thought."

With a sigh, Saga sat up. He was not wrong. Every time in the past when she had ignored the messages of the dead, they had hounded her relentlessly until she had finally taken the time to listen to them, or an adult had finally listened to her, allowing that person to be put to rest. "I don't understand him."

"Then be quiet and listen," Tremblay suggested.

"Upon the return of the maidens of war, the legend will become the core, the one great king," The nameless ghost of the disembodied head from Master Berfelan's office had been repeating the same words for three days now, and she had no idea what he was babbling about, just like she still had not deciphered the words he had spoken to her in the library all those weeks ago. *"Of whom they once did sing, the sons of gods will fight."* His voice was raspy, unlike Tremblay and the other house ghosts. He sounded dead. He sounded like he was missing his throat or like a long-time smoker, and she just wanted him to go away!

"Trembly!" Saga begged, but the house ghost held up a hand in silence before motioning back to the nameless ghost.

"Bring about an endless night, beware the shining jewel!" the ghost wailed, his voice getting louder, a warning she was sure, but against what? A shiny jewel?

She sat up suddenly and looked at Tremblay. "What shining jewel?"

"That's the bit that caught your attention?" he asked.

"Well, yeah-,"

"There's no time to be looking for pretty trinkets, Saga," Tremblay Jimpsee chided.

Saga sighed. "No," she exclaimed, looking over at the now-silent ghost on the other side of her room. "It's the only bit he's mentioned before."

"Oh," Tremblay said curiously. He stood and floated over towards where the mysterious ghost had situated himself in the corner by Saga's closet. "So, it's not you being interested in pretty things."

Saga looked at him, and Tremblay held up his hands in mock surrender. "When have I ever been interested in pretty things?"

Tremblay laughed. "Well, to be honest, I've only known you a few weeks, but you're right. Beware the shining jewel."

The nameless ghost looked at Tremblay. Sad, intelligent eyes looked from Tremblay to Saga. *"Yes, beware. Beware the shining jewel."*

"And tell me, good sir," Tremblay asked jovially, "What is this of kings you speak about?"

But the ghost said nothing more, just stared at them, moaning softly.

"See!" Saga exclaimed. "How am I supposed to sleep with that?"

"Solve his riddle."

Saga sighed and flopped back in her bed. She stared up at the ceiling and sighed loudly, trying to block out the moaning ghost. She looked around the room, spotting Tremblay still hovering where she had last seen him and sat up. "Tremblay?"

"Yes?"

"Why don't I see any others here?" she asked. The moaning, nameless ghost was so similar to the ghosts that had once followed her around that it reminded her. Everything had been so new and exciting that it had been easy to block out the times the dead had asked for her help.

"Other what?" he asked, and she waved toward him and the other ghost. "Ghosts?" he asked. "You see ghosts. You see me."

"Yeah, but where are the ones that used to follow me, tormenting me, like he is now."

"We don't have all that many unsettled dead here," Tremblay said. "The Angels of Death take the recently departed."

Saga frowned and lay back in her bed but couldn't resist glancing toward the moaning, cryptic ghost. "So, what about him?"

"I don't know," Tremblay admitted.

The door creaked open, and there was the gentle padding of paws on the wooden floor of the room. Nails clicked across the floor before Saga felt the bed sink as the large dog jumped up and settled beside her, stretching his long body beside her.

"Hey, Shadow," she whispered. "Where did you wander in from?"

The big dog huffed and flopped his head down on her pillow before both succumbing to sleep.

The off week from school actually allowed Saga to explore Nýr Ásgardr in a way that she had been unable to do since the beginning of the school year. They started early and finished late, and then weekends were filled with other activities that always seemed to take precedence over mere exploration.

Jimpsee House was practically empty. Almost everyone had returned home for the break. Jemima and her aunts had gone to Yggdrasil City to meet with her seven other aunts. Emory had gone home to his parents. Tymberlee and Onorati were around, citing — upcoming exams as a reason for not leaving so that they could get caught up before school restarted, but Saga had not seen them since the break started.

Much of her time was like Yggdrasil City, running around with Navi and her sisters. Ziva and Annis seemed to know everywhere in town that was worth going to. To avoid the loneliness of the empty house, Saga would join them at mealtimes at Dorbe Manor, where several students had stayed. Despite the dimness of the house, they were a lively bunch who seemed to enjoy each other's company. Their dining room was not half as depressing as people had indicated, and to Saga, the impression that Dorbe Manor was only for poor students rubbed her the wrong way, especially with what she knew about the ghost selections of first years.

"So," Navi said, lying on the floor of the main common room; the fire lit in the hearth, and Shadow stretched out before her. That had been the best part of the vacation, the return of Shadow. Saga had no idea where he disappeared or where he would come from, but she and Navi had speculated on his origins often. They were no closer to finding an answer than they had been when they had first met the big wolf-like dog. All Saga knew was that she had that him to thank for her new life. Saga stretched out on the other side of shadow and enjoyed the warmth that the fireplace and the big dog provided. "You decided about the Pentathlon team yet?"

Saga laughed. "Everyone keeps asking me that. Especially Donetta Coccio." She let her head flop over to the side to look at Navi over Shadow's nose. "I don't know."

"You might be the real deal, though," Navi speculated. "You're running aside, your horsemanship has improved by giant strides, and with actual lessons, your stick fighting is really something to watch. Not that Navi gets much opportunity to watch," she laughed.

"You thinking that I'll get that first in stick fighting instead?"

"Gods, no! That's Navi's!" she insisted. "It's all this one has coming her way. You're still thrashing every Were out there in Stadion. You can have that. What do you want to do tomorrow?"

Saga frowned, "Well, we should go see Pingu and Ephyra."

"We do that every day!"

"I know, I know, I was thinking of going to see Astrid. I've been trying, but I haven't been able to find her," Saga said. "I only have time during the class, and then there's no time to actually talk, no matter how fast we make it there."

"Especially with us going around the Rishi farm now."

"Yes... well... The crossbow bolts. Astrid wasn't kidding about those. But ever since I came here, I've been trying to ask her about what happened to the people I left behind, and there just never seems to be the time or the right time."

They met for breakfast in the morning at the Rolly Polly Kitty, where after months of speculation and rumours, talk of the Valkyrie at the school had finally died away. Some even speculated that there wasn't even a Valkyrie at the school and that someone else had made that up. It was good not to have to go through town hearing people blame her for the horrible fires anymore. After polishing off their food, they wandered off together to the stables to tend to their assigned animals. Shadow trotted along behind them, eager for whatever they gave him, but he did not enter either stall leading off to the specialised environments for their animals. Instead, he settled in the main aisle of the stables by the door to the pegasus enclosure and seemed to go to sleep.

Saga brushed Pingu's mane and tail, then checked each of his feet before filling his feed and allowing the large animal to eat. Gently, she ran her fingers down his white feathered wings. They flickered and rippled, but not in the same was as the other pegasi in the stable. She had observed them over the weeks, and even when they were at home in their stalls, rarely were they completely still. Moving their feet, shaking their heads, twitching their wings. She had felt them twitch ever so slightly during riding class when they were going over jumps, almost as though he knew that he could fly and that the feeling of leaving the ground and having nothing beneath his hooves was something familiar and innately him, but he never extended them out on his own. He never flicked them around as though they were itchy, not like the others who did.

"We'll go jumping again later, huh?" She suggested to him, and he nodded his big head as though in agreement. Her reading on Pegasi indicated that if exposed to enough human speech, they could understand what was being said to them. She liked the idea that Pingu understood her, but she was unsure just how true that fact was, especially for a young one like Pingu.

She gave him a pet on his nose and said goodbye, ready to meet up with Navi and Shadow to go find Astrid. It had been far too long since she had been able to spend time with her benefactor, and she wanted someone to talk to, someone to explore the differences between her world and this new world she had been living in. Astrid had been there, and they had talked back in Yggdrasil city, but their interactions had been restricted since the day of the choosing.

Navi and Shadow were waiting for her when she stepped out of the enclosure. The big dog was licking the girl's fingers, presumably from whatever meat she had fed Ephyra. "Ready?" Navi asked, looking up from the dog.

"Yeah."

They were in no hurry for once, and instead of running along the outskirts of town to get between classes, they strolled through town. They stopped and looked at the market, admiring the clothes for sale, but both realised pretty quickly that they had no money for such extravagances.

"Let's bring a pie," Navi suggested as they were about to pass the Kitty again.

Saga looked at her in surprise. "We have pie almost every day for lunch. You sure you don't want anything else?"

"Navi would say yes, but then she would be lying. lucuma pie and pacay. What do you say?"

"And a jug of jelly melon cider," Saga added, relenting to the other girl's desire.

"Of course. This one would never go without!" Together they went back into the Rolly Polly Kitty Eatery and ordered a pie to go with a side of pacay and the jug of cider. It was earlier and later than their usual times at the eatery. Too late for the breakfast they usually enjoyed when they did not have an early class and too early for the lunches they usually wolfed down between classes with Emory, Jemima, Tasso, and Yasen.

They were waiting in line for the group in front of them to order when a group of Ljósálfar elves entered. They were older men and women dressed in fine, brightly coloured clothes, and they talked loudly as though they had no concern for anyone around them. The change in Navi was remarkable. Suddenly she shrunk behind Saga as though they did not want to be seen by them.

"What is it?" Saga asked.

"Nothing," Navi whispered. "Let's just get our pie and go."

The space at the counter opened up, and Saga moved to step up as the next when one of the elegantly dressed men stepped up, pushing her out of the way. Saga stared at him in disbelief. "Excuse me, sir, I was next in line," she said as politely as she could, eyeing him with a distinct level of disdain as Navi sidled further behind her, trying not to be noticed. The man looked at her with a scowl, and when his eyes found Navi, the scowl turned to a sneer. He took in their clothes. Without the uniform of Toserra Sorose to give them any legitimacy, they were dressed plainly. Saga, in a long-sleeved grey shirt over trousers, and Navi, in a dull brown dress. It was a simple design, but it spoke of simplicity and, perhaps, a lack of money to this man. "Out of my way, girl. Slaves go to the back of any line."

Saga's eyes narrowed, and Navi cowered, grabbing Saga. "Don't!" she exclaimed.

"Take that back," Saga hissed at the man. "We are both students of Toserra Sorose Academy. We were in line first. Wait your turn."

The man scoffed and turned back to his friends. "Can you believe this? The girl says that that doxie is a student at the school," there was a burst of raucous laughter before he turned back to Saga. "And that is why my children go to Shamel Aiyeola. Good, reputable Elvan school that doesn't allow the muck in," she added with a sneer at Navi.

"I didn't even think they could read," A woman said. "I mean, mine can barely follow instructions."

"We can read!" Navi shouted over the woman. "We can do anything we want, but you can't be bothered doing your own cooking or cleaning, so you treat us like animals, no, worse than your animals." Saga blinked and looked back at her friend. She had never, not ever, heard Navi raise her voice and without a stutter as well. Navi was not finished, though. "It's you who are too stupid to cook your own food, brush your own hair or even put your own clothes on in the morning that you need to belittle and hold back an entire race of people to do it all for you! If someone isn't listening to you, it's because you're too stupid to use manners. It's because that task is so simplistic. They're laughing at the fact that you don't know how to do it—"

A slap echoed through the silent eatery, and Navi stumbled backward into a table, knocking the drinks and food situated there over the floor and the patrons sitting there. She looked back up at the man in horror as she realised what she had done.

The man stalked towards her, his hand raised to have another go at her, but Saga stood in his way. Despite his age and masculinity, her stature put them at an even standing. She stared into his eyes, daring him to try and move around her. It was not him, though. One of the others in the group rounded past her and grabbed hold of Navi. "I wonder what the going rate is for a young runaway like this one?" His eyes gleamed, and Saga whirled on him. Navi was still, fear riveting her to the spot. Around them, no one moved. No one said a word.

"She's free!"

"No such thing as a free Doxie!" the one holding Navi sneered, trying to haul her petrified form along with him. "Move!" He screamed in her ear, kicking her unmoving legs.

Saga did not think. She should have thought, but she didn't. Her fingers clenched into a fist, and she barely noticed what she was doing until her fist connected with the face of the elf holding Navi. The impact seemed to loosen his grip on her, and Navi stumbled free, her legs barely holding her up. The first elf that had hit Navi reached out and hauled Saga back by her hair. She felt herself falling until she caught herself and kicked backward at him.

The female elves ran from the Eatery, wailing about a wild slave being loose and attacking her betters. Their feebleness irritated Saga. Navi, on her feet again, picked up a nearby serving platter with half a Lucuma pie on it and cracked it into her assailant's head. The blond elf stumbled into Saga, and as a result, she fell into the man who held her by the hair. They all fell, a table collapsing under their weight.

Other people were screaming now as the fight proceeded to destroy tables and food platters. By the time the city guard entered the Eatery, there were broken chairs, plates, and Saga, Navi, and the two Ljósálfar men were covered in food and drink. A woman Saga presumed to be the owner was wailing to the guards about the state of her shop.

The four of them had been escorted out of the shop in shackles by the guards, and there was not a person nearby who didn't look on in anticipation to see what would happen next. Saga was glad that most of the school was on holiday and that there were very few students or staff to watch their walk of shame.

"Who should I have summoned up here?" The guard asked after sitting the four of them down in the tower.

"That Slave——" one of the men started, but the guard held up his hand.

"There are no slaves in Nýr Ásgardr, and I am well aware of the Dökkálfar students at the school. Who should I have summoned up here to take charge of you?" The man muttered that his wife would be right behind them and as the second elf mentioned that his sister would be with her. The guard then looked expectantly at Saga and Navi. "And you two? Who's legally responsible for you in town? House prefects?"

Navi nodded and sighed. "Ziva Jensyn, Dorbe Manor."

"You?" he asked Saga. Saga knew the game, though, and Tymberlee would kill her. "Astrid Grunborg, Weapons Mistress…"

Navi cringed "Mistress Grunborg? She's going to kill us."

Saga nodded slowly, all too aware of how right Navi was.

"You sure you want Mistress Grunborg and not your prefect?" the guard queried.

Saga nodded again. "Yes sir…"

"You're a new race at the school then, being sponsored by a staff member," The guard pressed. Saga nodded sullenly. "What are you?"

Saga looked at him. She remembered being told not to ask that question but guessed that she was in no position to complain. "Valkyrie."

The second elf's eyes widened in shock as he hit his friend's shoulder. "You picked a fight with a Maiden of War?"

"There's no such thing," the first elf insisted, but Saga stared at the second elf.

"What did you call me?" she asked, staring at him. The phrase rattled around in her head. Maiden of War? Had that not been what the ghost of Master Berfelan's strange head had called her?

"You're a Valkyrie?" The guard asked dubiously.

"That's what they tell me, sir."

The guard looked down at his parchment and then up at the four of them. "Who wants to tell me what happened rationally?"

Saga and Navi looked at each other, but Navi seemed to shrink. In the meantime, the two elves were bickering about the course of events. "Sir," Saga said, trying to find her manners back.

"Yes?"

"My friend and I were waiting for our turn in line. We go to the Kitty frequently," he nodded, "The person in front of us finished their order, and we were about to step up when that one," Saga pointed to one of the elves, "Pushed me, physically, out of the way. I informed him, politely, I believe that we had been waiting, at which point he informed us that slaves go to the back of the line."

He looked at Navi. "This true?"

She looked up, surprised to be addressed. "Y… y… y… yes."

"What happened then?" he asked.

"Why are you asking them?" The first of the elves complained. "We're the ones who were assaulted!"

"I'll get to you," the guard said before turning back to Navi. "Go on," he said.

Navi looked at everyone there, and she looked a little grey, perhaps the same way as Saga had gone white as a sheet when asked to do something she didn't want to. "Well... umm... Saga informed the man that we a... are students at the school, and one of the women said that Dökkálfar cannot even read."

"He then attempted to attack her, and that one actually tried dragging her out of the shop, even hurting her," Saga intervened when Navi went quiet.

"Lies! They lie! The doxie can't possibly be free!"

"Shut up," the guard said to the elves. "I have not gotten to you yet. He turned to Saga and Navi again. "And the fight?"

Saga sighed. "He hit her, and she fell. That's when that one tried to drag her out of there," she said, pointing at each elf. "Going on about what price they could get for her."

~*~

Astrid and Ziva stood in the doorway of the Guard tower staring at them. Both were looking harassed and less than pleased with them.

"This one just can't," Ziva said, turning away from Navi.

"Ziva!" Navi cried, but her sister waved her off.

"The guard told us a little of what happened," Astrid said, trying to placate the sisters. "They're not pressing charges on the two of you, although you will be required to pay back damages the Kitty—"

"Navi!" Ziva exclaimed. "We can't afford that!" Panic seemed to cloud the older girl's features as she fretted about what to do.

"I've paid," Astrid said. "While I disagree with how it was handled, allowing those," she paused, trying to find the right words, "People... to take Navi into custody as a runaway slave would have been far harder to deal with. Proving her freedom would have been far more complicated than what has transpired here."

"Thank you, Mistress Grunborg," Navi said in a small voice.

Ziva nodded, the reality of Astrid's words ringing true to her. "Free Dökkálfar are still too uncommon for many to accept it or realise that you are telling the truth," Astrid continued. She looked at Saga. "You threw the first punch?"

"After he hit Navi, but yes," Saga agreed.

She nodded. "It is you who will be responsible for paying me back." The thought seemed to weigh on Saga. She already owed Astrid for the school fees and everything she owned. The clothes on her back, the books she used in school, her tournament gear and now this.

"No," Navi gasped. "Let me help."

Astrid shook her head. "No, Miss Jensyn, Saga has a reputation for allowing her fists to do the speaking, and it is still a lesson she has yet to learn." Saga resisted the urge to speak up. That reputation was based more on her size than any actual event, and it had followed her wherever she had gone, even here.

That seemed to settle Ziva, but at the same time, seemed to set something loose in Navi. "We just wanted some pie!" Navi cried. She looked at Astrid. "Saga really wanted to see you, and we were going to bring you lunch." Tears were streaming down her face now, and Ziva must have relented a little because she pulled her sister into a hug, patting her back and whispering reassurances into her pointed ear. "We just wanted lunch."

Astrid sighed and looked between the girls. Her gaze settled on Saga. "I'm sorry that I have been so unavailable to you. Things have been... hectic since the beginning of the school year."

"You can say that again," Saga muttered. She had had so many hopes for the week-long break that was now never going to happen. She was still expecting further punishment for her part in the fight.

"Ziva, go on and take Navi home. I'll take Saga back to my place," Ziva nodded, and the girls said goodbye before Ziva directed her sister off in the direction of Dorbe Manor.

Astrid had a small cottage near the training grounds on the edge of town. Upon entering the place, Saga had been honestly surprised to find out that the woman lived so close to Jimpsee house, yet they never saw each other outside of class or on tournament days.

"Come in, have a seat," Astrid said, going straight through to a small kitchen at the back of the room to put on a kettle.

Saga wandered in slowly, taking time to look at everything. A suit of armour in the corner looked as though it had once been Astrid's, or still was, but it did not look as though she had worn it in a while. There were various weapons scattered around the place. Swords, bows, staves of various lengths, maces, and other weapons that Saga could not identify.

Astrid had barely returned to the small sitting area before a knock on the door. "Excuse me," she said before hurrying to open the door.

"There you are," a breathless voice exclaimed. "Where have you been?"

"Busy Vali," she said, stepping outside and closing the door behind herself, leaving Saga alone inside the house. "What are you doing here?" The small cottage did not do much to block out their voices.

"Freyr's heir is making moves again," the man said.

Saga edged her way close to the door to listen. "That would be far more useful if you had identified who Freyr's heir actually was," Astrid cut in. "Until you do, people will continue to die."

"Oh, am I supposed to be the only one looking, dear sister? I thought the whole reason you've been hiding out at this school was that you thought the heir was here or have you been too busy playing with your new toy?"

"The heir is here, Vali. Be assured of that. As for the Valkyrie, she is none of your business."

The man snorted in response. "A Valkyrie roaming this world again? That is everyone's business. Come find me when you are ready to take this more seriously. The wild hunts will only continue to grow fiercer each time they ride."

The man walked off; Saga could hear his heavy footsteps retreat from outside Astrid's door. Astrid cursed, and Saga took that as her sign to return to the seat she had been sitting in when Astrid had stepped outside.

"Who was that?" Saga asked when Astrid re-entered the small cottage. "Is everything all right?"

Astrid looked distractedly towards the door, "No one... that was no one important. Everything is fine."

Saga frowned slightly and wondered why Astrid was lying to her.

MIMIR

By the time everyone returned from break and school resumed, Saga had
still not been able to let go of Astrid's lie. Or ask her about the old world.
Sure, she may not have wanted to talk about private matters, but why lie about
the man at the door being her brother? It made no sense to Saga, but it seemed
that the more time passed, the fewer things made sense.

"Hey, the half-semester tournament scores are up," Emory announced,
pointing at the board in the town centre. Overall winners were announced and
posted on the first day of the week after the Tourney events, but a full tally
of everyone's positions by score had not been available.

"Odin's beard," Navi huffed, looking at the points list for the stick
fighting event. It was her only event and one she thrived in, but Saga had
overtaken her in the scores, having a mere five points more than the dark elf.
"How do you do it?" she asked.

Saga shrugged. "I don't know."

"Look at this," Emory said, pointing at the swordplay list. Saga was neck
and neck with him there. "She never even got to compete that first week
because of the jousting accident."

"And the stadion," Jemima said, pointing at the list, where Saga's name
was represented in the first place. Around them, several people were looking
at her as though trying to weigh her up and figure out what she was doing

that they were not. Week after week, she outran them to the point that Raphaella Damir from the hospital had been forced to test Saga for any enhancing herbal concoctions or magics. Finding none, the school continued to allow Saga to run, but the students, or more precisely, the Were community, felt like they were missing something. Jemima grinned though she found the dressage list. "Well, would you look at that."

"Show off," Tasso grimaced, finding his own jousting scores. He was somewhere in the middle of the pack, and he sighed. "If I don't get better at this, my father will tear me a new one when the semester finishes."

Saga, uncomfortable with the attention, looked at the scores and turned away from the board. "Let's get lunch. We need to get to class."

By habit, the group started towards the Rolly Polly Kitty Eatery, and when they realised that that was where they were going, Saga and Navi stopped still in the middle of the town square.

"Coming?" Tasso asked, looking back at them both.

The two looked at each other, then back at the group, who were all looking back at them expectantly. "Umm," Navi tried.

"Well," Saga started.

"What is it?" Jemima asked.

Emory looked between everyone as though he wanted to say something, but he stayed silent as the group awkwardly awaited what came next. "We want our pie," Tasso pressed, turning to continue.

"We can't," Saga said hurriedly.

"Why not?" Tasso asked, looking back at her.

"Well." Saga looked at Navi, who motioned for her to continue. "You see," Saga looked in the direction of the Eatery and sighed. She really did love their lucuma pie and pacay. She motioned to herself and Navi. "We've been banned from the Kitty."

Eventually, they procured their lunch from a street vendor in the marketplace, going for lotus chips and meatball skewers. They ate and walked to class after detouring for their afternoon materials.

Tasso and Jemima had extracted every painful detail about the encounter in the Kitty out of them, from their decision to buy a pie to Astrid and Ziva picking them up from the Guard Tower. Their incredulity turned to concern, back to incredulity as the tale tumbled from them.

"And now what?" Emory asked.

Saga shrugged. "I owe Astrid for the damages she paid for and I can't get pie."

"But those elves were in the wrong," Tasso said, his fists clenched so tightly that Saga thought he would draw blood if he did not release them soon. "They had no right!"

"They're Ljósálfar," Navi said softly, her hand stroking his arm soothingly. He unclenched a little, but not by much. "They will always get away with everything."

"It's not fair," Tasso spat angrily.

"No," Navi agreed. "It's not. But that is how things are and how they have been for a very long time. Ziva had an extremely hard time being the first and only Dökkálfar at this school. At any school, but we're here and quite frankly, we're only here because our mother made sure that we learned to read, and Ziva got caught in the Big House's library by the Mistress, who turned us into her little project."

Saga looked at Navi. She had never heard the girl or her siblings speak of their mother. Tasso spoke, his hands unclenching, revealing the fingernail-shaped blood marks on his palms to wrap an arm around her shoulders. "I'm sorry," he said softly.

"For us to go to school and have the life she never had. That was all our mother ever wanted," Navi whispered so softly that they could barely hear her. "Navi wonders, though... What good will any of it be after we graduate? How can anyone take us seriously?" She sighed heavily. "This one guesses Ziva will find out soon..."

~ * ~

It was late, and Saga was trying to keep her eyes open long enough to get some reading done, but she kept pulling out the piece of parchment that she had scribbled down the ghost's mysteriously cryptic words. She remembered the message he had repeated again and again in her bedroom over the break, but his words from the day in the library were harder to recall. He had only said them once, and all that had been amidst her insecurities about her ability to see and speak with the ghosts.

"Still looking at that?" Tremblay asked.

Saga peered around, making sure that she was, in fact, alone before speaking. "I can't get it out of my head."

"The odd one?" Tremblay asked, perching himself as well as he could on the corner of the table as though he were a solid being come in for a conversation.

"That and something one of those elves said."

"The ones that attacked you and your friend?" He asked.

Saga looked up at him in surprise. "How do you know about that?" she gasped.

"Oh, Amyra Dorbe was talking about how her prefect had it out with her little sister. Something about a fight and the guards."

"Well, there's a bit more to that story than that, but yes."

"So, what about those nasty snivelling elves?" Tremblay asked, his disgust evident.

"One of them called me a Maiden of War," she let her comment hang there as Tremblay thought.

"Well, I suppose I should have put that together sooner," Tremblay said thoughtfully.

"What do you mean?"

He shrugged and looked at her, assessing her before he spoke again. "Valkyries were called the Maidens of War."

"You don't think—" she started.

"That our mysterious friend was talking about you?" Tremblay finished for her. Saga shrugged back at him, but a thought settled in her mind, and it would get her into trouble.

~*~

"I cannot believe you managed to get another detention with Master Berfelan," Jemima said as they walked out of class. Saga, though, while she had not been trying, was happy about the fact. Another chance to see the head. Another chance to make the ghost come for her.

"What were you thinking?" Emory pressed. He looked as exasperated as Jemima did. "I mean, with everything at the Kitty and the multiple detentions already. What were you thinking?"

"I wasn't," Saga said, following along behind them, trying not to show that she was happy about the turn of events. Better was the fact that Berfelan did not want her to report in that night. He would be busy, out of his office busy. Her mind was reeling as the others scolded her for again getting on Berfelan's bad side.

"Are you even listening to us?" Jemima asked.

"Saga?" Navi pressed when she did not respond.

Saga looked up from where her feet were going, taking their concerned faces in as she said, "I'm... I'm listening."

"Ah, huh," Navi commented, the doubt audible in her voice. "What was Jemima saying then?"

She looked at them, realising that she had, in fact, missed something as she had been thinking out her plan. She planned to get back in and see the mysterious head without Master Berfelan being there. "I have to get into Berfelan's office," she said, ignoring them.

"Well, you get in there often enough on detention," Emory snorted.

"Without him," Saga elaborated.

"What?" Navi and Jemima exclaimed.

"There's a head in there, like an actual head, no body. He keeps it on a pedestal and talks to it."

"I always knew the man was barmy," Tasso said.

"It talks back," Saga told them. "It's... I don't know what it is, but I must see it again."

"Why in the Nine Realms would you want to do that?" Jemima asked.

"Because it keeps talking to me," Saga looked back towards the school building as they walked across the town square, and an idea sprang to mind. Berfelan was busy tonight, and he had classes this afternoon. She looked at the windows, picking out the one she was certain was Berfelan's office window and an idea began to form.

They made it back to Jimpsee House, where Tasso and Navi had taken to storing their extra class materials so that everyone could go together, and as she stood in the room she shared with Jemima, she stared at the corner that had been occupied most of the week by the ghost of the head in Berfelan's office. Navi was in there, changing into her riding uniform with them, and Tasso had followed Emory to his room.

"You girls ready?" Emory asked, knocking on their door.

"Just about," Jemima called.

Saga looked at the door and thought about Berfelan's empty office and the head just waiting for her. She glanced at the girls when Jemima double-checked that they were ready and opened the door to the boys. The idea was sudden, and her gaze looked back over the corner where the ghost had stood, wailing his message. "Tell Master Toshiji that I'm feeling unwell," Saga said, trying to get past them.

"Oh, hell no!" Emory exclaimed, grabbing her by the arm to prevent her from pushing past him and Tasso into the hallway. "Absolutely not."

Navi and Jemima stopped moving around behind her, and Navi gasped. "Do not do what Navi thinks you're about to do," Navi cried, standing up, only one riding boot on her left foot, the other clasped in her hands.

Saga looked at them. "You don't understand!" she exclaimed.

"Because you won't tell us anything," Jemima said, hanging back, the hurt look on her face saying everything. She knew that something was up. "You keep these secrets, like that day in the library and now."

"You are in so much trouble already after what happened at the Kitty. You can't afford to go off like this," Emory insisted, shaking his head.

Saga looked pleadingly at Navi. "Astrid is hiding something from me, and there's something about me, and no one will tell me anything. The answers are in Berfelan's office. I can feel it!" she insisted. She wrestled her arm free. "I'm not asking any of you for anything!"

"Saga," Tasso said, stepping up to take Emory's place in the doorway. Jemima was hanging back. They were missing something. Something more than Berfelan's cruelty. "Seriously," He muttered. "Talk to us."

"Go to class," Saga told him. "All of you! Go!" She pointed out randomly in the direction of the stables as she spoke, and she could see Tremblay form out of nothingness just over Emory's shoulder, a look of concern plastered across his ethereal face.

Jemima huffed and, without a word, turned, pushed past Saga and the boys. She walked away, her steps echoing down the stairs. Navi frowned. "Happy?" She asked. "You helped Navi. Let Navi help you."

Saga shook her head. "You can't. You're in too much trouble already."

"And you're not?" she cried, picking up her school satchel from Saga's bed. She walked over to stand by the door and looked at Saga. "This one does not know what's going on with you, but you could just talk to us."

Tasso frowned at Saga and tugged Navi out of the room. He looked over his shoulder, glowering at Saga. "Come on," he said softly. "She doesn't want our help."

"You sure that pushing us all away is the route you want to take?" Emory asked. He leaned against the doorframe, his arms crossed as he eyed her sadly. Saga eyed him cautiously but said nothing. "You're not alone now. You know that, right? That's what they're all trying to say." Sometimes Saga regretted the times she had spoken to him about her old life, but the fact that he was sad rather than angry told her he understood her just a little bit better than the others did at that moment.

"Maybe I need to be," Saga said, looking back into her room to find her belongings. "Who knows what I am?"

"You're you," Emory said simply. "That's all that really matters and look at us. The Angel, the dark elf, the faerie, and the werewolf. Not a group you would see at Toserra. Friends from different houses, it's not impossible, but it is unlikely. You did that." She looked at him out of the corner of her eye. "You don't need to give us plausible deniability."

"This is something I have to do by myself."

"Is it really?" Emory asked, leaving her with something to think about before turning and walking away after the others.

Tremblay glided into the room, his arms crossed before him as he stared at her. "I hate to side with the wolf boy, I really do, but he is correct."

"Don't you start." Saga huffed.

Tremblay sighed and swirled in front of her. "They are all right."

"Really," Saga said, rifling through her trunk for different clothes from the riding gear she was wearing. How could she get back into the main school building when it was known that her group was on afternoon activities outside of town?

Gedde.

The answer seemed so simple. Vampire students roamed the school with their cloaks pulled over their faces, protecting them from the harmful sun. She slipped out of her room, Tremblay following her. "Whatever it is that you are thinking of doing, please. Do not do it," he begged.

Saga slipped across to the room Gedde shared with Vespers and looked at the two sides, trying to decide which suited each of the boys. Eventually, it was the book on Vampire Law on the desk on the right side that decided it for her, and she opened the wardrobe on that side.

"Saga!" Tremblay called, his voice holding a warning. It was easy to find the Vampire's second cloak and draw it out of the wardrobe. "I swear, children these days just don't listen!"

Saga drew the cloak around herself and smiled. "There! Nobody ever looks twice at the vampires."

"She's not even listening to me," Tremblay cried.

Saga returned to her room, the cloak draped over her shoulders, and grabbed her bag. This was going to be easier than she thought.

"Saga!" Tremblay yelled after her as she ran down the stairs to the front door.

It was amazing, Saga thought as she walked through the streets of Nýr Ásgardr, the cloak pulled tight around her as she hurried through town. No one stopped her. In fact, people moved out of the way as though they knew just how important it was that the Vampire students be allowed to pass unimpeded to the school building.

The ease of her trip through town was perhaps a bad thing because it boosted her confidence in a way that should have been a warning. Saga had snuck in and out of plenty of schools and group homes over the years, but the ease of crossing the entire town without anyone stopping her should have been a concern.

Saga bounded up the stairs of the school building, blending in with crowds of students, no one taking notice of her as she weaved her way through them towards the wing where the teachers' offices were.

She neared Berfelan's office on the third floor. She saw as she approached that the door to Master Iacono's office was open. The Planarography teacher was sitting at his desk, pen scratching away at the parchment on his desk. He was likely grading papers.

"Hello?" Apparently, she had not been as silent as she had wanted.

There was a rattling of furniture as inside the office as Master Iacono pushed his chair back and walked to the open door. Saga looked around, trying to find somewhere to hide. She thought of those books she had read about the wizard boy who went to school in an old castle that had suits of armour lining the halls and plenty of alcoves to hide in. Whoever had designed the main building of Toserra Sorose had had no such whimsy. The hall was straight. Windows on one side and doors to the offices on the other. Benches to sit on and a few decorative tables occupied the space, but none were sufficient to hide behind.

"Can I help you?" Saga looked back from her search of the hallway to find Master Iacono standing in the doorway to his office.

"Oh, um," Saga said, trying not to look at the man. "I... umm..."

"Yes?"

"I was looking for Master Berfelan," Saga said, trying to disguise her voice into the low, emotionless tone of the vampires. Hell, she had no idea what else to say, so a half-truth seemed just as useful.

The Planarography teacher eyed her. "Master Berfelan has class now. He won't be in for the rest of the day, either. You will have to come back tomorrow."

"Right, umm... thank you," Saga said, turning to hurry in the opposite direction. If she had to reapproach Berfelan's office, she did not want to pass Iacono's office again.

She turned a corner, feeling the man's eyes on her the entire time. She dared not look back. She did not want to risk being recognised. Saga had no idea and could not explain what it was about the encounter with Master Iacono just now that gave her a solid case of the heebie-jeebies, but it was as though his coming out of his office was pre-emptive, just like the night of her detention, stepping out, before anyone could step in. Berfelan did not like him, which had been obvious since the first day of school, but he did not appear to like anyone, so that was not an opinion she could really trust, especially since everyone she knew loved Master Iacono.

Saga leaned against the wall of the corridor, breathing hard as she thought of what to do next. She had not thought this plan out, and now she was stuck. She did not know this wing of the building and had no idea how to get out of it without going back past Berfelan's office and that of the overly observant Planarography teacher.

She stared out the window of the corridor. It looked over Farnphrey House and past that to the school's farmlands. In the distance, she could see the swatch of blackened land caused by the ghostly hoard that had destroyed the farm there weeks before. She had to see that head. It had appeared to her that day. People had died; maybe that was why things were so dire to her. She had been waiting for another ghostly hoard to appear, killing more people. She had not known Sindre Mozhan, but Mannish had spoken fondly of the older boy and had been devastated by his loss.

The head.

Regardless of Master Iacono in the office next door, Saga had to see the head. Maybe she could get it to talk to her as it did to Berfelan. How would she get in there with Iacono in his office, though?

A ringing crash echoed down the hall suddenly and startled her. Saga peaked her head around the corner to look down towards where Berfelan's office was. A vase that had been sitting on one of the ornamental tables was now shattered on the floor. Flowers, water, and broken pieces of vase scattered the space. Master Iacono appeared at his office door.

"Who's there?" He cried. His head looked up and down the empty hall, trying to find the cause. Flittering just past the open window, more hovering in the air outside, Saga could see the translucent form of a ghost. She did not recall having ever seen that ghost before, but the woman, for it was a woman, looked towards Saga and winked. "The wind, I swear, I told them not to leave delicates in front of the open windows, but does anyone listen to me? No. Why would they do that? Now, look at this mess. A mess I have to clean up," Iacono huffed, hurrying down the hall in the opposite direction of where Saga was hiding.

The ghost swept in and pointed at Berfelan's office eagerly. Cautiously, not wanting to make any noise, Saga hurriedly tip-toed down the hall to the door. "Thank you," Saga said to the ghost woman. She just smiled in return, not saying anything, and Saga could not help but wonder who she was. She was not one of the house ghosts, that was for sure. She had seen all of them on the first day of school as they had bickered about who would get which student for their houses.

Hand on the doorknob, Saga turned it. Nothing happened. She sighed. Of course, it was locked. Fermin Berfelan was not about to leave his office unlocked for anyone to come and go as they pleased. He had more sense than that, especially with that thing in there. Saga looked up and down the hall again. The female ghost looked as well and nodded in agreement.

Saga turned back to the lock and removed one of the few things she still had from the real world from her hair. Bobby pins. A wayward girl's best tools. She had found nothing of the sort when looking at hair accessories in Yggdrasil city or the clothing store in Nýr Ásgardr. She would have to keep these and her remaining supply safe. At the same time, she wondered if hat pins would do the job. She bent them into shape, stuck the ends of the pins into the lock of Berfelan's door, and twisted the two around until she heard the lock click.

With a grin, she looked over her shoulder at the ethereal woman. She was beaming. Saga stayed low as she pushed the door open and scurried inside, closing the door right behind her. The woman glided through the door, joining her inside the room. Together, they looked around Berfelan's office. It was just as Saga remembered it. Scattered with piles of scrolls and stacks of books on every surface. The walls were decorated with large, ancient parchments and fragments that seemed to primarily tell the same story now that she had a chance to look. She turned, trying to take it all in, and a heavy sheet fell from an obscured tapestry as the ghostly woman passed by it. It was with a shock that Saga realised she recognised a scene.

A winged woman soared over a battlefield, and it looked to Saga as though it was the same image that her mother had embroidered with gold thread on the small white blanket Saga had been found wrapped in. She reached up tentatively to trace the wings of the Valkyrie shown in the sketch.

"That which cannot be understood is on those walls."

Saga spun around at the voice. "What?" she gasped. Her eyes fell upon the very thing she had come to see, and she now remembered why she had not noticed the artwork in the room. Set on a pedestal to the right of Berfelan's desk chair, as though he would sit there and converse with it, was a severed head. She had seen it before, heard it speak before, but always at Berfelan's behest. "Who are you?" she asked, stepping carefully around a stack of books to approach the desk and the head.

Eyes followed her every step. "I am the rememberer. I was, at one time, the smartest man alive. They called me Mimir."

"Mimir," she repeated the name hesitantly. "But, you're not... alive?" she asked hesitantly.

"Maiden of war that you are, you understand little." Eyes flicked towards the decorative parchment on the wall. "Róta and Ölrún. The final flight."

"The what?" Saga asked.

The hollow eyes set deep within the severed head on the pedestal flicked back to her. "The final flight of the Valkyries as war raged between the Æsir and the Jotun. They sought until the ends of the Nine Realms for warriors to flood the ranks of the Odin's chosen, but those slain again could not be returned."

"Astrid mentioned Róta and Ölrún to me, as though she knew them."

"Knew of them. They were long gone before the child was born into this world. Many questions must be raised with the return of the war maidens." The head looked as though it would have cocked its head to the side in thought if it had had a neck. "The Æsir and the Vanir once fought. You know this, yes?"

Saga nodded. "Master Berfelan told us in class."

"In the end, the Vanir become a part of the Æsir. But many were not happy with this. Blood boiled, and anger seethed under the surface. The coming of the end of the world brought many changes. Many chances too. Some squandered, some not taken, some not yet noticed. The return of the Valkyries though bears nothing but bad omens for what comes next."

"Bad luck wherever I go," Saga muttered.

"No, the Valkyries are not the cause of what is to come, but a sign that the time is nearer than any could have predicted," The head told her. "With the death of Odin, a struggle began. A struggle for power that has never been resolved. There are those moving in the shadows. Those who wish to see neither Æsir nor Vanir takes power for themselves."

"What do the Valkyries have to do with this?" Saga asked.

"For once again, the Æsir and the Vanir will need to unite. Unite to battle the evil that is brewing as they quarrel with each other. Before long, young Maiden of War, you will take your first soul to Valhalla. The first of a new army."

DREAMSCAPE

Saga shook her head adamantly. "No. No, no more dead people," she begged. Those weird hollow eyes just stared at her while the ethereal woman floated around until she hovered next to the head. Still, Saga shook her head. "I lost everything because I could see the dead. I'm not willing to lose it again here, not when I'm finally making a place for myself."

"You will have no choice in the matter, girl," Mimir said. "You see the ghosts of Toserra Sorose. It would explain why I have been drawn to you. It is an ability unique to Valkyries that even the Angels do not have. You see the lady beside me, yes? And the house ghosts." When Saga nodded, he went on. "What about other spirits?"

Saga shrugged. "Not so much here, but back home, the dead would talk to me, ask me to help them find peace."

The head hummed in thought, and maybe he had wanted to nod his head. Beside him, the ethereal woman did. "You are but a young one. And then, a young one in Midgard. It is not surprising that you could not lead them to the afterlife. That will come."

Suddenly the female ghost looked around, startled. She darted towards the door of Berfelan's office and through the closed door before darting back in and pointing at it in a panic. "What is it?" Saga asked her.

"Someone is coming," The head of Mimir said. "Interesting that you cannot hear her. It must have to do with the curse on her grave."

"Who is she?"

"You don't know?" The head chuckled. "Then I will allow you to discover that for yourself. That awful man from next door must be back. Fermin won't be in for the rest of the day."

The female ghost held her fingers to her lips, and everyone went silent. They heard the man outside muttering about cleaning up other people's messes and how there would be trouble when he found the student responsible. Saga barely remembered to breathe as she recalled the fact that the man, Master Iacono, had kept his door open as he had worked.

"Can you fly?" Mimir asked softly.

Saga looked at him dumbfounded. "Are you crazy?" she asked. "How on earth would I fly?"

The head sighed, and she could imagine the drooping shoulders of the movement. "Children these days. We will discuss this at your next, inevitable detention." Saga huffed and muttered something about him wanting to get her into trouble with Master Berfelan before she looked back at the door. She crept over to it and listened to the man outside. "Get back," the head hissed. Saga looked at him but moved to stand behind an overflowing bookshelf. Two more voices could be heard outside, talking to the Planarography teacher. She instantly recognised Berfelan's voice and gave a panicked look towards the head. The ethereal woman appeared once more and shrugged for him.

The other voice, also male, sounded familiar. She had heard that voice only recently, outside Astrid's house. What had his name been? Astrid had not wanted to talk of him, but Saga had heard a name. Vali?

The door to the office crashed open, and Berfelan entered. The mysterious Vali entered behind him. "I have already told her that this is too important to squander."

"Who is squandering it?" Berfelan snapped back, stalking towards his desk. He was focused on whatever he was doing, and Vali was focused on Berfelan. Neither of them had noticed Saga yet, but that would change the instant either turned around. The female ghost pointed at the door.

Saga nodded in understanding and drew the hood of the Vampire cloak around her head. She straightened, waiting for the two men to speak again. "You are, Fermin. Just as she is. Neither of you has a clue as to what to do with what I have given you."

"Given me? I've lost everything since you showed up. You haven't given me anything," Berfelan spat. "I am the son—"

"Yeah, yeah, yeah," Vali said, holding his hand up as he interrupted Berfelan. "You are Njoror's son, and we are Odin's—"

Saga did not wait to hear anything else. Holding the hood tight around her face, she dashed from the room, the cloak fluttering in her wake as she escaped Berfelan's office and darted past the open door beside it.

Berfelan's shouts echoed down the corridor as he crashed his way through his office, the sound of books toppling from their unsteady piles still audible under his shouts. Vali and Berfelan both tried to get out of the door at the same time, getting stuck.

"Idiot," Berfelan screamed. "Get that, student!"

Byrge Iacono bounded from his office and looked from Berfelan to the fluttering cloak running down the hall.

Saga ran. Running was her thing. Her true superpower did not involve the dead or being weird. Her hand was gripped tightly around the neck of the cloak, making sure that the clasp stayed fast and that the hood did not fall off.

She could hear them behind her. Squabbling with one another as they chased after her and intermittently shouted for someone to 'catch that vampire.'

Saga could hear laughter. A female voice filled the hall with a musical sound. She could not risk looking back. If Berfelan or Iacono recognised her, it would be more than detention. It would be expulsion, or worse. She was sure of that.

Her only thought was of putting one foot in front of the other as fast as she could. The stairs were coming, and she had to make sure that she did not go tumbling down them. Classes were letting out, though, and several doors opened on the far side of the stairs, students spilling out into the hall. She could lose herself in them. The other hooded figures of the Vampires would hide her from them.

Berfelan was behind her, Iacono mere feet behind him, but Vali was within a handbreadth of her. Suddenly, Saga tripped, the long flapping ends of the cloak catching under her feet as she tried to duck away from Vali. She went sprawling to the floor, skidding along the polished marble floor with a momentum she did not expect. Vali stumbled in his attempt to catch her, thwarted by her slide into the oncoming mass of students.

"Stop that Vampire!" Berfelan yelled, but Saga got to her feet amidst the stampeding students making their way to their next classes. She noticed several hooded figures looking in her direction before making sure they got between her and the oncoming teachers.

Saga had no idea who Vali was, but she was sure that he was betraying Astrid with whatever it was he was doing with Berfelan. It was something with that head, Mimir, but she had no idea what it was yet.

In front of her, the ghostly woman pointed her to a small staircase that led down to the first level of the building. Saga had never seen it before, usually taking the main staircase, but several older students were making their way up and down the stairs in a calm, sedate manner. The ghost held up her hand as if telling Saga to stop, and Saga slowed her fast jog to a slow walk to match the others using the staircase. She took several deep breaths; the run, while it had not tired her, had been exhilarating. She slowly made her way down the stairs and exited into a small foyer in the classroom wing of the building. Saga slid into the traffic of moving students making their way out of classrooms, getting lost in a group that headed out of the building, past a portrait of a smiling woman seated in a large, plush chair.

~*~

Jimpsee house was not empty when Saga returned. She recalled that the twins had a free class in the afternoon and would likely retire to the lounge room as they always did. She went to the back, deciding to risk the kitchen door rather than the front. She wished that she were the kind who would or even could climb up the trellis on the side of the house, but if she looked down even once...

No, sneaking in was a much better plan. She pulled the cloak off, rolling it up and carrying it as she slipped into the house. She could go straight up to her room, and as she crept through the kitchen, trying not to make a sound, she heard the front door open, and the boisterous voice of Mannish entered, Vespers right behind him, the older boy's musical voice resonating throughout the house.

Saga cursed under her breath. She would never get back into Gedde's room now. Vespers was his roommate. Saga looked around for a new plan and jumped out of her skin when Tremblay appeared.

"Trouble up at the school?" He asked smugly.

"Not now!" Saga hissed, looking out towards the hall. She heard Vespers and Mannish trudge upstairs, their heavy footsteps resounding through the house.

"Hmph," Tremblay said, hovering in front of her, arms crossed over his chest. "You might try the laundry."

Saga's eyes widened as she realised that he was right. There was a small basement in the house where they could go to handle the washing of their clothes, and it was accessible from the kitchen. She turned from the door to the hall and opened the narrow door onto the basement's top step. She carefully made her way down, closing the door behind her as she went.

With the door closed, it was completely black, but she kept her hand on the side of the wall and felt her way down each step, carefully feeling for each one, before moving. She had done this countless times, but always with the light. Tremblay appeared at the bottom of the stairs and watched her.

When she reached the bottom, she foraged for the baskets everyone stored their belongings in before they got around to washing and found Gedde's. She dropped the cloak in it, arranging some clothes on top of it as though it had always been there.

"Was it worth it?" Tremblay asked as she headed back for the stairs.

Saga looked back at him over her shoulder. "I think so," she started up the stairs before stopping and looking at him. He still hovered where he had appeared. "Who's the ghost at the school?"

Tremblay glided over and swirled around her. "What? You saw Miss Serra?"

"Serra?"

He nodded. "Yes. Serra... Toserra Sorose..."

Saga came down for dinner when the bell rang. She had hidden in her room for the rest of the day and had waited for Jemima's return. She had not returned to their room, so when Saga found her at the dinner table with Emory, she was startled. Everyone else was milling about, grabbing food, settling themselves down or talking amongst themselves, so Saga did not want to draw attention to the strain between herself and the others. She picked up a plate and filled it with food, her eyes cast downwards as she made her way to her usual seat beside Jemima and across from Emory.

"It was just the strangest thing, what happened at the school today," Onorati said.

"What was?" Mannish asked, shovelling a forkful of mashed potatoes into his mouth.

"Master Berfelan and Master Iacono, along with some guy I had never seen before, chasing a vampire through the halls of the school," Onorati explained. "I have never seen Master Berfelan look so angry before. He was all 'Catch them,' and he and Master Iacono do not get along to boot, then there was that mystery guy."

"Did they figure out who it was?" Gedde asked, sipping from a glass of red, syrupy liquid. Saga had grown used to his meal choices over the months but still found his food disturbing to look at.

Onorati shook her head. "Not that I heard. I think that Vitillon Hall is on lockdown tonight because of it... after that, I suppose they'll look at all the other Vampires in the school."

Gedde frowned. "And just like that, something bad happens, and it's all 'blame the Vampires' again. What did this one even do to get chased after anyway? Feed from another student?"

"No idea," Onorati replied, between forkfuls of food. "No one seems to know that one."

"And is everything all right with you three?" Tymberlee asked, looking down the table towards them.

"Yes," Emory said, not looking at Saga. "Just fine."

"And you Saga?" Tymberlee pushed.

"Fine."

"Really? I heard that you missed your afternoon classes."

Saga looked up from her food. She had not eaten much, just pushing it around on her plate as Onorati went on about the school incident. "I..." She started.

"Saga wasn't feeling well today," Jemima interrupted. "We suggested that she sleep this afternoon."

"Oh," Emory said, looking at the two girls before going back to their house Prefect. "Yes. We did."

"Ah-huh," Tymberlee said, eyeing the three of them cautiously. "Well, how are you feeling now?"

Saga eyed her food, her fork aimlessly picking at bits. "Actually, still a little a queasy."

Dinner had proceeded slowly after that, and as soon as they had all been dismissed, Saga had begged off study hall in the lounge area and had gone back to her room. Alone in her room, she wouldn't have the prying eyes of the others on her.

She prodded around in her trunk, looking for the book she was after, but stopped when her fingers brushed the soft material of her baby blanket. She pulled it out, caressing the material with her fingers as she always did. It had always amazed her that no matter how many years passed, it was still as soft and white as the day it had been given to her. Nothing had managed to stain it or discolour it, not like other things she had owned or been given. Maybe it was made of some weird fibre only found in one of the other Nine Realms that were not Midgard.

She carried the blanket over to her bed and sat down with it as she had done so many times before. She spread it out over her bed and looked at the picture that had been artfully embroidered in gold thread. She traced her fingers over the embroidery, just as she had over the wall hanging in Berfelan's office. They were the same picture. She rolled over on her bed, arm stretched out for her desk and looked for her history textbook. *Realities of Ragnarök* was not there.

"Oh... right..." She sighed, remembering that she had left it in her bag when she had decided to skip out on class and go find the Head – Mimir. She sighed again and sat up to search for her bag. It was where she had left it at the end of the bed. She leaned over, hauled the heavy bag up and opened it. The big book was in there, and she pulled it out. She put it down on the bed, just above the blanket, and she thought about the image in Berfelan's office. The one in his office was the same image embroidered lovingly on her blanket by her mother. The textbook he set for his class had the same Valkyrie depicted on the cover. Was it a coincidence? Did Berfelan just like the work of Oji Kamal? Or was there something that she was not seeing?

Mimir had told her that she was a sign of what was to come, but if that was true, nothing good was coming because all she ever saw was death. Book on her bed, Saga curled herself around it, the blanket spread across herself as her hand fisted in the soft fabric.

~*~

It was hot. So much hotter than she recalled summer being. An orange glow seemed to permeate the air as she tried to sleep, but it was not the hot night air that kept her awake. It was the sobbing. Heavy, heart-wrenching sobs pierced right through her soul. She pushed the covers of her bed aside and sat up.

She was alone, and everything was a burnt orange colour. Lights flickered all around her, and the sobbing continued somewhere nearby. Feet on the hot ground, she padded away from the solitary bed in the room of burnt orange.

"There are those moving in the shadows," Mimir's words echoed in her ears as she turned a corner. Just ahead of her, she saw a flutter of white hair. Someone had just turned another corner.

She ran. Maybe it was that person crying, sobbing so hysterically that it seemed nothing would ever soothe them again. "Hello?"

"A struggle for power that has never been resolved."

She turned the corner. Mimir's pedestal was lit by a spotlight she could not find. The head kept repeating his ominous words. "The return of the

Valkyries, though," he was saying as she looked around, trying to find the source of the incessant sobbing. "Bad omens for what comes next."

"Who is it?" she asked, turning to look at the head.

"Bad omens for what comes next," it repeated.

She ran past him, it was getting even hotter, but she had no idea how it kept getting so hot. A flicker of white hair in the distance. Who was it that she was following? Was the hair even white?

The sobbing seemed to follow the person she was chasing after, and she felt an even greater need to catch up to the mysterious figure, find out what was wrong, and what she could do to help. The floor was too hot for her feet now, and she had to take fast little steps, ensuring contact with the ground was as short as possible. Her feet were hurting, and each step she took seemed to take her further away from her goal. All the while, though, she heard the sobbing.

Even over the loud crackling that she had not noticed. She could hear the sobbing over the ringing of metal against metal, jeering, and the beating of horses' hooves. What was going on inside? The wall nearest her splintered into millions of pieces, and a gigantic galloping horse barrelled through the hole it had made, a huge barking wolf at its side. Two crows flew in, circling the helmeted rider who galloped past her as though she had not even been there. After the rider, hundreds of thousands of warriors, running on foot, mounted on horses and other gigantic beasts that Saga could barely name despite her time in the Mistress Anhora's classes flooded the room.

The other riders seemed to ride right through her as though she was not there. She felt the thundering beat of every foot, hoof and paw fall that passed through her. It shook her to her very core, but as they barrelled through her, she could not move, and finally, she could see that flames started to flicker up the walls around her, and tiny little curls of fire seemed to appear on the floorboards. That would explain the heated floors.

As the last warrior ran through her, her knees collapsed, taking her to the floor, where her hands and knees were singed by the mere touch of the burning floors. Breathe. She could not breathe.

"The wild hunt rides again," Mimir's voice echoed down the hall but was consumed by the air-cracking noise of the fire.

The flames licking at the walls seemed to follow set trails, going up and up and up until they reached the roof and started to spread along that, surrounding her in fire. And all the while, someone sobbed.

Saga awoke, panting for breath. Her bedclothes and sheets were drenched through, and her hair clung in wet clumps to her face, neck and back. She concentrated on breathing long, deep breaths, trying to force air into her lungs. She felt as though they were singed and that she had had all the air knocked out of her, just like that day on the jousting field.

On the other side of the room, she could hear Jemima shifting in her bed, stretching, before sitting up. "You ok?" She asked, "You sound as though you've run a marathon."

Saga looked over at her roommate. "I..." Further conversation was prevented by the high-pitched ringing of the town's emergency bell. Saga clambered from her bed, hearing Jemima doing the same thing, and they reached the small window in their room at the same time. They could see nothing from where they were, but they could hear the house waking up.

Tymberlee, Onorati and Siobhan could be heard running down the stairs. The twins emerged from their room, looking sleepy-eyed and tousled. Across the hall from Saga and Jemima, Emory and Mannish appeared.

"I smell smoke," Emory said without hesitation.

"From where?" Saga asked, the fire in her dream haunting her. "We couldn't see anything from our window.

"Outside the town gates, towards the Witch's Brew," Tymberlee said as she reached the landing. Onorati and she were somehow already dressed but not in their uniforms, and they barely stopped in their tracks to reach the stairs down to the first floor. Siobhan followed, her stout little form finding it harder on the steps than her tall, elegant roommate.

Tremblay appeared without warning; his already ghostly parlour even paler than Saga had ever thought possible. "It's a student house!" he gasped out as though he had run from the fire to Jimpsee House. "It's Dorbe Manor and no one can find Amyra Dorbe!"

Listening to Tremblay, she had missed Tymberlee changing direction from the stairs down to running into each room, trying to look out the windows to see where she had to go. "Where is it?" she cried.

"Dorbe Manor," Saga gasped out, repeating Tremblay's words.

"Navi!" Jemima cried.

Saga felt her chest constrict as images from the dream flooded her mind. Between Mimir's words, Tremblay's news, and the events of past fires, she could not breathe. "Navi... white hair... oh my god... oh my god..."

"What is it?" Onorati asked, pausing slightly to look at her.

"Come on!" Tymberlee ordered, returning to her quest to get out of the house. "We have some serious distance to cover."

"White hair... in the flames..." Her knees felt weak as she allowed herself to fall back against the doorframe to their room as she closed her eyes, trying to see the dream. "Navi and Annis and Ziva and Edun."

They started down the stairs after Tymberlee and Onorati, but Mannish grabbed Emory's arm. "You can't go."

"Like hell, I'm not going."

"We can't let you," Gedde said, trying to be the voice of reason.

Emory shook his arm free from Mannish's grip and looked at the girls. "Get dressed."

They did not need to be told twice. Saga and Jemima disappeared back into their room, putting on the first clothes they could find before meeting Emory on the stairs. Gedde was trying to block their way, along with Vespers and Mannish.

Perdita, always a voice of reason, spoke up. "Thirty students live at Dorbe Manor. There's also the bar next door. There will be many, many people in need of help. Let them go."

Mannish glared at her. "They're first years."

Saga stared defiantly at him as she stepped up to him, face to face. "My friends, our friends," she motioned to Emory, a sleepy Hermes now sitting on his shoulder, robbing at its eyes with its little, clawed hands, and Jemima. "They live at Dorbe. If you don't let me down those stairs, I'll just find another way. Now move."

Mannish stared back at her before turning his gaze to the defiant faces of Emory Harding and Jemima Dove. "Go, but for crying out loud, come back alive."

DORBE MANOR

It was chaos. The night sky was bright with the crackling flames of Dorbe Manor, and the only permeating smell was the sickening stench of smoke. People from the town and fourth years that Saga barely recognised were everywhere.

"Aunt Rafi!" Jemima cried, spotting the healer. Beside her, Dina Bess, their world religions teacher, knelt tending to a girl coughing up great, black gobs from the smoky fire air. "Aunt Dina."

"What are you doing here?" Dina exclaimed, looking over them. "First years should not-."

Jemima interrupted her aunt. "Our friends live here. We're here to help."

Dina and Raphaella looked at each other. "Ok, Jemima, you can help here," Raphaella finally agreed. "Remember the healing spells I taught you?"

Jemima nodded. "Yes."

"Good. Then follow me," she eyed Saga and Emory. "And you two, stay out of the way."

"SAGA!"

Saga turned at the agonised cry of her name. She turned, as did Emory and Jemima, but Raphaella pulled Jemima away. The figure was shrouded in darkness, and skin as dark as the night sky, making it almost impossible to see the person coming towards them from a direction away from the fire. Hair usually as white as snow was blackened with ash and soot.

"Navi..." Saga started, but as she approached the crying girl, she realised she was wrong. "Annis..." She realised.

"I can't find them," Annis wailed. "I can't find any of them!" Saga's eyes looked towards the inferno that was Dorbe Manor. The school residence housed all of the Jensyn siblings. Ziva, the house prefect, Edun, the troubled second year and Navi, one of Saga's closest friends. "This one's sisters... This one's brother..." Her hands grabbed Saga, the hysteria forcing her to seek comfort and control in her surroundings. "Annis can't find them!" She continued to cry.

Saga looked at Emory as she wrapped her arms tentatively around the older girl. The look of terror that Emory gave her, she was certain matched her own. Nothing. Nothing would be the same after today, of that Saga was certain.

Somewhere, far off, high above Annis's cries and the pained and sorrowful wails of the people around them. The shouts, the cries, the orders being given in the rescue attempt, Saga could hear another wail, another sobbing cry that seemed to echo in her ears with a cold familiarity. She looked around, desperate to see who it was, but she could not find anyone that stood out.

A cracking, creaking sound emanated from the student residence, and rescuers raced out. A man Saga recognised as the cook from the Rolly Polly Kitty carried an unconscious girl. Several others, farmers from the look of them, also ran out, helping coughing students or carrying unconscious or wounded students. Not one of them was one of the Jensyn siblings.

"Where are they?" Saga whispered to Emory.

"I don't know," he whispered back, looking at the sobbing Annis in Saga's arms.

"I..." Saga said, looking at the building. Sparks erupted as the south side of the building collapsed on itself, the fire weakening the structure beyond the point where it could stand on its own. "I need..."

Something. A feeling that she had never felt before pulled on her. It drew her gaze to the fire; it wanted her feet to walk in the direction of the fire. It wanted her to be doing more to help than cradling the distraught sister of her friend. "I have to find Navi," Saga said.

"You can't," Emory chided, but she could see that he, too, wanted to do more than just stand there, uselessly on the sidelines. Hermes had taken off shortly after that had arrived and was sending him images of the chaos from the air.

"Mistress Bess?" Saga said, looking towards the teacher who still sat with a young Dorbe Manor student.

"Yes?" she asked, looking up at them.

"Can you keep Annis with you? We're going to go look for Navi and Edun," She indicated herself and Emory."

"You-," Dina Bess started, but Emory cut in.

"Just amongst the crowds," he insisted.

"You won't go inside, right?"

They both nodded, not daring to open their mouths, and Dina took Annis' silently crying form from Saga and sat her down beside the other girls she was watching. Then, as quickly as they could, Saga and Emory left Dina's line of sight.

"We're not searching the crowds, are we?" Emory asked when he was certain they were out of earshot.

"You can," Saga said, looking at the fire, "But I'm going in."

That ceaseless sobbing from her dream kept ringing in her ears, and she could barely tell if it was a memory or really happening, but it was not coming from the crowd. It was coming from within the old manor house. Ziva, the ever-responsible, the first Dökkálfar prefect at Toserra Sorose, the epitome of courage in so many ways, would not leave the manor house without the students under her charge.

And Edun? Navi? Where were they? Where were almost half of the Dorbe Manor's thirty residents?

"You're not going in alone," Emory said forcefully. "I know that I don't always act it, but Saga, Jemima, Tasso, and Navi, you're my friends. I'm not letting you go after Navi and her family alone."

She wanted the tears in her eyes to stay hidden, but when he reached out to brush one from her cheek, she realised that she had been doing a terrible job all along of pretending she was strong enough to handle this. She gasped out a breath as more tears followed. "I'm scared," she admitted. "I'm scared of going in. I'm scared of not going in."

Surprising her, Emory pulled her close, his arms wrapping around her tightly as she buried her face in his chest. "I've got you," he murmured into her hair. "I'm scared too," he whispered, "But we can do this. You and me," and Saga nodded against his chest.

She drew herself from his embrace and rolled back her shoulders, standing straight as she angrily swiped at the remnants of her tears. "Let's go then."

There were people everywhere. Gawkers, of course, but so many people were trying to help. The inhabitants of the next-door bar trying desperately to prevent the fire from spreading to nearby buildings, townsfolk were helping where they could, and students looking for friends and helping. Tymberlee and Onorati were with other faerie fourth years, casting Arcana spells in the hopes of quelling the raging fire.

"This way," Saga said, pointing in the opposite direction of the faerie casters. Neither faerie would be happy to see them if they caught sight of the first years. Saga led Emory to a side entrance of the manor house that only had a few people nearby, mainly to see if anyone had come out.

"Do you hear that?" Saga asked, still looking for the source of the relentless sobbing she could hear from the noise of the fire and all the activity around it.

"Hear what?"

"The crying..."

"Everyone is."

"No. Not like this. I can hear it over everything else," Saga explained. "It's all I hear."

"Help them."

"Who's there?" Saga cried out, looking around. The sobbing had stopped for the mere moments it had taken for those two words to be spoken, so the source was the same. "Where are you?"

The ghostly apparition of a woman appeared in the flames. *"Help them!"* She cried before fading away.

"Inside," Saga cried. "There are still people inside, Emory!"

"You're seeing the ghost of the house, right?" he asked, following her.

He handed her a wet cloth that she had never noticed him pick up. They tied them around their faces. Hermes landed on Emory's shoulder, glaring at Saga with its toothy grin, and then together, they entered the inferno. The ghost of Dorbe manor, a woman who in life had been Amyra, a poor slave girl before it was discovered that she was a demi-god, the child abandoned and alone in the world until Toserra Sorose had found her, freed her and made a place for her to belong... Much as Astrid had done for Saga.

"That way," Saga said, pointing after the ghost. Amyra Dorbe seemed to blend in with her surroundings, but every time she got too far ahead and they had to stop to find out where she was, Amyra would return and hover just before them. Tears streamed down her ethereal face as she guided them through the burning halls of the Manor House that had been named after her.

Fire licked at the walls and floors of the once-great house. The cracking of wood, the raging sound of the fire was everywhere around them. The heat seemed to engulf everything around them. Emory was perspiring heavily, but despite the superheated air around them, Saga found that she did not appear to feel the heat, not in the same way Emory appeared to be.

"Must be because you are Valkyrie," Emory said, noticing her concerned look at him. "We werewolves are not so keen on fire." His hand swiped at his face, smearing ash and soot across his features. "Keep going."

"Hello?" Saga cried out, hoping that someone would hear her. Maybe then they could find their way. Something flew past her, a swift wind blowing the fire away from her face for a moment.

"Hermes can go ahead," Emory suggested, the homunculus leaping off from his shoulder, its large wings flapping a backdraft at them as it flew away from them. They followed along behind the creature, arms up in front of their faces, a weak effort to keep the fire from them. "I'm seeing something," he said suddenly. The ghost of Amyra Dorbe had stopped and was pointing frantically at what had once been an archway into a common area of the house. "Two people," Emory added. "I can't tell who they are..."

"Come on, we can get them out," Saga said, surging forward to the opening. Fire danced along the frame of the arch, and as they passed through the blazing portal, everything seemed to die away around them, the flames keeping mainly to the walls, except on the far side of the room, where they could see Emory's homunculus hovering over the two figures, he had shown

Emory. The inferno lit them oddly, and from so far away, there was no way to identify them from across the room. "Hello?"

"Over here!"

"We're coming," Saga called back as they began to pick their way through the debris. Looking up, Saga could see that the roof had fallen in, the remnants of the floor above them covering the room with roofing, furniture, and the things that the residents of Dorbe Manor had called their own.

"Saga?"

Saga paused her crossing of the room and squinted at the other side, trying to see who was over there, trapped by the debris. "Navi?"

"Oh, by the Nine Realms, it is you!" Navi cried excitedly. "Sarabia, we're going to be fine!"

"Just hang on," Emory added.

"This one is not going anywhere," Navi threw back. "Sarabia is trapped, and Navi can't get her free."

"We're almost there," Saga's foot slipped on a piece of debris, and she fell, cutting herself on some other broken piece of furniture that she could not identify.

"Saga!" Emory shouted, his hand reaching out to grab her back up to her feet. "You ok?"

She took a cursory look at the wound and shrugged. "Fine. We have to get to Navi and Sarabia." They continued, the homunculus flying erratically between Saga, Emory, Navi and Sarabia. The creature would circle the room, its wings pushing the fire in tiny little dances in the opposite direction of the people.

As soon as Saga and Emory crossed the room, Navi grabbed them both, her strong arms pulling them into a tight hug. "Oh, this one can't believe you're here."

Emory looked thoughtfully at Sarabia. "Caught when the roof came down?"

The girl nodded. "It just about killed us both, and Navi wouldn't leave me..."

Navi motioned to her staff, the beautifully carved staff protruding from the mass. "I tried to lever her free, but I couldn't do that and pull her out."

Emory pulled the staff out and handed it back to Navi. "I'll find something else." He walked a few paces away, looking for a long but thin piece of debris they could use. He picked up a piece of longish wood that might have once been a part of someone's bedframe and tossed it across the gap to Saga. She caught it easily and stuck it back into the hole Emory had retrieved Navi's staff from.

She stopped when she heard the thumping. "What's that?" she asked.

"What's what?" Navi asked, looking around. The walls that remained seemed to shake with the vibrations. "Oh... that?"

Saga looked at her in surprise. "You can hear it?"

"This one can feel it!"

Saga looked around. "Come on. We have to get Sarabia out! Now!" she cried.

"What is that?" the werehyena girl wailed, looking around frantically as, around them, the already broken and unsteady walls of the manor house shook with a ferocity like that of an earthquake or a thundering stampede.

The wild hunt rides again...

The image of the mounted warrior bursting through the wall of the burning house flashed before her eyes mere moments before the wall on the far side of the room exploded into splinters of fiery wood flying everywhere. At first, it was just that one mounted warrior, but then, just as in her dream, more and more descended upon what had once been the common room of Dorbe Manor. With no regard for the debris scattered across the floor, they rode, ran, and flew.

"EMORY!" Saga screamed, trying to catch sight of him. "EMORY!!!"

Hermes hurtled towards them, weaving in and out of ethereal warriors as they attempted to bat and swat at him with their weapons. The small bat-like creature crashed into Saga's chest, her arms instinctively wrapping around the creature.

"Hermes," she gasped from his impact. "Where's Emory?"

Not inclined to answer her in any way, he just looked back towards the horde riding through the common room. He crooned mournfully, his large, bulging eyes searching rapidly for any sign of his master.

"Saga!" Navi cried. "We'll look for Emory."

Reality set in. They still had to free Sarabia from the debris. Saga set Hermes on her shoulder as she had seen Emory do dozens of times since they had been paired during that first Animal Husbandry class, and the creature sat there, docile but crooning as he looked for Emory. She took comfort in the fact that Hermes was there. Homunculi formed unique bonds with their handlers, unable to be far from them for any length of time but also suffering if their masters were injured. Emory was neither dead nor seriously injured. They would have time to find him, and Hermes would help them do it.

She turned her attention to the lever they had set up. "Ok, ready?"

Navi nodded, her hands grasped under Sarabia's armpits, ready to haul the girl out.

"ONE!" Saga screamed, the noise of the fire, the noise of the hoard all too much to be heard. She saw Navi nod, though. "TWO!" She started to press on the lever. "THREE!" With all her might, she pushed down, and nearby, Navi pulled the tall and lanky hyena girl out from the pile of debris.

"Her leg is broken!" Navi screamed.

Certain that Sarabia was free, she let the lever go, the debris falling back to the ground with a crash they could barely hear over everything else. Saga scrambled around to where Navi held Sarabia. The girl not being able to walk was going to be an issue, and they had to get out. Her wet cloth was now dry and it was getting really hard to breath, but she noticed that Navi seemed to be having no trouble at all.

"Come on," she said, sliding her arms under Sarabia's legs and back. "Hold on," she told her, and without comment, Sarabia wrapped her arms around Saga's neck. As Saga lifted her, she cried out in pain.

"I can't."

Saga glanced at the homunculus. The girl was going to be useless anyway; Hermes could, but how would she get Emory's creature to take instruction from her? Homunculi were tiny creatures that did not have much fighting power. They were servants, messengers, and spies. But the one thing they did have was a power toxin that they could inject into an enemy that would put them into a deep sleep. Sarabia would be unable to feel any pain if homunculus bit her.

"Hermes..." She said softly as she stood, careful not to move, not wanting to aggravate Sarabia's injury. "Can you put her to sleep?"

The creature cocked its head to look at her, its large, bulging eyes assessing her, trying to decide what it would do without Emory there. Tears of pain streaked Sarabia's face, and the creature seemed to assess her, too, before turning its gaze on Navi.

"We can look for Emory as soon as she's safe," Navi promised the creature. That seemed to do the trick because as soon as Navi said it, the creature leaned down and bit the hand closest to him. It took only seconds for Sarabia's eyes to close and the pained lines on her face to smooth out.

"Thank you," Saga said to the creature. The horde, the warriors running through the building who never seemed to deviate from their path, only destroying everything that got in their way. It all seemed almost silent without them, the crackling of the fire, the creaking of the building. "I don't see Emory." The ghost of Amyra Dorbe appeared and pointed towards a gap in the fire. "We gotta move," Saga said finally.

They followed Amyra Dorbe from the common room, though Saga kept her eyes constantly peeled for Emory. There was no sign of him anywhere. "The front door is that way," Navi said, pointing down a corridor that Saga had not seen. Amyra nodded in agreement, and Saga turned, taking their advice.

They emerged from the house into the cold night air. Finally able to breathe, Navi and Saga fell to their knees, Saga careful not to hurt Sarabia. From the crowd, Raphaella Damir came running towards them. "What the..."

"NAVI!!!" The cry was from Annis. She hurtled past the healer and engulfed her younger sister in a hug so tight that Saga was not sure if Navi could breathe. "You're safe! You're safe!" A step behind her, blond hair practically glowing in the night, Tasso ran, his glistening faerie wings glowing red and orange as they reflected the light of the fire. He stood there awkwardly as Annis held onto her sister, not letting go. He looked rapidly from Navi, to Saga and with a start, he saw Hermes set upon Saga's shoulder.

"She has a broken leg," Saga told Raphaella as she passed the unconscious werehyena to the healer. "And the homunculus put her to sleep."

Behind the healer, Amyra Dorbe was beckoning to her. "Do not dare re-enter that house," Raphaella ordered. The words were stern, and the angel's eyes burned with a ferocity Saga had only seen on the field during Tourney events with other students.

"I have to," Saga said. "Amyra is guiding me to them." The words had left her mouth without any forethought, and when Raphaella's eyes widened in surprise, Saga realised what she had said. She handed Sarabia to the older woman and stood up. "I can help."

She ran back inside before anyone could stop her.

"SAGA!"

Amyra's wild hair and tear-streaked face hovered three feet in front of Saga at all times. She moved only when Saga needed to change direction. She still sobbed as she watched the house named for her burn. Saga had no idea how many students had been lost or how many had been injured, but she was not done yet. The homunculus, Hermes, sat upon her shoulder, looking this way and that, probably trying to find Emory. Who else was still inside the house? Had anyone found Ziva or Edun?

Suddenly, Hermes leapt from Saga's shoulder, diving down the hall, and Saga took off running after him. "WAIT!" she cried. She would never forgive herself if something happened to Hermes. Emory had become overly fond of the odd creature in the months they had been paired together.

He screeched in delight as from the fire came running a black wolf, large enough for a small child to ride on. "Shadow?" Hermes landed on the wolf's back, his clawed hands grasping into the long black hair of the wolf. Shadow bounded up to her, looking left and right as though searching for someone. One day she would have to figure out where the big wolf kept coming from. He was one of the oddest things about this world, and yet she always valued his presence.

"This way," she said as Amyra eagerly pointed her down one hall. It was a tunnel of fire. The floor warped, the walls and roof burning all around them. Shadow walked beside her, Hermes riding upon his shoulders. Amyra floated before them, leading the way through the burning building. She guided Saga when every direction looked the same. When the fire blinded her and the smoke clouded her vision and made her breathing hard. The ghost's loud sobbing had not receded, but she seemed more content now that some more of her students had escaped. She lifted her finger and pointed. A glimpse of white hair, just like her dreams, sent Saga running, Shadow breaking into an all-out run to keep up with her.

They emerged into a space that might have once been the dining hall of the house and given the demolished walls on either end of the space. Saga guessed they were near the common room where she had retrieved Navi and Sarabia from.

"Ziva!" Saga cried, wondering if the prefect could hear her over the roar of the fire.

White eyes in pitch-black skin turned to look at Saga and the wolf. "Saga," she gasped, coughing as she spoke.

"We need to get you out of here," Saga shouted as she moved closer.

The older girl shook her head. "Z... Ziva hasn't," she coughed. "This one hasn't got them out!"

She was standing before what looked to be two bodies. In her hands, she held her throwing knives and she looked as though she had been fighting. Saga looked around, wondering if she could see either Ziva's foe or the ghosts of the two unmoving students. Maybe they were hovering with Amyra Dorbe, but there was only one ghost in the room. An old warrior with a horned helmet and long beard. He swung a large axe in his hands and snarled.

Saga sidled beside Ziva, "There's something here," Ziva hissed.

Saga nodded slowly, eyeing the warrior as he snarled again and tried to menace her with his axe. Shadow snarled in his direction, and the old warrior recoiled. "Ziva—" Saga tried to say.

"We need to get them out!" Ziva cried, looking over her shoulder at the bodies of the two students. She looked at Saga, and she could see, reflected in the firelight, streaks of tears running down the older girl's face.

Saga crouched, her hand tentatively reaching out for the body of one student. The skin was hard and like nothing she had ever felt before. She found no hint of a pulse beating in the body and wondered if they had been killed by the rampaging hoard rather than the fire. Shadow snuffled at them and let out a piercing whine.

"They're gone," Saga said, her voice cracking. She had no idea who the two students had been, but she had to get Ziva out. Ziva threw one of her knives in the direction of the warrior. How could she see him? He deflected it easily with a spin of his axe and chuckled. Then he charged, his axe raised over his head. "Come on," Saga said, her arms wrapping around the slight girl.

Ziva struggled against Saga's strength. Despite being older, Ziva's slight elfin form was no match for the sturdy strength of Saga's valkyrie body. "NOOO!" she cried, throwing her other knife in the direction of the charging warrior. It struck him, and he roared with fury. The sound rattled the building. Ziva's plaintiff wail was muted by the roar of the fire and the creaking of the upper floors.

"We need to run!" Saga looked around, seeking out the ghost of Amyra Dorbe. Where had she vanished to? "Ziva!" The girl struggled, kicking and attempting to wrestle her way of Saga's bear-like hug as she tried to haul the prefect of Dorbe Manor out of the house the way she and Shadow had come in.

A bony elbow caught Saga in the stomach, and the impact made her loosen her grip on the older girl. Ziva pushed herself free, and Saga lost her balance as Ziva ran back towards the bodies of the two students who had huddled under the kitchen counter together. She fell right in the path of the ghostly warrior.

Saga fell to the floor, fire burning her skin as she skidded into the wall. Shadow bounded after Ziva, his large body flying through the air to catch her. Saga saw him collide with her and bring her to the ground. Ziva cried out, and Saga scrambled away from the burning wall.

"Ziva," She hissed. "They're gone. We have to get out." Saga motioned for Shadow to move, and he slinked off of her as though ready to jump back on at any moment if she tried to escape again.

A groan sounded throughout the building as something above them shifted. Dorbe Manor was a three-story house that was now structurally unsound. There was a lot that could be shifting. Saga hauled Ziva back to her feet, her burned hands screaming in protest as she grasped the other girl tightly.

They made it two steps towards the hall when the floor above them gave way.

VALHALLA

There were cries of horror from outside the house. Saga was almost certain that she could hear someone calling her name, but she didn't know from where. Beneath where she lay, Ziva in her arms, Shadow wriggled, desperate to escape the confines he had been trapped within.

Using what little strength she had, Saga pushed up, and Shadow wriggled himself free. As soon as he had turned on the spot, he started to howl.

"Ziva!" Saga cried, shaking the girl beside her. She did not move. "ZIVA!" Saga cried, hysteria burrowing itself deep within her. "ZIVA!"

Shadow howled, and as he did, a light began to shine within their tiny, caved-in space. Saga had seen many ghosts in the years before she had come to Toserra Sorose and even more since her arrival. The house ghosts hovered around them every time they were at home, but they had always, always died away from her; she had never in all those years seen a ghost separate from its body.

The ethereal form of Ziva Jensyn stood, despite her body lying beside Saga. Saga blinked away tears. "No! No, no, no!" She begged. "No!"

It took a moment for her to realise, though, that it was not Ziva that was glowing. As she reached out a hand to the oldest sister of one of her best friends, Saga realised that her already pale skin was luminescent. She was the one who was glowing. The ethereal form of Ziva smiled weakly as she looked at Saga and Shadow.

There were screams outside and Saga wondered what was happening there. She scrambled to her knees, getting a good look at Ziva for the first time. A piece of flying debris had pierced the girl's body and blood soiled her nightclothes. The stain had likely been growing for some time.

"Ziva..." Saga cried.

"It's ok," Ziva's ghost said softly.

"No! No, it's not ok!" Saga wailed. "Navi and Annis and Edun. They need you! Why didn't you listen to me? Why didn't you come when I asked you to?"

Shadow rubbed his head against Saga's shoulder as he howled, presumably, attempting to draw the attention of the outside rescuers to their location, but they would not come. Not until it was safe. Shadow paused his howling to lick at Saga. She looked down at her hands, disconcerted by their luminescent quality. Then suddenly, she felt herself being lifted into the air and tried letting out a scream. Shadow stilled, staring at her lifting away from him and resumed his howling. Ziva, ethereal and beautiful as the frayed edges of her spirit form started to become a reality. She watched, her ghostly hand resting on Shadow's head. Ziva watched on as Shadow howled. The change to Saga was sudden as wings erupted from her back. Wings of feathered light blinded her to everything around her.

Saga hovered in the air above Ziva and Shadow as the light started to dim; the huge wings seemed to keep her there. Shadow looked up at her, a smug look upon his doggy face as though he had done everything that he needed to do.

"Wow," Ziva said. "A Valkyrie to lead this one to hereafter."

Saga held out her hand to her, and Ziva took it. Shadow seemed to float up to sit beside Saga as they lifted out of the house, as they simply went through the remains of the old house, untouched by the flames of that still raged all around them.

"Heights!" Saga wailed as they left the roof to hover over the scene. People pointed up at them. They could see them, but worse than that, Saga could tell just how far up they were right now. "Oh god... oh god."

Ziva laughed that gentle laugh she had always used when Navi and Saga had said or done something she had found amusing but said nothing.

And then, all of a sudden, everything was gone.

~ * ~

The light died away and their feet touched the ground. Saga stumbled, the weight of the wings on her back disrupting her sense of balance. Her arms fell away from the girl beside her and they stood there, just staring at each other.

"Where are we?" Ziva asked.

Saga shook her head. "I have... I have no idea..."

They stood within a wide-open hall, lined on each side by gigantic pillars, that drew their attention to the end of the room, where a throne of marble and gold stood on a raised dais. No one sat in the throne, but between them and the throne were dozens of tables, each surrounded by a dozen chairs.

At their feet, they heard a groan. "Would one of you help me up?"

Without thinking about it, Saga reached her hand down and felt it grasped by a warm, strong hand. She drew him up and was startled to find Emory staring back at her, shirtless. Her eyes skirted just far enough to realise that he was in fact, not wearing anything.

"Emory!" Ziva gasped. She looked around. "You're not wearing clothes?" she added, "And... Where did you come from?"

Emory's hand went to his hair, scratching his scalp. Something he did when nervous. He looked from Ziva to Saga as he tried to cover himself. "You two look different."

"Why are you here?" Saga cried, looking away from him. "Where is here?" She added in exasperation, looking around. "We need to get back to town."

"How?" Ziva asked, looking around at the expansive space. The grandeur of it was like nothing Saga had ever seen before, but they were the only people present in the space.

"Listen to me!" Emory stated. "You both look different!"

"You do have wings," Ziva conceded.

"It's not just that," Emory interrupted. "You're glowing... and Ziva, you're... you are... well..."

"Well, what?" She asked.

"Welcome."

They all turned in surprise. Standing there was a solid form of a man only Saga recognised. "Mimir."

He nodded. He looked more solid than when she had seen him in the library or the house. His head was attached to his body for the first time. He eyed Saga cautiously. "You have truly become what you were destined to be," he said.

Saga shook her head. "I'm not anything special."

"I beg to differ," he looked at Ziva and bowed his head towards her. "I am sorry for your loss, but your valiant sacrifice is much appreciated."

"Sacrifice?" Ziva asked, looking from him to Saga and Emory, who was trying to back away behind the two girls. "I... I don't understand what you mean."

Saga shrugged, but Emory's presence beside her was distracting. How had he gotten there? Where was there? What was going on? And where were Emory's clothes? "Mimir," Saga said, looking around cautiously. "What... what is this place? And what do you mean by Ziva's sacrifice?"

The old man crossed his arms and gazed at each of them. "What is he doing here?" He shook his head. "Never mind him. You have no memory of what happened?"

They looked at each other and shrugged. "It's not that," Saga said. "It's more that my memories don't make any sense." He nodded at her. "Well... We were inside the house... and..."

"The roof fell in," Emory said, picking up a tunic that seemed to be folded over a chair as though waiting for him. He hurriedly pulled it over his head, his back turned from the girls, relieved to find pants on the chair as well, before looking at Saga and Ziva. "We... we couldn't move Ziva..."

"No... it was more than that..." Saga paused, thinking. There was someone else there... and... then..." Saga looked at them. Confusion etched on her face. "We were outside."

"No... this one... Ziva remembers looking... looking at herself... looking at you... looking at this one," Ziva murmured.

Mimir looked sadly at Ziva. "That was your spirit separating from your body." At the look of confusion that crossed their faces, he sighed. "My dear girl... you... you died tonight..."

"What?" they cried.

"No!" Saga said, shaking her head. "We... we... we got her out... we were outside! We got her out. Shadow and I, we..." Saga stared at Emory as she spoke, still trying to piece together what was happening. How was he there? Where had Shadow come from in the fire? "We..." She returned to Ziva. "We... we were..."

"Floating," Emory said softly. "We were floating above the house... you were all wings and light and... and I couldn't see Ziva... not there... I didn't see her."

"But you weren't there!" Saga cried.

Mimir held up his hand to silence them. "Perhaps I can explain..."

"I can't believe that it actually worked. The valkyrie awoke and opened Valhalla." The voice came from further down the hall, and Saga thought that she might have recognised the voice, but at that moment, she could not place it. There were too many things going on in her head for her to understand what was happening.

Mimir's already deathly pallor seemed to go as white as Ziva's hair. "Run."

"What?" Saga asked.

"Run!" he ordered. His tone left no space for argument or further conversation. "Run."

Emory looked over his shoulder and spotted the mystery speaker. He walked towards them, and it was the first time Saga had ever really gotten a good look at the man. He was tall, taller than anyone she had met, which was saying a lot since almost everyone she met these days was tall. His bulk made him look like a wrestler or... well... a Viking. Four others accompanied him, all similar in appearance to him.

"They're all armed," Mimir warned.

"Odin's beard," Ziva exclaimed.

They stalked towards them, the one in front, Saga recognised. His voice, his movements. He was the man that she had seen outside Astrid's home and in Berfelan's office. "The doxie's already dead. Kill the boy and bring me the valkyrie. My sister was right. She will have her uses."

The man to his immediate left rubbed his hands together eagerly. "And the old man?"

"Leave him. He's of no use to anyone," Vali said.

"RUN!" Mimir roared, and Emory grabbed Saga's hand. He ran, pulling her with him.

Ziva looked at Mimir, and he seemed to nod at her. "We'll hold them off," she said, pulling two small knives from beneath her long jacket. Mimir picked up a large hammer from the table behind him, and they stood there, ready to face the oncoming man and his crowd. "Go!"

Emory pulled Saga after him as she had difficulty deciding where to go or what to do. "Come on," he begged. "They're after you."

Saga shook her head and allowed him to drag her along. She had no idea what was happening or where they were. She also still had no idea how Emory was even there. The wings on her back made it hard to move. They changed her balance, and she felt herself constantly stumbling as Emory pulled her up three small steps and between large pillars lining the grand room. He pulled a sword from a rack they ran by, never letting go of her hand as they ran.

"Get me that girl!" The roar of the man Saga knew to be Vali echoed throughout the great hall just before Mimir's hammer crashed into the floor. Tables, laden with mugs of mead and plates full of food, awaiting the warriors who would serve again in the afterlife, were overturned, food and drink spilling everywhere.

Saga turned back to look, only to see Ziva throw first one knife and then another. They skewered the sleeve of one man to an upturned table and Mimir's hammer swung furiously. Saga never got to see what happened thought, because Emory pulled her past the large pillar and through a door.

He slammed it shut behind them, and together, they leaned back against the door. "Who was that guy?"

Saga shrugged. "I don't know. His name is Vali, he..." She shrugged again. "I have no idea. How are you even here?"

"I was always here," he said, his hand grasping hers tighter. "I never left you."

Saga rubbed at her eyes. "I can't figure anything out anymore."

"What do you know about him? Come on. What's his connection to Mistress Grunborg?" He led the way down a corridor, Saga following along, their hands still clasped. In his free hand, he held the sword before them.

"He was mad at Astrid for her interest in me and I saw him again in Master Berfelan's office," she exclaimed. "They chased me through the school..."

The door they had come through rattled, and Emory pushed her through a door to their left, closing it behind himself as they heard the door to the great hall give way under the assault. Footsteps ran down the hall just outside their hiding spot.

They huddled together, their ears to the door. "Where'd they go?" One of Vali's henchmen asked from the far side of the door.

"I don't know. Just find them!" the other replied.

"Yeah!" The first henchman said, his voice full of glee. "I was looking forward to skinning that werewolf."

Beside her, their hands still firmly grasped, Saga felt Emory shiver, and suddenly it clicked. She could not believe how stupid she had been. The answer had been in front of her the entire time. She had never seen Shadow and Emory at the same time. Not in Yggdrasil City and not in Nýr Ásgardr. She remembered Lady Harding complaining that Emory was never where she wanted him to be, that he was always running off. But Shadow had been with her. And then later, not being able to find Shadow after Emory had appeared in the various shops. There had also been Astrid's insistence that he was not her dog, but his appearance in Nýr Ásgardr when they left him back in the tree city. How he got into Jimpsee House and his apparent absence the night of her first detention when Shadow had walked her back to the house.

"You're Shadow," she whispered, eyes wide as she stared at him.

"Shh," Emory hissed, but he nodded.

"But—" She tried again.

"Not now," he hissed, pushing his ear even harder into the door.

With him listening to what was going on outside, Saga took the time to look around the room they found themselves in. It was sparse, but it appeared as though it had once been some sort of sleeping quarters. Furs covered pallets that were lined up like the rooms in some of the group homes she had lived in. There was another door on the far side of the room.

"Come on," she said, drawing him away from the door. Emory allowed himself to be dragged away, but he kept his eyes on the door just in case and his sword ready in his free hand. The handle of the door they had just left rattled.

"This one's locked!" The man who wanted to skin Emory exclaimed.

"Probably lots of them are locked," His partner insisted.

"Or this is where they're hiding."

"Thor's Hammer!" Emory whispered while Saga muttered, "Crap!" They were halfway across the room when the two men outside went to the door with what sounded like a giant hammer. An axe blade came through the door. It would not be long until they got themselves through the door.

"There!" Saga said, pointing at a pile of furs. They dived for it, pulling the furs over their heads and trying to ensure they were covered before the door caved in. Emory pulled his foot in and wrapped his arms around her, making them as small as possible. She remembered snuggling with Shadow and realised that Shadow and Emory actually smelled similar, or maybe it was the fact that they both smelled like smoke and ash and death.

The door crashed open, and they tightened their grip on each other. They could hear the two men moving around in the room. "There's nothing here."

The other one did not seem as sure, though, as he walked around the room, with slow, heavy footsteps. They heard him stop by the pile of furs they had buried themselves in. He picked something up from the floor. Emory seemed to tense as they waited. "What about this?"

"It's a sword. What about it? Look around. We're in a hall of fallen warriors. There are weapons everywhere." The other man grunted and tossed the sword onto the pile of furs. It landed harmlessly on them.

"What is going on in here?" Vali's booming voice filled the room. "Nap time?"

"No, my Lord. We were looking for the girl."

He was given no time for further explanation, though. "Leave the girl to me and find me Odin's spear."

"Saga? Emory?" Ziva's tentative voice came from the broken door. "Are you guys in here?" Saga shifted awkwardly. She had no idea how long she and Emory had been holed up in the pile of furs, but with Ziva's appearance, she suddenly realised just how close she and Emory were. They scrambled apart, and the furs that were covering them fell away. "Oh, there you two are," her voice trailed away as she tried to hold back a giggle.

"Are they gone?" Saga asked, climbing up and out of the furs while not looking at Emory.

"Yeah, Mimir says that they'll be a while looking for Odin's spear. That is what Vali really wants, something about solidifying his claim to Asgard."

Emory scrambled down the furs behind Saga and reached back for the sword. His face was as red as he inspected the placement of his feet on the floor. Anything to not look at Saga and to not look at Ziva's grinning face. Ziva led them back through the main hall, where Mimir half-heartedly picked up fallen chairs and looked up when they entered.

"Oh, thank Odin's beard, you are all right," he exclaimed. "You must leave this place! At once."

"We don't even know where this is," Saga told him.

"This," Mimir motioned to the hall they stood in. "Is the Hall of Valhalla. No, do not speak. No one living has stepped foot in this place since Ragnarök. No spirit of the dead has been brought here since the last valkyrie disappeared from the Nine Realms."

"Who were those people?" Ziva asked, craning her head to see if they were coming back.

"There is an enemy faction stirring things up amongst the descendants of the Æsir and the Vanir. They believe the deaths of Odin and Thor left a power vacuum and now believe that a new Ragnarök will secure them a new leader."

"That's ridiculous," Emory said. "And what's that got to do with those men following us here?"

"Only three types of people can enter Valhalla," Mimir explained, holding up his hand, and he ticked off each point by raising a finger. "The chosen dead like Ms Jensyn, a Valkyrie like Ms Carolle or a Demi-God."

"What about me?"

Mimir looked at Emory, who held his hand up as though he was trying to ask a question in class. "Yes, well... You, like the men who accompanied Vali, are an interesting fourth party. The invited. Presumably, a weakness caused by the hall opening for the first time to welcome Ms Jensyn."

"But what happened at Dorbe Manor? And all the other places?" Emory asked.

Mimir sighed, but it was Saga who answered. "The Wild Hunt, but I do not understand, if The Hunt was ridden by Odin and the Einherjar... Well... if they died at Ragnarök..."

"Then how have they ridden through Nýr Ásgardr all those times since you came to town?" Mimir asked. "By calling on the memories of the spirits. All across the land, there are remnants, embedded memories of past events. Some of these exist from a time long before the great war. The Hunt used to ride those paths. Those memories, those echoes... They... they were summoned from the depths of the realms to wreak havoc and ultimately to kill people," he looked at Saga, "All so that you would bring a soul here, opening the hall."

"Wa... wai... wait," Saga said, holding her hands out. "Do not tell me that Ziva and all those other people are... that they're dead because... because... because I..." She backed away from the group, "No..."

"Saga!" Ziva exclaimed.

"No... I'm so... so... sorry... Ziva... Oh my god... Navi is never going... Ziva!"

"Saga!" Ziva called as she continued to back away.

"No... No... No... all those people dead... Because of me..." She was gasping for breath, tears streaming down her face. She stumbled on a platter strewn across the floor. Without her even realising it, Emory was beside her, ensuring she did not fall.

"None of this is your fault," he said softly. He looked towards Mimir, "Right?"

"Right," The old man agreed. Ziva moved to join them, but Mimir rested a hand on her shoulder, keeping her in place. "None of this is your fault. As I have told you, the return of the Valkyries was inevitable. Their belief that Odin's spear is here is the true problem. Their belief that the hole left by Odin needs to be filled by one of them. No, none of these things needed to happen except that the two of you must go. Vali does want you," he stared at Emory. "And you, boy, take care of her."

Disappearing and reappearing against their will was becoming something of a habit. When they opened their eyes again, Saga found herself, still held by Emory, on the grass outside Dorbe Manor. The fire had died down to a smouldering mess that displayed a hulk of rubble that had once been the house.

Around them, people were screaming, crying, and shouting orders.

Saga clung to Emory; her fingers wrapped tightly in his shirt as sobs wracked her body. "I've got you," he said into her hair, burying his face there so that passers-by could not see his own tear-streaked face.

"Emory! Saga!"

Emory looked up, looking for the caller, and he spotted Tasso, flanked by Navi and Annis. Behind him stood a tall, willowy elf boy with a Prefect's uniform jacket worn over his nightshirt. Navi broke from them, falling to her knees beside Emory and Saga.

"What happened in there?" She asked, reaching out to grip sagas arm. "Where's Ziva?"

Saga looked up at Emory and tried to sit herself up rather than stay safe and secure in his arms. She didn't want to face this, but she would have to. She knew that. Her failure would irrevocably affect her best friend, and there was nothing she could do about that. The chill from the ice and water spells was starting to permeate the air. Saga shivered. She didn't know if it was from the growing chill in the air, fear or something else, but Emory gripped her tighter against him.

"Saga? Emory?" Tymberlee asked, the voice of calm reassurance amongst all the chaos and disaster, despite a burning desire to tell them off for not only being there but for going inside the burning house. "Did you manage to find Ziva or anyone else?"

"We found her and two others," Saga said, but as she tried to speak again, it was as though the words would get stuck in her throat, and nothing but harsh choking sounds would come out. The words that needed to be said, along with their impact known, physically cut at her even as she tried to tell Annis and Navi the fate of their oldest sister.

"NAVI! ANNIS! ZIVA!" The panicked voice cut across everything as Edun came pounding over to them, his clothes singed, his hair covered in soot and maybe even burned shorter in some parts. He grabbed Annis, hugging her tight against him, before pulling Navi to her feet and crushing her to his chest and bear-hugging her. "You're ok, you're ok, he murmured again and again.

"Breath," Navi coughed out. "Can't breathe."

Edun let go and looked around. "Where's Ziva?"

While Edun had grabbed at his sisters, hugging them close as though the world was about to end, Saga struggled out of Emory's grasp, to wind up sitting next to him on the grass. Saga tried to push herself up, but her hands burned at the touch of the ground beneath her, so she stayed where she was, willing the pain to go away.

Emory tried to accept a hand from the willowy elf with the Prefects' jacket but his own hands stung at the contract. Saga wasn't sure, but she was almost certain that she had seen him several times with Ziva. He looked worried and drawn, as though he was bursting to ask a question, but showing restraint in favour of the three dark elves. He let go, his hands burned and blistered. Saga looked at her own, realising that they looked the same.

"Guys," Edun pushed, "Where's our sister?"

Saga and Emory looked over at each other and Saga tried again to form words, but they just kept catching in her throat.

Emory looked at her, the sadness present deep within his eyes and he nodded to her as though to say it was ok, he would do this. He could do that for her. "Ziva... she... was trying to get two students out," he started.

Edun clutched at Navi and Annis, but the willowy, nameless prefect's hand went to his mouth. He glanced at Tymberlee who looked as though maybe she was catching on. She reached out, put her hand on the boy's shoulder and together they waited.

"She either couldn't or wouldn't accept that they were dead," Emory added, his voice thick with emotion. "We tried... we tried to haul her out," he bit his lip, looking at Navi and Annis. "We tried..."

"She wouldn't come," Saga managed, all eyes shifted to her as they waited for more of the story. Anything to finally tell them what had happened. "When we pulled her away, she fought us." Saga closed her eyes, replaying the scene in her head. Ziva's refusal to come, her refusal to believe that they could not save those two students despite the charred feeling of the skin. The roof fell in, burying them beneath burning rubble. Saga tried to rub at her face, but her hands burned at the contact and she cringed.

"The roof fell in," Emory said, picking up the story when it became evident that Saga couldn't any longer. "The roof fell in—"

"And what?" Edun demanded.

"She didn't make it out," Saga whispered, almost hoping that they wouldn't hear her, but they did.

The silence was deafening. It was as though all of the noise and chaos around them just ceased at that moment as everyone stood there, staring at them. And then Navi let out a heart-rending wail that Saga was sure she would remember for the rest of her life. The little dark elf collapsed against her brother, who struggled to hold her up on hand as Annis seemed to stare at the remains of Dorbe Manor, her face a landscape of anguish as silent tears rolled down her cheeks, the drops falling from her chin.

Edun struggled with Navi, her wailing cries loud enough and so full of heartbreak bringing people over from around the sight. "Navs," he said, letting go of Annis to try and hold his youngest sister up, but Saga could see that he looked ashen, his ebony skin looking dirty grey, even in the uneven light of the night. He breathed heavily, as though he was restraining himself from a bigger, more volatile reaction as he tried to pull Navi tighter against him.

"No, no, no, no!" she wailed, fighting against his attempts to comfort her. "ZIVA!"

The boy with Tymberlee seemed to sag against the fairy girl, his lips mouthing Ziva's name as he tried to not let his obvious grief show.

"Sid," Tymberlee said softly, "Come on."

He shook his head as he dragged his hands down his face, creating streaks in the soot that had gathered there. "Not yet."

Tymberlee nodded and looked over the scene, not sure what to say to any of them. Finally, she asked. "How did you get out?" That caught almost everyone's attention. Edun was still holding it together, although barely, and Navi was sobbing into his chest now as Annis just stared. "And what was with the light show? What happened up there?" She nodded towards the night sky above the house.

"I don't know how we got out," Saga said, glancing over her shoulder towards the remains of the house. It would be a recovery effort now to find the bodies of those they hadn't been able to save. The two in the kitchen, Ziva.

Tymberlee looked ready to ask more questions. She seemed to be the only one that could, but before she could, Jemima appeared, followed closely by her aunt, Raphaella. "Saga! Emory!" Jemima gasped.

"Make some room," Raphaella demanded. "Stop badgering them. All of you. Those burns on their hands and the smoke they took in. I'm taking both of them to the healing house."

Emory stood slowly, realising that while he may not have felt anything while they had been in Valhalla, his hands and his feet were actually burned. He stumbled, only to be caught by Saga. "Ow," she gasped, the pain in her own hands becoming unbearable.

"Come on you two," Raphaella ordered.

The boy Tymberlee had called Sid stepped away from the fairy girl and slipped his shoulder under Emory's arm. "Come on. I'll help you." Tymberlee appeared on Emory's other side, removing his weight from where he had fallen against Saga. She nodded to him, and together, they led Emory away, attempting to keep his burnt feet free from the ground.

Jemima looked between Saga, who was staring at her hands and Navi and Annis, who was still cradled against Edun, then to Tasso. "You'll take care of them?" He nodded, going to Edun and extracting Navi from him so that the older boy could concentrate on his other sister. Jemima nodded, looking around, the devastation again bringing tears to her eyes. She had work to do to get her friends through this night.

Saga allowed Jemima to lead her away, but her eyes stayed fixed on the remnants of Dorbe Manor, where she could still see, when she closed her eyes, the bodies of those two students Ziva had been trying to save, curled up together in the kitchen. Ziva's spirit separating from her body.

Around them, she could still see the ghost of Amyra Dorbe. Nearby her, she saw five other ghosts. Five, no six people had died tonight—all students of the house. The students looked around, scared and afraid as Amyra tried to guide them, as several glowing, winged forms began to appear. Angels of Death. Amyra pointed them out to the children who had once been in her care, and one by one, the angels took them hopefully to that somewhere better that was so often talked about.

"Jemima," Saga said right before her legs gave out. She slid almost to the ground before Jemima was able to get a grip on her, but Saga barely noticed as the world went black around her.

AFTERMATH

"They're coming along nicely," Raphaella said as she inspected Saga's hands. "Impressive, seeing as how it has only been a week."

Saga did not react. Behind her, Tymberlee waited, arms crossed over her chest, concern etched across her face. As house prefect, she had visited Emory while his feet recovered and brought Saga in for her appointments. "It's getting emptier in here," she commented, looking around at the beds that were no longer constantly filled with the victims of the Dorbe Manor fire.

"Many have gone home to their parents, others off to temporary accommodations at other houses," Raphaella agreed. "Many more from the school and the city are receiving recurring treatment for injuries they sustained that night." Raphaella stood up, "I'm just going to get some ointment," she directed her next words to Saga. "You need to use it day and night, but I don't think you need the bandages anymore."

"I'll make sure she uses it," Tymberlee stated.

"The boy too. I'm sending him home with you today. I also want him to avoid using his feet as much as possible."

As Raphaella walked away, Tymberlee patted Saga on the shoulder. "I'll be right back," and she followed the old angel down the long row of beds to the cupboard and workstation on the far side of the room for medicine dispensing and creation. "Matron Damir?"

"Yes, dear?" She asked, bustling around with ointments.

"I'm... I'm worried about Saga," she looked back over her shoulder at where the girl sat, unmoving on the bed, her hands resting in her lap.

Raphaella paused her movements. "Yes... Jemima has told me that she, too, is concerned. I can't say that I disagree with your concerns."

"What should we be doing?"

"You're doing it," Raphaella insisted. "Caring. Being there. She will talk when the time is right."

"I can't help feeling as though none of it is enough," Tymberlee said with a frown.

"This situation is inexplicable. It is not something anyone ever expected to be in your job description as a house Prefect. I also understand that you have some of the survivors staying with you?"

"Yes, the Jensyn sisters. Their brother didn't want to stay with us," she sighed heavily. "They are as reticent as... well... they're grieving the loss of their sister... we all are... Ziva was..."

Raphaella Damir put a hand on Tymberlee's arm. "Perhaps your main concern should be caring for yourself, dear girl before you are unable to function. You lost friends. You are watching people you care about suffer greatly, you are taking extra responsibilities in their care..."

Tymberlee looked back at the girl she had brought in. Emory sat beside her. Perhaps having the boy back home would help her. He seemed to have a remarkable ability to bring her out of her despondent moods, but it was as though she had not even noticed his appearance. Tymberlee sighed, "I'm fine. Or at least I will be in time."

Raphaella nodded, and together, they walked back to where Saga and Emory waited. She handed both of them their ointment. "Use. Twice a day. On your hands, and you on your hands and feet." She said first to Saga and then to Emory.

"Yes, Matron Damir," Emory said. Beside him, Saga nodded. Emory looked from Saga to the others, his own concern evident even though this was the first time he had seen her since the night of the fire. He could tell that not all was right with her.

~ * ~

The loss of Dorbe Manor lingered over the entire town of Nýr Ásgardr. The hulking mass of the house stood outside the town as a stark reminder, and pictures of the six students lost on the night of the fire hung on the notice board in the town square. Flowers filled the immediate area, and somehow, it still smelled like smoke to Saga. She stood before the signboard. Their names and sketches of each of them in life, holding her attention.

The sketch of Ziva was of her in uniform. A standard one done of all house prefects. It did not do her justice, Saga thought. In her mind's eye, she could see the older girl laughing, smiling at her siblings as they had messed around. The stern, displeased look as she had accompanied Astrid to pick her and Navi up from the Guard's tower. This picture... It did not, could not, show everything that Ziva had been. She guessed that the same could be said for all of those who had been lost.

Gone from the Nine Realms too soon.
In the hearts and memories of Toserra Sorose forever.

-Ziva Jensyn-
Dorbe Manor Prefect. Dökkálfar.
The first Dökkálfar to attend Toserra Sorose Academy.
Beloved by all who knew her, she is survived by her sisters,
Annis and Navi and her brother Edun.

-Euseph Chernus-
Fourth Year. Angel.
A talented swordsman whose skill will be missed on the field.
He is survived by his parents and younger brother, Sendhil.

-Sandrine Zuaiter-
Fourth Year. Siren.
A much-admired songstress who delighted any crowd.
She is survived by her mother and older sister.

-Efremova Nzeky-
Third Year. Faerie.
A talented arcanist with a love of adventure.
She is survived by her parents and siblings.

-Laitila Panthaky-
Second Year. Werebear.
Always there with a helping hand for anyone in need.
She will be sorely missed.

-Elimu Sinyor-
Second Year. Werehyena.
Always quick with a joke. His boisterous laughter will be missed.

"It will be many years before we recover from this," a voice said behind her.

Saga craned her head to see Raphaella Damir standing beside her. She, too, inspected the names before sighing and adding one more to the list. Together, they stood and inspected the seventh addition to the list.

-Omar Barzilay-
First Year. Ljósálfar.

No comment on who he had been in life was added. "He died this morning," Raphaella explained. "I want to tell you that your friends need you, but you need to find peace within yourself first."

"They're all dead. Ziva and Omar and all the others," Saga said, her fingers reaching out to trace the boy's name. She hadn't really known him, but she remembered facing him in her one and only disastrous joust. "They're all dead because of me. Because people wanted to use me," she pointed at the older notices listing the names of the dead at the previous fires. "They're all dead. All of them, because of me... they're dead, so I could bring my best friend's sister to Valhalla. Where is that fair? How can I ever look at Navi or Annis or any of them with that hanging over me? This is all my fault. All of it." Her voice had risen as she had spoken and she was almost screaming her anguish by the time she finished. Fresh tears rolling down her cheeks as she stood there before the town notice board.

"Ziva went to Valhalla? Not to Fólkvangr?" Raphaella seemed surprised. "Fitting, I suppose. She was that kind of girl."

"And what about the others?" Saga asked. "Sindre Mozhan died rescuing those from the Jisook Farm fire. Was he not worthy?"

"They were all worthy dear girl," Raphaella said, wrapping an arm around Saga's shoulder. "That is not on you."

"Maybe not," Saga said. It was nice to hear it from someone other than Emory. "But I will stop them."

"Make right with your friends. I see what you and Navi and Jemima, and Emory are doing. That is where you can help," Raphaella insisted.

Saga's eyes blazed with a fire no one had seen since the night of the fire. "No... I know who caused this, and I'm going to stop them."

"Saga..." Raphaella tried. "That... that was not what I meant."

"Thanks, Matron Damir," Saga said before turning and heading back for Jimpsee house.

There was a strange silence over the town, and it seemed as though the townspeople eyed each of the students that neared them with a wariness born of concern and despair. The burns on her hands identified her as someone who had been at the fire that night, and people gave her a wide berth. She had heard talk of the glowing girl in the sky and knew that they were talking about her. She wondered if they knew it had been her, and every time she heard the talk, she felt the need to shy away from the conversation before someone had the opportunity to realise it. She heard everything, always listening in for news of Vali and his men.

This was why when the fist meant for her face came towards her, she could easily step out of the way, leaving her attacker to stumble past, trying hopelessly to reclaim their balance. Then she reached out and grabbed his arm, preventing him from falling to the ground. He shook her off.

"I don't need your help," he sneered.

"I wasn't offering any," Saga said before turning and continuing on her way back home.

"Is that all you have to say?" he cried, running after her. "After what you did, is that all you have to say?"

She had been dreading this day somewhere in the back of her mind whenever her thoughts had managed to dredge themselves up from the depths of self-loathing and despair. The thought of what would happen if she allowed herself to come face to face with one of Ziva's siblings. She had actively avoided Navi and Annis since that day, not able to look either girl in the face. Edun, no one had really seen him. His appearance, though, was not unexpected, at least not to Saga. He was quick to anger and blame and had no idea who was really to blame, so of course, he would turn on the only one he knew for sure had failed his sister.

She did not want to talk to Edun. The hot-headed boy had never liked her and had resented his sisters engaging with her during their time in Yggdrasil. Still, she had heard just how worried they were about him. She had seen his bouts during Tourney and the effects of his victories. Edun had been an angry young man before his sister's death. She had no idea what would happen without Ziva holding him in check.

He grabbed at her, his hand clasping around her elbow, swinging her around to him. "You're seriously just going to walk away from me?"

"I don't know what you want from me, Edun," she said softly.

"I want to know why my sister is dead. I want to know what part you played. I want to know what you did to her!" He screamed in her face, "You did something to her!"

Saga looked down at her feet. Looking at him was too painful. He looked so much like his sisters... or maybe it was her and an inability to really see the differences that were there. "I...." His grip on her tightened, and she saw a glint of silver, no, steel in his other hand. "Edun," she gasped.

He shook her, the knife in his hand becoming more visible. "I need to know!"

"You're not looking for answers," Saga said, "You're looking for someone to blame. I failed to save her, so I'm the easy choice." Maybe it would be easier if she let Edun have his way. She would not have to live with the pain of her failure. She would not have to fear seeing her best friend. This weight would not follow her around anymore. The scars on her hands would always be a constant reminder.

What neither of them noticed was another head of white hair observing them. When the knife came out, she turned and ran, only one destination in mind.

Saga wrenched her arm free and turned away from him. He stomped along, following her every step, neither of them noticing where in town they were going.

"You want to blame me, Edun? Go right ahead. I'll take it. I deserve it for not doing more but get out of my way so that I can find the people who are really responsible for taking Ziva from you."

Edun's step faltered, but he continued to follow her. "Why are you avoiding Navi?" It was Saga's turn to pause, but she shook her head and continued. "Why?" he cried. "She needs you!"

Saga shuddered. "No, she doesn't."

"How would you know? Have you asked?" He pressed.

Saga turned on him. "It's not like you've been around either, Edun. You abandoned Navi and Annis long before Ziva died." She poked him in the chest with each of his sister's names. "And it's you they want with them, not me."

She sensed the blade before she saw it. She ducked, falling into a roll, and she came up in front of Edun. Lost in their world and concentrating only on one another, they had never noticed the group coming in to surround them as they had proceeded down a dark street of Nýr Ásgardr. They dressed the same as Vali's men in Valhalla, each carrying a sword.

"What are you doing?" Edun snarled, pushing her aside and brandishing his dagger at them. Saga was unarmed, having not taken her staff with her when she went into town to see the memorial. Her hands, still sore from the burns, had not been able to handle carrying it. "Who are these idiots?"

Saga narrowed her eyes at them and shifted into a fighting stance. "They're the ones responsible for Ziva's death."

Edun's eyes flashed with rage before he launched himself at the nearest man. Saga ducked as the one nearest her swung his sword at her. He had the reach, and she had nothing. Edun only had that small dagger. They were screwed. Edun's bravado in battle would only get them so far.

"Saga!" She turned her head, and there stood Astrid, Navi at her side. Navi carried her staff, and Astrid carried not only the sword on her hip but one in her hand that, after slashing at the man closest to her, she tossed to Saga. As she leapt into the air to try and catch it, she felt one of them tugging at her, pulling her back down, trying to prevent her from acquiring a weapon of her own. She tried to kick at him, her foot connecting with his knee, not only knocking him to the ground but giving her a little extra height. The hilt of the sword slid into her hand, the soft leather wrapped around the hilt rubbing painfully against the healing burns on her hands, and she came back down to the ground with a slash of the sword. A grungy woman with dreads piled high on her head caught on the arm, a dark gash welling with blood. She screamed in agony. She fell back, not wanting to be in the midst of the fray anymore.

Astrid, the weapons master that she was, easily held her own against two of them. Navi had her staff spinning around her, fending off anyone that attempted to approach. As Saga scanned the melee, though, she spotted Edun struggling against a man twice his size. It appeared that Edun had to rely on his smaller size and his natural speed to avoid getting hit and was not making any headway. She skidded under the feet of one attacker, and he fell to the floor at Navi's feet. Saga did not wait to see what the small elf girl did with the man, though. Instead, she came to her feet just as Edun took a blow to the head from a sword pommel.

He staggered, his hand releasing his grip on his dagger. It clattered to the floor, only to be kicked away by the foot of the man who had hit him as he raised his sword above his head, ready to take Edun's head off in one foul sweep.

Saga ran. She found herself in front of Edun, sword above her own head, to take the blow that rang with steel on steel. The man pressed harder against her. "Move!" She hissed at Edun, and he scrambled back up to his feet. She knew that hand to hand, he was a ruthless fighter.

He moved so that they were back-to-back. "Now what?" he asked, eyeing Astrid and Navi.

"Now you give us the girl," The man closest to Edun said. "Give us the girl, and everything ends.

They turned so that Saga was facing the speaker. "You want me? You're going to have to kill me first." They did not want her dead, and that she knew. They needed her alive. They needed her to open the way to Valhalla, not that she knew how to do that. "Edun, now!"

Together they separated and launched themselves at the fighters directly in front of them. Edun's small, lithe form slid past the blade of his attacker's sword, and he could round on the guy from behind while Saga clashed, sword against sword.

"Guards! City guards!" One woman screamed. She had not been a part of the confrontation, turning out to only be their lookout. Her words halted the battle until the group's apparent leader ordered them to flee.

"You lot, too," Astrid ordered. "Meet back at your place," Astrid directed towards Saga. Saga nodded and grabbed Edun while Navi and Astrid took off in the other direction.

"He could have killed you," Edun panted. "Why did you protect me?"

"Why wouldn't I?" Saga cried. "Come on, run! We don't want to get caught by the guard."

"What? Don't want to get caught with me?"

"No, you don't want to get caught with me after the trouble Navi and I got into at the Kitty!" And with that, she ran, pulling him along behind her. Edun, for once, shut up and allowed her to drag him along. She dragged him around through the back entrance of Jimpsee House. They burst into the kitchen, startling the twins. Perdita dropped her plate of sandwiches. The plate shattered across the floor, sending pieces of crockery, bread, and salad everywhere. Percival knocked two glasses of orange juice from the bench, and the glass shards and juice were added to the mess.

"What in the Nine Realms are you two doing?" Perdita cried, her hands on her chest. Her nose, reminiscent of the rabbit she was, was twitching. She leaned in. "You two smell like blood and adrenaline. What happened?"

"Nothing!" They chorused together.

Percival raised an eyebrow. "You're waving that sword around like there's something wrong."

Saga looked down at her hand, startled to find that he was right. She was wielding a sword. She had never taken the chance to have a good look at it. Astrid had thrown it to her in the heat of battle, and it had felt like an extension of herself. She had always performed well in the swordplay tourney matches, but this sword, unlike any she had ever wielded in the past, had felt as though it had been an extension of herself. She had barely thought about the action she intended to take, and her body had moved. There had been unity between herself and the weapon, the kind that Astrid had spoken of, the kind she had read about in novels.

She had forgotten that it was still in her hand. Beside her, Edun attempted to discreetly resheath that dagger he must have managed to reclaim during the battle. Saga looked around awkwardly. She had no sheath for the weapon. "Umm..."

"Is Navi here?" Edun asked.

Perdita frowned. "I don't know."

The front door slammed, and they could hear thundering footsteps coming in. "Saga? Edun?"

"Navi!" Saga breathed out in relief.

Edun pushed past her and into the hall. "Navi!" he exclaimed, and Saga followed him out, leaving Percival and Perdita standing there staring.

~*~

"What in the Nine Realms happened out there?" Astrid asked when the four of them stood in the hallway. "Navi comes bursting into my place saying you two are fighting, and when we come back, you're under attack from that mob."

Edun started to speak, but Saga cut him off. "We were just having a bit of a disagreement," she smiled sadly at Navi. "Nothing to be worried about."

"But—" she tried, but nothing else came out.

Edun looked at Saga but nodded when she glared at him. "Yeah... we were just..."

"Y... y... you," Navi stammered, pointing at Edun.

"Thank you for showing up when you did, though," Saga said, "Here," she held the sword out to Astrid.

Astrid eyed her. That mysterious look she sometimes got over her features as she thought about something. Instead of taking the sword from Saga, she removed the sheath she had strapped to her back and held it out to the girl. "Why don't you keep it?" she suggested.

Saga blinked in surprise and confusion. "Huh?"

"It's a Norse blade," Astrid explained. "You looked good wielding it. Keep it." She looked as though she wanted to say more but instead asked. "Who were those people?"

Edun shifted so that he was leaning against the bannister of the stairs, arms crossed over his chest. "You said that they were the people who killed Ziva."

Navi gasped in surprise, her hands covering her mouth and tears appearing in the corners of her eyes. She said nothing, waiting for Saga to speak.

Saga gulped. "When... when... when Emory and I were in Valhalla with..." she trailed off, looking at Navi and Edun. She knew that Emory had explained to the others everything that had happened between disappearing from the fire to reappearing back outside that night, but that didn't make saying the words any easier. Then, she took a deep breath and said, "When Emory and I were in Valhalla with Ziva... we... we were attacked... this man... Vali... he appeared with men dressed just like them... they... they said that they had been waiting... waiting for me to open Valhalla so they could find Odin's spear."

Astrid cursed under her breath. "You have got to be kidding me, he thinks it's in Valhalla," She shook her head. "The sheer insanity of that man."

"But..." Navi interrupted softly. "What does this have to do with Ziva?"

Saga sighed. "The fires... all of them..." Saga's throat felt tight as she tried to speak. "They... they were all intended for people to die... for the person..."

"For the person worthy of Valhalla," Astrid finished for her. "Ziva was worthy of Valhalla, and so it opened." Saga just nodded. "And they did it all because they think the spear is there. Damnit, Vali is such an..."

"How do you know him?" Saga asked in a small voice. "And how does Master Berfelan know him?"

"So... why exactly is our sister dead? What is this spear?" Edun asked, looking between Saga and Astrid.

"Gungnir," Astrid said simply. "Odin's spear. Vali is the head of a group that believes Odin's throne must be filled. The group itself has two factions. Those who think it should be an heir of the Æsir and those who think it should be an heir of the Vanir."

"What does that even mean?" Edun asked harshly.

"To you? Probably nothing. To those whose blood runs with that of either faction, much," Astrid sighed. "All was supposed to be fixed with a child born of both bloodlines." A deep sadness seemed to consume her. "I know the loss and the grief you are feeling. Ziva's death was as meaningless as many others have been."

"This makes no sense," Saga said. "Why are we just standing here? You know where to find this Vali guy!"

"So, how do we get back at them?" Edun asked.

"We?" Astrid asked. "There is no we. You all have enough to deal with. I will bring this to Headmaster Gotts. We, the staff, will deal with this." She turned and headed to the door of the house. Hand on the handle, she turned to Saga. "Keep that sword safe. It's no ordinary blade."

Then she was gone. Edun shuffled his feet awkwardly, looking up and down the hall. "I'm uhh," he said, "I'm going to go."

"You could stay here," Saga said, "With your sisters. Tymberlee said it would be fine."

Edun shook his head, though. "Nuh... I uhh..." He shook his head again. "No thanks."

He headed towards the door. "Edun!" Navi cried. "Edun."

"Navi," he said, turning to her. He pulled her into a hug before kissing her on the forehead and walking out the door.

"But," she sighed and cried as Edun hopped down the front stairs, looking both ways before heading off down the street.

Saga stood there, watching as her friend seemed to deflate into herself at her brother's departure. She wanted to say something to make her feel better, but what could she say? This was all her fault. She stepped backwards, trying to retreat, but the sword banged against the rack of shoes in the hall, and Navi turned to face Saga, her face glistening with tears.

"W... w... where are you going?" she asked, and Saga hated herself for being the cause of the stutter.

"I..." Suddenly, her feet were the most interesting things, and she stared at them as they shuffled uncomfortably, itching to get out.

"W... w... why won't you talk to Navi? D... d... did this one do something wrong?"

Saga's feet moved without conscious thought as she crossed the hall and took Navi's hands in her own. The small dark elf was trembling." No!" Saga exclaimed. "No, no, you haven't done anything wrong."

Navi stared at their hands, intertwined as they were and gripped Saga's harder. "Then why?"

"Because of... of what you must think," Saga said softly.

"Navi doesn't understand." Saga swallowed hard as Navi's fingers delicately traced the burns on her hands. "You saved this one, and you... you... you tried so hard to save Ziva."

Saga sobbed, "But I didn't. It's all my fault, Navi... if I'd never come here... if I wasn't what I am... if—" She was cut off by the resounding sound of a slap echoing throughout the room. Then the pain hit, and Saga's hand went to her cheek, pain blossoming as she tenderly prodded the stinging flesh. "Navi?" she breathed.

"Don't you dare say that!" Nave exclaimed. "You're not allowed to talk like that."

"But..."

"NO!" Navi screamed, her chest heaving with deep, ragged breaths as she spoke. "No! Wishing yourself away will not bring Ziva back!"

"Navi... I..."

"It's not your fault!" Navi cried. "It's not! Just come back! Please, just come back and be Navi's friend again."

Sobs wracked Saga's body as she fell towards her friend, hugging her with everything she had. "I'm sorry, I'm so sorry," she kept murmuring again and again.

THE SPEAR, THE HEAD
AND THE VALKYRIE

Pingu nickered in Saga's ear as she brushed him. His wings flapped restlessly against his side, and he restlessly stomped his hooves against the ground.

"I know, boy, I know," She murmured, brushing him in long, arching strokes. "I'm sorry that it's been so long." He whinnied loudly and snorted. "But here you are, looking all pretty for everyone to see. What do you say we go join the rest of the class, huh?"

She slipped the halter over his face, and he accepted it, waiting for her to tighten the buckles. Then she led him from his stall, saying her goodbyes to the older pegasi as she did. She had done it every time she had led Pingu from the stall for riding class or Tourney. The big black pegasus, Pingu's father, whinnied in return before she led Pingu out into the barn with the rest of the class and their animals. Harriet's owlbear stopped attacking her on sight and was now standing docilely beside her, only occasionally trying to swipe at one of the other animals. Emory's homunculus sat on his shoulder, eyes always on Navi as her bezkira wrapped itself around her, almost as though it was comforting her.

Even Mistress Anhora had laid off her criticisms of Navi. This icy hostility had been present since the first day of class, having magically evaporated with the tragedy of Dorbe Manor. In many ways, the entire school had changed. That morning in World History, Master Berfelan had not made a single snide remark about Valkyries or Dökkálfar. When Navi had tentatively raised her hand and asked him about Valhalla and what he knew, instead of berating her for interrupting his lesson, he had told them to do the reading over the next week and had, to everyone's surprise, given them a detailed history of Valhalla, the Valkyries and how those warriors who died in battle were chosen for Valhalla over Folkvangr.

All the while, he had eyed them curiously, Navi, Jemima, Saga, Tasso and Emory. His gaze had constantly strayed to Saga as he had spoken. At the end of the class, he had returned to his usual grumpy and disreputable self, hurrying them all out of his classroom with his regular insults to everyone but those five.

"You will now take your teams and your animals into the forest," Mistress Anhora decreed. "This is a test, not only of your knowledge of your animal but of how you have trained them. It is a chance for you to see each other's animals and work in a team with them. There are twenty of you, so four groups of five."

Saga stayed where she was, next to Navi and Jemima. Emory and Tasso made their way through the crowd to join them. Things were nowhere near back to normal between the group, but after the fight in the street and, in particular, her talk with Navi, Saga had started to join back in with the others a little. Navi had refused to allow Saga to isolate herself from the group again and, along with Emory, had sometimes physically forced her out of the house with them. She was beginning to stop blaming herself for Ziva's death as well, but that may have taken a few knocks to the head from Navi before it had sunk in. Navi slept on the floor in their room, a makeshift bed between hers and Jemima's. They would talk long into the night about anything and everything. Emory would sometimes sneak in and sit on Saga's trunk at the back of the room. More often than not, though, he would pad in in his wolf form, jump up on Saga's bed and fall asleep there.

Mistress Anhora threw her hand up, and several small eyeballs flew into the air, each one hovering over a group. "I will be able to see you from here. Go."

"Any idea what we're expecting?" Tasso asked.

They shook their heads. The assignment had come out of nowhere. They walked through the magic portal within the barn doors. Jemima sat upon Kia's back, the Dragonne, dragon-like with its brass scales, had a cat-like face and lion's mane that were the same brassy colour as the scales. It padded along beside Pingu. Jemima was busily flipping through the student guidebook about Animal Husbandry until she gasped, looking up at the others. "I can't believe her," she exclaimed.

"What?" Emory asked, handing Hermes a stick of berries. The homunculus took the twig, grasping it in its clawed hands and eating at the berries with razor-sharp teeth.

"This is the final exam for this class!" Jemima cried.

"What?" Anger was only a small fraction of the emotion Saga felt when she spoke. "I thought that-."

"That every exam had been cancelled," Emory finished for her.

Saga looked up at the magic eye following them and frowned. "Why would she do this?"

"Could she really not care?" Navi asked softly. "I mean... I... she... she never really..."

"No," Jemima said, reaching out to take Navi's hand. "Even Master Berfelan was... well... He was nice today."

Everyone nodded in agreement. "That was really disconcerting," Saga said, looking around them. "What are we supposed to expect?"

"No idea," Tasso said. Cronin, the big blink dog that followed him everywhere, appeared and disappeared from their sight in the blink of an eye. "But this is eerie."

He was right. They had not ventured far into the forest that had appeared from the doors of the far side of the school barn, but it had quickly turned from the bright walk in a pleasant forest to a dark and ominous one.

"That was quick," Jemima whispered, her voice dropping as they realised the drastic change in their environment.

Emory sniffed. "Something is off," he said slowly. "Hermes," the homunculus looked at him suddenly, beady eyes waiting for instruction. "Go, scout out. All directions."

The creature bobbed its head before stretching out its bat-like wings and leaping from Emory's shoulder.

"What are you seeing?" Saga asked. He shook his head and waved her question off, concentrating on his link with Hermes. He slowed his walking pace, unable to concentrate on what he was seeing and where he was going. Around him, the others slowed as well.

"In front of us, everything seems, it seems to get darker. It's weird. He's circling to our left. Everything seems dark that way too. Behind us..." Emory gasped and stopped walking altogether.

"What is it?" Navi asked.

"It's... the barn... you know whenever we do this, you can always see the barn."

"Yeah," Navi agreed.

"I can't see the barn. I can't see the other groups either. I can't find them." Hermes reappeared, landing on Emory's shoulder in an exhausted heap and nuzzling into his neck. Emory absentmindedly raised his hand to scratch the creature behind his ears. "I... Where are we?"

"You don't think that Mistress Anhora is, you know... one of Vali's, do you?" Navi asked.

"I would never have thought so," Saga said. "Master Berfelan, sure... but Mistress Anhora? No... I wouldn't have thought so."

"Well, there's something odd going on around here," Emory said. "I have no idea how to get back to the school."

Eyes seemed to turn towards Pingu, but as if knowing what they were thinking, the pegasus shook his head and whinnied in disagreement.

"Still can't fly?" Jemima asked.

Saga nodded. "It's not like Kia flies either."

"So, what do we do?" Tasso asked, looking around them. "Do we try to go back, or?"

"There's nothing to go back to," Jemima said, fear growing in her eyes.

"Wait," Saga said, a thought coming to her mind. "Hermes!" she exclaimed. The creature looked at her but stayed where it was on Emory's shoulder. She pointed up at the magic eyes that were staring down at them. "Grab it!" Hermes looked at Emory. Emory nodded, and the homunculus launched itself from Emory's shoulder.

Hermes grabbed for the magic eye. The eye bobbed around, desperate not to be caught. The clawed hands of the homunculus clutched, stretching out his sharp fingers, barely grazing the magic eye before it flew out of his reach.

"It's not working!" Navi complained. "Bring it down to the ground, Hermes!" The creature shot her a dark, glowering look but focused not on capturing it himself but on herding towards Navi. "Cronin! Ephyra!" she cried.

The large, shadowy cat at her side looked up at the incoming ball. Ephyra's eyes darted back and forward before setting on the magic eye. Cronin appeared beside the big cat and then disappeared again. He reappeared a few feet away, blinking in and out of existence, all around the spot where Hermes was herding the eye.

"We don't have time for this," Jemima urged. "We need to find a way out."

Surrounded by Hermes, Ephyra and Cronin, the Eye was trapped between Ephyra's giant black paws. Navi crouched down beside Cronin and stared at the small, magical eye.

"What exactly is it?"

"An advanced Arcana spell," Tasso said, following suit and crouching between her and Cronin. "As a Ljósálfar, there was a chance that she could do Arcana. I guess Mistress Anhora can," he poked at it subtly with a stick. "Now, what do we do with it?" he asked, looking up at Saga.

"Ummm..." She patted Pingu's neck and left him beside Kia, who still had Jemima on her back. "Well, Mistress Anhora said that she would be watching."

"And if she did this, what good will that do us?" Emory asked.

Saga sighed. "I don't know!" She exclaimed, throwing her hands in the air. "It seemed like a good idea at the time!"

Suddenly, everything happened at once. Pingu reared up, shrieking in fear and pain. Beside him, Jemima fell from Kia's back. An arrow whistled past

Emory's ear and barely missed Hermes, who hovered around his head. Cronin barked, blinking to position himself between Tasso and the arrows.

Pingu bolted into the forest, almost trampling over Navi and Tasso. Ephyra swiped at the large, winged horse, but her claws missed his hind leg as he raced past her.

"Pingu!" Saga cried. Another arrow slammed into the ground by Navi's feet. She stumbled backwards, only to be caught by Tasso.

"Run!" Jemima cried, scrambling back to her feet, using Kia to haul herself back up.

~*~

Saga had leapt upon Pingu's back as he bolted and before she knew it, she and Pingu were deep within the forest's depths. Around them, the trees were tall gnarled and twisted. The bark was a dark grey-black colour, and no light seemed to permeate the dense canopy of shadowy leaves. Pingu nickered nervously, scraping his hoof against the ground. Saga patted his head.

"It's ok, boy... We just..." She looked around, not spotting any of the others. "Jemima? Navi? Tasso? Emory?" She called out. Wind whistled past her, blowing her hair around her face and rustling leaves, but she heard nothing until—

"Ahhhhhhhhhh!"

A golden, brassy streak of colour ran past Saga and Pingu, the scream emanating from the back of the streak.

"Jemima!" Saga cried. The grasped Pingu's reigns tighter, "Go!" Without further instruction, Pingu bolted off after the brassy streak of Kia the Dragonne. "Hyah!"

Heavy hooves beat the ground, the noise thundering in her ears as she ducked another low-hanging branch. The sound of Jemima's terrified cries kept drawing them after Kia's panicked run, but they never seemed to close in.

"Jemima!" Saga cried, trying to alert the other girl that she was coming, but over the sounds of the animals and Jemima's terrified cries, she had no idea if she could even hear her. Twigs and thin branches cut at her face as

Pingu galloped through the forest, which seemed to continue growing increasingly darker, beyond what she had thought was possible.

A screeching cry of pain filled the air, followed by the thud of a large body falling to the ground. "Kia!" Jemima's cry confirmed Saga's worst fears.

"Where's the dog?"

The harsh male voice seemed to make everything stand still as Pingu reared to a sudden halt, Saga having to use every ounce of riding knowledge she had accumulated since starting school to prevent herself from falling off the startled pegasus.

"What dog?" Jemima's panicked voice was now high-pitched with fear. Her eyes stared at Saga.

"What was that?" one of the men asked, starting to turn his head to look.

"I don't know what dog you mean," Jemima cried out, drawing their attention back to her.

"The big black one. It's always spotted around your little friend." Jemima's eyes widened in realisation as she continued to watch Saga. Saga had dismounted from Pingu and was creeping towards the tree nearest to the two men holding Jemima. She recognised both of them from the day she had been attacked with Edun. They had been among the group that had fled when the City Guard had been sighted coming towards the fight. Kia lay on her side, mere feet away from where Jemima was held. Saga's fists clenched and unclenched as she saw the knife held to Jemima's throat as the second man interrogated her.

But why were they after Shadow? He had not been present at the fight and had not been there in Valhalla because he had somehow turned back into Emory. That had been a shock.

"Ohhh! That dog!" Jemima exclaimed, a little louder than necessary. "I have no idea." The Angel groaned in pain as the man holding her dug the knife harder into her throat, a prick of blood appearing.

"Don't lie to me, girl!"

"I'm not lying. He's not my dog."

The bushes behind Saga rustled, and she turned to see what had made the noise. Cronin stood there. Saga looked around. "What are you doing here? Where's Tasso?" Suddenly, Hermes popped up from behind the dog's big head, and Saga blinked in surprise. She had seen the homunculus ride Shadow, but that had been completely different. Cronin? Where had be blinked in from?

Hermes took flight, flapping his large wings and going high in order to inspect the immediate area. It should not have been a surprise when Tasso, Navi and Emory stumbled out from the bushes. The appearance of Cronin and Hermes had given that away.

Emory opened his eyes, obviously having been watching through Hermes. "Well... that's a predicament."

"You don't know the half of it," Saga muttered, turning back to see what was happening with Jemima. "They're after Shadow."

Navi gasped, eyeing Emory, but Tasso spoke. "Why would they want your dog?"

"He's not my dog!" Saga shot back, awkwardly eyeing Emory as she spoke.

"He uh," Emory started awkwardly. "Does always seem to be everywhere you are. How far away could he be?"

Saga shook her head, looking meaningfully at Emory. "Not today, he isn't."

Tasso frowned, looking between them. "Am I missing something?"

"Nope," Saga said before either of the others could say anything. "We need to figure out how to get Jemima back without handing over Shadow."

"Well... yeah... that," Emory said, biting his lip as he looked past her to the clearing. "You know, they're probably not after—"

"Shhh!" Navi hissed, "They're talking."

"What do you want with Shadow anyway?" Jemima asked. The talkative one was walking up and down, pacing before Jemima as he thought of what to do next. His friend, the only restraining Jemima, watched him eagerly, awaiting any instruction.

"We don't want the stupid dog," the pacer said. "We want the girl it protects."

"Oh," Jemima said, her eyes flicking to where she had seen Saga. Her eyes widened when she spotted the rest of the group. "Well... I mean... Why didn't you just ask about her?"

"How do we get Jemima out of there?" Navi asked, "Kia's hurt."

"Hermes!"

"Cronin."

Saga nodded. "Yeah... yeah, that could work. Hermes circles around to come up behind the guy with the knife, and Cronin appears in front of the talkative one."

"And then what?" Navi asked. "Kia looks bad. It's not like any of us can carry her."

"Do we still have the magic eye?" Tasso asked.

Emory pointed at Hermes. "Yeah... he keeps playing with it."

"Maybe help is coming?"

"Let's deal with those two first and get Jemima," Saga decided.

Nodding in agreement, Emory ordered Hermes to fly around to the other side of the clearing. Always quick to respond to commands, he flew off, and they lost sight of the small creature. Tasso, meanwhile, was instructing Cronin on his part in the plan, the large blinkdog panting away in excitement over what would come next.

"What do you want with Saga?"

They turned their attention back to Jemima.

"The road to Valhalla, of course," the one with the knife laughed.

"You idiot," the pacer shouted. "We got that already. Remember? Vali told us all about them gilded halls and the new dead girl there, some Doxie girl from the house fire." Navi tensed, her hands going for the staff she usually carried with her, but it wasn't there. Instead, she clenched her hands into fists by her sides. Tasso's hand rested on her shoulder, giving her a supportive squeeze as they waited for Hermes. "The spear wasn't there. Vali thinks the girl has it."

"Saga doesn't wield a spear," Jemima said without thinking.

"Hermes is ready."

Looking at Emory and Tasso, Saga nodded, letting them release their creatures upon the two men holding Jemima. They spotted Hermes flying into the clearing as Cronin blinked in, cutting off the rhythm of the man pacing up and down before Jemima. He stumbled, never looking to see the small bat-like creature wrap its tiny hands around his partner's head and bite his razor-sharp teeth into his neck. It took mere moments for him to slump, the knife dropping from Jemima's neck. She struggled to get herself out from under his weight, allowing him to collapse to the floor. She ran for Kia, running gentle fingers over the creature's scaly skin. The Dragonne whimpered in pain.

Saga emerged from the bushes with Emory right behind her. Hermes flew back to him and landed on his shoulder, a smug look on the little creature's face. Tasso patted Cronin, who had blinked back to his side.

"How's Kia?" Navi asked, walking over to Jemima and crouching beside her and the big Dragonne.

"I..." Jemima shook her head. "I don't know... my healing spells are... I'm not good enough," she sobbed. "I can't help her..."

Navi wrapped an arm around Jemima's shoulders. "You were amazing on the night." She hesitated, swallowing back her desire to cry. "You were amazing that night, if anyone can help Kia, it's you."

While they worked on Kia, Saga walked over to the man Cronin kept blinking in and out from. He had tried several times to attack the dog, but every time he tried, the dog was no longer there, and the momentum of his attack would send him flailing around the clearing.

"Get that mutt away from me!" he screeched as Cronin reappeared behind him, growling.

"Weren't you looking for a dog?" Saga asked, cocking her head to the side. "He's the only dog in this group." Cronin barked in response. She crouched in front of the spot where he had fallen and looked into his eyes. "Or were you looking for me?"

Pingu nickered nervously behind her, his hooves scraping at the floor. Hermes bared his teeth at the man, and he recoiled in horror. "Our Master wants the Valkyrie."

"Why?" Emory asked, teeth clenched and fists ready to pummel the man.

Saga held a hand out to him, telling him to hold back. "It's ok, Emory. Let the man speak."

"But—"

"No," Saga interrupted. "It's about time we had some answers. Navi deserves that. So, what is it that Vali wants from me?"

"I don't have to answer you," he sneered.

"Navi?" Saga called.

"Yeah?"

"Is Ephyra hungry? This man is offering himself up as her dinner." The big shadowy cat padded over quietly, her large feet barely making a sound as she walked. The hell cat stalked around the man, looking towards Cronin with a sneer, showing that this prize, this prey, would be hers even though the dog had captured him. "Oh, look, they're going to fight for you."

"Continue on into the woods, and you will know all," the man said, warily eyeing the two wild beasts. "He waits for you at the centre of the woods, the divine guiding light of his vision will be realised."

"Divine guiding light?" Saga questioned. "Is he a god?"

"Descendent of Odin himself. Vali will rule over all the Nine Realms. With Valhalla awakened, the new world order shall come!"

"He makes me sick," Tasso grumbled. "He can't really believe this crap, can he?"

"Sounds like he does," Emory murmured back. "But what did this have to do with anything? Why the fires?"

"They weren't fires," Saga said, looking back at them. "They were hordes upon hordes of warriors riding through those properties. Ghosts, warriors long dead, the Einherjar most likely..."

"But the Einherjar are all dead... like... DEAD dead," Navi called over. "They... they died their final deaths at Ragnarök."

"Mimir said that they were an echo... A memory of what had once been. Not even of the Einherjar themselves, but of The Wild Hunt."

The man in front of her sat up and reached for her. Before anyone could react, his fingers were wrapped in her jacket lapels, pulling her towards him. "What did you say?"

Emory shifted and grabbed the downed man. "Let. Her. Go."

Instead, he shook her. "What did you say?" He cried. "You have spoken with... you... he told you... the great wise one himself."

"You saw him yourself," Saga said, hands scrabbling to release herself from his grasp. "You and your people tried to kill him in Valhalla."

He fell back in surprise, falling back further than he had intended when he let go at the same time Emory attempted to haul him away from Saga. "The... the old man? But... Mimir? He's a head!"

"Yeah," Saga said.

"Who has the head?" the man begged.

Saga grinned. "Not Vali." She stood up. Emory now held the man, and she paced, much as he had done, while his still unconscious friend had held a knife at Jemima's throat.

"Wait," Tasso said. "Who's Mimir?"

"The old guy in Valhalla," Emory answered.

"He was one of the Æsir, gifted to the Vanir in the aftermath of the Æsir-Vanir war," Jemima interrupted, walking over. "I mean, it was more an exchange of hostages, but still, Mimir and Hoenir were given by the Æsir in exchange for Njoror and Freyr. The Æsir and the Vanir considered these men to be their best and finest men. Strong, intelligent, and capable of many great feats. Hoenir relied heavily on Mimir's guidance, and without him by his side, people started to believe that they had been cheated in the exchange. Mimir was beheaded, and the head was sent back to Odin. For many years until Ragnarök, the head of Mimir is said to have still guided Odin, providing him with much wisdom."

The man nodded eagerly. "Yes, yes. The head of Mimir will guide us to victory. The head and the spear. That is what we need."

Saga frowned, turning back to him. "But Vali knows where the head is."

The man stopped nodding and blinked at her stupidly. "What?"

"And if you want the head and the spear, what do you want with Saga?" Emory pressed.

The man sneered at Emory. "You think Valhalla is the only place Valkyries can transport you to? They can travel without the Rainbow Bridge!"

"No," Saga said. "I plenty like the bridge, thanks."

He scrambled towards her, desperately trying to escape Emory's grip. "Don't you see? he who wields the spear of Odin, hears the wisdom of Mimir and travels with the wings of a Valkyrie shall rule not only Asgard but all of the Nine Realms."

They were left with no time to contemplate what the man had said because, in the next moment, Mistress Anhora, Master Iacono and Master Toshiji rode into the clearing, several city guards behind them.

"There you are!" Mistress Anhora cried out.

Navi sagged against Tasso in relief. "Navi didn't think it had worked."

Mistress Anhora turned to Jemima, who instantly led their Animal Husbandry teacher to Kia. Looking at who was left, who did that leave? Master Iacono? What was he doing here?

Tasso whispered into Saga's ear, a sudden thought occurring to him. "He's faerie!"

Her eyes widened in surprise. "You're right," she whispered. "Mistress Anhora isn't the Arcanist. Not today anyway."

"But what does that mean?" Navi asked.

Saga shrugged. "I have no idea, but I think we can write Mistress Anhora off the suspect list."

"And what? Add Master Iacono?" Tasso asked. "That seems a little... well..."

"This one liked him," Navi added.

"We all like Master Iacono. He's one of my favourite teachers... but why is he here?"

"Where's the head?" the man they had captured cried. "Tell me where the head is!"

"What head?" Iacono asked, walking over to them.

They looked at each other before shrugging, and Saga said, "No idea, Sir. He sounds like a raving madman if you ask me."

ILLUSIONS

"Are you saying that we're still close to town?" Jemima asked in surprise.

"That's what Mistress Anhora said," Tasso explained, petting Cronin as they waited. They had made a stretcher for Kia, and Pingu would have to pull it. He was the only one of the creatures big enough to do so. It had taken time, but the dragonne would have a way of making it back to the school stables.

In conversation with the trees, Mistress Anhora had asked for wood that had come, not only without them having to search but in shapes and lengths that allowed them to merely assemble the contraption. Vines suitable for use as ropes were also asked for by the old elf woman. She had not wanted to waste time returning to the school for supplies.

Master Toshiji had helped her, following every order she had given, while Master Iacono had assisted the city guard in questioning the two thugs.

"What do you think he's saying to them?" Tasso asked, watching Master Iacono.

"You know that we're only guessing... I mean... at the beginning of this, we thought it was Mistress Anhora," Navi reminded him.

"And we still think Master Berfelan is involved in this somehow," Jemima added.

"Astrid." She had spoken so softly that it took a minute before they stopped, and all eyes turned to look at Saga. Disbelief appeared on each face.

"What?" Navi asked in disbelief. "Mistress Grunborg?"

"What in the name of Odin's beard makes you suspect her?" Jemima added.

Saga stared pensively at the teachers. They were busy getting everything ready to return to the school as Saga and the others waited, having been ordered to stay out of the way. She said slowly, "Well... what was it he said that they needed?"

"The head... this... this Mimir character," Tasso said.

"Odin's Spear," Emory added. Beside him, Navi nodded solemnly.

"And the Valkyrie," Saga finished for them. "They wanted me... and who brought me here?"

"Astrid," Navi said.

Emory shook his head. "No."

"What?" Saga asked.

"It wasn't Mistress Grunborg." He looked away, thinking hard. "I..." He glanced awkwardly at Jemima and Tasso, then said. "You said it was Shadow who pushed you that day, that Mistress Grunborg was going to come back for you. But Shadow pushed you, and you fell on the rainbow disc..."

Saga stared at him in surprise. He was right. Astrid had been about to leave when Shadow had leapt onto the platform, knocking Saga over. It had been a harrowing ride through the sky until Astrid had been able to pull her up. Still, she shook her head. "True as that may be, it was Astrid who came. It was Astrid who ultimately decided to go to Midgard and find me."

"Bringing the Valkyrie into play," Tasso said. He tapped his finger against his lips, thinking. "And you said that she knows this Vali character."

"Huh," Navi said, looking at them all. "That does change everything."

"So, who can we trust?" Navi asked.

They looked back towards the teachers, realising that there was no one they could trust.

"We're moving out," Master Toshiji announced suddenly. "Kia is ready to be transported."

"You lot will have to tell us everything," Mistress Anhora decreed. "Headmaster Gotts is going to want to hear about all of this. I have no idea how the test was taken over. Who would do this?"

Master Toshiji looked back at the students, his eyes lingering on Navi before turning to Anhora. "Why were you even running that blasted test? End-of-term exams were cancelled after the fire." He motioned towards Emory and Saga. "They went into the house, rescued people lost people." He pointed towards Jemima. "That girl worked with the healers." Finally, he pointed at Navi. "That girl's sister died. What were you doing?"

Mistress Anhora huffed, arms crossed over her chest. "My class. My students."

"Seven children died," he hissed. "Seven." He looked towards Master Iacono. "Would you weigh in, Byrge?"

Before the faerie man could answer, though, Anhora spoke up. "Perhaps it was a mistake to run the exam, but how was I supposed to know it would be hijacked?"

"Hijacked or not, Gretchen, this test should never have happened. We have barely finished burying those children. That hulk of a building remains on the outskirts of town as a constant reminder. Flowers and toys litter the town square. The town and the school still grieve. Half of the survivors are no longer here, taken home by panicked parents or still lying in their hospital beds, and you try to run an exam?"

"I already said that it was a mistake!" Mistress Anhora hissed.

Ephyra mewled and pawed at Navi's leg. She crouched down and picked up the large, shadowy cat. As she stood back up, the last few remnants of sunlight glinted off the tears that had streaked her face when no one was looking. Realising that people were looking at her, she buried her face in Ephyra's dark, shadowy fur.

Tasso, as always, was by her side, ready to lend a hand and be her shoulder to cry on. Saga shook her head. It would only be a matter of time before one of them finally admitted how they felt. Kia groaned, and Jemima went to sit by her, riding on the litter that had been made up and harnessed to Pingu for the trek back into Nýr Ásgardr.

"What are you thinking?" Emory asked, walking beside her. Hermes sat upon his shoulder, and Saga kept her hand wound tightly through Pingu's reigns. She bit her lip, not wanting to draw attention to her thoughts as she fought not to look back at the man walking behind the guards' horse. "Saga?" Emory pushed.

"Nothing," she lied.

He shook his head in disbelief. The feeling of fear grew within him as he watched her untangle her hand from the Pegasus' reigns. The animal would follow Mistress Anhora. That fact was certain. There was no need for Saga to lead Pingu anywhere.

"You're not going to go... I mean, I heard what he said about finding out deeper in the forest," Emory said softly, not wanting anyone else to overhear them.

Saga nodded. "I have to, and now might be my only chance. I have to find out the truth. I have to put a stop to this."

"Why you?"

Her eyes widened at the question, and she faltered for a moment. "Well..." She glanced towards where Navi and Tasso walked. "For her... for... all of them... for you and..."

"You don't owe any of us anything," Emory hissed. "If anything... if anything at all, we..."

Saga shook her head, and before he could say anything else, she wrapped her arms around his neck and hugged him. "Thank you," she whispered in his ear, "Thank you for being my friend."

He tried to turn his head to look at her, wondering where this was going. What was she doing? At this, her lips were on his. Had she just kissed him? Saga held him closer, realising that while it had not been what she had meant to do, it had been something she had wanted to do for a long time. Emory was stunned into near paralysis, unable to move. He wanted desperately to wrap his own arms around her, but just as his arms began to heed his orders, she pushed him away.

"I'm sorry, but I have to do this alone," she whispered before running off, leaving him standing there, surprised and stunned by her actions.

~*~

Running. It had always been her thing. Her speed, maybe a speciality of her Valkyrie powers or maybe just years of expert coaching. She ran like the wind. While usually a sprinter, Saga performed well on long-distance runs during school competitions. What was needed was different, though, stamina and endurance to last the distance rather than bursts of speed.

She could barely see where she was going as she descended deeper into the forest, running back the way they had come. It was getting darker and darker with every step she took, just as it had when they had traversed that path the time before. She hoped that by heading back to the clearing where Mistress Anhora had found them, she would be able to seek out those answers she so desperately needed.

She rubbed at her eyes, trying to clear them, and when her hands came away wet, she realised that she was crying. What had she done? Had she really kissed Emory? Oh, could things get any worse?

The rhythmic feeling of her feet hitting the ground, again and again, soothed her though, or maybe that was the distance from him? He was one of her best friends. What had she been thinking? She had not. That was the only answer. That was the only way that this could have happened.

Had she passed the clearing yet? Dragging the stretcher with Kia had been slow going, even for Pingu. She ran fast, and there was no doubt in her mind that she should have found the clearing by now. Had she been so stuck in her head that she had missed it? Or had she gone the wrong way? How hard could it have been to run back the way they had come? Not only that, the man had only said, *"Continue on into the woods, and you will know all,"* What else had he said? *"He waits for you at the centre of the woods."*

The centre of the woods. Well, how big were these woods? There were no woods near Nýr Ásgardr. She had seen that when they had flown in on the great airship, but the magic portals used in the school barn had been something else altogether. A phenomenon she had not been able to explain as of yet.

So, where was she?

She needed to breathe. She slowed her run to a gentle jog. She did not want to stop moving completely. There was no guarantee that she would be able to resume that pace again if she stopped completely.

The forest around her was pitch black. Exactly as they had imagined the forest turning, had they not stopped, only to be startled off by the attack. Where was she going? There were forest noises all around her. She was not used to that, except maybe from school camp when they had stayed in those forest cabins. Yggdrasil had just sounded like a big, vertical city with people everywhere, talking, laughing, and living their lives. It had not felt like a giant tree in the middle of a forest.

This place though, this place gave her the creeps. The rustle of the trees, the groaning of branches that seemed to bear too much weight upon their limbs to remain on the trees. A wolf howled somewhere in the distance, and she shivered.

She looked around, trying to figure out which way to go. Everything looked the same. The same dark, mangled trees, the same all-encompassing darkness. Where was this centre of the forest?

Maybe Emory was right, and she should not have gone off alone. Alone was the only way she knew how to do things, though. She was so used to never asking for help that the thought of putting any of them at risk for her made her sick to her stomach.

A light. A light glowed in the distance, and she started to run again. The light bobbed up and down, left and right. A person with a lantern? Maybe it was Vali. Maybe she would finally get her answers.

The closer she got, the further the light got away. "Wait!" Saga called. Yet, the person carrying the lantern did not seem to hear her because they kept moving further and further away. Every step she took, no matter how fast she ran, the lantern bearer moved away. "Hang on! I just wanted to ask if-."

Paws and claws, followed by the heavy body of a wolf, hurtled into her body, sending her crashing to the ground, the heavy weight of the animal on top of her. Heavy, panting breath blew in her face.

Saga stayed still, not daring to move a muscle. Was this the wolf she had heard howl? Had it come to eat her? Why didn't she have at least a knife on her? Behind the large dog-like animal, the lantern bearer seemed to return, walking past the bush that the dog had pushed her into as if looking for her. But, even with the light illuminating the space, she could still see no person. No one was holding the lantern. It just floated by. Bobbing up and down, left and right.

The rustling in the bushes across the path had her trying to sit up, but the large animal would not let her. "Emory? Emory? Shadow?"

Saga's eyes widened as she tried to get a good look at the big animal that still sat atop her. "Shadow?" she hissed. In reply, he licked her face before launching himself off of her. The impact of his hind legs leaping off her left her winded for a moment before she could finally sit up. Shadow sat there, panting in innocence and beside him crouched a figure with glistening white hair that was supposed to glow in the moonlight but just looked a lighter shade of dark in their lightless environment. "Navi?"

"Hey!" the other girl said, still trying to catch her breath. "Wow, you can really run."

"What are you two doing here?"

"Looking for you," Navi said before reaching out and slapping Saga on the shoulder. She followed that by giving the large wolf beside her an ear flick. The animal, Emory in his wolf form, yelped in pain and surprise before looking up at the girl with sad puppy dog eyes. "First, you run off, and Tasso and this one just are stuck staring after you like we've missed something, which by the way, we did not miss 'seeing' anything," she emphasised, and Saga immediately felt her cheeks heat up. She looked away from Shadow, concentrating on Navi. "Then the big guy here starts to change. Like Navi has never seen a Were change before. They're always so secretive about it and then, before we could stop him, he was off."

"Are Tasso and Jemima going to show up in a minute?" Saga asked in disbelief.

Navi shook her head. "No. Kia was doing poorly, so Jemima decided to stay with her, and Tasso wanted to try out some spell he had learned and said he would cover for us. When this one left, you and Emory walked silently beside Pingu. It was disturbing but Navi guessed that it was some sort of illusion. This one doubts it will fool Mistress Anhora or Master Iacono for long."

Shadow barked, and both girls looked around. They heard nothing, but the light started coming back into view, wandering down the path as though it was looking for them.

"Damned Will-O'Wisps," Navi whispered.

"A what?" Saga asked.

"Will-O'Wisps," Navi repeated. "The way you followed it before Shadow knocked you off your feet would indicate that it had found a way to feed on you."

Saga eyes the bobbing light. "Feed on me?"

"Well, yeah, that's what they do. They feed off powerful emotions. Particularly negative emotions," Navi explained. She eyed the light cautiously. "We see many of them around the Ljósálfar homes where we work."

Shadow's paw rested on Navi's thigh, and she looked at him with a sad smile. "Thanks."

"So, how do we get past here?" Saga asked.

"Daylight?" Navi suggested.

"Daylight?" Saga repeated. "It was daylight when we stepped into these woods for our exam. I don't want to spend all night out in these woods."

"Well, neither does Navi, but you're the one who ran off without a plan," Navi shot back. Guilt flooded Saga. "And you could change back and say something, you know?" She shot at Shadow.

The wolf looked from Navi to Saga before he barked and resettled himself into a laying position. Navi huffed. "Great. Just great! Now what?"

A growl from low in Shadow's chest brought their attention back to the big wolf. He sat up again, alert and turned to stare at the path. Saga looked, too, and gasped.

"What?" Navi cried.

"The Will-O'Wisp thing is the least of our problems," Saga murmured.

"What is it?" Navi asked, peering over the bushes.

Saga looked at her. "You don't see them?"

"See what?"

Shadow growled beside the girls, his eyes intently on the scene on the path. "You can see them?" Saga asked the big dog. He had not been able to see Amyra Dorbe back at the fire, Mimir at the library, or Tremblay Jimpsee at the house, but was it because he was in his wolf form? No, if the Were community could see ghosts, someone would have said something long ago. She rested her hand on his neck and smiled to herself. "You can see them," she murmured in wonder.

"See what?" Navi cried.

"The Wild Hunt..." Saga whispered. The light of the Will-O'Wisp had originally hidden them from view, but now, she could see them plain as day.

"What? Like the rampaging warriors who destroyed Dorbe Manor?" Saga started to nod but then shook her head. "What's that supposed to mean?"

"I have no idea," Saga said. "I recognise the one in the lead. He led the ride when we were separated from Emory in the common room, with Sarabia, remember?" Navi nodded, still staring out at the forest path, trying to see what Saga and Shadow were seeing. "Well, he's also... well... he looks like Odin or at least the depictions of Odin in our books, but they're all just milling around like they don't have a care in the world. Not! It's not like all the other times I've seen them."

"All the other times? Girl, we have got to talk about you and your ghosts. Wait... why can Emory see them?"

"I don't know."

"What are they doing?" Navi asked, staring over Saga's shoulder, trying to see what she was seeing.

"I don't know... just walking up and down... patrolling, maybe?" Sage replied. Her eyes followed the movements of the ghostly warriors. What were they doing there?

"Hmm... Between the wisps and your warriors, should we stay here, wait until we get some light or something? Do you see ghosts in the daytime?"

Saga thought. "Well... I have seen ghosts in the day... The house ghosts at the square on the first day of school... That was the oddest one, full sunlight... Usually, I only see the house ghosts inside the houses... But the hunt... They only ever happened at night... except Jisook Farm. We were at the library when that happened."

Shadow watched them as they spoke. He had not changed back, and until he did, he could not contribute to their conversation. Frustration gnawed at him. He had things he wanted to say, and his dog's mouth would not allow it.

Navi frowned, not sure what to make of all the information they had. "Let's head further into the woods. Maybe set up camp and wait until morning?"

Saga nodded even though she was unsure. She wanted to run in. She wanted to find Vali and get those answers she needed. She needed and wanted all this to be over so that she could concentrate on school and tourney. She wanted to enjoy her friends and her new life, but how could she do that when her appearance had caused Ziva's death and countless others? "Yeah... let's do that."

Navi led them away from the path, away from the Will-O'Wisp and away from the ghostly forms of the Wild Hunt. "We'll need some wood for a fire and something to eat," Navi ordered.

Shadow barked and ran off, leaving both girls just staring at each other. "I guess he's going hunting," Saga said, though she was uncertain of that. "I'll look for firewood."

She wandered off, not far from the spot Navi had chosen. She started picking up pieces of wood that she found. A few small logs, branches, and twigs. She knew the theory of setting up a good fire. She had heard talk about it. The perfect ratio of logs to twigs to keep a fire burning. She could still see Navi from where she was, and she could see her picking up the beginning pieces of the fire, trying to get it started.

A growl emanated from where Shadow had disappeared, followed by the terrified squeal of a small animal. In that instant, Saga dreaded what was to come next. What camping she had done in the past had not been much; there had always been tents and shopping supplies. A lighter for the fire, blankets. There were things about this world that she could still not get her head around, and this, the ability to go out completely unprepared and still survive, was one of them.

Navi seemed, for once, so confident in her ability to direct them at this time so Saga was happy to sit back and allow her to do exactly that. Saga returned and dropped her supply of wood down next to the firepit Navi had created.

"Spréach a adhaint," she whispered, her finger pointed at the collection of sticks and twigs she had created. To Saga's surprise, a flame sparked at the end of her finger. The flame caught on the twigs of wood, and Navi blew out the flame on her finger before fanning the tiny flame she had created, helping it ignite the fire.

"Wow," Saga murmured.

Navi jumped back in surprise, falling to the ground before recovering her composure. "Saga," she gasped. She looked around wildly, seeing if anyone else had seen her do Arcana. "I... I..."

"You can do magic?" Saga asked.

"Arcana," Navi corrected. "And... maybe."

"Maybe?" Saga asked incredulous. "You just had a flame coming from your finger."

"Shh, keep your voice down," Navi hissed. "No one can know about this."

"Why not?"

Navi frowned. "N... Navi does not want to be put in the Arcana class. If it comes out that this one can do Arcana, they'll make this one take the class, and Navi does not want to... Navi just cannot...."

Ah, that made a little more sense. Arcana classes were reserved for faeries and elves who showed an aptitude for Arcana. "None of your siblings?"

Navi shook her head. "None of them," Navi whispered. "They don't even know. Only Tasso knows." She grabbed Saga's arm, her fingers digging into the flesh. "You cannot tell anybody, Saga. Promise me."

Saga winced but nodded. "Of course."

"Navi does not want to be stuck in that class," Navi hissed. "Navi just can't!"

"Navi," Saga said, her hand resting on Navi's. "I won't say anything. I promise."

After several deep breaths, calming herself, Navi nodded. "Ok," She released her hand and flexed her fingers. "Oh, Saga... Navi is sorry! This one didn't mean to hurt you!"

Saga chuckled. "It's ok, really. I shouldn't have startled you."

Navi looked around awkwardly. "Navi just... well... yeah," she shrugged. "Let's cook dinner."

"Dinner?" Saga asked.

With a shaky hand, Navi pointed to the far side of the clearing where Shadow stood over two dead rabbits. Saga gulped, her thoughts straying to Percival and Perdita, the wererabbits of Jimpsee House.

"Oh and what exactly are we supposed to do with them?" Saga asked, shaking off her disgust.

"Skin them, skewer them, cook them," Navi said, getting up and collecting the rabbits. "Nice work. They're big ones."

"Is that it?" Saga asked, staring at the rabbits. Where was the rest of the meal? They weren't seriously only going to eat those rabbits? What about spices, at least?

"What else do we need?"

"Right," Saga tried to hide the groan from her voice as the other girl extracted an intricately carved knife from within her tunic and began to skin the dead creatures. "I'm uh... I'm just going," she mumbled something that didn't make sense to her own ears and backed away from the sight. Navi was too engrossed in her task to notice, but Shadow watched her with a smug look. "What are you looking at?" she hissed at him.

The meal, or what Saga managed to eat of it when she managed to forget that Shadow had only literally just killed the animals and that they reminded her of her housemates. She glanced at Shadow as he munched away at the chunks of cooked meat that Navi fed him.

"You know he could just change back and eat it himself."

Navi shook her head. "This one does not think that he can. Surely, he would have by now, if he could." Silence settled between them. Neither felt the need to talk. The friendship between them had always been comfortable like that, ever since that first meeting at the weapons shop in Yggdrasil. "Oh, crap."

"What?" Saga asked, looking over at her.

"We ran away from school."

"Yes."

"Tasso hid our disappearance from the teachers... Saga. We have no idea how to get back! I mean, the magic portals, where in Idavoll are we? Are we even still in Asgard, or are we on one of the other planes? Do you know? Because this one does not!" Panic laced her voice.

"We'll..." Saga bit her lip and looked at Shadow. She shrugged. "I have no idea." She finally admitted.

VALASKJÁLF

The first rays of sunlight were dimmed by the dense canopy of the trees above them. The small clearing Navi had selected for their campsite had not been big enough to allow the surrounding trees' branches to separate and the sky to be truly seen. Still, small rays of sunlight streamed down and hit Saga's face, warming her.

She had expected it to be much colder overnight without blankets or bedrolls. The fire had died down to smouldering embers hours ago. Still, she had not been cold. The heat nestled against her was soft and... furry?

Eyes opening slowly, she saw Shadow's big black, furry head curled up against her. Trying to look without moving, she could not help but smile when she realised that Shadow had spent the entire night curled up against her.

Emory had spent the entire night curled up against her.

That thought had her turning bright red in embarrassment. Though why it mattered now when he had done it several times before back at Jimpsee House, she did not know. It seemed different now. She sat up, trying not to shift him, but maybe it was the lack of warmth against his back because he stretched his legs, a groan emanating from his body as he did so. He looked up at her with doggy eyes. Was he sad? Was he sad because of the loss of contact?

No. That could not be it. She turned away from him. "Navi?" she called out. Next to her, Shadow barked, also calling out to their friend.

"Oh good, you're awake," Navi said, emerging from the bushes. She had a cloth full of berries in her hands. "This one didn't think you would be interested in more rabbit, but Navi found these."

Saga nodded. "Uh... yeah..." Shadow slinked away from her, his haunches low to the ground, his tail down and sweeping in the dirt. "Good thought," Saga said, looking away from him as he disappeared into the bushes.

"So..." Navi said, sitting next to her to share the berries. "What next?"

"Well, we go back and see if I was right about the ghost warriors vanishing in the sunlight," Saga suggested. "I wish we had our weapons, though. I feel naked without them."

"Navi too," Navi agreed, popping a berry into her mouth. "Maybe we can find some or steal some?" Shadow barked in agreement, his head popping back out of the bushes. Navi shook her head. "This one wishes he could speak to us."

Saga was about to agree when the thought of looking Emory in the face again after what she had done struck. She felt her cheeks go red with the thought. Damnit, why had she had to go and ruin everything by doing that? She had never even kissed a boy before that and why did it have to be Emory? Emory, whom she could talk to. Emory, who always knew the right thing to say, even when she was mad at him. Emory, who accepted her for who she was and what about their friends? Would there be this whole Emory's side versus Saga's side? She could not imagine anything worse. She had seen it before when people had believed her or had not believed her about her visions of ghosts, and she had no interest in being put in the middle of such a thing ever again.

Worse than that, it was all her fault.

~*~

"Are they there?"

Saga poked her head over the bushes that lined the path to the clearing, where only the night before they, well, Saga, had seen masses of Norse warriors, long dead, patrolling the area.

Elongated shadows fell over the road, but the clearing where she could see the shimmering doorway within the ruins of a building destroyed some time ago. No one walked, no one patrolled. There was no sign that anyone had been there at all.

"Clear," Saga confirmed. "Or at least, I don't see anyone."

"Good enough for this one," Navi stated. Shadow barked in agreement and bounded out onto the path. "Hey!" she called after him. "Wait up! We still haven't found any weapons!"

"Well, we're not going to find any out here," Saga stated, following Shadow towards the ruined cottage.

"W... w... wait for Navi!" Navi cried, scrambling out of the bushes after them. Shadow glanced back at her but kept walking. Saga kept her walk tentative, as though waiting for the ghosts of long dead warriors to jump out at them and attack. "Anything?" she asked in a whisper as they got closer to the ruined cottage.

What used to be the door into the cottage shimmered in the light and looked like the barn portals they took to see their animals during animal husbandry classes. Saga shook her head. "Looks like a clear run." Shadow barked long and intent in what he was trying to convey. Saga nodded along. "You're right, we have absolutely no idea what's on the other side of the portal."

"You can understand him?" Navi asked, grabbing onto Saga's shoulder and looking down at the dog.

Saga shook her head. "Of course not, but it's totally something he would say." At her feet, Shadow whined. Navi laughed, but the way her fingers dug into Saga's shoulder told everything of how nervous she felt.

"Into the unknown?" She asked.

"Into the unknown," Saga agreed. Now, if only she could embrace her inner Elsa and be just as brave.

It was dark. Saga could not see a thing. She could feel Shadow pressed up against her legs and Navi clutching her shoulders as they stood there. The silence was engulfing, and it did not seem as though they wanted to be the first to break the silence or draw attention to themselves.

"He waits for you at the centre of the woods." The words echoed in her mind. Who was Vali, and what was she to his plan? She had barely figured out what she was in this world, let alone how she figured into grand plans of world domination.

"Whew," Navi murmured. "Looks like we're in a corridor of some kind."

"Can you see?" Saga whispered.

"Yeah, can't you?" Navi hummed when Saga shook her head. "Well. that is a nuisance, something our valkyrie can't do. Can you see Shadow?"

He let out a little yip of affirmation, and Saga sighed in relief. "Well, as long as you two can see, I guess..."

"Come on," Navi said, dragging Saga along. "We'll go this way."

Something about Navi's stance as she walked made Saga think that she was armed. "Is that the knife you skinned the rabbit with?"

Navi nodded. Saga could not see it, but she felt the movement in the other girl's body. "They were Ziva's throwing knives. Navi's not exactly good with them." She pushed one into Saga's hand. "There, now we both have something until we find something better."

Oddly enough, the weight of the knife in her hand actually did make her feel better. Saga had not been expecting that, but here she was, some of the tension and panic that had been building up within her, alleviated by the presence of the small knife.

They carefully made their way through the dark corridor until they reached an intersection. Suddenly, Saga pulled Navi to a stop. "Wait," she gasped out.

"What is it?" Navi whispered.

"Ghost," Saga hissed.

"Crap, Navi cannot see them. Now what?"

Two warriors walked past them. Saga's eyes followed them. "Well, we wait. What else do you see?"

"Well, there are these big silver doors in front of us, and the corridor in front of it runs down in either direction. I can see other doors, smaller than the ones in front of us, though. Where did the ghosts go?"

"Down that way," Saga pointed to the left. "They came from there," she pointed down the right.

"Well," Navi said. "Where do we go?"

"Centre of the woods," Saga murmured to herself. "Centre of the building."

"Big silver door it is!" Navi declared, about to step out into the hall, but Saga pulled her back. "What?" she hissed.

A group of Norse warriors passed by, banging their weapons. They laughed at something, and Navi had almost walked right into them. Saga remembered all too clearly what it had looked like inside Dorbe Manor when the warriors had ridden through the house, destroying everything in their path. Killing without even noticing what they were doing. Would that happen if one of them walked into the warriors without noticing? She had no idea. Saga breathed deeply and finally said, "They don't appear to come from anywhere, in particular, they just... appear."

"Oh goody," Navi replied sarcastically. "So, how do we get across the hall?"

Saga watched the boisterous group disappear down the corridor and wondered. Would anyone come through their corridor? Either find them and turn them in or maybe incinerate them as though they had never even been there. She had no idea. There were so many things that she did not know.

Like what was on the other side of those doors.

She took another deep breath to steady her nerves and stepped into the hall. Shadow growled, low in his chest, as he watched her. Saga stepped quickly over to the silver doors. They were massive, as though meant for people she could barely imagine.

Frost giants...

That had to be it. These doors had once welcomed the frost giants before Ragnarök had come. Before, the world had been destroyed and reborn without a ruler. Two statues guarded the doors. They were as tall as the doors, carrying weapons as big as a house. Never in her life had Saga ever felt as small as she did, standing before that door between those gigantic statues. Not even with everything that had happened to her before this day had she felt so small and insignificant, and if she was small and irrelevant, then what were her friends?

Shadow appeared to her left, and Navi on her right. "Ready?" Navi asked.

"No," Saga admitted. Shadow barked, and with that, Saga pushed the doors open.

For doors big enough for giants to walk through, they flew open at her touch, crashing into the walls. The sound reverberated through the hall that opened before them and down the corridors.

"I think they know we're here," Navi whispered.

Lights appeared, and the two pillars nearest to them were suddenly aglow, then the next ones and the next ones after that, until the entire room was illuminated.

"Uhh... yeah, they do," Saga agreed.

Together, they took another step forward. The pillars were all lit from their bases, not from torches as she had expected. Instead, it was the pillars themselves that illuminated the room and the light reflected off a ceiling of silver.

"Wow," Navi gasped. "It's so... so..." She cut off suddenly with a pained gasp, and Saga whirled around to face her. The girl was staring wide-eyed, her mouth trying to form words, but nothing came out. Navi started to fall, but before Saga could reach for her. Shadow launched himself at Saga. She fell to the floor with a heavy thud, the big black wolf on top of her, breathing in her face as a knife went over them. Beside them, Navi lay crumpled and unmoving.

"Navi!" Saga cried out. "Move!" she ordered, pushing at Shadow. She shoved at his massive body, but he stayed still. Footsteps. She could feel footsteps. They rumbled through the ground. "Navi!" she begged.

"Well... I had wondered when you would make it here," that voice. She recognised it. "Welcome to Valaskjálf. My home with my father, Odin himself. King of all the Gods, Lord of the Nine Realms. The All-Father, the Storm Bringer himself."

"You are Odin's son? I thought that was Thor."

Vali sneered at her. "He had more than one. Why is it that all anyone ever remembers is that brute, Thor?"

Saga shrugged. "He was the one everyone liked?"

"No one liked Thor, Girl," Vali spat. He turned but spoke over his shoulder at her. "Unfortunately, since you did not bring the spear, I have no time to deal with you."

"Wait!" Saga gasped out. "What is it you want from me?" Shadow shifted so that she could sit up.

She glared as he stepped over Navi's still form and crouched down before her. "Why don't you ask your father?"

"I'm an orphan," she spat.

"Are you?" he asked. "Really?"

"You look so much like your mother. It's remarkable, really."

"You knew my mother?" Saga scrambled towards him. "You... you have to."

"I have to do nothing, girl," he spat as he stood back up. "Bring me the spear of Odin, Gungnir, and then we can talk."

"I don't know how!"

"Find a way. Valhalla has reopened, and a new Ragnarök will come. A new king will be decided upon, and it is my rightful role as the son of Odin... And there is nothing my sister or the children of the Vanir can do to stop me." Then he walked away, stepping back over Navi's prone form as though she was not even there.

Shadow bounded after him, barking. A club carried by one of his ghostly guards slammed into Shadow's side, and he went flying across the room with a cry and whimper. "Shadow!" Saga cried.

"Control your mutt!" Vali sneered. "I'm not my father. I have no affinity for wolves."

As he left, Saga was torn. She should run after him and end all of this, but Navi and Emory were injured. Navi was the closest to her. She scrambled over to her and, for a moment, could have sworn that she saw Ziva lying there amid the fire, that piece of wood protruding from the back of her neck and Saga had to hold back her cry of despair. "Navi!" she cried. She could finally see what she had missed all along. A knife protruded out of her back. Saga skidded to her side, not knowing if she should touch her, move her, or take it out. "Navi! What do I do?" she cried.

A hand reached out and touched her neck. "She's still alive," Emory gasped, his voice pained. He cradled his other arm against his ribs. "What just happened?"

Saga shook her head. "I don't know," she started to get to her feet, finally noticing that Emory wasn't dressed. She blinked and looked away from him. "But I'm going to find out."

Emory reached out over Navi's still form and grabbed Saga's hand, apparently not fazed by his lack of clothing. "Where are you going?"

"For answers," Saga said, trying to free her hand from his grip.

Emory's grip tightened around her hand as he tried to pull her back down to the floor. "Don't go."

Saga looked out the giant silver doors that Vali had disappeared through, then back at Emory. "He knew my mother! He knows who my father is..." She frowned. "He implied that my father is still alive! Emory, I can't let that go. I have to find out more."

"Let me come with you then," Emory insisted, starting to get up, but Saga pushed him back to the ground. "No. You need to stay with Navi and..." She waved awkwardly at him. "Umm... deal... you need to... umm..." Her cheeks flushed red as she tried to find the words.

"Saga," Emory pleaded, ignoring her obvious embarrassment. "There's nothing I can do for Navi, but I can protect you—"

"No," Saga cut him off. "I don't need protecting." She wrenched her hand out of his grasp.

She headed for the door, intent on following Vali before he got too far away. She could hear Emory behind her, getting up and following her. He would never let her go alone. That was just the kind of person he was. He would never let a friend walk into danger alone. She bit her lip as he grabbed her again, trying to pull her back. "Saga!" he begged. He wanted to say more, but his voice kept catching in his throat. "I can help you."

She slowed her step and shook her head, not daring to look back at him. "No, you can't." She could not bear seeing Navi lying there, motionless and near death and for what? Because she had followed Saga? Hadn't Navi already lost enough because of Saga? Her best friend in this strange and wonderful world had lost her sister because of her. She could still lose her own life. How could she let Emory continue to take those same risks for her? She couldn't. Not even as he looked at her in a way no living person had ever done before, his face full of earnest hope and his eyes full of undying loyalty/ To her?

"I will always be there when you need me," he promised.

"Stay with Navi," Saga begged. Why wouldn't he listen to her? Why was he doing this?

"Saga, you're not listening to me! There's nothing I can do for her!" he begged, pulling her close to him. "Don't ignore me."

She shut her eyes tight, not wanting to see the world around her. "I don't need you," she gasped out. Yes, she did. She needed his friendship. She needed his strength and his thoughtful words. She needed the comforting presence of Shadow by her side. She was not sure how to do this without him anymore, but there was no way she was going to let him be another person who risked himself for her. "I never needed you." She pushed him away from her with her last words before running from the great silver-roofed hall after Vali, neither one of them noticing the tears falling from the other's eyes.

She hated how weak crying made her feel. No one had ever cared before when she had cried. Cried for the mother who had abandoned her, cried for the lost souls who had begged for her help while everyone around her had patted her on the head and told her to stop making believe. None of it had ever mattered. She had always been alone. Just as she had told Emory, she did not need anyone. She had never needed anyone.

She followed the hall where she had watched all the ghostly warriors go down. She realised when she could see clearly again, after brushing away the tears, that the hall was now dimly lit. Perhaps Vali could not see in the absolute darkness either?

The hall seemed to go on forever and ever. What had happened to the doors down each side that Navi had mentioned? She found nowhere to turn. Where had the ghostly warriors gone? Where was Vali now? Should she turn around and try one of the other doors? Like the one directly across from the great silver hall that they had come in from? That would mean going back past Emory, and she had no idea if she could resist him a second time. And if Navi was... The thought gripped at her chest, making it hard to breathe.

"I will leave you to handle the children." Where had that come from? "The dark elf girl is practically dead, but the wolf boy will be fine." *No...* Saga thought. *Not Navi... Not Emory...* 'Kill the boy and bring the Valkyrie to me after she has retrieved the spear."

There was silence before another person spoke, and Saga realised that she knew that voice too. "I can't just go killing students."

"The boy is a distraction. You said so yourself. I have no use for him."

"But my Lord, haven't enough people died, after Dorbe Manor... they're children!"

"And the boy went to Valhalla with her. He is not normal. Remove him from the equation and bring me the girl." Who was the man talking to Vali? She crept closer, needing to know.

"This ends!" Saga screamed as she launched herself into the room. She could not afford to wait any longer, and if she continued to think about it, then Vali would get away. The room was empty. Hadn't they just been talking in here? She had heard them plotting to kill Emory. "VALI!" She screamed as loud as she could. "Come and get me!"

Laughter echoed in the chamber. Everything was so dark that she could not see anything but a shadow standing there on the far side of the room from her. The laughter mocked her with its joviality. "He doesn't come when called. My lord is far too important to come for a mere child."

Saga cocked her head to the side, still trying to place the voice. "He seems awfully keen on having me brought to him, so here I am."

The shadow stepped towards her. "You miss the point, Ms Carolle. He only needs you to access the Spear. The spear that is within Valhalla. Valhalla, which was closed until now, until you brought the soul of the Dökkálfar girl there. Interesting that a doxie girl would be the first inhabitant of the new Valhalla."

"Don't call her that!" Saga hissed, her hand tightening around the hilt of the knife in her hand. "Ziva was my friend!"

"I'm sorry about that. I'm sorry about all of it, really." Saga gasped and stumbled backwards in shock when he stepped into the light.

"I... I don't understand," she whispered. "What about... why are you here?"

Master Iacono laughed. "Everyone needs maps Ms Carolle. Maps to guide them to the halls of the Gods. Maps that can tell you which realms you have dominion over and which you don't."

"Maps?" Saga asked incredulously.

"I have seen firsthand the lawlessness that was left in the wake of Odin's death. Æsir against Vanir. Faeries fighting faeries, the enslaved Dökkálfar being freed to enrol at a school like Toserra Sorose. Next, you'll tell me that the frost giants would have been allowed in. Don't make me laugh."

"But, Master Berfelan," Saga muttered.

Byrge Iacono laughed. "Fermin Berfelan is a weakling. Nothing but a cowardly Vanir. He couldn't even save his wife, and he doesn't have the guts to fight for his right to the throne of Asgard either. Vali, Lord Vali does. Lord Vali sees what the future could bring, not just for my kind but all of the Nine Realms."

"But why try to kill me, though?" Saga asked. "If he needs me to bring you the spear, why try to kill me?"

Iacono laughed. "We weren't trying to kill you, Saga, we were trying to awaken you. To bring out your full powers, to see what you are capable of. That's why I signed you up for the Tourney events."

"That was you?" Saga asked. She remembered thinking that it had been Tonya or maybe Konishi. The idea of a teacher doing it had never even entered her mind.

"You being taken out like that during the joust was unfortunate. But your matches since then have been inspired. You will be a real asset to our cause." Iacono walked towards her. "Come, little Valkyrie, we are of your people. You belong with us."

HER PEOPLE

"We are of your people?" Saga repeated in disbelief. "What on earth does that even mean?"

Iacono's finger trailed down her shoulder and arm, and she flinched at his touch. He chuckled. "You are the answer to everything."

Saga backed away from him. He was not the same teacher she remembered. "None of it makes any sense!" Saga cried.

Byrge Iacono sighed dramatically, "To proclaim his right to ascend the throne of Asgard, Vali needs to possess not only the blood of the gods, which he does as Odin's son, but so do many others." Ok, that made sense. "But he must also show that it was Odin's will, and to show that it was Odin's will, he must possess Gungnir, the spear."

"Right," she said. Iacono was walking circles around her, and she found herself following him. He had always been an engaging teacher in his circular classroom and could keep everyone's attention.

"Good, good, you're keeping up," he praised as he paused his pacing to observe her. "My Lord Vali has been searching for Odin's spear for centuries."

"It's only been two centuries since Ragnarök," Saga muttered. See, she had learned something from Master Berfelan. "Why?"

"When the Einherjar rode the lands defending the glory of the gods, they vacated the Great Hall of Valhalla. Their duty was fulfilled, and their time to truly rest upon them with their second deaths, glorious deaths in battle. The Hall was sealed, and then Odin died, and no one could find Gungnir. There was only one place it could have gone, returned by the last of the Valkyries before she departed this world."

"But you didn't find it there!" Saga sneered. "All those people you killed, and it wasn't there!"

Iacono shrugged. "Sacrifices for a greater good."

"You killed innocent people," Saga cried, "Those farms... Arsinee and Jisook, Dorbe Manor... All of those people dead. Your students, dead. People from town. Good people just wanting to help, dead. And for what? To reopen the hall of the dead?"

"You are young, and you have not had the lessons of our young, but you will, in time you will come to understand the power you have over life and death," He was trying to justify those deaths, but all she heard was senseless and could never explain, not to her anyway, why they all had to die. "The great war took many more lives than we did, and everyone has to make sacrifices for a new world order. Lord Vali's vision will be realised," he passed behind her, ever so close. Close enough that she could feel him against her back, and she shivered.

The knife was still in her hand. "Ziva Jensyn," she said, turning to face him, Navi's sister, always first in her mind when she thought of the dead.

"What are you doing?"

"Sindre Mozhan." Sindre had been the prefect of Pouinie Cottage and he had run into Jisook Farm trying to rescue people, only for the entire house to collapse upon him before he had had a chance to save even a single life.

"Stop!"

"Sandrine Zuaiter and Euseph Chermus," whom Ziva had been unable to leave as the ghostly warrior had come for her, even though they had already been dead, huddled together in the remnants of the Manor's kitchen.

"I don't want to hear this!" he screamed.

"Latila Panthaky. Elimu Sinyor," She had made an effort to remember the names of everyone who had died. Died because of her. She would not let him forget those names either. If she had to carry their deaths on her shoulders, then so did he. "Omar Barzilay."

Iacono covered his ears. He could not face the realities of his actions. If Saga had to live every day believing that these deaths were because of her, so would he. "Stop it!" he begged.

"No," Saga said, turning to face him, her confidence returning. "Steensel and Benedet Arsinee, their daughter Kinney, age twelve and their baby boy Helias, three."

She brandished the knife at him, making him keep his distance, but with his hands to his ears, trying to block out her words, he did not even notice. "Just stop talking!" he screamed.

"Hisaishi and Rahnuma Jisook, their sons Bruun and Datu. Bruun's fiancée, Ria Samadova. You killed all of these people and more." She had never been able to learn the names of all the farm hands working the farms or the names of any Dökkálfar slaves, but everyone on those farms had died when the hordes of dead warriors rode through. "You did that! You!"

Byrge Iacono looked up at her, their eyes meeting, his insane denial and her determination. Something sparked within him. "You!" he hissed before launching himself at her.

She brandished the knife toward him, but she preferred the distance that her staff or a sword provided between herself and an attacker. The knife in her hand was suddenly gone and in its place was a sword. Was it her imagination, one last delusion before he killed her? But no, she could feel the weight of the weapon and looking at it, she realised it was not just any old sword. It was the sword Astrid had given her when she and Edun had been attacked on the street. The strange one that had called to her as though they were meant to be together, as though it had wanted her and only her to wield it. Navi's knife clattered to the floor at her feet, the sound echoing off the walls around them.

Iacono stumbled backwards when confronted with the blade of the sword instead of the knife, and he laughed. A raucous, insane laugh. "I'll be the one to bring you and the spear to him!" he crooned, *"Claíomh na sióga,"* he murmured. Golden flowers and butterflies whirled through the air, forming a shimmering golden form of a sword in his hands.

"Wow," Saga murmured, not wanting to seem too amazed, though she backed up, making the distance Astrid had hammered into her head during class. What she should have expected, though, was that a magic sword created by the Arcana of a faerie did not need to meet her own sword.

"*Cumhacht na gaoithe,*" he murmured, and suddenly, the butterflies and flowers that had come to form the sword in his hands broke apart, flying towards her. She had no chance to escape, half of their effectiveness coming from their mesmerising flight before they hurtled right into her, sending her flying across the dark room. She crashed into a wall and crumbled to the floor. The sword in her hands clattered to the ground. Byrge Iacono walked towards her, the sword of golden flowers and butterflies reforming in his hands. The beauty of the sight seemed so at odds with the fact that she was about to die.

~ * ~

Saga was warm. She was comfortable, too, except for the fact that she hurt. She hurt everywhere, even in places she did not know that it was possible to hurt. She was sure this was worse than the jousting accident during her first tourney.

There was something important that she had remembered. Something that she had to remember... No, someone! Her eyes shot open, and she sat up. Ignoring the agony that ripped through her body with the movements, she gasped out, "Navi?" breathing was hard, and the pain in her ribs and back threatened to send her spiralling back into uncertain darkness. "Where's Navi?"

"Careful, girl," Raphaella Damir ordered, her hands pressing against Saga's shoulders, trying to force her to lay back down as gently as she could while still compelling her patient to obey.

"Navi?" Saga begged. "Where is Navi?" The image of that knife sticking out of her back flared before her and fear gripped her even more than the pain did. "Please!"

"Right beside you," Raphaella finally said, and Saga craned her neck to see. Relief flooded her at seeing her friend, and all resistance left her as she allowed Raphaella to push her back down to her bed. Her bed? "Do you remember what happened?"

Saga thought. "I... we... Navi was hurt and... and I went after... Vali! I went after Vali!"

"Calm down," Raphaella ordered. "Or I will not allow your visitors to enter. They've been trying to bang down my door for three days now to see you and Ms Jensyn."

Saga allowed herself to take several deep breaths as she lay back down. "Three days?" she asked. "I've been here for three days?"

"Why don't I let Mistress Grunborg and your friends explain everything? Yes?" She nodded, "Ok, I will go and get them."

Saga turned her head and stared at Navi's still form. The other girl looked a dirty shade of grey rather than her usual deep black colour. She blinked several times when an older girl walked up and sat beside Navi.

"Annis?" No, she did not look like Annis. Saga gasped. "Ziva?" The girl smiled at her but put her fingers to her lips before taking her sister's lifeless hand in her own.

"She is unable to speak outside of the Hall," Mimir stood behind Ziva, "But she wanted to be here."

Saga gulped. "Navi's not..." The thought was too painful.

"No," he promised. "Navi will awake and continue as though nothing has happened." Mimir paused before continuing. "The Hall has been reopened now. It will only be a matter of time until he tries to re-enter the hall to find Gungnir."

"What do we do?"

"I will think on that. For now, Vali will need to regroup and find a new course of action to achieve his goal."

"Mimir?" she said hesitantly.

"What child?"

Saga glanced at Ziva, hovering over her youngest sister for a few precious moments. "What made Ziva more deserving than Sindre Mozhan?" The Hyena prefect had rushed into a burning building looking for survivors, why hadn't his death warranted a grand and purposeful afterlife?

Mimir frowned, glancing at the two sisters for a moment before answering. "More deserving? Sindre was brave and valiant, there was no doubt about that, but Ziva was courageous and fought to the last. She saw the hoard and instead of running or cowering, she fought. I do not believe that Sindre Mozhan ever had the chance to prove his valour in battle." Apparently able to tell that she was about to object or argue, Mimir held up a hand and continued, "I'll see what I can do."

"Saga!"

"Navi!"

Mimir nodded to Saga before putting his hand on Ziva's shoulder. She looked up at him sadly before the two of them faded away into nothingness, the places they had been suddenly filled by Annis, who looked so much like her two sisters that it was disconcerting, and Tasso, who stared in distress at Navi. Jemima settled herself next to Saga, and standing at the end of her bed was Astrid. Someone was missing, though.

"Where's Emory?" she whispered to Jemima.

Jemima frowned, not entirely sure of what to say. "He uhh... he had something to do," she said unconvincingly. Jemima was a terrible liar, but that was ok.

"Ready to talk?" Astrid asked.

Saga nodded. "How did we get here?"

Astrid chuckled. "Well... instead of returning Pingu to his stall, these two," she motioned to Jemima and Tasso, "Rode him to my place after Mistress Anhora had returned them to the barn. You all still need to apologise to her and Master Toshiji, but they told me about what had happened in the woods and how you had gone back for answers. Why did you go?"

Saga looked away, ashamed for believing the promise, "The man in the woods said that Vali would give me answers." Tears sat in her eyes, and she tried hard to blink them away. "And Vali said he knew who my father was..."

Astrid took a deep breath. "Oh." She looked away, letting the silence hang between them for a long moment. "Saga... we... we will."

"No," Saga interrupted. "It's ok. It was stupid. I should have known better." Years of waiting for someone to come and get her from the endless number of foster homes had taught her to stop wishing for her mythical parents to reappear. For someone to come and take her away into a warm and loving family where she would be wanted. The mere mention of her father, though, and suddenly she had been that insecure child who wanted her happily ever after, and she would have done anything to find that connection. Her people, as Iacono had said. Iacono and Vali were not her people. Siblings, a mother, a father, aunts and uncles, they would have been her people. Her friends were her people.

"What else happened?" Astrid asked, pulling her from her thoughts.

"Umm..." Saga took a deep breath, thinking. "I went after him, but he ordered Master Iacono to kill Emory and let Navi die," she sobbed, "He... he wanted me to find the spear and Master Iacono kept saying how I was the answer and that they really needed me for it all to work" She looked at Astrid, her face full of distress. "They're going to keep killing people, aren't they?"

"Byrge Iacono won't be doing much of anything anymore," Astrid replied smugly. "Vali, though..."

"Do you know him, Astrid?" Jemima asked.

Astrid frowned as she thought. "Yes, I know Vali. I..." She shook her head. "He's not the man I remember anymore."

"Mimir said the spear he's looking for is not in Valhalla," Saga started.

"It's not," Astrid agreed. "But that won't stop him. He was told it would be there. Therefore, it must be there."

"Who told him that?" Tasso asked incredulously.

Astrid sighed. "Odin told him that the spear would be returned to Valhalla, to be locked away. Perhaps it was Odin's plan for the spear to be locked away, hidden so that new world order could be established."

"But what?" Annis asked, listening in intently. "He took the fact that Odin told him this as what? A message that he was the one supposed to retrieve it?"

"Yes," Astrid said simply. "That is exactly how he understood it."

"That's ridiculous," Jemima added. "So, he's what? Spent the last two hundred years looking for a way into Valhalla to find the spear that Odin locked away and so, he... he..." She looked at Saga, "What did you call it?"

"The Wild Hunt."

"The Wild Hunt. He summoned up the Wild Hunt to cause murder and mayhem to open Valhalla," Jemima finished.

"You don't just summon up the Wild Hunt," Astrid interjected. "The Wild Hunt has not been seen since Ragnarök. The Hunt was Odin's way of allowing the dead out of Valhalla, a reward and essential training to keep their skills sharp. It was said to be a regular occurrence in the days before Ragnarök. But the Hunts happened with such regularity, upon the very same paths, in those days, Nýr Ásgardr should never have been built here. The paths of the Hunts were known, and they should have been known now."

"Master Iacono would have known them?" Jemima suggested.

"Possibly," Astrid agreed. "Among others, yes."

"What happened after Master Iacono knocked me out?" Saga asked.

"Oh," Tasso threw in. "That's when we arrived! Found Emory and Navi. We made sure Navi was all right." His voice grew thick with the mention of the small dark elf girl, and his gaze unconsciously moved towards her. "All the while, Master Berfelan not only clubbed some bad guy over the head with a wicked-looking club, but he also did something to stop the Wild Hunt from riding through Nýr Ásgardr again. No idea what."

"He does not like to answer questions," Jemima added.

Saga narrowed her gaze at them. "Berfelan knew how to stop the hunt?"

"Master Berfelan," Astrid corrected. "And yes. He knew about the memory echoes and how to stop them. It was his job to figure that out."

Saga frowned but said nothing. Something did not sit right with her. Her memory of the fight was hazy, especially after Master Iacono had brought out the sword. "How did we get out?

"Well, after Astrid thoroughly beat Master Iacono," Tasso was having too much fun talking about this battle, but she should have known that after the way he talked about her and Navi's fight against his sister. "She secured him, Emory and I carried Navi, and Master Berfelan carried you out."

"He what?" Saga asked, surprised by that information. Astrid looked pained as they spoke. She stayed silent, allowing Tasso his story time. Saga was confused, though. Despite her hazy memory, she recalled feeling, at one point, warm. Warm and safe, carried in someone's arms. But if Master Berfelan had been the one to carry her out of Valaskjálf. No, it did not make any sense. It had to have been someone else. Emory maybe, he always made her feel safe.

"You were out cold when we arrived, and Master Iacono looked ready to kill you," Jemima added. "But we got there just in time." Her voice was small, almost scared. "What did you say to him? He... he was..."

"Mad," Astrid said from behind her. "He looked practically mad, near insanity."

"Names," Saga whispered.

"What was that?" Astrid asked.

"Names," she repeated. "I recited the list of the dead they had caused in Nýr Ásgardr."

"Ziva," Annis whispered.

Saga nodded. "And all the others."

"All of them?" Astrid asked. "How did you learn all of their names?"

Saga looked up at her with tear-filled eyes. "I learned them. I ensured that I knew the name of every person I could."

"Oh, Saga," Astrid murmured.

~*~

"Visiting hours are over," Raphaella Damir's voice dominated the large room as she stalked down the rows of beds, shooing away her patients' loved ones. The hands wrapped around Saga's tightened. "You too, boy."

"Just a few more minutes Matron Damir." Saga opened her eyes to see Emory sitting beside her, his hands wrapped around hers as he looked pleadingly toward the healing house's matron.

"That's Matron Damir, young man," she said jovially as she walked past, winking at him. "Make it quick. She needs her rest."

Quickly, she shut her eyes again, not wanting Emory to know that she was awake. He had been sitting there for the last ten minutes, and she was not sure what he was doing. She felt him shift in his seat to face her again.

"Ok," Emory breathed out. He sounded tired. "I... I don't even know why I'm here. I mean, you don't need me, right? You don't need me to protect you. Yeah, that might be true, I suppose." He sighed. What had she done? "I don't know if anyone's telling you anything, but Navi's doing fine. She was even talking to Annis when I came in. You were right, I did need to be with her. Leaving her alone would have been the worst thing. She was so afraid, afraid of dying there in that place, afraid for you. We were both so afraid for you and Tasso and Jemima when they came..."

He paused, and Saga contemplated opening her eyes and talking to him, but what could she say that would make this better? *I'm sorry, I'm used to being alone... you wanting to be there scared the living daylights out of me more than the thought of dying.* "Yeah, no, that was not something that he could understand.

"I don't get you," Emory whispered. He held her hand against his mouth and kissed her knuckles. "I just don't get you. You kissed me. You kissed me, and then you left... was that... was that something? Or was that just a way to distract me? I don't get you and then you don't need me. I don't know what to do with that. What do I do with that?"

She had to talk to him. She had to apologise.

"Mister Harding," Matron Damir called out. "It's time to go."

"Right," he replied, his voice sounding choked. He turned his attention back to Saga and said, "I have to, you uh, you get better, and then we'll talk. That's probably the best idea. Yeah..." He unwrapped his hands from around hers and gently placed hers on the blankets, smoothing them down as he did so.

Then he got up and walked away without saying another word. She opened her eyes and followed his form as he walked away and was about to say something, to call out for him to come back, but Matron Damir appeared before her with a frown on her gentle face.

"You really did a number on that boy," she said disapprovingly. "He has waited outside my hospital since you were brought in, only to vanish when your friends appear."

Saga blinked in surprise. "Really?"

She nodded. "Young people," shaking her head as she walked away. "Friends like you have don't come easily."

When Matron Damir disappeared from the ward, Saga curled onto her side, ignoring the pain from doing so. She buried her face in her pillow and cried. What she would not have done for the feeling of Shadow curled up against her like he had done so many times in the past. She supposed that in losing Emory, she would also lose Shadow. Her first friend in this strange world. The one who had brought her here.

~ * ~

Saga was allowed out the next day. She dreaded the prospect of returning to Jimpsee house. There was only a week and a half left in the semester. The last tourney day was ahead of them and the team selections for interschool competitions. Maybe after the holiday's everything would suddenly make sense. Or at least maybe the dust would have settled.

"No fair," Navi said from the bed beside her. "Navi wants to go—" she cut herself off though, realising what she had been about to say.

"With us," Saga said confidently. "Tymberlee said that she's working on getting permission for you and Annis, and Edun if he wants to, to stay at Jimpsee House."

She smiled sadly. "Thanks. This one has no idea what we're going to do, though." She frowned. "We would umm, well... we worked for this family... they were ok. Navi means they let us come to school after all and the others would come back there over the holidays, you know, work and accommodation. It was also where this one stayed until this year. This year was going to be different."

"We'll figure something out," Saga promised. "I, too, have to find some way to make my own money. I can't rely on Astrid forever."

Navi smiled. "Then together, we will find a way, huh?"

Saga nodded. "Always!"

Saga sighed and looked around at her bed, ensuring she had tidied up all her things. She began stripping the bed.

"What are you doing?" Matron Damir asked, coming to stand at the end of the bed.

Saga looked around awkwardly. "Cleaning up after myself."

The old angel sighed. "Dear, this is a house of healing. It is not required. I have people who will do that."

Saga looked around awkwardly. "Umm... ok... I don't mind... really..."

Matron Damir put a chair down next to Navi's bedside. "Sit. Be a friend."

"Yes, Matron," Saga said, lowering herself into the chair. Matron Damir harrumphed and walked away, shaking her head.

"What was that about?" Navi asked.

Saga scratched her head with a sigh. "Whenever I had to move houses or left the group homes or, well, whenever I left somewhere, I had to strip the bed. Leave it ready for the next kid."

"Oh," Navi said. "Did you move a lot?"

Saga nodded. "Yeah... particularly in the last few years before coming here. When I started seeing the dead. No one wanted to believe me and thought that I was too much trouble for them to handle."

SEMESTER'S END

There had not been a crowd this size at the Tourney since mid-semester. Even for the early morning events, there had been an unprecedented turnout. Many had come to see if Saga could run an unprecedented, undefeated season in the Stadion.

Or at least that was what Tillson Everard had said.

"No pressure or anything," Saga replied, actually wondering if she could, after everything that had happened. Raphaella Damir had insisted that she was well enough to compete though, and Saga figured that the woman would not say that if it wasn't true. Her fingers rubbed at her palms, feeling the scars left by the fire, something the old angel had been unable to remove. The scars were a constant reminder of that night and something that she and Emory had in common.

"None at all," the Tourney judge said. "Just watch out for all of those jackals."

"Hyenas!" Shot back a fourth year, who was stretching. "We're hyenas."

"Same difference!" Everard called as he walked away.

"What I want to know," the girl said, walking up to Saga, "Is the secret of your magic shoes."

Saga looked down at her runners. They were one of the few things she still had left from Midgard, and she wore them every month for the stadion event.

She finished lacing up the first one before looking up at the girl. "They're not magic."

"Uh-huh..." She responded doubtfully, crouching down to get a good look at them. "I don't know about that. You sure run like they're magic." She stuck her hand out to Saga. "Zibby Amin."

"Saga Carolle."

"Oh," Zibby said with a smirk. "I know! We all know."

"We all... Who?" Saga asked, looking around.

"Hey there!" A familiar voice said, and Saga grinned.

"Hey, Donetta!" Behind the girl stood a boy who towered over the elegant girl. Saga recognised him from previous events. He was skilled in most Tourney events, a master of the sword, staff, and bow.

"I see you met Zibby," Donetta said, her grin getting wider. "And this is Deluca Goett."

Deluca held his hand out, and Saga took it tentatively. She had only beaten this fourth-year boy the month before when they merged the races. With so many students from all the year levels now excluded due to poor placement, they had merged the year levels into one race in the hopes of making the competition more exciting. It had been that. There had been raucous cheering when Saga had overtaken the tall boy just before the finish line for the win. It had been her toughest race to date, and she looked forward to racing him again.

"You using some kind of witchcraft to win?" he asked, releasing her hand.

"Nope."

He, too, like everyone else, glanced at her shoes. Those multi-coloured runners had drawn a lot of attention. She rarely wore them, only bringing them out for the Stadion before changing for all of her other events. She had been barred from the Joust, but that had been no great loss. Running was still her happy place.

He chuckled. "Glad to hear it."

"Starting line, everyone!" Everard Tillson called. "If you are not running, get out of the starting area!"

Donetta ducked away, but Zibby and Deluca got in line. There were ten racers left from the entire school. Saga, as always, got down into a runner's crouch. Several had tried to imitate her but had had issues launching themselves from the position.

"Witchcraft Zibby," Deluca called from his position. "The girl's using witchcraft!" Zibby laughed, and then they were running. Saga let the feel of the wind against her take her away to the space in her head where she went when she ran. "Oh! And Carolle," Saga looked towards Deluca beside her as they ran. "If you beat me again, you're on the Pentathlon team."

Shock ran through her, but as Deluca appeared to get ahead of her. She pushed on, pumping her legs as hard as she could. Behind her, she could hear Zibby laughing.

"The pentathlon team?" Navi exclaimed as she sat beside Jemima, her hands weighed down again with food. "Did this one hear that right?"

Saga shrugged. "I don't know. For all I know, he could have been joking."

"Deluca Goett does not joke," Annis stated. "Well... not about Pentathlon, he doesn't."

"Really?" Navi asked.

"Really. He is..." Annis glanced at Saga with a smirk, "He was the school's Stadion champion."

"Oh," Saga whispered, staring out at the field. "I... umm..."

"Sooo...?" Navi drew the word out, the actual question unasked, but they were all thinking it as they stared at her.

"What?" Saga cried, looking at them. When they just eyed her expectantly, she stuck a lotus chip in her mouth and chewed loudly, refusing to answer.

"She'll do it," Jemima said confidently.

"What?" Saga exclaimed.

"Yeah," Navi agreed. "Definitely."

"Who says?" Saga cried.

Annis chuckled. "Yeah, Annis can see it. You've done too well in the other events not to do it. Plus, Deluca and Donetta won't let you get away. Donetta's going to be the team Captain next year, and she's had her eyes on you for a while."

"The first tourney, right?" Jemima asked with a laugh.

"Exactly!" Annis agreed. "She's been all over this one about you."

"You know her well?" Saga asked.

"Yeah, we were in the same class set, and we still have some electives together," Annis explained. "She's noticed that you and Navi are joined at the hip."

"That's an over-exaggeration," Navi stated and then stuffed several chips in her mouth.

"Tasso's up!" Jemima exclaimed, turning their attention to the jousting match on the field before them.

Annis leaned down between Saga and Jemima and whispered loud enough for Navi to hear, "Either of you know what that faerie's plans are for this one's baby sister?"

"ANNIS!" Navi shrieked, causing several nearby watchers to look at them critically.

Saga laughed. "Oh, complete and utter devotion."

Navi looked around, taking her eyes off the match and her companions. "So," she started innocently. "Where's Emory?"

Saga stiffened. When she had returned home to Jimpsee House, Emory had not been there. After that, he had avoided her at mealtimes, and whenever they passed each other in the house, he had ignored her.

Jemima shot Navi a look, but neither said anything else. Annis raised an eyebrow at them but did not know enough to add her own thoughts to the conversation. Saga stared out at the jousting match, not really watching but not wanting to look at her friends or be caught searching the stadium for him.

It was better this way, anyway. Away from her, he would be safe. It was not like his overbearing mother would approve of her precious darling cavorting with the Valkyrie of no stock. Emory's family were nobles. He would likely already get chided for hanging around with them. It was better to let him go now before she fell too deep for her werewolf.

Her werewolf. She could not think like that. No, that would only come back to bite her painfully if she did.

~ ✿ ~

Saga sat on her bed, not entirely sure what to do. Should she pack? Should she not pack? She had no idea. Jemima was packing, preparing to head home for the holidays with her aunts after the school assembly that evening. All through the house, everyone was packing. Everyone except her and Navi, and Annis. Navi and Annis had nothing to pack, but Saga was at a loss.

"Are we even allowed to stay here?" Navi asked, tucking her bed away under Saga's so they had free movement around the room.

"I don't see why not," Jemima replied. "Have you spoken to Mistress Grimaldi? Or maybe our household ghost?" She looked hesitantly at Saga.

Saga shook her head. "No, he hasn't been around since... well, he just hasn't."

Navi frowned. "What will happen to... to..." She frowned, obviously feeling uncomfortable about saying this. "What will happen to the ghost of Amyra Dorbe?"

Saga shrugged. "I don't know."

"What usually happens?" Jemima asked, and Saga raised an eyebrow. "I mean, you've dealt with ghosts before."

Saga frowned. "The unsettled dead. The spirits of people who had been murdered. Amyra Dorbe and Tremblay Jimpsee, all of the house ghosts, really. I have no idea about them. Are they here because the realms of the dead were sealed? I mean, if Valhalla was sealed, what about Folkvangr? I don't know enough about this place to answer those questions or are they somehow sealed to their houses, in which case is..." She looked sadly at Navi, "Is she another victim of that night?"

"You have to talk to Aunt Dina!" Jemima suddenly announced.

"Huh?" Saga exclaimed. "Why?"

"You aided the unsettled dead, right? Well, Aunt Dina, before becoming a teacher here, was an Angel of Death. She might have some answers. In fact, her speciality was the unsettled, the lost, the... the troubled."

Saga nodded thoughtfully. "That sounds like the ghosts I dealt with back home."

"Angels are one of the few races to descend to Midgard," Jemima added. "In various religious roles."

"Does that mean that she can see them too?" Saga asked curiously.

"I know she could when she was working. I don't know if she still can."

"So, how does this Angel thing work?" Saga asked. "I mean, I was always taught that God created the Angels, and they served his will and so forth. Church was never really my thing, though. I could never fathom the idea of some all-knowing being dictating my life, but there are so many gods, and Angels are an entire race with children that go to school."

Jemima laughed, stuffing two more books into her trunk. "Well, it's kind of like, umm... places of employment, you know, like working at this school versus one of the others. The culture is all completely different, and the Gods are our employers. They just only hire Angels, and you can specialise. One of the things the World Religions Class does is differentiate between world religions. An angel can specialise or keep it general. We're not forced into working for the Gods, but it is considered the ultimate goal for any Angel."

"Weird," Saga murmured, watching her friend pack.

"You say that as though your own ideas are not weird," Navi said.

"Hey!" Saga exclaimed. "I'm perfectly normal!" With that, the three of them burst out laughing.

There was a knock on the door, followed by Siobhan sticking her head in. "What's all the racket in here? Are you lot leaving or what?"

"Just about," Jemima answered for them.

"Well, actually," Saga started, but Siobhan quickly cut her off before she could get the question out.

"Good, good. Move it along, then. The sooner you're packed, the sooner we can all head for the assembly and get to the boat," Siobhan said before hustling out of the room.

Only a few seconds later, their door opened, and Saga called out to the person without looking. "We're coming!"

"Good," Mannish said, his voice causing them all to look at him. "But have any of you seen Emory?"

"No," Jemima replied. "Why?"

Mannish frowned but shook his head. "Nothing. Come on. The others are getting antsy to be off."

"We're coming," Jemima said, closing her trunk finally. "Right, what else?"

Saga tossed Jemima her uniform jacket and jumped up from her bed. "Let's go."

Monday night assemblies had not become any more familiar or normal to Saga in the months she had spent at Toserra Sorose. Students from every house made their way into the great auditorium, and teachers milled around, waiting for everyone to settle.

Up high on the side of the room, accessible to people only by ladder or wings, the seats usually reserved for a choir during performances were full of ethereal beings. Saga recognised the household ghosts, and among them, the form of the silent ghost who had helped her escape from Master Berfelan and Vali. Serra, Tremblay had called her, the ghost of the woman who had started the school. Tremblay had also said something about her being cursed. Saga wondered what that was about.

"Toserra Sorose," she murmured to herself. Jemima and Navi looked at her, and before either of them could ask her what she had said, she saw her. The ghost no one had seen since that dreadful night. "Amyra Dorbe."

"What?" Navi asked, looking around as though she would be able to see the ghost.

Saga shook her head, a sad smile on her lips. "She's here..."

"Who?" Jemima asked.

Navi's eyes widened. "Where?"

"She's with the house ghosts in the choir area up there. They're all there."

Navi smiled as she looked toward the empty choir stalls. "Good," she said. "Navi's glad."

"Seats, everyone! Seats," Mistress Athanasios ordered.

"Talk more after the assembly," Navi declared before disappearing into the crowd to sit with the other survivors of the Dorbe Manor fire who had stayed in school.

Saga took her usual seat beside Jemima and had half expected Emory to take his on her other side, so she was surprised when Vespers sat down, shooting a glare towards the far side of their row where she spotted Emory sitting.

"You need to put that dog back in his place." The usually melodic voice of the siren was harsh.

Saga glanced at him. "What makes you think I can do anything?"

"He always follows you like a lost puppy."

"No, he doesn't," Saga protested. "I'm not his keeper. You have an issue with Emory. You deal with him."

Vespers held his hands up in defence. "Geez... I'm sorry... I guess the gossiping girls were right. You and wolf boy are fighting."

"We're not fighting," Saga hissed.

"You're something," Jemima said from her seat. She leaned over Saga and looked at Vespers. "It's been over a week."

The male siren nodded sagely. "Yes, I thought Onorati and the others were just sprouting random gossip, but it would appear as though they were correct."

"All rise for the school song," Mistress Athanasios announced.

As one, the students of Toserra Sorose Academy rose to their feet, *"From the fires of war, a school grew."* The combined voices of every student echoed off the walls of the auditorium. Saga had to bite back tears at the thought of the fires that had plagued Nýr Ásgardr. She felt Jemima's hand grasp hers. *"We're going to do just the same."* Yes, they would heal from what had happened. It would take time, but the school and the students would heal. Nothing would be as it was, but they would heal.

As the song's final chords faded, they sat, and Mistress Athanasios handed the podium over to the hardly-ever-seen Headmaster Gotts. Aside from that night in Yggdrasil city, Saga could not remember any time outside school assemblies that she had ever seen the man.

He strode sombrely to the podium Mistress Athanasios vacated and took a moment to look out at the students seated before him, his gaze moving from one side of the big room to another. "In many ways, this was a fine first semester for Toserra Sorose Academy. We saw students show incredible feats of bravery, camaraderie, and resilience. The way you have come together as a community has inspired not only myself but all of your teachers, and the entire town of Nýr Ásgardr," he sighed dramatically. "That camaraderie and bravery came at a great cost to Toserra Sorose. It came at an even higher cost to the students of Dorbe Manor, and we cannot close this semester without remembering those lost. Two prefects died, young students about to embark on the great journey of life in the Nine Realms. Students who showed not only great feats of bravery but embodied the spirits of their houses. The loss of those bright lives is a loss to the Nine Realms."

There were murmurs of agreement throughout the hall, even a few sobs of grief. Saga closed her eyes, not wanting to see the room around her. Instead, she listened. It was easier than witnessing the grief of the school. It had only been a few weeks since the loss of Ziva and the others.

At the podium, Headmaster Gotts recited the names of the dead. To her surprise, Saga saw Ziva standing there when her name was called. Then Sindre Mozhan, beside him, Omar Barzilay, and the other students of Dorbe Manor. Their ghostly figures looked back over the school and their friends, and Saga had to choke back a cry of despair. Beside her, Jemima took her hand and gave it a reassuring squeeze.

"What is it?" she asked.

"They're here," Saga whispered back.

"Oh," Jemima whispered. "Wow."

Saga bit her lip as the house ghosts descended from the upper seating area and surrounded the students and the teachers on the stage. Saga breathed a sigh of relief when she saw Amyra Dorbe between her students and Patani Pouinie next to Sindre Mozhan. The ever-silent ghost of Toserra Sorose herself stood beside Headmaster Gotts. Behind them all, Saga noticed the teachers seemed not to notice, except for two. Mistress Grimaldi, the residential advisor, had definitely been able to see the ghosts during the choosing on the first day of school and, as Jemima had suspected, Dina Bess, the former Angel of Death.

Mistress Grimaldi held her hand in front of her mouth, trying to hide the gasp of surprise, but Dina Bess, could not hold back the tears that streamed down her face.

"Your Aunt can see them," Saga whispered. "All of them."

Jemima glanced sideways at her in surprise but said nothing.

"This town, this school, we reside within the plain of Idavoll, in the realm of the gods. Idavoll was the first land to return to Asgard after the great war, and as has been done, time and time before, we will rebuild, and we will remember."

They held a minute's silence for the lost, and when it was done, Saga looked upon the stage to find it empty of all the ghosts. Not just the lost students but the house ghosts too. Looking at where they had been sitting, they were not there either.

"The end of term is still meant to be a celebration. A time to reflect back upon your successes and your struggles. I will now pass you over to the Master of the Tourney, Tillson Everard, for the student's rankings."

The air turned electric as anticipation overwhelmed the grief that had been almost like a physical force in the air. "It was a semester with many ups and downs. The Tourney season saw feats we had never seen before. From the most spectacular jousting fails to the greatest streaks and speeds in the stadion that Toserra Sorose Academy has ever seen, let alone from a non-Were. So, beginning with the first event of any day, The Stadion, I will—" a chant cut off Tillson Everard from the students.

"Carolle! Carolle! Carolle!"

Saga blinked in surprise. On either side of her, Jemima and Vespers eagerly took part in the chant. They all were chanting her name, even Emory, who was looking at her. Their eyes met momentarily before he smiled briefly and then looked away.

"Yes, well, I suppose the leading runner in stadion for the semester comes as no surprise as she won every race that she ran. Saga Carolle, Jimpsee House."

Jimpsee House went crazy. They were standing and cheering. From the seats of Knightrich Dormitory, she could see Tasso doing the same; from Dorbe Manor's seats, she saw Navi and Annis cheering, Annis hitting Edun, trying to make him join in.

Saga shrunk in her seat, the attention making her more uncomfortable than she had ever remembered being in her life. It was not the first time she had received awards for running, but looking around her, it was the first time she had done it with friends who so enthusiastically cheered her on at every race and who wanted to share the joy of the win with her.

From beside her, Vespers pushed her out of her seat. "You actually have to go down and receive your award."

Students streamed out from the auditorium, mingling with friends, congratulating one another on accomplishments they had won during the semester and saying their goodbyes.

"If the students making their way to the ships would please come this way," Mistress Grimaldi announced.

Tasso looked around with a frown. "Where is she?"

"Tonya?" Saga asked.

"Yeah, she's probably already gone off without me," he sighed. "Ah well..." He took the handle of his trunk, then dropped it again and hugged each of them. "This semester was so much better than I expected it to be," he said with a grin. "See you next semester?"

They nodded. "Yeah, way better," Saga agreed.

Navi nodded in agreement, even though she was still wrapped in Tasso's arms. "So much better," she whispered in his ear, and Tasso blushed a furious shade of red as they separated.

He swallowed before looking back at Saga and Jemima, who were grinning at him. "I'll uh... yeah... bye," he waved.

"Wait!" Jemima called. "I'm going too."

"Not waiting for your aunts?"

"Aunt Raffi and Aunt Dina are meeting me on the boat," she explained. "I'll keep faerie boy here out of trouble."

"Good idea!" Navi grinned. Then she frowned. "What about us?"

"No idea," Saga answered.

"Well," said Astrid, walking up behind them. "You head on over there to talk to Ellora Tayyip, the prefect of Queenette Dormitory. Navi, tell your brother to talk to Ehren Kennemore over at Knightrich."

"Why?" Saga asked. "Can't we just go home to Jimpsee House?"

Astrid shook her head. "No, not over the semester break. The school prefers to know where any students still in their care over the break are, so they move all those who remain into the dormitories."

"Oh," Saga murmured. Beside her, Navi looked just as crestfallen, but they would still be together, at least.

"You didn't pack, did you?" Astrid asked.

"Umm..." Saga tried to look anywhere but at Astrid.

"Saga lives out of her trunk," Navi said before Saga could stop her. "She doesn't have to do anything."

"Saga? Is that true?"

"Umm," Saga stared at the ground. "Well, it's like," she shrugged. "It's not that bad... there's stuff on my desk."

Astrid shook her head. "Go, talk to Ellora and get yourselves places at Queenette. Then we'll go and get your trunks."

It was Navi's turn to look uncomfortable. "I... umm... well... you see..."

"Right!" Astrid said, looking embarrassed. "Let me see what I can do about that for you and Annis and Edun, ok? Meet you at Jimpsee House."

~ * ~

Saga tossed the last schoolbooks into her trunk and closed the lid. She looked around her room and frowned. It was already odd that Jemima was not there, but the house around her felt empty. Dragging her trunk out of this room and out of this house made her feel sad. It grabbed her in a way that she had felt when she had been forced to leave one family for another. She had a horrible feeling that she would not see this room again, which scared her. What if this entire world, this entire semester, had been some overly complicated dream that was now being ripped away from her?

"You'll be back," Tremblay said, hovering behind her.

She whirled on the spot to face him. "What makes you say that? How can you be sure?"

The ghostly young man smiled at her. "I chose you."

Saga scoffed. "No one else wanted me."

Tremblay waved his hand as though waving the thought away. "Pish posh dear girl. You will be back."

Saga shook her head and took the handle of her trunk. "See you next semester Tremblay?"

"That long? Of course not. I'll pop round to Queenie's to see you," he said with a smirk. "She does hate it when we pop on by to look at her girls."

Saga laughed. "You're incorrigible."

"Who me?" Devil horns appeared on top of his head, and she laughed. "Where's the tail?"

"Oh! I can do that too!" A tail appeared before all of it was replaced with an angelic halo. "I would never do anything wrong!" Saga finally took the trunk handle and pulled it out of her room. "Take care, Saga Joy Carolle," the ghost of Jimpsee House called from within her room before fading away.

Navi waited for her downstairs with Annis. Edun, as usual, was missing. When Astrid returned, she pulled two old and battered trunks with her. She presented them to the sisters, who then quickly packed the few belongings they had scavenged from the kindness of friends, the school's lost property and the townspeople.

"Thank you, Mistress Grunborg," Annis said when she was done.

"Astrid. School is out for the next few weeks. Just call me Astrid. Come on. They'll be waiting for you over at Queenette."

Together, the four of them left Jimpsee House. Saga closed the door behind her, locking it. The feeling of dread that she had felt back in her room was not there as she turned away. Who knew what tomorrow would bring? The next Semester was only a few weeks away; until then, they had the town of Nýr Ásgardr to explore.

ABOUT THE AUTHOR

Annie Mars was born and raised in Melbourne, Victoria. From a young age, she was a voracious reader, loving anything from epic fantasy to crime thrillers and hard sci-fi. She's always had animals around her and currently enjoys the company of two cats, the grumpy Sammy and the eternally energetic Pawla.

Saga of The Wild Hunt is her first book and the first in the *Toserra Sorose Academy* series. Annie's other works include *The Kahzer Chronicles* for Mythrill Fiction.

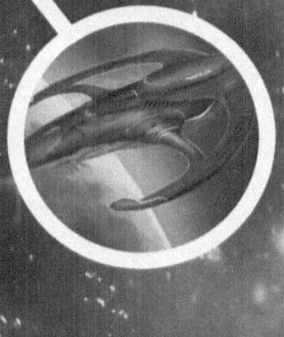

www.ingramcontent.com/pod-product-compliance
Lightning Source LLC
Chambersburg PA
CBHW030517120726
47904CB00005B/1510